NOT
ALONE

NOT ALONE

A NOVEL

SARAH K. JACKSON

DOUBLEDAY
New York

All rights reserved. Published in the United States by Doubleday, a division of
Penguin Random House LLC, New York, and distributed in Canada by Penguin Random
House Canada Limited, Toronto. Originally published in hardcover in Great Britain
by Picador, an imprint of Pan Macmillan, London, in March 2023.

www.doubleday.com

DOUBLEDAY and the portrayal of an anchor with a dolphin are
registered trademarks of Penguin Random House LLC.

Library of Congress Cataloging-in-Publication Data
Names: Jackson, Sarah K., author.
Title: Not alone : a novel / Sarah K. Jackson.
Description: Originally published. | New York : Doubleday, [2023]
Identifiers: LCCN 2022041678 (print) | LCCN 2022041679 (ebook) |
ISBN 9780385548434 (hardcover) | ISBN 9780385548441 (epub)
Subjects: | LCGFT: Novels.
Classification: LCC PR6110.A2685 (ebook) | LCC PR6110.A2685 N66 2023 (print) |
DDC 823/.92 23/eng/20220—dc30
LC record available at https://lccn.loc.gov/2022041678

Jacket illustration by Clément Thoby / Dutch Uncle
Jacket design by John Fontana
Art on the title page and recto chapter openers © aksol / Adobe Stock
Art on the verso chapter openers © flowersonthemoon / Adobe Stock
Art on the epilogue opener © jenesesimre / Adobe Stock

MANUFACTURED IN CANADA

1 3 5 7 9 10 8 6 4 2

First American Edition

For Duncan (Dink) and Dad.
The whole world died with you,
And began again, painfully, anew.

"And when we do find each other again, we'll cling together so tight that nothing and no one'll ever tear us apart. Every atom of me and every atom of you . . . We'll live in birds and flowers and dragonflies and pine trees and in clouds and in those little specks of light you see floating in sunbeams . . ."

Philip Pullman, *The Amber Spyglass*

This book contains references to suicide
and scenes depicting sexual assault.

NOT ALONE

1

"There's nothing there, Harry."

"You were staring. Your eyes are all big."

"Sorry," I say, whispering—to remind him to use quiet voices next to the open window. "It's nothing you need to worry about, just grizzling up to rain I think." I force myself to smile. Get a grip, Katie.

And still, I can't help but glance outside. Eyes scanning the same flat hard ground that always looks up at me from four floors below, snaked with algae and moss. The same grey buildings that press in on us all around, with dappled ivy-strewn alleys running between them. Searching amongst the rowan trees and snowberry bushes, thick and wild along the crumbling walkways. Pausing over the leaves piled up where they've been blown. Everything is alive, pink-red, yellow and golden out there, fluttering in the pale orange light. A scattering of something that could just be fine, powdery grey snow, if I pretended, swirling across the open air.

Harry shrugs his delicate little shoulder and I realize I'm clutching it tightly, as if I only need to hang on to him to keep him safe forever. The kitchen-lounge comes back into focus. Together we lower the sloshing tin bucket to our feet. The cloudy water swirls with debris and the shield bug—iridescent-green shell that so mesmerizes me with its precious rare colour, red "socks" up to its ankles—still thrashes on the surface.

I catch Harry's wrists before he scoops up the tiny creature. His face crumples, the bug's six legs desperately flailing. "You know you mustn't—we've been washing stuff that's come from outside in there!"

Harry flinches, scrutinizing the almost-clear water fearfully. "There's bad in it, Mummy?"

"Could be. You know this. We must always be careful..." I glance at the woodstove behind me.

"What if he's breathed it or eaten it?" Harry says, a whine creeping into his voice, the shield bug buzzing at the sides of the bucket.

"Try this." I grab the heatproof glove from beside the stove. Harry's little hand is swamped by the thick padded material, but he gently rescues the shield bug and we watch together as it wobbles out onto the railing with the disorientation and weak limbs of something too clogged with dust to live for much longer. Too sick from inflammation or the toxins leached or bloated by the foreign particles—the slow way. Or just plain suffocating—usually quicker. Yet creatures like this that can reproduce fast, before they succumb, seem more successful at surviving in the world After.

"I'm going to call him a green," Harry whispers.

"A green?"

He nods, eyes bright. " 'Cause he looks like emerald-dragon-green from the book. Emer because that's a brand-new secret name and only we know it."

"How do you know it's a he?" I smile, thinking about Harry's dragon book and feeling that tug towards make-believe.

Harry peers closer at the shield bug. "How do you tell?"

"Actually, I don't know, usually male animals are prettier though, so they can attract females."

"He *is* very pretty. Maybe that's what dragons are, just lots of tiny pretty bugs all together. That would be cool! So dragons are not-real but kind of real in the end?"

"Yeah, it would," I say, wondering when Harry became this sweet imaginative little person.

Emer opens his wings—a film of grey on the unevenly swollen and oozing lung-like vents underneath—and jumps out into the open air. Gone. One way or another.

"Was it the only friend?" Harry whispers gently, peering into the bucket, as if he might rupture tiny insect eardrums with his voice.

I try to return his grin, but the make-believe feeling is already seeping out fast. Harry hurries back towards the kitchen, skipping and bouncing off the arm of the sofa on his way, as I shut the window and smooth down the seals.

"Did you see, Mummy? I added these when you weren't here." He points at one of his artworks, stuck to the front of the defunct TV—some old hooped earrings of mine I loved wearing at uni and foreign coins have been added.

They make his collage of gleaming red and yellow leaves look like the insides of an expensive glossy watch—an artistic autumnal leaf print beneath tiny perfect cogs.

"Where did you find them?" But I know instantly. He's been in drawers and cupboards I'd rather he left alone.

He looks away.

"I don't want you going through that stuff, Harry." But then I spot a pencilled motif repeated across several of the collages. "What are those overlapping circles supposed to be, rain?"

He shrugs, eyes avoiding mine. "Raindrops on raindrops."

"You didn't uncover the windows when it was raining, did you? Go right up to the glass to trace it?" I glance at the window—where there are the remains of vague smudgy circles where rainstorms have hit the other side of the glass.

"No, Mummy," he says, his voice flat—hiding something— and throwing me a worried glance as he hurries to wait by the counter.

I clutch my forehead. Maybe it's just been a long time since the Fear has settled inside me—that unbearable quality of fear, running deep and laced with dread and blind panic, that coloured most of that first year, and still threatens to drown me again every now and then. Different to what I think of as healthy fear, with its brief surge of adrenaline and sharpness in a moment of trouble that feels better at helping me act. The Fear only saps and overwhelms. I'm not sure why it's there today, growing heavy in my gut, putting me on edge.

Trying to focus on the task instead, I haul the bucket back to the kitchen area. The fruits are warm and sticky as I rinse them over the bucket, pouring clean—filtered and boiled—water from my flask over and tilting the sieve to carefully inspect the delicate skins for grey residue. The blackberry harvest is late this year. And these, the first, early fruits—bitter-berries, Harry calls them—are always tart and sharp, almost inedible, and Harry winces with each mouthful. Yet he stuffs them down. One after another as I pick out clean ones for him.

I think back to the first few weeks, when I still had chocolates and cake and actual sugar in the flat—boxes of supplies stashed in the kitchen from the panic-spree in the last winter Before—and I would go from periods of barely eating to periods of stuffing down mouthful after mouthful, even though I wasn't hungry, even though it didn't make me feel better, because it tasted good for just a second and it was filling me up.

I squeeze his shoulder again. "Sure you've not had enough?"

He doesn't answer, instead swallowing down more berries without appearing to chew at all.

"OK, let's save the rest for tomorrow." I shut the lid on the still-dirty ones.

"Mummy, I want them." He looks so desperately sad for a moment that I nearly give in. And besides, we need to eat plenty; everything, I have long suspected, is less nutritious than it once was. Yet he looks flushed, his eyes a bit wild, and he's eaten nearly a bowlful.

"Remember how you were really sick last year because you ate too many damsons and redcurrants? Doesn't it feel full?" I kneel to rub his tummy, putting my ear to it. "Oh my, Mr. Tummy *is* complaining."

Harry's beautiful little face breaks into a grin and a grimace at the same time.

There's just enough filtered water left in the glass barrel on the kitchen counter for dinner tonight. I tip the dirty bucket into the top, where it trickles slowly down through the layers of magnetized gauze and charcoal and drips clear into the bottom.

"Come on, I should have got properly washed straight away." I suddenly feel sick by having broken that rule—and risked contaminating Harry's airspace—no matter how calm and safe it seemed outside, no matter that my overalls and boots were left out on the landing outside the front door, no matter how upset and desperate for berries Harry was, no matter how guilty at his waiting tearful face I felt.

I tread softly on bare feet along the hallway towards the bedroom, relieved when Harry follows quietly this time. Please, no tantrums, not tonight.

Outside, the wind is now a constant rustling in the tall poplars beyond the blocks of flats opposite, but our flat feels still and stuffy—it always does in the summer, even at the tail end of it. My T-shirt and shorts cling to me, clammy and uncomfortable from wearing my outer gear over them, and I yank them off, draping them over the chair by the window.

Harry—eager to copy—struggles to get his T-shirt off. "Mummy! Alistair's got me stuck!" He jigs on the spot, increasingly frantic, as I pull it up his small frame and over his head. I grin, tickling him as he reappears, and Harry dashes to the chair to turn his T-shirt back the right way and lay it next to mine, lovingly stroking Alistair's faded red dinosaur crest from his forehead to the tip of his tail. Harry's naked chest is delicate, and he *is* small, his clothes sized for three-year-olds, not the nearly five that he is.

"Perhaps I should raid the shops again for something new for us—"

"I like Alistair," Harry says.

"I like my stuff too." Makes me feel like me, having things that are ours, that we wear over and over. It tethers us, this flat, and everything in it. Safe.

In the bathroom, I crouch in the bathtub and lather up the soap. This batch is heavy on the lavender, making the ash lye and animal fat a little less unpleasant. Harry insists on coming in too, shivering—goose-pimpled—close to me, watching as I cup cold water over myself from the bucket I filtered and boiled yesterday and grinning as I gasp. I wonder if this counts as cold-water therapy—there was a craze for that once. Before.

Harry makes wet handprints on the stone-effect tiles and marvels at the way the water drips down in little droplets, getting slowed by limescale and the criss-cross network of grouting.

I let down my hair and tease it loose, the mousy-blonde strands falling to my shoulders. The water shivers through my scalp.

"Do me." Harry bounces on his toes, knees knocked inwards, arms scrunched to his chest.

"Tip your head back."

He blinks as the water dribbles through his hair, eyes clear and healthy, unlike mine, which sting from the rinsing. He giggles: such a soft, beautiful sound.

We splash the remaining water over each other, chuckling, until the bucket is two-thirds empty and I upturn it over the both of us— another shock of cold as it runs down my back. Harry squeals—the sound echoing off the tiles—then clamps his hands over his mouth. Both of us fall silent.

"Sorry," he whispers between his fingers, eyes going from shining bright to watery and worried. He stands there rigid and dripping.

"It's OK," I whisper back, leaving him wrapped in a towel in the tub as I walk down the hallway towards the front door, still drying myself, my wet feet slopping across the thick muffling rugs. Harry's delicate scuffs soon trail after me. I pull on the Yale lock, just twice, and try to take a few slow, deep breaths.

"I'm sorry, Mummy."

"It's alright." I try that smile again, for Harry, hoping that despite my face feeling weary and the muscles twitching out of place, it might be comforting.

In the bedroom, I rummage for fresh clothes, my heart still pounding. My eyes are drawn to the top of the chest of drawers. To the last photo I took of Jack. His face smiles and squints out at me—the camera lens flooded with the kind of bright daylight that I can only half-remember now. I can bear just this one thing, this one reminder, the rest is tucked, safe, in drawers and cupboards. My fingers graze the bottom dresser drawer where the most unbearable things are hidden from constant view, all the painful pictures, diaries and keepsakes I have secretly pored over like carefully catalogued treasures so many times when the urge comes over me.

"Mummy?" Harry's looking at me, beautiful rich amber-brown eyes frowning, that thick chestnut hair unruly and in need of a cut, just like Jack's intense gaze and beachy mop in that photo. His still-wet fingers trace the edges of the seed packets in the basket by the door, his face falling further into bottom-lip worry as he catches me looking at them. And yet it reminds me that I must harvest the beetroots and carrots from my little polytunnels tomorrow, start sowing the spring cabbages and onions in trays in the stairwell—my seedstock is thin these days. It's late summer now, and winter is coming. It always feels like winter is coming.

"Saying hi to Daddy?" Harry whispers, joining me on the edge of the bed.

My eyes flick once more to the photo but slide straight off Jack's face, unable to stay looking at those sparkling eyes that don't know what lies ahead, that remind me how utterly alone I've been now for five years.

Awful possibilities fill my head, as they often do when I look at his photo, imagining exactly how he died and where . . . It matters, not quite knowing—it eats at me. But I shove on a fresh shirt and shorts and leap off the bed.

"You're it!" I race up the hallway, Harry right behind me, and he tags me before I reach the other end.

"Now you." He grins, hurrying to the kitchen doorway, so we can start over and race towards the front door, the sound of our feet muted by the thick hallway rugs. Harry smothers his squeals this time with both hands.

Up and down we go, until I'm a heap on the floor, my chest suddenly tight and wheezy. But I'm smiling and pretending that it's all OK and Harry has me beat fairly and squarely.

"I win today, same as yesterday!" he sighs, happy and curling towards me, his breath gone sour from the blackberries.

My eyes close, I'm still trying to catch my breath. Worry flickers. This is the third time in as many days where I've struggled to breathe. I try to dismiss it. I was running. I'm tired.

Instead, I let a familiar yearning creep to the forefront of my mind before I can stop it, imagining we've just run to the door because Jack got home from work, pleased to see us, and us him. Imagine us all hugging on the threshold, my face pressed against Jack's chest, his arms wrapped around me, his breath slightly foul from the coffees that got him through the afternoon slump, but I wouldn't care. Even now I can remember how good he smelled post-shower in the morning, of cedarwood and sage. I imagine him scooping Harry up.

A twinge inside my chest.

Think of something else.

The meat I caught for dinner—I need to prepare it.

I peel myself up and head down the hallway towards the front door. "Go put some clothes on, Harry."

"I like no clothes."

I sigh, trying to sound nonchalant.

"Alright!"

Barely a few seconds pass before he rushes after me, still shrugging on my sweaty T-shirt. It's so big it falls to his knees. He sniffs at the collar, beaming up at me when he sees me looking, before he realizes where I'm heading.

"Harry . . ."

He gets there first and stands at the front door, smiling, as if that will make me stay, make me play with him instead. And there's a slither of guilt that I make myself swallow down.

"I'm tired, come on, Mummy has one more job to do today."

He stares, the smile shrinking, and that frown that's mine creasing his forehead.

"I won't be long this time, I promise."

"Do you love me?"

My resolve crumbles a little. "Of course I do." I squeeze his hands and kiss the top of his head and each cheek; kneeling down, I hug his face to my chest.

As soon as I get back up, I open and close the front door quickly, before we get into something more. I blink back tears on the landing outside. Come on, Katie. I think I can feel Harry on the other side of the door, pressed against it like I am. I know that's not right, that I can't really feel that, because this is a full-thickness fire door. He could just as easily have disappeared to the bedroom on soft quiet feet without my hearing. But I think something strange happens when I leave Harry, it's like there's a piece of elastic connecting me to him—thick, the kind my mum sewed our gloves to as children and threaded through our coat sleeves—and every time I leave, even if I'm just the other side of the door, it pulls.

There's a smear of blood beside me on the blue vinyl floor. The limp cat I left here earlier stares at me with big dead eyes, one of which is just a bloody hole, making a dark dribble down the tarnished brown fur of its neck. With time now to inspect it, I can see its nose *is* gungy, eyes bloodshot, and when I squeeze the paw pads, its uneven claws stand out creamy white against the darker fur—a scattering of pink-red veins running through the cracked keratin. But it looks no worse than rabbits I've caught previously. And everything is thin, same as us. It must have been scouting the same burrows I'd set snares at.

My boots, overalls and gloves hang from their hook out here on the landing and I put them back on, before lifting my catch by its cold hind feet and walking across to the neighbouring flat, the black tips of its soft ears brushing my legs. The door is wedged open with a shard of wood, as I left it yesterday, but no matter how many years have passed alone, I check out each room before I start, eyes drawn to the corners and shadows of the empty spaces, ignoring the stink of damp. Two monochrome bedrooms, a stark white bathroom and the kitchen-lounge done out in grey and dusky pink, all streaked with mould. The ceiling joists creak worse in this flat, unnerving me. But there's nobody here.

I focus on the job then: wetting the cat's coat to safely damp down and brush away the worst of any debris, cutting, carefully but firmly peeling back fur, pulling out the innards, chopping the joints, saving the heart—not time yet to also risk eating the liver, kidneys and brains. I clean up as best I can, frowning at the permanently stained grain of the table.

As I do, I realize I can't get a good lungful of air in again. Worse than earlier. My chest is tight, my feet and hands tingling. I drop my tools, gasping at breaths, trying not to panic, but the lack of air is making my head dizzy too. This feels like how it gets in winter, ever since the first damage was done. But only in winter—with the cold and damp and polluted air pushed low. I cough, lungs itching. Fuck.

I force myself to squint outside through the pocked grimy window, groping for a distraction. Above the rooftops opposite, the bright erratic canopy of the poplars trembles in a breeze that's just picking up, carrying away leaves like golden flakes of snow. The River Hiz is flowing beneath them, hidden behind the flats opposite, the more intense yellows and reds following its route, like a vein of black magic. Across the pavements and car park below me, on the far side where it often floods, the amber of the rowans and bronzed leaves of the snowberries are the most fierce, loose leaves dancing and swirling like sparks, making my eyes fuzzy, as I try to remember how things are supposed to be in late summer. But now I can't quite imagine that that much green ever existed. Even in leafy Hitchin and the fields and hedges and woods of Hertfordshire, or anywhere else.

I think of Harry's earnest little face as he asked if I loved him.

I fall to my knees, coughing and wheezing.

My eyes flicker up—watery—in the direction of Harry and our flat. I can't move. I place a hand over my chest, dread—cold and shivery—coming over me with each short, shallow breath.

Last winter was the most certain I have felt that I was going to *die*: the first time I'd coughed all that blood and my heart winced with that horrible searing pain. I've been tired all year really—not just in the last weeks—like everything takes slightly more effort and foraging is that much harder going. Harry more difficult, sleep never rejuvenating—making me slower to get up. Like this time the damage in my chest didn't really ease in the milder spring weather at all.

And if it's getting bad again already . . .

I can't help it, worrying about Harry. This winter suddenly looming worse than ever.

What happens to him? If I can't forage now in the last of summer and the autumn, can't build enough winter stock, can't get out of bed, can't breathe—

I can't finish that thought. There's no one.

The horrible dark despair of last winter yawns open inside me.

I need more time.

I lower myself onto the soothing coolness of the hard floor, letting my muscles go and relaxing my chest to help me breathe— letting the ground hold me up instead.

All I have to do is keep breathing. For Harry. Just fucking breathe.

2

Vague squares of evening light move across me as I lie here in the flat next to ours, the room cooling around me. Wind whips at my sheeting repairs in the loft space overhead and the joists whine, like they're old and grumpy. I blink, alert again. The noises scare Harry when he's in the flat without me. I check my chest, taking increasingly deep and careless breaths. The tightness has passed and I'm able to haul myself up to my feet. Grasping hold of my knife with one hand, I press the cleaning rag over it with the other, Harry's little voice replaying in my head: Do you love me, Mummy? The more I'm away, the more he asks. I rush to get finished.

A torrent erupts above and against the glass, loud like spitting oil in a hot pan. I yelp, the knife jerking in my hand as if I mean to throw it. It bites across my left palm through the cleaning rag instead.

A stupid "mmm" sounds as I press my lips together, toes curling to absorb the stinging, blood pooling out through the rag: a shock of too-dark, rich crimson.

Always turn the blade away from you! My dad's voice comes to me, hurried and whispered as if we're stood at night on land we shouldn't be on, rabbiting, and I nod, guilty, sucking in a breath.

The gash runs right across my palm—superficial, only shallow, but I know that doesn't matter, it will be slow to heal. Holding that hand clear, I scrape the meat into a pan, the bones into a dish—abandoning the unwanted body parts into a bucket for now—and head back to our flat.

As soon as I've closed our door behind me, Harry's at my side and following me to the kitchen.

"Mummy, bad rain! Are there nasties in it?"

"I know. It's OK, it didn't get me."

There's a dull tingle of discomfort in my chest and I try not to let it show.

He bumps into my legs as I put everything down on the counter, right at the back out of his reach. I rush to make sure the windows are properly shut, the sky outside grey and thick with heavy pearly drops. Next I secure the boards with their sponge edges, which stop anything creeping in through the cracks and friction-eroded holes of the mouldy brittle frame, or through the taped-shut vents. Harry pulls the curtains to for me last of all. Even so, I can smell it—the whiff of chemical bitterness.

Reluctant, I turn to the bookcase in the premature gloom, full of toys and creations of Harry's now, including his current favourites—a caterpillar string of broken shells and a polished selection of pebbles. I reach for the little wood box at the top to select one of my precious scavenged lighters. Once we get a resin-moss candle going with one careful strike, the flickering flame is just about enough to see by, the mirrors on the walls helping to spread the light.

"Just a small cut, it's fine," I say as I pour clean water from my flask into a bowl and rinse my palm. Tendrils of deep dark red dance out.

Harry whimpers.

"Get one of those bulrush roots, will you? And grab my book."

He hesitates, peering into the grey hallway, but bravely scampers off to the other end and soon races back. I flick through *Wild Foraging* one-handed, the pages soft and worn, and check the information on poultices. My left hand stays held over the bowl, Harry staring at the red drops.

He does his best to help me pound the bulrush root with the pestle and mortar, taking turns when my right arm gets tired. The fleshy fibres slowly become a jelly.

He leans over the bowl. "Is this what Outside smells like?"

I smear some over the cut: earthy and bittersweet.

For a second, it seems exotic and unnerving, like it does for Harry perhaps—something from the otherworldly unknown territory out there. "Sometimes," I say.

"Why doesn't it always?" Harry brings me one of the sterilized cloths from the middle drawer, which we use for cleaning, and I tear off a strip.

"You *know*, sometimes bad rain or air comes—"

"But why—"

"Harry, please, we don't need to talk about it, we're safe inside." I wince, binding the strip around my palm.

"What does it do?" He prods the bulrush jelly. "I thought water and charcoal was for cleaning."

"It'll pull out anything nasty and seal the wound to help it heal. Stop me getting sick."

Harry looks to the ceiling, the rain easing to a lighter patter. "Can I have some too? Just-in-case?"

I open my mouth to answer, but pause, holding my chest, worried my breath is catching again, sounding ragged.

Harry's eyes grow larger. "Shall I get the leaves, Mummy?"

I nod. It's been a long day of foraging, non-stop walking. This is how it starts in winter—coming on after exerting myself.

Harry plops the rosette of small oval leaves—dried greater plantain—into my mug of flat-warmed water. The soothing tea is bitter, always reminding me this was considered a weed, Before. I sip at it as we kill time until it's properly dark outside and we can light the woodstove.

"Hide-and-seek?" Harry suggests, already edging towards the door, eyes bright. He won't go far from me and the candle in the gloom, yet still my hands become sweaty and the emptiness of the buildings all around us seems to press in on me. "Harry, no, you *know* you were too good at that. Just Luna."

He grins, but pulls Luna the reindeer out of his pocket ready

14

without argument and I close my eyes. This keeps us busy for a while. The hallway cupboard is one of his favourite spots and I take my time getting there, Harry giggling. "Cold! Nope, colder!"

When it's finally fully dark outside, Harry hurries to wait excited on the hearthrug.

I let him hold the ball of kindling as I ignite it with the candle, which he solemnly does, sitting very still. We blow on it together until delicate grey smoke curls out of the wood shavings, and I add it to the seasoned split wood already neatly piled in the stove.

We wait for the wood to catch. Harry stares, eyes wide and glassy, the orange flickering glow repeated there. Wood-burning stoves were popular, Before, supplementing the unreliable and expensive central heating. I watch as smoke winds upwards into the silvery flue, which juts up through its bodged and much repaired hole into the ceiling and loft space above, imagining the smoke emerging, hidden in the dark, from what's left of the roof.

Some of the wood snaps and fizzes trails of toxic thick white, I spot a yellowy puff at the back, and then a streak of blue-black bitterness—and I reach for the door.

"Can I do it?"

Harry imagines the door like the great maw of a dragon's mouth opening and shutting.

"No, only Mummy can touch—it'll be hot soon."

Once the stove is shut, the sooty glass throws the room into suffocating darkness, leaving just a faint gleam around the square of the stove door. It's soon stuffy in here. We sit listening to the crackling wood and the gentle bubbling of the heavy pot above it, meat and roots cooking in a stew of water and dried herbs—rosemary, thyme and wild garlic. We always eat leaves, roots, seeds or nuts, as much variety as I can find, and meat every day if we can get it or have enough stored, for the calories, though I worry about particles and toxins accumulating up the food chain.

"Can we do a story now?" Harry asks after gulping down two bowlfuls and a spoonful of rosehip syrup for vitamin C. In the gloom, he seems even more scrawny and small, his hunger too urgent, as if I've not been feeding him. "Could we find a new one? Maybe there's one in the drawer in the bedroom—"

"No, I told you, there's no other books—"

"There is . . ." He trails off, looking guilty again.

"How do you know what's in there?"

He looks away.

"Those things make me sad, you know that. You leave that drawer alone, OK?"

"OK," he mumbles.

"You'd find those books boring anyway, I promise." Full of things we can no longer have.

"But I want a new one." He hugs Luna to his chest. The reindeer toy looks scuffed from years of play now, ears uneven from being chewed. I regret it for a second, because it's losing the carefully carved shape it once had. But I feel warm too, the sight of it in his hands.

"I think I've told you every one I know." I place a cool hand on my weary forehead, not sure there's enough brainpower for inventing a good enough, new story tonight.

"OK, tell me the one about the hungry reindeer?" Harry wobbles Luna across the blanket.

I hesitate. I only told that story to try to make Harry understand that many things aren't safe to eat outside and how hard I have to try—why we have to make do with what I can find. "Alright . . . What's the name of this reindeer in the story?"

He thinks. "Badger! Because he's got stripes and he's not afraid of going in the Wild Wood by himself."

"Alright, so Badger the reindeer's really hungry and he's been looking all over for some lunch." We play a game of thinking of all the places he might look, from up an old tree protected by leafy coppice bushes, to a pond thick with filtering bulrushes, or the hedge-shaded edges of a field, and imagine fine snow's coming down.

"With nasties in it?" Harry asks, wafting his hands through the air, as if it's wraiths and ghosts that he imagines lurking amongst smoggy rain or haze, waiting to suck your soul away. "Will it sting him if he touches it?"

"I was pretending it was just snow . . . Eventually, Badger the reindeer goes into the woods—"

"The Wild Wood."

"—and he finds lots of nice smelly herbs and roots just under the ground—"

"But underground is bad! Nasties can live there."

I frown, wondering how he's picked up on that idea. "Well, he eats hundreds of plants because the soil is so thick and rich and wet from all the decaying leaves, plants and trees. But he doesn't know if he should eat them or not."

"Because some are bad."

"Normally, the brighter it is and more snow it's surrounded by, the more poisonous it might be. And the woodland floors are like a sea of flowers: red leaves, yellow, alien blue-grey, or purple-streaked, bright bleached white . . ." We have fun imagining what it might be like to have four stomachs and be able to eat all sorts of things that Harry never could—tree bark, colourful fungi, even, in Harry's wild imaginings, window ledges and curtains . . .

"But even with four stomachs," Harry continues, "and eating sticky soil to help him poop out the bad bits, stuff covered in the 'snow' dust gives him stomach aches and aches all over his body—"

"OK, yes—"

"—and bleh!"

Harry mimes being sick: a rainbow of leaves. This time Luna the reindeer lurching about before lying down to have a "sleep."

I shiver. We don't usually end it like that. "Come on, we need to swallow some charcoal and brush our teeth."

Harry shakes his head.

I open the stove to relight the candle. "We don't have four stomachs, so we definitely need a bit of magic powder, don't we? To carry away any toxins, or any dust, *we* accidentally ate. What if you get to choose a new toothbrush tonight?" I pad down the hallway to the bathroom and open the cabinet. Inside the grass-woven basket we made for fun earlier in the summer are four pieces of fresh, sappy willow twig. Eventually, I hear the pitter-patter of Harry hurrying to see. He takes his time selecting his stick—the piece bending slightly in an s-shape, and one for me too—bumpy with knots. We make a good go of chewing an end, really gnawing at it. "I think that's enough," I say.

"By myself." He shrugs off my help, brushing the frayed end over his front teeth.

I make a show of getting right into the corners of my mouth, and he copies. The bitter taste makes me wince and Harry giggle. The charcoal isn't too bad either, washed down with a glass of water.

One final pee in the bucket of wood shavings where the toilet used to be, and then we're in the bedroom, Harry insisting I help with his pyjamas—the blue ones with clouds of what could be jellyfish floating across them but which remind me of plastic bags.

Harry grabs my hand and squeezes it.

"OK," I say softly.

He leads me from room to room, touching things, the dragonfly curtains in the lounge, the rug we were sat on, the boxes of supplies in the spare room, and whispers goodnight to each. The precious candle flickers low and smoky, but I try my best not to rush him, moving him on gently if he tries to say goodnight to too many things. Yet my fingers reach out to touch the kitchen counter where Jack last set a coffee cup and the nick in the hallway where we manhandled Dad's old oak desk towards the spare bedroom on moving day, Jack and I both worn out, making us laugh too hard about something I can't remember now.

In the spare bedroom, Harry counts the boxes and sighs, as if reassured. We don't go back inside the bathroom, as it has no windows and is often a pitch-black hole that Harry avoids. But he whispers goodnight anyway, touching the edge of a floor tile.

"What if it was dark when I was born, Mummy, or there was bad air or bad rain and the nasties tried to disappear me . . . would you have lost me?"

"No, I would have sniffed you out." I twitch my nose through his hair and he giggles and bats me off.

Finally, we curl up under the duvet together with just enough candlelight to open up the quote book. Harry flips through, pressing his fingers across the glossy pages, choosing one with a faded rose blooming across it, just grey in the darkened room.

"It says: 'Don't live in the past, it's already gone.' "

"That's a good one," he says, nodding, in a perfect mimic of me.

"A sad one, pick another?"

He flips and points and I shake my head, so he does it again.

" 'A river cuts through rock, not because of its power, but because of its persistence.' "

"Is a river sharp like a knife?" Harry asks.

"No, it's like when we brush our teeth and the bristles pick out all the bits of food that got stuck—water chips away pieces of earth and rock—"

"And bad things?"

"—as it flows past. One day, the Hiz outside might flow right through the car park all the time, not just in winter when it floods. That's what it means."

Harry twists his mouth to one side, frowning.

"Will it get inside, scratch all the way to our bedroom?"

"No, no. And it won't happen for a long time yet, Harry. The words just mean it's good to keep trying to do something, to not give up."

Harry scrunches his eyes shut, long eyelashes fluttering.

"What are you wishing for tonight?" I ask.

"For a rainy inside day, so you can play more games with me."

When he opens his eyes again I bend down to kiss his forehead. "Night night." I put the book back on the bookshelves above the bedside table, placing it so the cover faces outwards, so the ten books in our "safe" collection fill the space.

"You forgot the rest."

"Night night, sweet dreams."

"You won't go, will you?" he whispers, his skin hot and sticky as he snuggles close, taking up the middle of the bed.

"No, I won't. It's just our room, Harry, nothing different about it now than in daytime."

"It *is* different. There's dark shadows and I don't want to fall in one by accident."

"You can't fall anywhere, where do you think you'd go?"

"I don't know," he says fearfully. " 'Cause you can't see. Like the nasties in the rain. But you might get disappeared—gone!"

I swallow, feeling that familiar tremor of reaching the edge of things I don't want to talk or think about. "It's still the same as it is always," I say, the words calming me, "the same wood floor and cream-painted walls and ceiling, the same wardrobe and dresser. And they're not scary, are they?"

"And woolly rug on the floor—sky blue-grey."

"Yep."

"I don't want to fall in the shadows anyway, just-in-case."

I try not to focus on the darkness in the room, in case Harry's fear rubs off on me. It has always felt the safest in here, especially as I watch Harry, asleep as he is now, his eyes twitching as he dreams. I feel as if I'm in that secret place between reality and sleep, where everything is kind of hazy and soft, and sort of OK. And it doesn't matter what happened today or what might happen tomorrow. At the moment, in this soft warm bed in this darkened bedroom that's always been ours, everything is alright.

My mind ticks over the minutes, until I feel safe to gently roll to the edge of the bed and carefully lever myself up. Padding softly back to the kitchen-lounge, I make sure to leave all the doors open so that I can hear if Harry stirs.

The fire must have shrunk down to black and red embers, only the faintest tinge of red is visible around the stove door. I set filtered water on to boil, ready for the washbowl and drinking water tomorrow, and slump onto the sofa with the balcony doors open— the dust boards down and curtains a few inches ajar—cool evening air seeping inside. It's calm and still now, and often safest after rain has damped everything down. Just the brightest stars glinting through the night haze, the moon hidden behind the flats opposite but bathing everything in cold light.

I let myself imagine I could be drinking a glass of wine beside Jack, our legs tangled together as they rest on the coffee table. We'd be talking about whose family we'd go and spend the weekend with, what friends we might see the following night, all the little things that happened at work that day. Everything's all rosy and perfect, looking back, and painful, but right now I want to hold on to that warm feeling, imagining the wine taking its effect, making me relaxed and slightly fuzzy-headed.

After a moment, something kicks me back into alertness.

I set my water flask down and inch the curtains open a little more. Under the night sky, the blocks of flats look darkest grey and indistinct, the trees blurry and fluttery black. When the wind isn't blowing, it's always quiet outside. I spot just one bird, an inky flutter against the navy sky, circling the poplars for a place to roost. My throat tickles, the cool air itching right down into my lungs. My eyes scan left to right, right to left. I look down. A silhouette shifts between the cars. I immediately drop to the floor, banging knees and elbows.

I can hear, in the back of my mind, a sort of desperate scream that echoes all round my head, making the blood pulse in my hands splayed on the hard floor.

I fight against that itchiness creeping in my throat.

I dare myself to take one more look—please, not now, not this too—just to double-check I'm not seeing shapes in the shadows that aren't there.

Steeling myself, I inch forwards on my front, until I'm within inches of the Juliet balcony. I peep over. I can't see the shape that I saw before. I search the edges of the car park, around the crumpled rectangular forms of rusting cars in the dark.

I pace the hallway, thinking. I check on Harry.

In what used to be the spare bedroom, I open up a locked chest. Jack would have laughed at my collection: a hammer, a sturdy piece of wood with five-inch rusty nails sticking out, the classic baseball bat, and an assortment of knives. Like I'm a player in one of his computer games, only in real life you don't get to restart and try again.

3

"Mummy?"

I flinch, but it's only Harry coming to squat next to me by the window. Familiar soft round cheeks, clear amber-brown eyes, and thick chestnut hair.

"Morning, baby," I whisper, smiling over the twinge of sadness and worry as I look at him, reaching, out of habit, to check his eyes and his throat.

He wriggles. "I'm not a baby, remember we said—"

"We did. Morning, my big boy," I say, beaming.

I ease myself up, body aching from sitting here all night, and take tentative deep breaths—wary of finding stiffness in my lungs—and crack my neck as I scan the ground below again.

"Breakfast time?" Harry asks.

Breakfast is always cold, unless it is wintertime and still dark enough to get the woodstove going and make a pottage with whatever vegetables and meat we have, the soup getting increasingly watery the longer winter goes on.

So Harry eats cold leg meat and the succulent bulrush shoots I gathered yesterday, which give off a bitter cucumber scent as he tears into them. And I sip cold greater plantain tea and tear at the white starchy fibres of a cold cooked bulrush root. Always reminds me of sweet potato and winter comfort food, but this morning I can hardly stomach it.

It's cooler today, the rain yesterday breaking the warm spell, making autumn feel suddenly closer. But it looks calm out there, the sky bluer than normal. I should take advantage of it. I fidget my hands over my chest and search the doorways and windows outside for movement . . .

Maybe it *is* safer to stay indoors today, though.

Still achy and tired, I sit on the sofa while Harry cuts up deep-red bulrush root husks.

"What are you making?" I ask.

"I don't know yet."

"You could add them to that collage in the middle, they could be tree trunks."

"No, they can be slugs."

I lean on the arm of the sofa, grabbing the box of chalks from the end of the kitchen counter. We don't use them often; there are only stubs left. "You could use a white to make some of them snails?"

Harry grins and reaches for one. "Yes, and the blue and pink to show all the holes 'cause their houses are too thin, like when they were on everything Outside, all at once, remember? You got mad."

"Oh yeah, of course. Well, they ate everything. And then they all keeled over after bad rain making an awful goo!"

Harry giggles and I shuffle off the sofa to help cut and hack with the rusted scissors. Mid-morning, we share a small cup of cold mint tea—the last drinking water in the flat unless we break into what we've put aside for the winter—and head to the spare bedroom.

We might as well put this time to good use by checking our winter stocks. Harry helps make sure everything is stored neatly, inspecting for mould and damp. Carrots preserved in airtight, heat-sealed glass jars, wooden crates of bulrush roots, turnips and onions. Malformed crab apples layered between old towels are sweating— I spread them out. I crush dried orange-brown pine needles, cheered by the faint green tinge at the sheath end, and seal them in jars to make "tea," pound roasted dandelion roots for "coffee," rotate the emergency containers of water to prevent bacteria or algae growing, and even start the laborious job of grinding dried bulrush roots into flour, bit by bit with the pestle and mortar.

The sweet chestnuts I picked last week already smell mouldy.

They weren't ripe, but I took them because some years they just rot on the tree with the sudden onslaught of the cold autumn rains. Yet they must have been damp—they'll be bitter when we eat them, if they're edible at all. Damn.

"Can't you get better ones?" Harry frowns as he sniffs them too.

"We have to be happy with what we can find, you know that."

Harry lines them up on the desk by the window for me so today's sunlight might dry them out.

"Mummy!"

His yell makes my mind race and I glance beyond him through the glass. All morning I've felt drawn to the windows, looking for human shapes in the shadows under the trees and in doorways. Harry's been absorbed in helping me, but I've caught him looking fearfully across at the windows too.

He points at the desk. "No, there, get it!"

I spit on a cloth and wipe the far corners, where fine dust has settled, and then continue round the room and the whole flat. "Not all dust is scary, Harry, some of it in the flat will be tiny pieces of your skin and mine or bits of our clothes."

He touches his face, checking his fingers for evidence.

"When the bad stuff's in the air or rain outside, I can smell it, but settled and undisturbed on a surface like this, it's hard to tell. So—"

"Better clean it up, just-in-case," Harry says, with an exaggerated nod.

We pick at rabbit jerky and the wilting shoots for lunch, watching the blue-grey sky outside. I worry about my traps in Nathan's Coppice. Unchecked, any trapped rabbits might attract dogs or foxes or rats to my best spot.

"We could have a feast tonight?" Harry says, eyes warming. "We could have baked potatoes and turnips, mashed up, with chestnuts all hot and yummy. Smoked-rabbit stew with pancakes . . ."

"That does sound good, but no, we have to save lots of food for the winter."

"Why?"

"You know why, summer and autumn are when the food grows outside."

That dread I felt yesterday rises up again. We have to gather enough to last from the autumn berries until spring, with only scant fresh meat to be caught in between, provided the flooding isn't so bad I can't leave the flat, and the air meter isn't hitting too deep into the orange danger part of its dial and I stop trusting my mask and gear, which it does more often than not in winter with the cold seeming to push bad air to the ground. And my lungs aren't too sore, inflamed and breathless, the cold thick air triggering it, so that we have to stay in bed.

If they're sore already . . .

All I've collected so far just isn't enough.

"Yeah, I don't want to be hungry," Harry sighs, nodding.

I stare, as if he's heard my thoughts.

He shrugs. "I remember my tummy hurt."

Biting my lip, I can picture his hungry face and tears at the end of last winter.

I make myself get up, guilt and worry fuelling me to the front door—I should at least collect water today. We must not dig into our winter stores if we can help it, especially not now. My rainwater butt is only just the other side of the flats opposite.

I shove my favourite knife into my back pocket where the point of the sheath pokes out the hole in the corner. I run my fingers over the roughed-up leather and up the curved hardwood handle, tracing my father's initials engraved there. It's a good knife, fixed blade, five inches, full tang, proper pointed tip. It doesn't feel like a weapon though, so I also pick up the rusty-nailed piece of wood, and head out, jittery, shoving boots and overalls on on the landing outside our front door, and leaving Harry stood in our hallway as the door closes on him, more peelings to stick to his collages in his hands.

I grab the empty water containers on the landing, and head down the stairs, kicking the sandbag dust and draught excluders out of the way at each internal door, and frowning at the bitter chemical-like smell of our building. I imagine it's from leaks of bad rain and the smoke drifting in from our woodstove flue in the roof above, which I removed from another empty flat and fitted as best I could into ours. Finally, I step out into what was the communal garage. The cool shade makes me pause. The weapon in my hand is heavy, but I clutch it tighter. One whack if I need to, to give me time to run. That's all.

Dark silhouetted cars still sit between the grey columns of concrete—glass glittering on the ground, wheels missing or tyres pancaked, fuel caps sticking out. I wait until I'm certain there's nothing moving in here and then lock the stairwell door behind me, hurrying to the heavy metal shutter that once used to roll up and down electronically to let you drive in and out, and carefully slide through the half-metre gap at the bottom. I avoid nudging it, but the slight lip on the ground where the self-rising floodgate is still clips me.

Stepping outside, rubbing my shoulder, the dial on the handheld air meter springs up but settles in the green—less than ten micrograms per cubic metre—so I leave my hood down and my mask dangling from my neck—it can get hot and moist underneath it, and I'm scared of it triggering a coughing fit. Clicking the meter off again, I clip it to my overalls, so its solar chip can charge. A familiar heavy feeling rises alongside the worries as I walk. At least inside the flat, it can feel like Jack was only just there—that I'm less alone, or things might not be so bad. But out here, he always feels long gone.

My breathing seems loud and wheezy in the quiet open air, throat tickling. How far and how fast can I run if my chest flares up? I pause, squeezing my weapon, looking back the way I've come. Just the water. Just get that and then I can lock us inside the flat.

I tread carefully over the broken tarmac with its drifts of yellow and browning leaves and webs of bile-green algae, careful to avoid disturbing the glossy brown mounds of fungus.

Down the ivy-shaded alley between the two blocks of flats opposite ours, holding my breath until I reach the dappled daylight on the other side, kicking through the deepening carpet of leaves. I look both ways. Nothing but the bright limey-yellow grass on the banks of the Hiz and drifts of golden leaves and the lurid acid yellow of the poplars above, rustling softly.

My water butt is on the left, tucked inside what used to be a corner of communal garden, a sweet nook with semi-circle benches and box hedging. Now it's full of ivy—all washed-out green edged with deep red. The metallic front of the water butt sparkles in the sunshine, the deer of the Hertfordshire crest wet. The lid rests on the floor. The mesh filter too. Larger particles caught in the weave stand out, grey against the dark silver.

I snatch the lid up, checking the clasps in case it's broken and been blown off. Yet condensation drips off and further wets the crest as I go to put it back. Worry gnaws at me.

The pebbles at my feet form two heavy indentations, as if a larger person has stood here. That trembling I felt last night kicks in. *I* could have kicked larger depressions myself, and I could have forgotten the lid last time I was here . . . Yet I'm not convinced I did.

I fumble the first container beneath the little tap at the bottom. Hitchin Town feels like a lurking presence at my back—beyond the poplars are supermarkets, rows of terraced houses, shops around the market square, where a survivor, if they came here, working along what were little commuter towns between London and Cambridge, might go scavenging. So I stand up, turn around to face it as water trickles into the container, but I feel very aware of the blocks of flats then, their tall looming masses and big dark windows at my back. A few broken doors and windows clatter in the breeze.

I try to focus on the familiar soothing sound of the poplars instead, leaves rustling like rushing waves on a beach, and how the air under the yellow canopy is golden as if shimmering with heat despite the cool day. I hear the Hiz trickling below the trees too, bankside grasses scratching.

Yet my eyes snag on a path trampled through the grass and fallen leaves to the river. So close to my water butt and the worry of tampering, that I leave the container still filling to follow it. The thick tufts of limey-yellow grass are unsettling as I brush past, orange-splotched, as if that imagined heat is real and the whole undergrowth about to ignite.

I find just deer prints and snuffle holes left in the moist earth at the water's edge. Spots of the animal's dry blood on the trampled leafy carpet too. It was too ill and disoriented perhaps to find a better source of water or food—the water thick with clotted clumps of that bile-green algae, and sparkling with suspended spores and plastic dust particles, like turquoise and grey glitter.

The moment I relax I lose my footing, one boot sinking into one of those soft holes, and I let myself topple backwards to my bottom to stop myself plunging forwards into that water. The snuffle hole sloshes with pearly mud and torn roots, now coating my boot too. From my place on the ground, the layer of grey in the soil profile is clear, an inch down, licking loose where I've disturbed it, below a thin line of the richest, blackest soil, and a thick pile of dark, decomposing leaves. It reminds me of cutting into cake and recoiling at decay and mould inside.

From this spot, too, the light catches the mist rising from the river. Droplets forming where the moisture clings to the hundreds of delicate threads from which hang moth cocoons. And I can imagine it all rising—water, plastic dust, and chemicals leached from the dust or runoff from elsewhere—only for it all to be rained down again, plastic and pollutants spreading through watercourses and groundwater into every crumb of soil, all caught in the cycle now and we'll never be rid of it.

4

I haul myself up, a few triangular leaves drifting down to land in the thick carpet at my feet, where they fall in a continuous cycle all year round—lurid yellow, golden-orange, pale buttery-green. Slugs and snails are in a bust year, but woodlice are thriving, tiny armoured bodies scurrying around in the decomposing leaf litter.

I'm reaching for a particularly bright unmarred leaf, thinking of Harry's collages, when a breathy bark freezes me to the spot. It's followed by a low gravelly howl that rips through the air and through my chest.

They're close. In town.

All thoughts of colours and collages and water-butt tampering drop out of my head. The hoofprints glare up at me, a third, more ragged grunt echoing off buildings—all their vocal cords damaged and inflamed by exposure. As far as I know there are five deer in the pack—frayed silvered roes, scavenging the kills. Maybe they're good lookouts and can hold their own, that's why they're accepted by the dogs, I don't know.

Water is overflowing my container when I rush back to it—not clear, but milky. The mesh wouldn't have done much against last night's grey rain anyway perhaps. I pour it away in a hurry, letting the tap run until the flowing water narrows and clears and I manage to gather a few inches. The dogs and deer are still calling to one another, and I hear two more dogs, whining. Yet, even if they're close, they sound like they might have made a kill. That will keep them busy.

I haven't heard them in town since the spring.

I try hard to convince myself that perhaps that's all I saw in the dark last night. Just a dog or a deer.

The blocks of flats look especially grubby from the west as I retreat back through the ivy-strewn alley: roofs gappy, brickwork specked with grey and the vomity runs of algae, and the mortar sprouting with bright blood-red weeds and moss, making it look like some underwater rusting relic from much longer ago. It looked new and modern and soulless when Jack and I first moved in, with a rented van piled full of our hand-me-down furniture—all smart red bricks and white PVC. I wince: imagining how all the rooms beyond all those windows are empty now makes me nauseous.

Yet I'm afraid to look, in case I'll spot one that isn't.

And I'm afraid for Harry. I can almost feel him watching me, even though I tell him not to, and it hurts not to look up at our window, not to smile and wave. Because what if I *did* see someone last night? What if they're watching us right now? That thought makes my stomach drop.

I wait in the shadow under the ivy, watching, listening to the dogs and deer in the distance.

The light is waning—the haze always making the descent to evening drawn-out. Behind me, the horizon is tinged orange-pink, not so intense tonight because the haze isn't so thick.

Every one of my limbs is shaking. I run out from under cover and across the car park, heat and breath and my pounding feet. There's an echo of the Fear I felt that first year after the very last time I saw other people. When I'd failed to get to the Midlands to see if Mum or my brother Paul had survived. And instead, abandoning the weeks of effort to get nearly halfway there, and the ragged tent on some dark hill behind me, I'd limped back here through the rain on a great wave of sickening adrenaline—days without sleep, sobbing, hunched over throbbing ribs and wheezing lungs, blood in my mouth and trickling down my chin. Scared in the dark and the dim grey days, of footsteps, hands reaching to grab me. The smell of an unwashed body, blood, sweat and smoke still vivid.

30

Nearly sobbing now as I roll back under the metal shutter, I dash to the door, just as I did back then. Swollen finger joints and torn fingernails made me fumble the key then, the Fear making me do it again now, checking over my shoulder.

That big car in the corner looms in the dark, as it did that day too, when I saw it for the first time. It had jolted a fresh surge of panic, in case looters and people had arrived here. I still hate its badly parked front end, always intruding into Jack's spot, wheels missing, leaving big gaping holes, but otherwise intact with its powdery uncracked windows, its body jacked up off the ground, too solid and unbroken compared to the other rusting, shattered, slumped vehicles. Its big dusty headlights and chunky metal vents seem to grin at me, its thick bull bar like a muzzle. I shiver, stopping mid-step. The logo gleams beneath layers of dust like a nose—two perpendicular ovals inside a large one—so like Harry's raindrops on raindrops upstairs.

Finally, I get through the door and lock it behind me. The handle's wobbly in a way it didn't used to be, so I restrict myself to one wiggle to check it's locked. Yet I feel that irrational compulsive need to keep checking and wonder how long I did stand here that day before managing to wrench myself away, terror turning then to the possibility of looters being in the building right at that moment.

I feel a little better now I'm inside again, yet worry still makes me double-check that the smashed windows on the ground floor are still barricaded.

Then I'm racing up the flights of stairs, kicking the sandbags back into place, remembering how finding the flat looted had blown open that big black hole inside me. Jack's life, and mine, as I lurched sobbing from room to room, wrenched off walls and counters and in a mess at my feet. As if they were here for something more than just snatching food or clothes, and revelled in the destruction while they searched. My eyes couldn't skip past anything: Jack's face smiling up at me, our adventures captured in the holiday snaps and collected fridge magnets, the postcards from Mum and our friends, my diaries, our books, films . . .

The dead anniversary flowers in a smashed vase. And ultimately, the wedding planner—that beautiful silver-white keepsake folder, full of pages of my ideas and lists, and sleeves stuffed with RSVPs—spreadeagled on the floor amongst letters and cutlery and broken plates. My ribcage had felt yanked open, the pain just roaring up out of it. The final unbearable reminder that it was all over, everything I loved: gone.

I couldn't bear to put things back. Instead, I'd scooped it all up, placing every memory of Jack and our life Before in drawers and cupboards, even the notes and shopping lists in our handwriting, our favourite coffee mugs. Everything except that one precious photo of Jack that I kept out, scared to lose that clear image of his face from my head.

Sometimes, I find myself kneeling at that bottom drawer in the bedroom, touching an image of us in the mountains or secretly reading a memory in a diary, but it cracks open that hole inside me every time. And I push the drawer shut again. It keeps a lid on that roaring pain.

"Mummy!"

I stop dead at the landing between the first and second floors. It takes a moment to find my voice again. "What are you doing out here?" I glance left out of the window. The tall houses opposite the front of our building leer in at us. I hold him back from me as he barrels towards me, tears in his eyes. "Harry, how did you even get out of the flat?"

Dust and mould cake the walls of the stairwell, crumbs of mud and dead vegetation littering the stairs. Particles drift in the air, blinking in and out of the muted light.

"I wanted to show you I'm big enough, I'm not scared to come with you," he says, through tears and a full body tremor that makes his voice all wobbly. He looks down at his feet, his legs jigging.

His toes are at the very edge of the landing; the next step would have been the furthest he's been from the four walls of our flat. It tugs at something primal in me, and I shove my mask round his face and push him up the remaining stairs to the fourth floor, squeezing his little shoulders tight.

"There's a key in the special drawer . . ." He offers it up as we get to the landing outside our flat door.

I grab it, a little crack opening inside me.

It's Jack's, his army-green lanyard and the electronic fob to the building attached to it. I've always thought he must have forgotten it on that last morning he was here.

"You didn't take anything else, did you?" I cling to the lanyard, that crack making my voice thick. It's silly, I know it is. Hoarding this stuff doesn't make Jack any less dead.

Yet I'm relieved when Harry shakes his head, even if he does it too fast, cheeks red.

"The front door shut behind me and wouldn't let me back in!" Now he cries properly, great gasping sobs and hot tears streaking down his cheeks.

"You're the bravest, sweetest boy I know, Harry—"

"We went out onto the stairwell once on my birthday. Why can't I—"

"Because I need to keep you safe!" I snap. I strip off my overalls and boots, hands still trembling, hanging them on the hook outside our front door.

"What's so scary Outside?" Harry says, staring at the last glimpse of the stairwell as we step inside.

I lock the door behind us, yanking it over and over to be sure.

"Is it like the Wild Wood, with scary shadows and animals? Nasties always in the dark and grey places to get you?"

I finally calm down enough to wonder what he imagined while he stood there all alone—formless monsters eyeing him up from the dark, dirty windows opposite? Something creeping closer with the creaks of the building? I've probably been gone nearly an hour.

"Nasties pointed at me!"

"No, nothing like that." I pull off all our clothes, pushing him to the bathroom. Brushing us both down with a soft-bristled brush—which I use when we're low on water—and use the few inches in the washbowl and a wetted cloth to work at Harry's face and hands, a sick sweat breaking out at the thought of his little fingers touching grimy banisters or breathing in the wrong specks of dust. "Wait, what do you mean something pointed at you, did you see a person?"

"A nasty!"

I nearly shake him. "Did it look like a person, like you and me?"

He shakes his head. "I didn't touch anything, Mummy!" he says, but I still get into every crease and under every nail.

"Alright," I relent, finished, and work on myself, brushing, lathering and scrubbing my skin and hair aggressively in the bathtub, until Harry can bear it no longer and I step out so he can launch himself into the hug and I squeeze him tight.

"Don't do that again, please," I whisper. Shuddering on the cold bathroom floor, bare skin goose-pimpled and pink; I hate that it reminds me of how hard I scrubbed that day that first year too. Nothing but spit and soap and rough abrasive cloths and desperation, hurting myself almost as much as they ever did.

That silhouette moving in the dark of last night replays in my head. Harry's "nasty" could have been anything. So why does it make me feel sicker . . .

"I won't . . . Hey, look, a ladybird!" Harry says, pointing at my hair as I walk to the bedroom.

We stow Jack's lanyard safely back inside that bottom drawer.

Harry picks the beetle out of my hair while I'm crouched. "I wonder if this one's bad-tempered or friendly."

"I wonder," I say, trying to smile at how quickly things are forgotten for him, while I'm still worrying as I throw on a T-shirt and head to the kitchen. The ladybird trundles up his delicate little arm as I pour the few inches of gathered water into the filtering barrel on the counter. Once it's boiled too, the last step to make it safe, there won't be much. "Don't go near the window, let's just leave him inside for now."

"OK! He can be our friend, then. Don't stamp on him, Mummy."

"I won't."

"I'm always going to be friends with every single creature."

The ladybird starts up the wall as I glance at the pot of cat bones that will be the base of tonight's meagre soup. I'm reluctant now to borrow anything from our winter stocks, yet I think we might resort to doing just that in order to lay low in the next few days.

5

Five Years and Eight Months Ago

Whinbush Road is busy with traffic as I hurry home on foot, drivers peering through dusty windscreens, wipers swishing back and forth. Even the lavender bushes and green wall outside our building, still blooming and buzzing with bees despite the season, look powdered. My coat, unbuttoned because of the mild winter day, is splattered too from the march from the station.

I nod a greeting to our neighbour as I race up the stairwell to the top floor, the rumble of cars fading. And I feel the tension leaving me as I step inside our flat, and change out of my smart things, blinking back the tears that I've held off since I left the interview. I forgot everything. I know about carbon calculation matrices, have plenty of planting scheme and advocacy ideas, so why did I sound so unsure and apologetic, as if I knew I shouldn't be there?

I put on the black dress I picked out for tonight and shake myself out. I've had jobs in my field now, and I did do well to land an interview for a more substantial position, and with the council too. A four-on-one interview *is* intimidating. Next time . . .

In the hallway, our suitcases from our bittersweet, strange Christmas still lie unpacked—Jack's mum and my dad absent from the festivities for the first time.

And yet, I feel that undercurrent of warmth that I've felt all day as I step into the kitchen. It smells of the soft-pink roses displayed front and centre on the counter, opened into beautiful layered rosettes now. Expensive anniversary flowers. Jack had them waiting there to surprise me this morning as I walked in. Four years, though the last two, moved in together, have felt more official.

I switch on the TV to catch the government announcement. They're confirming the dust in the air does contain plastic, but at less than ten micrograms per cubic metre, it's not considered a significant health risk, though those with respiratory conditions may be vulnerable and should stay inside.

I can't help grinning as I hear Jack at the front door: there's something wild and comforting about the way he blows in, backpack, jacket and shoes all shrugged and kicked off—those eyes bright and hair always messy and flyaway as I rush to meet him. He pulls me up into a swinging hug, his skin hot and thick with wiry hair, beard and lips brushing my forehead, his "Central Private Hospital" nursing scrubs rough and itchy.

"I've missed you today," I mumble into those scrubs.

"Me too, first day back always sucks."

As he stills and I sink into him, the formal stilted speech of the minister continues to blare out from the lounge. The high winds from these record-breaking North American hurricanes—Storm Stewart—are expected to dissipate dramatically as they travel across the Atlantic, but will start to hit tomorrow.

"I don't like the sound of all that," I whisper.

"Nor me."

"I suppose once they re-establish communication and get aid in, we'll know how bad it really is over there."

"Yeah—can we turn that off?" Jack groans. "The journalists on next will make it sound like Armageddon. It's just a storm, a big one."

I squeeze him harder to make him stay in this hug. "It's not, Jack—"

"It'll blow over before it reaches us." But he stays, wrapping his arms tighter.

And I remember our first proper hug four years ago today—the one that had lasted longer than either of us meant it to, as if we weren't capable of letting go. After weeks of chatting before and after the ethics lecture we had in common—Jack six years older and a postgrad, already on his second career as a nurse post-army, and me, an undergrad—we had that Christmas break, which had lasted an age, everything in me waiting and longing. So when we did see each other again, it was as if we were drawn together magnetically.

"How did it go?" Jack whispers, finally releasing me.

"Disastrous," I say, as we head to the kitchen and open the fridge. "But it's OK." I shake away his efforts to make me feel better before he even voices them. "How was yours?"

"Messy—post-op care was vomitus and shitty today."

"You win, then," I say, snorting.

"Thank you," he says, a hand to his chest and head tilting, as if accepting an award. "Now, this looks like a fridge filled in January." He laughs. "You got all this this morning?"

I laugh too. The shelves burst with greens, reds and yellows, and vegan cheeses wrapped in paper, soya yoghurt and almond milk in reusable glass jars.

"Jack's special?" He pulls out peppers, onions and tofu.

"Yes, please."

I dice the onions while he gets the rice started. This reminds me of those first at-home dates at Jack's place in London, where he'd cook and we'd watch movies.

The onions go in the pan to sizzle, Jack flinging in the chilli and fresh ginger next with a flourish.

"You can drink it, if you want," Jack says then, nodding at the wine Anna gave me at the weekend for our anniversary.

I wince; I'd forgotten I left it on the counter. "I don't think I want it anymore, doesn't feel fair." I put it under the sink in the recycling box, then feel bad for making a big deal about it, as if Jack's past is shameful.

Suddenly, the awfulness of Christmas and the interview nip at me again, making those tears prickle. I feel desperate to hang on to the sweet feeling of the anniversary instead, not to spoil it. I try to hide my face, focusing on slicing peppers.

"Don't turn away from me," Jack says gently, angling my face back towards him. "What's going on in there?" He smiles.

"I wish we always felt like we do today," I say, thinking of all of Mum and Dad's bickering and blowouts over the years, how that's all ended too now. I wish they could have loved each other at the end the way it looked like they did in their wedding photos. Is that always how things turn out?

"What?"

"This bubble, like when we were first dating and you were all I could think about, you know how you're half holding your breath until you see each other again?"

"I think it's a sign of a good relationship if after several years you can still find that feeling." Jack smiles. "I know Christmas was hard . . ."

I nod.

"Kate, you know I'd never choose not to have you in my life, don't you?"

"Dad loved me, but—"

"But he was ill and so many things seemed to be troubling him. I know it doesn't help, me saying it, but . . . him taking his life had nothing to do with how much he loved you."

"I hate how fragile things feel now, like I'm waiting for more things to break? Like everything's uncertain?" A person alive one moment and gone the next.

"I know," Jack says softly, and I see that shiver of melancholy. "Life is."

I grimace but I'm glad he doesn't contradict or gloss over that unsettling feeling. It would leave me alone with it.

Things have been harder this last year, grief making things rocky sometimes—each of us snapping at the other, irritable and sad. Far from those first carefree perfect years, or at least that's how they seem now. But our own wedding is only a few months away . . . when all I want is to feel all the good stuff. "I just want everything else to fall away. And for us to feel happy and loved-up, just like we did when we first met."

"How can we, though?" Jack says with mock seriousness, a glint in his eyes. "After I finally let one rip in front of you!" He laughs, making me laugh too.

"Or you've cleaned up my vomit after I got that stomach bug that first winter?"

"Yeah—I know I'm a pro at clean-ups but . . . thanks for that."
He smirks. "That bit at the start is the fantasy bit, isn't it?"

I nod a small smile. "I know, I know." Both of us on best behaviour, hormones making us see each other in a fog of gold. "And we've each got to make ourselves happy too, right? Chase our own dreams down."

"I admire you for chasing down what you really want to do—"

"I wish they weren't all short contracts though, so I didn't need to do all these part-time retail and bitty jobs."

"Yeah, but you've had the stamina to do that, keep the money coming in. Many people would give up—"

"I can't not do something meaningful with my life."

"I know, it's one of the things I love about you."

We go back to our chopping, before Jack suddenly slings down his knife and the greens he was shredding. "Fuck it." He sweeps me up, arms tightening around me like mine around him, like there's still space to be extinguished between us, like we can't quite get close enough, his mouth moving in sync with mine, eyes closed. Carrying me down the hallway, stumbling past the unpacked suitcases and feeling for the bedroom doorway, our eyes only opening when he accidentally clocks his head and mine against the door frame, which only makes us laugh harder, still trying to kiss. "Been thinking about this all day."

The black is liquid and heavy, suffocating. Outside, the furious thrashing wind, everything rattling, scouring, shaking and clonking as if I'm at the centre of a too-full washing machine manically spinning its drum.

My fingers—numb and sore from taping sills and vents, hammering rugs and blankets across windows, moving furniture to barricade—find the lid of my laptop. The bright white screen hurts my eyes as the familiar bathroom reappears around me—gleaming tiles, enamelled tub and glittering taps, shower curtain printed with rainbow fish. And I gulp in air, able to breathe again.

I grab a book from Jack's "toilet library." The first is just full of stoic quotes. I flick at random to: "I am calm while the storm is raging around me." I snort, imagining how Jack would laugh. But there's a shudder as the building creaks, followed by a great crash, and I skim a few other volumes before pushing away the books. I need something that can distract me.

I light the candle Anna bought me. As maid of honour she keeps buying wedding-planning gifts and sending me ideas and quotes and colour samples, joining me at all my dress fittings for moral support. This candle is sickly sweet and citrusy—not my taste— but it fills the room and makes me think of her.

There's just enough light to cut little songbird-sized holes in the bamboo segments I've piled in the corner, and to staple down the miniature bark roofs, then cut and tie fifteen inches of wire into bored holes for hanging it. Popular table favours, these crafted bird boxes—I like them. Anna's going to burn "Lovebirds" on them. Just sat there in the hallway, I piled them in at the last moment, for something to do.

I imagine incorporating this night into my speech on the special day, now I've decided I'm going to stand up beside Jack and Adders and give one, not sit silent. And I smile—it might get a good laugh. Maybe I'll also be laughing at having to alter my dress around a bump too . . . I hope not. Ever since we spoke about maybe trying after the wedding, we've not been careful and I feel silly wondering if I feel different—achy and cramping—after our anniversary two nights ago, as if you can tell you're pregnant that quickly.

Pausing, I realize my eyes sting. And my breathing is exaggerated, the air thick and dry. The laptop blinks at me.

I saw the warnings on the news: particles breathed in can clog and damage the lungs. Some are so small they could pass through tissues and into bloodstreams.

Is it inside the flat?

Four in the morning. I suddenly feel heavy.

I type another message for Jack into my phone, though the ones I sent yesterday and the day before still show as unread.

Jack, you OK? Where are you? Please let me know you're alright. Am
barricaded in the bathroom! I did as much as I could to the windows,
like they said on the TV. Wish you were here with me. Love you XX

There's probably several of his waiting to ping to my phone
too. His amused tone—often how he responds to things going
wrong—at how no one could have predicted something of this
scale. About the hug he couldn't wait to give me. That he loved
me too.

Jack must have slept at the clinic the previous night instead
of coming home. I imagine him weighing it up again yesterday,
whether to attempt the journey despite the government lockdown
and get back to me before the storm hit properly, or whether it was
safer to stay put, shuttered up like I am, but at the hospital, trolleys
and boxes of medical supplies used for barricades, ward curtains
pinned across windows. All that glass to cover.

Maybe there are patients he had to stay to care for, or people had
walked in, ill, and he's trying to help. The hospital is a small private
one, no A & E, but still, they might turn up as they did during the
flu scare.

I shut the laptop, just the flickering flame and sharp scent for
company in the grey gloom.

Images of damaged lungs, bloodied faces, bodies in the streets,
covered in dust, a shape falling from the balcony opposite, and
buildings levelled in the London borough Jack's hospital is in—all
keep dancing in the dark. It's all felt unreal, but now I'm trembling
again, sick as it washes through me.

The previous night—when I spent my evening waiting fruitlessly for Jack to come home—they were calling it a "plastic dust
storm": extremely high levels of particles and toxicity. They kept
showing that great swirling mass of Storm Stewart on the surface
of the globe—huge hurricanes—and kept talking in trillions about
all the minuscule plastic specks and flakes to be lifted up out of the
ocean, vast red algal blooms caused by chemical pollution lifting
with it. How they've recorded bigger hurricanes each year too—
climate change—making all this feel inevitable.

This will be the warning, I think, big and awful enough to make everyone really act, this time. Surely. I tick off in my head all the things I will do differently—convince Jack to give up his Subaru, do more research on what I'm buying, join a regular clean-up group, use that microfibre wash bag every time and not just when I remember, persuade family to go vegan, sign petitions to change the laws, join more protests . . .

The candle flickers, the flame and smoke stretched out long and thin, sizzling with a chemical bitterness as if there's something burning in the air that's too small to see. My throat is dry and sore, like the beginnings of a cough. The key symptoms replay in my head: irritation to skin, throat and lungs; trouble breathing; stiff painful chest; coughing blood. Leading to asphyxiation or heart attack. Emergency medical places were set up, but the advice soon changed to hole up at home and not to venture outside. I itch at the scarf around my face, knowing the thin cotton weave is useless to protect me.

And suddenly I remember, probably only six foot from me in the loft above, is Jack's old army gear, including a proper particulate-filtering mask!

I hesitate, heart pounding, my throat dry and itchy—wondering if that mask is the thing that's going to save me—before peeling away my tape and towels and pulling the bathroom door open, the thrashing wind getting louder as I do.

It's definitely inside. In the candlelight, I can see the vents above the window in the room opposite have been thrust open, and little trails of grey have worked through the seals around the window too, my tape peeling, barricades half fallen over.

I drag a chair into the hallway, and the loft hatch swings down after one sharp shove—along with a great snowdrift of thick grey dust! Coating me. I flail, wobbling on the chair, screwing my eyes to slits and holding my breath under the hopeless scarf, my nose blocked, a bitter taste in my mouth. In the seconds it takes me to grab the rucksack and push the hatch back up, I see a grey miasma of smog howling through the great holes in the roof.

I'm crying as I stumble back inside the bathroom, wedging and sealing the door behind me with tape and towels, grey swirling inside, head aching, washing my eyes, nose and mouth out with bottled water . . . before ramming that precious mask on my face as tight as it will go.

I huddle in the corner, the candle snapping and shrinking before winking out. Turning the ring on my finger, Jack's face as I saw him just the day before yesterday—smiling wearily—is clear in my mind.

I just have to hold out here. Jack will make it back. He will.

———

I peel the curtain aside. It's still thick out there, daylight dulled to twilight. But as I stare at the moving swathes of red-grey dust, the flats opposite appear in a ghostly outline. And beyond them, where town should be, sporadic glowing dots—street lights. I shut my eyes to take careful breaths in and out—I keep getting breathless, my throat and lungs burning as if sore and inflamed, my nose blocked and crusted. Imagine something else. Don't think.

It's like a film set. A well-established colony on Mars. That's all. Pretend it's nothing more.

I open my eyes again. Martian dust storms can last a while. Every day that passes, though, it *is* dissipating.

Squinting upwards, the sky seems brighter too. A pale warmth to it. Hard to tell, but it feels like the twilight-daylight is lengthening too.

I shamble towards the sofa—standing up feels too exhausting—and sink into it, absently flicking the lamp switch, but of course, nothing happens. Peering down at the coffee table, I trace my finger over the neat rows of crosses on the paper chart I made, each cross marking the food I'd rationed myself for that day used up. After those first thoughtless weeks, I've tried to make it last as long as possible. I've been able to stretch it to ninety-two days. Three months.

Fuck. *Three months* since I saw Jack.

A horrible heavy dread thuds in my sore chest, tears prickling behind blocked ducts creating a pressure around my eyes. I feel dizzy. I suck in another wheezy breath. And cough out pink phlegm.

But three fucking months. I try to make my tired brain calculate whether that means it's close to May, or if our wedding day has already come and gone. I cling to my phone suddenly, though all my devices ran out of power a long time ago. I sob, my eyes prickling and twitching. All of our family and friends who should have come together on that day are probably all gone. Dead, dead, dead. The noise of those last news broadcasts that I watched and rewatched once nothing new came in reverberates round my head. Snippets of it gouging through my mind. A military voice. Death tolls in the first twenty-four hours. Do not leave your home. Repeat. Do not. Repeat. Do not.

Slowly I notice a soft pitter-patter. Familiar and soothing. Not the irregular whooshing and battering of the dust-laden wind. I look around the dim room, before turning to the window. Tiny droplets of grey-red mud pepper the scratched grimy glass. Outside is thick with falling threads of mud.

I sit and stare out at it for days. Until the clouds dry up and the air bobs and dances with grey and red particles again as if nothing has changed. But I can see the splattered rooftops of town some distance beyond the flats opposite now! The row of poplars behind the flats opposite visible too, bare limbs sodden and splattered grey-red. I hadn't even considered that: trees and plants dying too. I blink, counting up those ninety-two days again. It should be spring.

The car park four floors below has disappeared under mud. Nothing moves out there but the haze. My hands find their way to rest on my chest, to feel that strained beat of my heart beneath the whistling and rattling of my lungs, to feel at least one thing still living. And absently stray across my too-small stomach too.

Yet past the poplars, there's the supermarket, and as I watch I slowly rise to my feet. There's movement in the car park.

With more energy than I've felt in weeks, I hobble to the spare bedroom and grab the binoculars off the bookcase. Wearing a dust suit and face mask, hood up over their head, someone is pausing at each car, checking for fuel, ignoring the electric-only skinny ones. Then they head towards the supermarket.

I scan the shopfront as they disappear inside, adjusting the lenses until the image clears again. Empty shelves and turned-over baskets, all the glass frontage smashed through. A big white army-style four-by-four—the splattered grey almost obscuring the blue UN lettering on its side—is parked across the entrance. I flinch the binoculars away from my face. There was something slumped in the front seat.

I rush to put on my shoes and coat. But at the front door to the flat, my fingers tremble on the cold metal of the lock and I can't catch my breath, lungs tight and coughing up that pink phlegm. My head feels dull—bleary and tired. I imagine myself outside. Air still heavy with particles. Bodies visible through glass and under debris. Empty black windows and grey splattered walls bearing down on me. The 150 metres up the road, across the Hiz Bridge, and the same distance back down to the supermarket car park—achingly far. The words of that last broadcast blare in my head: do not go outside. And the energy that propelled me to the door leaks out of me.

A sickly smell, like rotting fruit, is coming from the cracks around the door.

I heave, sagging backwards against the hallway wall.

Not yet not yet not yet. Words pinging round my fuzzy brain to the rhythm of my short tight breaths. Not today.

Once the red-grey haze clears more, Jack might still come home. I know what he'd say. *You're hurt, stay put; I'll get back to you.* He trained for stuff like this in the army. He'll get back. He will he will he will. Words echoing round my skull. Yet it's followed by that other fearful voice in my head: he didn't train for *this*. Not this not this not this.

And what if he doesn't come back? What if he doesn't?

I think of Mum and my brother, my eyes drawn down the hall-way to that useless phone on the kitchen counter.

Please. Let us all live.

Making it back to my spot on the sofa, I paw at the maps laid out beneath my chart. The route to the house in Birmingham. To Mum and Paul. I imagine Mum, desperate to know I'm alright. And part of me wants to run out there right now and sprint off in her direc-tion. I start coughing once more, burning through my lungs. I feel like a child again, wanting my mum to hold my hand for the needle or dentist, except now I'm scared of what happens if my lungs keep burning and my stomach keeps growling.

How long will I wait here on my own? I can hear a sort of keening in the back of my head.

The day I leave for Birmingham will be the day I accept Jack didn't come home. That he is covered by rubble or dust somewhere in his clinic or what's left of it. That Jack is dead. Dead dead dead.

6

Rain thrums on the windows, smearing the glass and obscuring the sunset, making dusk feel closer than it should. Harry and I sit on the sofa, staring, hoping it doesn't turn. So far it's good, clear rain. I try to imagine the water butt filling up, inch by inch.

"Is it time?" Harry whispers.

I adjust the plinking bucket in the corner, pulling him clear.

"No, it's not really evening yet, not dark enough—"

A muddle of sharp echoes sounds over the rooftops.

Harry's eyes widen. "What is it?"

"I'm not sure." I can't make it out, but there's yowling and bark-ing too. I creep down the hallway to the front door of our flat, and hesitate, listening, before I step out onto the landing and shove on my boots. I pull our front door closed—Harry hanging back in the shadows of our hallway—and push on it, just twice, to make sure it's locked. I pace, the noise growing louder. I tug on the lacing of my boots and finger my knife, still in my back pocket, before finally heading out into the stairwell and deciding I'm going to look out the front of the building.

At the second-floor landing, where I stood with Harry only an hour or so ago, I can taste vomit in my throat. I can see on the road outside: long arms and legs pumping, broad shoulders. There's the sound of boots sploshing through puddles and slapping against hard ground. It's as if my brain can't quite put it together after years of not seeing one, but it *is* a person. A man. At the top of the road. And running in this direction.

I can't see the dogs yet.

Something roped over the man's shoulder flaps as he runs— dead rabbits, badly butchered and hacked apart, bits of hide and entrails flying off them. Idiot. And I would never trigger a chase by running.

My feet take me down to the first-floor landing without me realizing it. Until I'm suddenly there.

He is almost at our building now. I can see grey-streaked black hair, tied in a topknot. I blink away an unwanted memory, which makes me imagine it greasy and lank, skin unwashed and sweaty against mine.

Three dogs whine round the bend at the bottom of Whinbush Road, just as two more and two deer appear from left and right from terrace alleyways. The dogs seamlessly join the chase. The deer are giddy, eyes wild, bucking, throwing their antlers about so much that they lag behind. The dogs, however, will soon catch up.

I see the man reach this conclusion too, and he jettisons the rabbits. They bounce behind him into a shallow puddle. The dogs don't slow down.

The distance between them closes. The collie-mutt leading the chase passes the rabbits without pausing. The man's not going to get away.

I'm on the last staircase. I find myself stepping towards the front door of our building, leaning to hide against the door frame.

His face is distorted through the splattered and scratched double- glazing, his expression blank. But he's running towards the door. He hasn't seen me yet, he can't have. I feel myself growing hot, wondering if the "nasties" Harry saw were real after all. And if this person is heading to our building for a reason.

The black and brown Labradors behind the collie snarl as they give chase. They're joined by the angry barks of an Alsatian, its teeth bared, and the excited whines of a large shaggy mongrel. They'll all be on him in seconds. Their ears and noses are nicked, their coats weathered. Time slows. If I open that door, there will be a man inside here with me, with us. And the door may never lock again. The mechanism was entirely electronic—automatic—in the past. Part of my defence here, to our flat, will be lost.

I bite my lip and turn back towards the stairs. My legs are ready to run. I can already imagine closing our flat door firmly shut, my arms around Harry.

Yet I can't help another glance outside as I stride up the first three steps.

The man waves—just a half-stretched-out hand, as if in greeting, as he nears. So achingly normal that my own hand nearly rises in response, but instead I freeze: he's seen me. The dogs are howling, yelping so close now. The man's hair isn't greasy, but combed back neatly and tied tight. He's thin like us, probably late twenties like me. He's wearing a short-sleeved shirt—clean, not grubby—the collar and shoulders neat as if it was hung as it dried. The sort Jack wore as "smart casual." I imagine the dogs tearing into that shirt, ripping it, exposing skin; the pack mauling, biting and suffocating him like they do rabbits and foxes, until he is spreadeagled and still on the cold wet ground. More dead staring eyes.

What would be left of him next time I came past?

Vomit churns again at the back of my throat.

I hurry to crunch down the door handle.

The mechanism clicks but the door sticks in its frame. Crumbs of dried rubber scatter at my feet as I keep throwing my weight into it, yanking the handle harder. Finally, the door flies open, hurtling me forward with it, the handle clattering across the paving slabs outside.

The man rushes past me indoors, the dogs within metres, whining, teeth snapping, wild eyes bearing down on me. I haul the door shut by what's left of the handle. The collie-mutt smacks into the glass, closely followed by the others. The force of their weight on the double glazing reverberates through me, and I nearly fall backwards. But I hold stubbornly on to the sheared piece of metal handle even as I feel it reopen the cut on my hand.

"Got any crap to barricade it?" The man projects his voice deep and loud over the snarling and clawing.

I jump, instantly hot and sweaty.

He shouts it louder, as if I didn't hear.

"I have an idea," I finally manage, my voice stretched and high as I force the words out. His hand slides over mine—rough and calloused—to take hold of the metal spike, and I snatch my fingers away.

I take the stairs two at a time, and burst into the flat.

Harry's in the hallway, biting his little fingernails.

"Hide in here for me, OK?" I scoop him into our bedroom and deposit him on the bed—dazed at the too-dark red smearing my fingers and staining his T-shirt. Harry stares at it too.

It crosses my mind to stay and lock the flat, wait this out. Yet I can still hear the growling and whining as I rummage through the baskets for gardening twine and, finding it, press the door wedge into Harry's hands.

"Push this in place, just like sometimes on bad stormy days when we hide in the bathroom, where it's safest? But this time you wait here on the bed, don't come out and don't call out, promise?"

He nods.

"It's a just-in-case, OK? I'll be back really soon." I force a smile, kiss his head, and close the door on him.

I pause to hear the wood being pushed under the door, then make myself lock the flat and race back down the stairwell. Now there are dogs at the internal door to the garage too, sniffing and yowling.

"Here." I pass the man one end of the twine and he frowns, confused, before winding it round what's left of the door handle. I tie the other end off at the banister rail, binding the door shut.

"They'll soon give up," he says—shrugging—in a posh, refined voice I hadn't registered earlier.

"Depends how fixed they are on your scent." My words come out harsh and short.

"And how hungry, I guess," he says and smirks, as if his life wasn't really in danger only a few minutes ago.

The bottom landing by the door is a small space, a metre by two. The odour of damp and dust is overpowered just now by a rush of fresher air laced with wet dog and delicious sweet rain—no trace of telltale dangerous bitterness. But quickly all I'm aware of is the musky scent of male sweat.

He is only slightly taller and broader than me, but the difference feels suddenly glaring.

My mouth is dry. I'm still catching my breath, lungs stiff and tight. There's a flash of shock and knowing pity on his face at the slight whistling of my airways and too-dark red on my fingers, making me feel smaller still. Blood is pulsing in my arms and legs, readying me to run.

I start up the stairs.

"You live up here?" He hurries at my heels, and that dread lurches up a notch. He continues when I don't answer, "You can call me Sim, by the way."

I stop, forcing him to halt on the step below me. He wrinkles his nose, looking up, as if he's sensed something I haven't and is inviting me to look too.

"Stay here until they're gone," I tell him, not taking my eyes off him and gesturing vaguely down at the bottom landing where we just stood, my hands then curling into tight fists, my toes too.

"Come on"—his hand on my elbow—"you want my company, surely?"

I pull away, my arm tingling, slamming boots onto each step, legs pumping.

"Wait!"

I dash to the flat door, smacking the key in. Feet pound behind me as I charge inside and turn to fling the door shut, breathless and wheezing. My hands skid off the wood, dark purple-red blood running down my fingers like warm paint, my head dizzy.

I open my eyes to find I'm lying on the floor in our hallway. In the gloom, I'm relieved to see that the door is shut, until I hear Harry sobbing and a soft upper-class voice whispering to him. Sim is in our flat!

Scrambling to my knees, swaying, I pat my trousers, at first to reassure myself they're still on, still zipped. Then to pull my knife from my back pocket with shaky fingers.

"Give him back."

"Fucksake, I wasn't doing anything!" Sim laughs, setting Harry on the floor as I struggle to breathe, my lungs still tight and heavy. Harry bursts into fresh tears, running to hug my leg. I push him behind me, unable to look away from Sim.

"Get out," I growl.

Sim's eyes—bright honey-brown—stare back at me, before flicking round the hallway, as if taking it in properly.

"I was only trying to help . . . You look like you haven't seen anyone in a while," he says, half chuckling. "Oh, you haven't?" He self-consciously fingers the stubble along his jaw, his stance widening as he straightens up. "You live alone then, the two of you?"

I want to make up some story about Jack out hunting. But my throat is constricted, my thoughts all bleary and unfocused as my blood pounds—making me panic more, because I can't think.

"How do you get by, then?"

There are a few breaths of silence before I answer. "I forage and I trap meat." The words bring me strength, help me ease my shoulders down a little from their rigid arching. "I've managed."

"Surviving like in the dark ages?" he scoffs.

I bite the inside of my cheek, feeling hot again, conscious of my creased and stained baggy combat trousers, the thinning shabby T-shirt, and the stuffy air which smells of vegetables and woodsmoke and burned resin.

"I thought I had *the life*, you know? And one of my mates survived, so it felt a bit like that for a while too. We played PlayStation all through it on a backup generator until that went dead!" He laughs.

I wince at his casual use of the word "dead."

"And then we, you know, were drinking ourselves silly, bonfire parties, eating whatever we wanted—can you believe we ate all the food from the freezers at Harrods? It was fucking epic." He leans against the hallway wall, resting his hands behind his head, one foot sliding to cross the other, like he's getting comfortable. "But I don't know if I'm suited to it, I start thinking about the detached house in Surrey my parents had, in Godstone, and it just sounds pretty and quiet, you know? I never thought I'd be craving that, ha! Did you ever try to find your family?"

"Yes," I find myself answering, moving my tongue around my dry mouth.

"And?"

The words swirl round my head. I've never wanted to go back over it. Not that I've ever had anyone to tell. "I never made it to Birmingham." I swallow, stumbling over the syllables. "It—it took weeks to reach Northampton—nearly halfway . . . but I had to—to turn back . . ." I trail off, surprised to have spoken aloud. But he stares at me expectantly. "After that, Harry was too small and . . . well . . . they'd have tried to find me here by now if . . ."

"You're really pretty, you know that? Bet guys were always saying that in the old life, weren't they? You must feel lonely."

Cold prickles down my neck. I run my thumbs over my tense sweaty fingers, pressing harder to try to keep my expression neutral, uncomfortably aware of my T-shirt loose from my trousers and flimsy, no bra underneath.

When Harry whimpers, I pick him up and he wraps his arms tightly around me, great heaving sobs wracking through him. I take a step backwards, not that *one* step makes any difference in this confined space.

"Would be better for him, you know, in the city—different people to talk to." He smooths the front of his shirt.

"Children to play with?" I find myself asking tentatively. "Families to share the—"

"There might be, yeah . . ." he says vaguely. "But when's the last time you did anything civilized—*lived*—music and drink round a fire in the evening, reading whatever books we like, practising on the best guitars . . . I've gotten pretty good." He flashes a grin.

My back is against the bedroom door now, I'm not sure why my feet have edged me here, it's not like I can rush inside and feel safe in there right now. It's the last place I want to go with *him* here.

And I suddenly consider that Harry doesn't even know what music is. I don't know if I've ever so much as hummed next to him. Not since he was a baby and I'd sing bits of nursery rhyme to try to settle him.

"Alright, I'll go check on the dogs for you." He steps towards the door and I press myself into the wall to avoid being too close.

"Perhaps—perhaps I should stay with you?" He blurts it out, his honey-brown eyes excited, but I think I spot fear in them too.

I don't answer.

"I was a stockbroker, you know, previously. Two years of the dream—doing deals and dining clients, studying the markets, making more money than my parents . . . I must be good at this life too, getting by, having good times—but it can drag, can't it? Days of the same shit. Oops, sorry!" He laughs, looking at Harry. "I haven't met anyone living like this." His eyes flick around the hallway again, lingering on the doorways.

Don't, something inside me screams.

"We in the city tend to have formed little groups." I glance at the gun holster attached to the belt of his jeans. He notices, whips the weapon out with a flourish, its dull grey metal scarred. "Was too slow to load it, damn dogs. We protect each other, scavenge for the group—it works. Mostly. Good to have people that have your back."

"Why would you want to stay here, then?" I bite down on my lip, regretting saying it almost as soon as I start doing so.

He rests his hands behind his head again, looking across at me like he doesn't see my shoulders tense, or the Fear in my face— maybe I'm hiding it better than I think. Or maybe he does notice. Maybe he mistakes it for nerves or maybe he's cruel, I have no intuition for these things now. He smiles. "A lot of the guys go hunting for a special girl in the summer; none of them have got lucky, though. What was it that fucked you over—that cancer of the vagina?" He laughs but his eyes drift down slightly.

Wincing, I find my energy fading, the bedroom door behind me holding me up. "No, it wasn't . . ." I grope for a response before my face gets too hot. "It was a big scandal—female health crisis— wasn't it? Women not able to get healthcare. And if they did, standard treatments still not working for them, or making them sicker. Took ages for people to believe it—do more, proper research. Heart attacks and serious illnesses. And yeah, female things being misdiagnosed too, women just seen as—"

"That was a load of bleating about nothing, surely," he cuts in. "Men are just more robust," he laughs, joking I think. "The hunter, right?"

"They said after the first twenty-four hours that it might have been something to do with why women were dying faster—"

"Nah, they were out faffing with kids and old people and not shutting themselves inside like they should have!"

I'm careful to smooth my expression.

Sim salutes as he walks out onto the landing. Holding my breath, it's not until he's through the stairwell door and his footsteps sound on the stairs that I feel safe enough to rush to our front door and push it closed with as gentle a clunk as I can.

I sit tight then, one hand on the lock, as if checking it isn't enough, waiting for my blood to stop thumping, listening to his footsteps fading.

"It smells funny here now," Harry whispers. "Like when you come from Outside, but different."

I nod. I hate it: Sim's male scent invading the hallway.

"What's dark ages mean, Mummy? Is PlayStation games we can play? Who tried to find you? Was it before I was in your tummy—"

There's a sudden rush of footsteps and a knock on the door, throbbing through my hand and making us both jump. I shake my head, finger near my lips. After several more knocks there's a heavy, frustrated sigh.

"I guess you're busy," Sim calls, snorting. Harry clings tight to my leg. "Come on, I'm being perfectly nice! The dogs are gone; I'm going to head out. It was nice to meet you!" There's silence a moment. "By the way, your building smells of leaked fuel or something—didn't you know?"

His tone makes me feel embarrassed and stupid. But I don't open my mouth, don't get drawn into talking. I am not opening the door again.

I listen as those footsteps fade away once more.

"What did he mean about children, Mummy?" Harry says, persistent. "Could I play—"

"Nothing," I whisper, "just stuff from Before." I force a grim smile.

Harry opens his mouth to ask more but shuts it again, scuttling closer.

My eyes slide to the spots where Sim stood—though it's so dark in the hallway now I can barely make them out. I can still feel the pressure of his fingers on my hands from the struggle at the door downstairs.

When I can move again, I clean the crusted gash on my hand first. It's oozing and hot—bad, and goes easily the whole width of my palm now, torn deeper and wider. I feel hot thinking about the wound being exposed to the open air outside. Retrieving the bulrush poultice we made yesterday, I slather it on, covering my palm with a fresh dressing. And yet I still feel restless and uncomfortable, a sickly feeling swirling in my stomach.

I take a soaked cloth and scrub the hallway. Every spot I recall him touching: where his boots met the floor, his shoulder the wall, and where his hand traced the inside edge of the door as he left. I strip and use the last water in the filtering barrel to wash myself too, to scrub him off me, no matter that we will have to eat *and* drink from our winter stocks for dinner now.

"Mummy?" Harry tugs at my arm.

I recoil from the touch.

In the gloom I see his face fall.

"Sorry," I whisper. "We're alright now." I gather him close and we go and sit in bed together, the door shut and the duvet pulled up around us.

"Was it a nasty that came in?"

"Harry—no, what do you mean? Your nasties are just—like in the stories we read—imaginary monsters, aren't they—?"

"No," he whispers urgently. "They hide in the dark, in grey air and in bad rain. They can get you and disappear you. Isn't that why Outside is so scary?"

I swallow, trembling. Thick grey dust swirls outside in my head, amongst bodies and bloody images. "Harry—" I start, that warning note in my voice. We don't talk about what's out there, about the past. But Harry looks tense and shivery. "It's not monsters in the rain, there's *just* thick dust that can hurt us," I say, though thinking too of invisible pollutants falling with it. "That was a man that came in, a person, like us, like Daddy."

Even mention of Jack makes surprise register in Harry's face.

"Are there more Outside? How many?" He gets up to look out the window.

I tug him back, hugging him close. "No, there's been no one out there—" That ache inside me is threatening to open. I wish we *could* have someone, that I could know we'd be alright, if I can't do everything. I inhale, try to stretch out the stiff parts of my lungs, fretting the race upstairs has made it worse, feeling sore and tired.

"It's just you and me and our safe flat," I say, but it doesn't make me feel any better. "He surprised us, didn't he, that's all, just like when there's an autumn spider suddenly running along the floor in all directions?" I run my fingers up Harry's sleeve, trying to make him laugh, knowing that if he does, I might feel lighter too.

Yet he just looks uncertain. "What if he surprises us again? Are there doors where a man could be if we look Outside?" He dashes up to check the window is secure—the dust board there, covering the glass, repaired seals and vents, and the blinds and curtains pulled to—and patters to the front door to tug at it like I do. Over and over, as if that's the magic trick to it. "Nothing can come in, can it, Mummy?"

Harry's questions ring in my ears. I should have followed Sim, checked he'd left Hitchin, or if not, seen where he went. If there were others. Already I know we'll eke out whatever we have up here. I'm not going outside for now. Not leaving Harry alone. My blood fizzes with panic. I can't believe I have ever left Harry alone. All the times run together—all those times as a baby I'd overfeed him so he slept, when I came home terrified to hear him crying, when he was a toddler and just down for a nap and I'd creep out, hurrying to try to get back before he woke, all the sad kisses and faces at the front door, all the times I stayed out longer than I meant to—it all makes me feel sicker. Anything could have happened then, each and every time.

And every time I've been outside, picking berries, digging roots.

Vigilant. But thinking I was alone.

Lying awake in our bed after a cold dinner as Harry tosses and turns, I'm trembling despite the warm covers, anxious thoughts flitting from Harry and my chest, to Sim, to milky rain and red and yellow leaves, to grey matter lying in soil and drifting on breezes, to another man in the dark, heavy, weighing me down, and back to Harry and my chest. Head full and racing, making me think of that cat in the snare, thrashing and wailing to get free so I couldn't get close enough to dispatch it, having to lump over a heavy paving slab to smash down on it.

I have to be able to go out. Forage. Get water and wood.

But the panic is right, isn't it? Can't rely on myself to be able to do all that, to make sure Harry survives.

And now it's even harder. Can't ever leave Harry alone again to go out there. Can't take Harry out there either. It's not safe, it was never safe.

There's no way out of this.

7

"I can feel your heart," Harry whispers in the dark. "It's going boom-boom-boom."

"Have you slept at all yet?"

"I don't know."

"It's alright, the man's gone." But where did he go so late in the day?

"Can we have the fire on? We always have it every day but not today." He shuffles closer, drawing the duvet over his face.

"Not now, Harry." I can't bear to leave our bed.

"The dark makes it like a cave. And there's always trolls or dragons hiding there."

"It's still the same room," I say, but my voice is wobbly. I locked our front door but it still feels possible in my sleepless state that Sim could be here in the dark somehow. "There's the four corners of our bed."

"And the wall with the mirror on it."

"And the dresser in the corner."

"With Daddy. And by the door, the baskets with magic for making food."

"And the door is shut and we're all cosy and safe in bed."

I can't bear to close my eyes to try to sleep. We're not safe here.

I don't know how long passes, but I feel hollowed-out and tired. There's a sharp but lyrical sound somewhere distantly outside. Birdsong! Perhaps a blackbird, but sharper and deeper than I remember—mesmerizing for a few notes, then jarring, as if off-key.

Didn't I always know it was hopeless? I curl my hand around Harry's little fist, and shift position, testing my lungs.

Eventually, too restless, I creep out of bed to the kitchen-lounge, and peer out through the curtains at the darkness outside. I watch it turn purple, then pale grey and yellow.

The flats opposite are visible in the early morning light, grey and ghostly. I remember staring out that day Jack left for work, sky heavy with dust, wind circling and clattering all afternoon. Eight p.m. Jack should have been home hours ago. A car screeched into the car park, a woman flying out before it stopped, no mask on—I remember thinking, didn't she know it shouldn't be breathed in? I watched the flash of her red coat up the stairs to the top floor where branches and debris had already broken windows. Screams, for Ethel, then Ryan, his name over and over, escaping through the gaping glass and puncturing the low whir of the wind.

The air seems to whoosh past me as I pull our window open.

The way she stood at her balcony, looking down, coughing painfully.

How I watched that red coat falling too fast. Staring, frozen in horror.

It would be easier if we weren't here too. No more of this.

There's nothing to look forward to, is there? Harry doesn't yet know just how much he is missing—he has no play dates with friends in his future, no school, no football teams, no university acceptance letter, no learning to drive, no gap-year trek through Africa, no bringing a special someone home to meet me. No love, no family, without me. Even if I can stay healthy and we manage, would he still struggle every day just to survive? No vaccines, no supplements, no clean air or water or soil—always vulnerable. Always knowing that this isn't how it's supposed to be.

If we weren't here there'd be no more waking up remembering what it's like outside, how much I have lost, that Jack is dead, that I am alone. No more fear, of any sort.

No more memories that won't fade from my mind: dead bruised faces, the feel of a stranger where I did not want them, the desperate emptiness of hunger.

And this dread for winter . . . If we weren't here, there'd be no more worrying about how much time is left or how much I might have to suffer. Or leaving Harry entirely *alone*.

I feel sick.

That coat, heavy, had splat like a bag of wet compost.

Done.

I can feel the big gawping blackness that Harry imagines shadows to be, where you might fall in and never escape, "nasties" there to get you. And the wonderful whoosh of cold air the way out. I just want it to be over.

He'd be safe from all of this.

We'll both be gone one day, what's the difference if it's today rather than another day? There's no one to leave behind who would be left with the awful grief and questions. It's not like there'd be ambulances, police, a family to deliver gut-wrenching news to; no body bags, no picture in the newspaper, no coroner's court . . . So perhaps it's not such a big deal, not much of a ripple in the scheme of things at all. All this would just go away for me and Harry.

His little feet slap softly as he pads towards me, fists rubbing bleary, sleep-filled eyes.

I gather him up, still warm from the bed, his heat seeping into me.

"It'll go back to normal," Harry whispers, "now the man's gone, won't it?"

I snort. "No, nothing is normal. It never will be."

I lean right up to the Juliet balcony, the cold air gently tugging at us.

"It's tickling, all soft and cool," Harry whispers in awe, little hand reaching out.

Flakes of dust dislodge from the door jamb above us, floating down around us. But I don't care anymore, even when Harry yelps.

It can't hurt very much. Just for a second. I feel loose, sort of dreamlike, relieved it could all be over.

"Mummy? I haven't got my mask!" He struggles in my arms, shrinking back from the railing and the breeze, eyes scrunched closed.

I frown, the relief I was feeling rightly disintegrating. The dawn horizon is intense melting orange where it still sits within the band of haze, bleeding out above it into yellow then grey then darkness. Grey specks bob around us in the cool air, the breeze shifting loose golden and bronze leaves far below us, little bushes fluttering.

The ground below seems to pulse. So terribly far down, yet stomach-churningly near.

And my little Harry. Who's scared of the dark and wants to treat little bugs like friends. Who likes sweet things and wearing my T-shirts because they smell like me. Whose nose wrinkles when he grins.

I imagine the pavement rushing up to crash into us. Cold terror. Pain. One or both of us broken but slow to die. Dogs and their strange deer finishing us off. Teeth and warm carrion-breath.

Oh God, Harry!

There's breath in my lungs. I feel very aware of it again. Blood pumping. Fingers flexing. And that intense shock and relief I've felt every morning since that first night of the storm: of finding myself alive. I am still here.

And the woman opposite *didn't* fall with her coat, did she? It hit the ground hard, the wool saturated and heavy as it must have been with rain and storm-particles. I force myself to look back up to where she'd clung to the balcony, and scrambled back inside. Knocked on *every* door in her block until someone answered.

I push Harry behind me, and shove the windows shut. Pushing on them once, twice, again and again; they're locked. We're safe.

Harry steps towards me.

"Don't go near the windows!" I snap, tears springing into his eyes.

They brim in mine, too.

My head feels so heavy, every limb suddenly completely exhausted. I fall forwards onto the floor, knees and elbows smacking into the hard flooring. I don't care. Bang. My forehead. I hear the loud crack, but don't feel it, even though the impact reverberates around my skull in a dull roar. Bang. Again. Stupid mean bitch.

"No, Mummy, don't!" Harry's tugging at me, crying in little gasping wails.

I pause with my head resting on the ground. Child's pose. Now the pain floods into my head, blackness edging my vision. A high-pitched tone in my ears above the roar in my skull.

"I'm nothing. Just a stupid useless bitch."

"You're not, Mummy," Harry sobs.

Suddenly there's numb silence, like falling asleep to battering high winds, heavy and scouring with particles, and waking in the morning to strange otherworldly silence and peace. I feel myself slipping in and out of a black place full of white noise.

Harry's mouth moves as I blink in the silence each time I come to.

I lift myself up without choosing to, in time to vomit, then slump down again. Harry snugs right into me, and I hug him hard, yet stroke his face gently, as if this conveys everything I can't find words for. And still the awful crying keeps bubbling up and out of me, and into Harry's jumper.

And those words roll round my mind in that deep, gravelly desperate voice that the years have not faded—the last other voice I heard until today—morphing now into Sim's posh cadence. *Useless stupid bitch. You're nothing. Nothing.*

"I love you, Mummy, don't be sad."

I squeeze him tight. Dying has to be worse than this. It has to be. I've tried so hard. Death wouldn't solve anything, it would just end any chance I have at making things alright. "I love you too," I whisper, "so much. Did you really think I might not?"

He shrugs. "Sometimes you don't say it back."

A knot of emotion slacks and pours out of my eyes.

"Did I make you cry again?" he whispers.

"I'm sorry . . ." I flick away a powdery flake of dust caught near his scalp, making my heart leap, and smooth his hair away from those beautiful amber-brown eyes. His pupils expand as we lie looking at each other. "It hurts sometimes . . ." To be alive when others are not. To feel worthy of hearing those words. "You and me are the only things that matter, OK? I love you, from the centre of my heart right to the edges. Wholeheart."

"Wholeheart," he repeats.

We lie like that until the fuzziness fades from the edges of my vision and my head stops spinning.

"We never lie here," Harry says, giggling. "Everything looks different!"

We look up at the ceiling, Harry pointing out patches of damp and mould that look like elephants on a hillside, escaping the crack-like earthquakes in the plaster. Trunk-to-tail so they don't fall.

The hazy dawn light makes me squint. I turn my head, forehead still throbbing, and my eyes land on the collage Harry has stuck right at the bottom of the TV. Something glued to it gleams softly in that hazy light.

I reach out for it.

"No!" Harry squeals, jumping up.

But I've already pulled the collage free, touched the unfamiliar silver and leather key ring stuck to it and the raindrops on raindrops symbol cut into the stainless steel panel.

I still Harry's grasping hands.

Underneath the symbol, I frown to make out "LAND CRUISER" etched into the shining metal too.

My heart is thundering. That dark looming car with its wide grinning vents and dusty headlights eyeing me from the corner of the garage is suddenly clear in my head.

I judder up to sitting, forehead pulsing heavy, angry pain, hands gripping the paper tight so it crumples. "Where did you get this, Harry?" I say, but I already think I know and I'm staggering to my feet.

"I'm sorry, Mummy," Harry sobs, following me down the hall-way, still trying to take back the collage, as if he can undo me seeing it, and at the same time tugging me towards the bathroom to get clean, fretting with his hair and his T-shirt. "What if I got some on me?"

"Was there a key with this, Harry?"

He shrugs, shaking his head.

"Was there *anything*?" I kneel at the bottom drawer in the bedroom, my hands shaking as I reach to creak it open, Harry hovering next to me, shifting from foot to foot, wiping at his shoulders and itching at his scalp.

"I only borrowed, Mummy, I was going to put it back safe . . ."

The drawer is heaped full of treasure. I paw through the piles of diaries and books, postcards, fridge magnets and photo frames, grabbing at bits of paper for anything I must have missed that might explain the key ring—I know I've never seen a car key but I search for that too—fingers sorting through a shopping list, a Valentine's Post-it, old mail that has Jack's name on it right at the bottom of the drawer, all just mundane pieces of our lives Before.

"There, Mummy . . ." Harry points sheepishly.

I pick up a small stiff cardboard envelope—the kind an Amazon delivery might have arrived in—with my name in huge letters scrawled across the front, obscuring the neatly printed address underneath. I've looked at it once or twice. It has never pulled me in like the photos or diaries of course, which gnaw at me to recall all the moments of my life Before. I only kept this because it was in Jack's handwriting—few things are—treasuring the distinctive untidy and right-leaning slant of his lettering. We used to write each other's names like this on used envelopes and scraps of paper, to leave on top of leftovers or the last slice of vegan cake, or on top of make-up chocolate after a fight.

KATIE!

But now I stare at it, a hot feeling of worry and regret soaking through me, my stomach squeezing tight.

"I didn't scribble your special things." Harry jigs beside me, picking up on my feelings, his voice high and worried.

"I know, it's OK." I turn the envelope over, scrutinize the blank card, and tilt the opening towards the light to look inside.

"It was in a secret place," Harry whispers, cheeks still flushed and guilty. He pushes his hand inside the stiff folds of the envelope and pulls out a playing-card-sized piece of torn cardboard—the envelope flap—from the bottom. I have glanced inside this envelope before, perhaps when I first threw it in the bottom drawer with all the other mail and odd notes. But it was empty. I didn't even notice the torn rectangle of card, or if I did, it wasn't of note—just rubbish. Harry unfolds it, unsticking the jarring bits of festive gift tape holding it to, and showing inside where the key ring was.

I grab the torn envelope flap from Harry. On the outside, there's writing that I've never seen before. Faint on the dark brown card—as if the pen used was nearly out of ink.

Katie! I'm so sorry it took me so long to get back. I've waited here now as long as I can. I've left something for you where I know only you would find it—find your phone! If you read this—please follow me north. Please. I love you, so much. J xx

A jolt goes through me, but even now I stare, frowning, as if it's a note from a long time Before—because Jack died with the storm, he's gone. And it must be a post-fight make-up note—*I'm sorry . . . I've left something for you*—from back when his mum was still alive and he'd get those worrying calls and race north to check on her as soon as he got home and I'd follow later when I got in.

But the words are too urgent, making my skin prickle. The car downstairs—partly in Jack's parking space in the corner, awkward to reverse into and not the empty spot you'd pick by choice, especially for a big car like that—and the key ring pulsing in my hand, missing its key . . . make the words twist round and come clearer. The looted flat when I got back from that failed trip to Birmingham in the first year . . . someone searching for something specific. As if they saw that car—and hadn't driven it and abandoned it here themselves—and hunted each flat in our building for the means to use it . . .

But what the fuck did he mean? Where only I will find it? My phone is amongst the treasure—black dead screen. I found a council building with solar power still working once and charged it up—so I know there's nothing to see. Nothing came through then, no signal, no messages, nothing but old photos I could only look at until the battery died again, taking them with it.

"Mummy!" Harry whines, squirming on the spot. "Have I got it on me?"

I turn, my tired brain still trying to work out what the hell Jack's message means.

"We were only outside there a moment." My voice gets thick, Harry's eyes big and worried just like they were when he was squirming in my arms out in the open on the balcony. "OK, it's OK, let's get you cleaned up, just-in-case."

In the bathroom, I dab Harry's face and hair with a moist clean cloth in a daze. Jack wrote that. He came back and left that and I shoved it in a drawer unread. Fuck! My head throbs angrily.

When Harry begins to look a little less scared, he wants to wipe me down too, so I accept the cloth daubed across my face—poked too close to my eyes—and my hair tugged through as he slops and squeezes at it with the cloth. Should've, would've, could'ves have started whirling round my head. If I had not left the flat for Birmingham and been gone those weeks, if I'd been here . . . Or if Jack's message hadn't been swept onto the floor by looters and I'd read it five years ago . . . I can just picture exactly where he might have left it, the card envelope perfect for leaning upright against something on the kitchen counter, waiting clearly and in plain sight for me. But discreet enough that looters might—even if that envelope flap had come flying out—overlook it, or even if they didn't, they wouldn't know exactly what Jack's message inside meant, where the missing key was . . .

The looters tipped everything everywhere, searching this flat and all the others in this building . . . How could I know to look for a note from Jack in all that mess? Or to realize what the car in his spot meant? Jack was dead. He was dead. That's why I'd left the flat—ill and in an awful state—after those four months of waiting and slowly realizing it.

If he wasn't . . . It's too big, my head too fuzzy, my stomach too swirly—I can't think straight. I stare at Harry instead and his beautiful pale clean skin, that chestnut hair, that little worried smile as he looks back at me, triggering that heavy lump in my throat again, knowing where on the ground outside we might have been right now. However much I wipe Harry's warm soft skin clean, I can't get that image out of my pounding head.

It can't end like that.

8

Four Years and Six Months Ago

I stare out across the rooftops, sagging against the glass. It's cold and dead out there: bare trees weeping dark stains from their cracks, like bleeding sores; grey skies. The thick smoggy daylight is lasting longer though. And it's milder—my lungs have cleared once more, the cough gone—so it must be nearly spring again. I squint, desperate to pick out any bud or fresh shoot. Any life.

I rock on my hands and knees as another wave ripples through me, sucking air between my teeth. I want this to be over. It's been two days. However it ends, I just want it done now.

Smoothing my hand over the hard bump, it feels an age since I started watching it grow.

"Please don't hurt me. Please don't hurt Mummy." My voice cracks. Mummy. If I survive, I'm going to be a mummy.

If I don't . . . Dread rises up my throat again. All this past year I have felt it, the big black void of death all around me. I don't want to face it alone. I don't want to die.

I rest my head on the floor. I wanted this so badly with Jack; we talked about it . . . but I don't want it like this. Not alone. Not in this world. Not now. I shouldn't have let it get this far, should have braved the grim medical centres for some method. But I just couldn't . . . Pilfering through medicine cabinets already well raided by their previous owners was enough—bathrooms are often awful places to go.

Nothing grows outside either, so no rue, feverfew, pennyroyal . . . anything that my foraging book says could have helped curtail it.

Idiot. I've been living in a fog, swinging from trying to forget to imagining what I could do to get rid of it, to a strange comfort in feeling movement inside me that made me feel less alone . . . and now I'm here. They said, Before, that fertility had declined, that most women's bodies struggled to carry to term anymore—

Pain throbs and I hold my breath.

I'm not going to die. I'm not.

But I've felt hot and uncomfortable for days, my waters leaking for the past week—the book says to call the midwife immediately if that happens, in case of infection.

I choke down a sob and nibble at some stale raisins. My hands look childlike and thin as I reach to touch the clean towel spread over the floor and smooth the pages of the books, clipped down to the sections on childbirth. I'm supposed to stay calm. That makes it easier, reduces the risks.

How the fuck—

The moaning is out loud now; I can't help it. I almost have this urge to shout out for help; I'd almost take anyone—God, even a complete stranger.

I try to take deep breaths, think of the muscles surging and tightening.

It's getting dark. I don't want to do this in the dark of all fucking things! I think of hands grabbing me. The swish of nylon against nylon. Me running, barefoot, no mask, having lost my pack, everything. What if this life inside has grown wrong or damaged somehow because of how they hurt me that night? And we're both going to die now?

No, I wouldn't want a stranger here now.

Only Jack.

I can't help the long, low moans and ragged gasps.

Down the hallway, I can see the door to the bathroom. I hesitate, before pulling the blankets and towels—my books bundled up inside—my water flask and the gas lantern I found and have saved, and crawl towards it, stopping twice, biting into my fist to stay quiet, and trying to breathe deeply. Don't pass out, Katie.

I feel safer when I get there, the gas lantern throbbing beside me. A duvet and some pillows are in the tub from the last heavy rainstorm.

I can't remember how dilated you're supposed to be to push or if I should lie down. The lines of writing in the nearest book seem blurred in the dark with only the flickering light.

Pain races across my stomach and I try to push. Pressure builds against my lower back and bottom, but nothing happens, and I come gasping to a stop, sweating and wincing and laying myself down for a second on the nice cold tiles.

I clutch the pages of the book. But I have no idea what I'm doing. This doesn't feel right. Nothing feels like it should.

I miss hospitals. And doctors. And Jack. He'd hold my hand and tell me it'd be alright, that I was capable of doing hard things. I miss my mum, and my best friends, and knowing they'd be waiting for me. I don't get to have anything. Not them, not even a wedding day, not the career as an environmentalist that I wanted and worked so hard for—I wanted my life to mean something, to do something worth something. And even though she's likely dead, I envy my friend Anna. At least she got to feel that flood of happiness when she had her baby—I know I won't. At least she had her husband, "her rock," to support her—and they got to hold their child in their arms together afterwards. At least she got to have a fucking epidural!

By first light, the instinct to push is there, and I remember that is just like the books said. On hands and knees, I try to. Following each wave of pain, face muffled in the blanket. A dull white noise keeps sounding in my ears. It's so dark in the bathroom with the door shut and the lantern gone out now that I feel a panicky urge to scramble out. I try to remember the squeeze of Jack's hands around mine at Dad's funeral, the way it held me upright in the pew, giving me strength. I try to imagine it's his hands wrapped around mine now, instead of the towel I'm clinging to.

One more push. A hot burst of pain and movement, and then agonizing fullness and tearing. I groan into the towel, feeling with my hand: a head, a tiny shoulder. I pull at it, pain making a horrible dizziness swirl in my head. I get a finger under that little shoulder to pull. Please. I don't know how long I tug. I roll on my side, on my back, trying to get it moving.

And finally I feel it, along with another hot wrenching pain: a slimy weight falling onto the back of my legs, the umbilical cord snaking between us.

I kick the door open a crack and the dim grey light helps me breathe. I stare at the tiny wrinkled shape behind me, my body twitching and smarting, blood still flowing out of me. A scrunched-up face, slick with gunk and wet. Limbs all bunched up tight. I'm crying again, trying to breathe. Don't faint, Katie! Yet the darkness is racing in.

I hold the little thing and rest myself down on the floor, gently, shivering against the tiles. My focusing on those tiny delicate little arms and legs against my chest, miniature fists balled up tight against my collarbone, just about keeping that fuzzy dark at bay. There's a feeble birdlike wail. A tiny heart beating beneath my fingers. I kiss its soft wet skin.

"Sorry, baby, to bring you out here."

And it does come: a weird liquid sensation of warmth, right in my stomach, swirling, even though everything's cold and smarting. And I know: I have to make it all alright, for this little precious thing. I have to.

9

Shaky and tired, and shivering from the cold wet cloths, Harry and I decamp to the bed—I can't face looking at that balcony window again just yet. And I need time to think—reading and rereading Jack's note.

Yet after days of no appetite, there's suddenly a gnawing emptiness in my stomach. So I bring Harry whatever he wants, anything to make that little smile appear on his face and dull the awful guilt of this morning.

And with a breakfast feast of rabbit jerky and bulrush cakes and a big mug of cold tea set before him—all from our winter stocks—he cheers up, the fog lifting from my head too. Harry wants *The Lion King* and as I read softly, I realize that Simba never saw his father's body in this picture-book edition, never confirmed to himself what Scar said was true; this edition doesn't even use the word "dead"— probably why I let Harry keep it. But what if it hadn't been true? And Mufasa lived? And Simba didn't need to despair and feel so alone.

What if it's not too late to find Jack?

A crunching and squelching sounds across the grit and leaves four floors below, and voices—clear in the quiet morning.

"This where she lives, then?" a male voice rings out.

"Let him go up by himself, if he wants to—"

"Dreaming of secret assignations, ha-ha! Girl all to himself."

My mind is still on Jack, thoughts all jumbled up, before I grimace, my heart racing again and palms sweaty.

"Romantic sod."

Their voices are too similar to distinguish at first: deep, somewhat gravelly and damaged, London accents.

"Ah, let him—pretty, young couple like that, odds were stacked against them, weren't they? Lucky to find each other."

The others whoop, and Harry flinches, his little shoulders shuddering against me as I wrap my arms around him.

"I wanted to get a look at her—mousy blonde and petite though, Sim said, didn't he?"

"Bit haughty if you ask me—not coming back with him or coming down to say hi. Hope she don't string that lad along; be awful wouldn't it, to reject someone when everyone's fucking dead?"

"Well, I'll try my luck if she don't fancy him!"

"Nah, Sim said she was just shy is all, couldn't keep her eyes off him. She's already got one kid—be nice to have littlies in our group, wouldn't it? Miss that—sound of kids playing, laughing."

"We'll meet her soon enough. Come on, lads, let Sim introduce her. Give him some respect."

I find myself shaking my head, embarrassed and strangely guilty—if Jack were here I'd hate for him to think I'd led another man on. But why don't they consider I might be scared of them? If I say no, or hide, I'm just a haughty bitch? Yet that voice that's stayed stuck in the back of my head for the past years rises up: *bitch*.

"Might not want any of you," an older, gruffer voice says. "Leave the girl in peace, come on."

Maybe not all of them would think so. I feel grateful for that last voice, hoarse and slow, like an old man. Part of me wants to call out, to hear my voice out loud and have that strange pleasure of being part of a conversation, like they are. But it's not them I want to speak to. Jack's message pulses in my tight grip.

Their footsteps crunch away, voices fading, and I leave Harry on the bed to peep out of the bedroom window at four men, taller and broader than Sim. All lean, clothes hanging loose, and I linger on the one that could most resemble Jack, his hair shoulder-length and messy.

Harry and I both swivel as hard boots pound up the stairwell inside the building. Getting louder until there's a sharp rap at our front door.

"A nasty!" Harry lets out a frightened sob, sinking low.

This morning's sickly panic flares, and, bringing a finger near my lips, I whisper, "The man's back already."

Harry stays wide-eyed and frozen.

"Hey!" Sim shouts through the door. "Hello? Why aren't you answering the door? Come on, we're friends now, aren't we?"

"Hello?" he calls louder, irritated, as if he has his hands cupped to the wood. "You know, I swear this building is probably danger-ous . . . and you shouldn't leave your shit about, by the way, anyone might take it! Come and get it back off me—we're at True Organics during the day, getting it fixed up for proper crops and stuff, and a nice place just round the corner from here at night. I'll keep my eye out for you." He laughs. "See you soon!"

I wait at the window, still frozen there, watching until he's out of sight, his boyish walk stiff. Swung over his shoulder are the things I need to protect myself—my overalls, my mask in the pocket, and my only pair of proper waterproofed boots! I blink back tears.

"He looks sad," Harry says, peeping up like a little meerkat, hands held fisted to keep from touching the windowpane.

"Maybe," I say. Or getting frustrated.

I pad out of the bedroom and along the hall to check the front door—and stop short, noticing shadows under it. I feel a desperate hope that maybe Sim didn't take my boots after all.

Harry bumps into my legs, clinging. "Don't go out there, Mummy." And I see him looking fearfully at those two shadows as well—still but solid, like a person stood right there.

"Why don't we play a game? Any game you want, to make you feel better?"

"Hide-and-seek!" He grins slowly, eyes still puffy and pink from crying.

"Alright." I find myself smiling back, turning him around.

"OK . . ." He twists Luna in his hands, shifting from foot to foot.

"Better hurry and hide Luna!" I make a show of facing the wall and counting, rushing as if I hope to catch him out, and I hear him dart off down the hallway.

Looking out through the peephole, I see the landing—empty—and let out a held breath.

Unlocking and pulling the door open as quietly as I can, I find two tins of food and a note wedged between them at my feet.

My gut says to leave it all undisturbed, as if taking them is some kind of agreement or encouragement. But I can't help opening up the paper, part drawn by the unfamiliar feeling of contact with someone, mostly dreading what it might say and therefore needing to see it.

He tells me he can't wait to see me again, *sweetheart.*

I watch for you now wherever I go—I saw you, a week ago, you know. But you didn't see me! Killing rabbits in that woody bit just north of town—little wild girl.

Nearly said hello, but the guys were just round the corner and I wanted to meet you alone.

You are so pretty up close.

I feel sick imagining him eyeing me up as I lay passed out on the hallway floor. What might have run through his head.

Don't be so shy. It's cute, but it's also a little rude, you know, waving knives about and this silent treatment—it's not like we're several months down the line and I've actually done something to piss you off! You really better answer my knock next time, or I might be the one to get pissed off first!

Meeting you puts all the shit to rest. Now you're all I want to think about.

He doesn't even know my name.

I frown, staring at the words, wondering if he expected me to find it funny. Or not.

I return the note to its place, wanting to shrink quickly back inside, but I pause. I can smell it too now, just for a moment before my nose habituates to it—the faintest odour of fuel beneath the damp and chemical bitterness of dust. It wasn't just a ruse, yesterday, to get me talking or opening the door. It's stronger as I step towards the water-stained metal doors of the lift, which Jack and I barely used: too wasteful to flash the key fob and get charged for the power, and with barely any hills round here, the four-floor burn was our daily little hill climb.

Except on moving day! We bundled our belongings up in it all afternoon. Me and Jack.

That's what he means! I lost my phone that day and got in a flap about it. He'd ribbed me for it for ages after that, any time anything got mislaid. I'd bagged my first ever interview for a proper environmentalist job. It was right up my street—if, actually, out of my reach six months post-graduation—researching effective carbon storage in green roof designs. It should have been that Friday afternoon, but then the key exchange and moving day was confirmed, and I'd fretted in case there was a problem pushing the interview to Monday.

I burst back into the flat and Harry's right there, waiting in the hallway, scared wide eyes looking over my shoulder.

"Let's do a finders game instead," I say, tugging on the deadbolt and running to spit-clean my hands with a cloth in the bathroom.

"But I hid Luna in a good place!"

"But—" I squirm on the spot. Yet Harry's little face is pale and drawn as he peers round the bathroom door, looking dangerously close to over-tired and tears. "Alright."

As I search the hallway cupboard, I feel not only for Luna's time-smoothed wooden body but also for something small, cold and metallic. I snaffle through the coats, scarves and odd keys on the coat hooks opposite the front door too, in case after all this time I've overlooked something else. Where did we find my phone in the end?

"Mummy! You're not doing it right."

"Sorry."

I'm sure we eventually found that phone inside furniture or a cupboard, where it had slipped while we'd manhandled stuff into the rented moving van. I can almost see it: the shiny ocean-blue case wedged in a dark corner as we unpacked . . .

In the bedroom, I peer under our bed and rifle inside the wardrobe.

"No, Mummy! You're cold! Very cold!" Harry is giggling and shaking his head.

In the kitchen-lounge, I open cupboards and look under sterile cloths and jars filled with flours and shove my hands to the back and pull out toys.

"Warm!" Harry says.

I pull apart the sofa, before my eyes catch on a lump under the rug.

"Hot!"

Still feigning a struggle to find it, I turn up the corners of the rug and act confused, until he finally says "Hotter, hotter!" and I uncover Luna.

I wait what feels a polite few seconds for Harry to relish the ending of the game. "OK, now let's play a finders game. We're looking for something small and metal, similar to the door key."

"OK," Harry says, already scanning the room.

"Let's think differently. Places that we haven't looked before."

"I think I know *all* of the hiding places."

Walking along next to the kitchen counters, which Jack fitted with second-hand units he'd hung on to for months before we moved in, I kick the skirting board at the bottom and drop to hands and knees to peer into the cavity, nervous of the dust.

Harry flinches as I stand up, staring at the dark gaping space as if something nasty might wriggle out from it.

"I don't like the new secret places, Mummy." Harry turns to scrutinize the room with serious eyes, brows scrunched together with worry. "I don't like not knowing! And it's like Outside is inside—I don't like it."

"It is a bit, I guess," I say, giving his shoulder a little squeeze. "We must be careful, you mustn't touch." Reaching for my pocket,

I turn Jack's air meter on, the black hole of grief beginning to reopen and make my earlier bleakness nip at me again. Already there's that awful feeling of hope being crushed, an echo of those days and weeks and months waiting for Jack when he never came back.

"It's alright, Mummy, you tried hard to look," Harry says. He rubs his eyes, weary, and I realize how exhausted I am too as I push the boards back to cover the dusty crevices.

But, limbs heavy, I haul myself from room to room . . . even turning over picture frames holding Harry's renderings of red and yellow foliage and grey swirling skies, in case something is taped to the backboards.

"*You* drew this, Mummy?" Harry is rummaging happily through my desk in the spare bedroom, an old university sketchbook in his hands, opened to a rewilded—the buzzword then—city street: crisp blocky architecture with panels of sprouting green wall, lollipop neon-green trees and a trickling stream meandering through the pedestrianized street. Happy people and bright primary colours that make it all look so stupidly simple to achieve and harmonious. And sterile—nature allowed on our terms only, in neat little strips. At least Harry's drawings are wild and windswept, as if the built world is truly part of the wild, not separate from it.

Harry discards the sketchbook and kicks at the base of the drawer unit, seeming relieved when it doesn't give.

"That one's fixed with screws," I say. And yet . . . while the desk in its window position is cracked and paled from sunlight and damp, the still-rich honey of the wood by Harry's foot jogs my memory. Jack and I stood here, knackered and splitting into hysterics at the lucky audacity of my phone to have made it all the way here—stuck inside the bubble-wrapped upside-down desk—and at the *hundred* missed calls I'd forced Jack to make flashing on the screen, above an email notification: interview moved to Monday. *See, all OK!*

"Stand back, Harry." I tilt the desk towards me. It heaves down with a sickening crunch.

"Ow!" Harry drops to the floor.

"What?" I throw myself down to check his toes, yet he's not cry-ing, but pulling up broken carrots and pointing at the squashed row of apples and the scattered chestnuts.

I should curse myself for being so careless, yet I'm clambering over to look at the base of the drawer unit instead and its preserved rich, dark underside. And there, taped in the corner, is a black and red box with wires curling out of it. So like bombs you used to see on the news, stuck to the bottom of planes and oil drills, that my mind automatically goes to Sim. But I think it's some sort of jump-starter.

A piece of black electrical tape is gummed up in another corner, easy to miss. I pull it up, strip by strip with my fingernails, until I see it—the tip of something metallic against the reddish wood, gleaming Snitch-like gold! Waiting for you, only, it seems to say to me, right where we'd once laughed.

10

"Is that it?" Harry peers at the key in my hand, running a finger across the brassy metal with its notched tip and the smooth plastic fob trunk. I pull a second key free—the crisp all-silvery spare presumably, its nickel coating still intact—and finally, a rectangle of folded white paper from the centre of the base board.

Katie

In a blur we walk to the bedroom and I sit cross-legged on the bed, Harry kneeling and eager beside me as I look down at that familiar leaning scrawl.

"Please, Katie," I remember Jack saying in the kitchen as he gulped down coffee on that last morning, "we've been through this. You know why I have to go back to London today." I can picture him, his eyes slightly wide and downcast. Tired and needing to hit the road to avoid being late. So important to him not to let people down.

"They've put out a severe weather warning."

"For the day after tomorrow. I promise you, nothing is as bad as they're saying, or the army would be out on the streets."

"Jack—"

"If I don't turn up, people could die, Katie."

I remember the hot desperate feeling that churned inside me

then. "What if *I* die while you're gone?" Instantly, I'd hated that I'd said it—I knew how his army career had ended, with a dead teenager that he couldn't save and an injury that got him hooked on pills, because guilt and pain became depression and addiction. Guilting him was a very low blow.

"Katie . . ." His voice had sounded worn out, all soft and breathy. "I would never leave you if I thought it was all going to shit. You know that, don't you? Stay off work today if it makes you feel safer, but it might do you good to go out, not dwell on the news?"

I'd shrugged, like a child not getting her way.

"This isn't the end of life as we know it, come on." He'd nudged me in the ribs, snorting, pulling that grin.

"I know, but—"

"The media is fearmongering, sensationalizing it, as usual. It's not even a storm, just some pollution blowing over from a storm across the globe."

"We don't really know how bad it was over there, I guess—"

"Exactly, communications are whacked because of it. It'll blow over."

"People *have* died here though, Jack, respiratory problems, in the last few days—"

"But people do at this time of year; if only we had the immune systems our grandparents had, eh?"

"Jack—"

"I've made my decision." He'd said it deliberately softly, walking towards the front door. "You disagree. We'll just have to live with that. Let's not get overemotional about this, Katie, I have to focus today."

Later, days later, I'd wondered if I *could* have persuaded him. Layered on arguments—I knew the hurricane season in the Atlantic and in North America had been record-breaking, that the readings suggested a big secondary environmental impact. I could have told him more of the worrying things I'd read—about airborne dust levels ramping up in those last few days. If that didn't work, emotional blackmail might have been worth it . . .

But outside, people had been leaving for work and school like normal, on the news in the background they'd been discussing the election, and there was the usual rumble of tyres on the nearby motorway. Everyone had panicked over the bad flu season a few weeks before, over that last Christmas—myself included—and that hadn't been so bad in the end, that time—at that point I'd still got the panic-bought supplies stuffed in our kitchen cupboards.

High winds and a bit of air pollution had seemed inconvenient, but not dangerous. And yet there was that feeling of unease. The grief counsellor had said it would feel like that sometimes after Dad's death—more vulnerable to worry, lower threshold to stress. Jack had looked calm, sounded balanced and rational, always the one with a stoic head on his shoulders. Maybe that's why in the end I'd nodded.

How could he have known? No one had really known.

I remember running up the hallway and putting my arms around him. He'd hugged me back, tight, warm, a few seconds longer than we might normally. I love you, I remember thinking. But did I say it out loud? Or did I keep it in, not wanting to seem overdramatic. In the weeks and months that followed, I'd tortured myself trying to recall whether or not I did. That same spiralling tugs at me now, except it's wondering if I'll see that face again, if Harry could have the daddy I've always wanted for him and now feel desperate for, if it's possible this car could start and we'd be able to find him, five years after he wrote this. If I'll get to say I love you, after all.

"Is it a story?" Harry squirms on the duvet, eyes lingering on Jack's letter in my hands, a spark of warmth igniting inside me.

"Sort of." My eyes race over the words, trying to absorb every one. Jack really didn't die in the storm. He didn't die! The realization rocks around inside my head, dislodging everything—lungs, food, Sim. And those months I waited here, was he somewhere else, clear of the hospital and that levelled bit of London, or somehow safe within it, ill, trapped, helping others, waiting for it to clear to make the journey? I reread in case I missed something, a new wave of not-knowing consuming me, but this is better than imagining all the ways he could have died.

"A new one?" Harry asks, matching my smile, waiting. Yet his face falls as he begins to guess that this is another story I won't share with him. He squeezes his arms tighter to his chest, Luna disappearing beneath elbows and forearms.

"OK, I'll tell you. Daddy wrote it."

"But . . ." Harry's confusion makes me feel dizzy too. "Will he come, like Sim the man?"

"He's not scary, Harry, it's Daddy, it's Jack—we know him."

Harry frowns.

"Being a daddy is like being a mummy—he'd look after you, love you, like I do. You understand that, right?"

There's silence between us, my thoughts racing, as I look down at the letter again. The last two-thirds are a list of practical instructions about fuel and getting the car started, keeping the vents shut, and the best routes to drive north, but it's the first paragraphs I pore over.

Katie—I choose to believe you went looking for your family, and that maybe there's still a chance you'll come back here. The Cruiser was just sat in front of the supermarket—too good and so close not to haul back here, for you, just-in-case. I've used these military-grade Cruisers before—there's a hack on the underside to get the door open.

In a stupid way it feels like I've done something for you by doing this. I know Adders and the others are probably right, finding your body would have made the goodbye final and in some ways it's unlucky not to get that closure. The hospitals are full, the makeshift ones too, and I know you might have gone there in the final days for help. I tried searching for you, there and at Anna's, and all over town, but it is grim, hard to make out faces or recognize features. Too grim. So I choose to live on just-in-cases and hopes, right now, until I've searched every place you might have gone to.

"We have to go," I say to Harry, our eyes fixed on each other. "We have to find him."

"Outside?" Harry whispers. "Where will he be hiding?"

"It's not hide-and-seek, silly," I say, smiling, but Harry remains serious, fretful, tugging his bottom lip. "I know where we'd need to go. Let me show you." Excited, I retrieve a couple of crumpled OS maps from the bottom dresser drawer and spread them out on the bed.

Harry stabs a finger at the top-most, local map. "Are these all the places you go Outside?" He scratches at the fine blue line of the Hiz, next to the flats, then follows the thicker, deceptive blue of the motorway down to the edge of the paper. My eyes follow its path on the smaller scale—zoomed out—England map next to it, right down to the sprawling grey and black of what was the capital.

"No, I don't go far normally. This plain bit is where the fields and hedgerows are—where the damsons and blackberries grow, and that little blue dot there is the clean bulrush pond—where I get bulrush roots and sedge seeds, and that's Nathan's Coppice, which is lots of trees together where there are rabbits."

"Why is it all green here?" He peers at the tree motifs marking the fragments of woodland, scattered over the map, that in reality are mostly now shrubby yellow-red-leaved bushes and saplings, only a sparse regiment of mostly dead trunks to show something older once grew there.

"Because that's what colour trees were." I can't help it, eyes drifting about the maps, wondering if we go if we might yet see something green in the flesh. They did speculate, during the storm, whether there'd be more shelter and dissipation of the winds further north.

He frowns. "Why? Yellow is prettier. Yellow is warm and happy."

"Green was pretty."

He snorts. "Would we only go really quick Outside and never in the dark? Promise?" He holds his breath.

"Well, we might have to sleep somewhere else—"

He frowns. "Like the sofa?"

I walk to the window, remembering the steep steps up to that house in Derbyshire, the views over the Rother Valley, Sheffield— the nearest city—far enough away that it felt like the countryside there, but its civilization only a tram-ride away. *Follow me north*: to his mum's old house.

I stare outside at our familiar view of rooftops and yellow poplars, feeling suddenly sick at the thought of actually packing our things, leaving the flat behind, and heading off *out there*. Would we try even if the car doesn't work? To reach *Jack*? My thoughts whirl again.

Beside me, Harry's pale cheeks are rising in colour.

I close my eyes, visualizing us leaving. "Going in a car wouldn't be as bad," I whisper. "It would be like a safe little room on wheels."

When I look down, Harry is wide-eyed and scared, scratching his chin with Luna's antlers.

"Come with me," I say, tugging him into the hallway. We take a box up and down across the rugs, Harry riding inside like he did when he was a toddler, when we fashioned them into magic castles and space rockets and special sledges pulled along by make-believe creatures. This time, we whisper about wheels and windows and a roof, weaving the box as if round streets. Harry looks unsure, but as I push faster—the friction from the rugs making my muscles burn—there's some chuckling and grinning as we hurtle down the hallway.

Harry stretches out his arms. "I'm flying!"

But a voice at the door makes us both freeze, Harry's arms snatched back inside his box. "Sorry to disturb—wanted to bring your stuff up—thought you might want it back." It's the older voice. "You OK, love?"

I creep to the door, cold and sweaty as I wonder how long he's stood there and how much he heard. Through the spyhole I can see—with great waves of relief—my priceless boots and overalls being set down on the landing.

Silence stretches out.

"Thank you," I manage finally.

"I'm sorry for the sound of your voice," he says, kindly I think, though I feel like I'm waiting to be accused of being ungrateful or haughty again, and rude for not opening the door . . .

"Look, if you're not interested, just tell him to fuck off—he'll get the message. He's just being a silly sod—set him straight, don't worry. Would hate to think he made you feel like you had to leave your place here."

I look at Harry, conscious of the car keys in my pocket. "He hasn't," I say, a little more calmly, starting to feel the joy of speaking to someone, though I keep my hand on the reassuringly solid door. And the words are true: a stronger warmth rising inside me as I think about Jack and I flash Harry a small smile.

Through the spyhole, I see the man outside nod. "Then just tell him. He'll get over it. We've all had to get over the motherfucker of bigger things, haven't we?"

I wonder if we have, any of us, "got over" it, if it's even possible. All of us capable of being the hurt person hurting people. Sim's last line: *Meeting you puts all the shit to rest. Now you're all I want to think about.* As if getting over it is simply putting your sadness into someone else's hands to take away. And be accountable for. His words leave me cold; stark against the real, deep pull to Jack.

Opening the door once the man is gone, I pull our things inside, Harry sidling closer to peer at the faded mandarin segments on the labels of those tins Sim left earlier. I imagine Harry's joy at the sweet citrusy juice, lips smacking happily together—there is nothing he has ever tasted like it.

But I shake my head. "Not yet."

"Why?"

"Sim might keep bothering us." Perhaps if I do nothing, he might back off just a little. Enough to give us time to prepare to leave.

Harry steps away from the door as I shut it, clambering back inside the box with Luna.

"I can ride in the car now," comes his little muffled voice, "but not Outside, OK?"

I twist my mouth, that warmth still swirling in my stomach. Maybe if it was possible to consider something as huge as ending our lives, doing something as huge as taking Harry out there is also possible, no matter what, to get him to Jack.

I breathe out the words, barely conscious of saying them aloud. "Maybe we *can* be brave, Harry, and try to find Jack."

11

Seven Months Before the Storm

I follow Jack up the trail, blood pumping deliciously hard as I stride up the glacial till, all the soreness in my back and arms from the days of tree planting starting to loosen. The Canadian Rockies—pink and limestone grey—peek out above deepest-green forest on the opposite slopes. Despite the heat in the air, there's a blizzard of gently falling snow around us, blowing in from the north to meet the warm front from the south, giving the surreal sensation of summer snow. It barely peppers the rich green scrub—cold-stunted aspens, pines, spruces and firs—either side of us on the narrow trail, melting almost as soon as it touches down. I feel sticky and warm in short sleeves, arms swinging to match Jack's rhythm.

He grins back at me. "We're doing it!"

"We are!" I chime, feeling that same giddiness. We're actually here. Now it's the last day, I feel like I'm looking at the green spread of wilderness afresh, sad to leave it on that unnervingly quiet hybrid plane tomorrow. I've felt strange all this trip: happy, excited to be here, yet worried and wanting to be back home to prep for the job now waiting for me, and also unable to let go of thoughts of Dad at the hospital and hoping he'll look more comfortable when we get back.

Jack walks backwards up the trail, dissecting the look on my face.

"Thank you," I say. "For agreeing to all this, coming here instead."

We postponed our plans for a year out because of me. But this short trip, instead, the first of several to make up for it, I have loved. To get to be in the conservation zone—in the forests of the Rockies—we had to book onto a volunteer rewilding trip. Understanding the species we're planting, so the forest as a whole can cope with whatever strangeness climate change brings, and perhaps, still, slow down those changes, has made me all the more excited for the position with Green Earth when we get back. Lobbying for rewilding projects back home.

"Norway's still waiting for us," Jack says. "*We* made the right choice, with that job and your dad's health."

"Promise you're not too disappointed?" I can't help feeling guilty. Jack's mum's death had galvanized his desire for a big adventure and a break from his job at the hospital. Making those year-out plans had helped bring him out of the downward spiral he'd fallen into.

"Only a little."

And what if we never find a good time to go again? "It's only a temporary position . . ."

"That could lead to something permanent, you never know."

I grin. I did bounce up and down like a kid after I got the call. "I had to take it."

Jack laughs. "Yeah, you did!" He throws his arms up and around at the view then. "And are you kidding? Look at this!"

There's lots to sort out when we get back: signing on for another year at the flat, unpacking everything we'd started to box to put into storage for a year abroad. Part of me is glad we don't have to say goodbye to our flat yet, our first home together.

Jack sounded upbeat about getting home when he was on the phone last night with his sponsor, Liam. Wary, though, that he needed to get straight into good habits—exercise and making time with me—so that the job he thought he was having a long break from doesn't take too much out of him. I understand now that helping people—however much he wants to do it—takes energy, and discipline too, so he doesn't overbalance.

Gale. The kid that died in his arms on that last army tour. If one good thing came out of Jack's relapse it was all these stories he'd never told me—I have more pieces of him than I did before.

"You must have felt trapped and hopeless," I'd whispered as he'd finally told me what had led to that first spiral into depression and addiction.

He'd nodded. "I waited all night next to Gale's body, a gun to my own head, waiting for militants to find me before my own soldiers—"

"What would they—"

"Shoot me dead at best . . ."

He'd told me how he'd willed that trigger to make the black hole of fear and the pain in his shot knee go away. When he was flown home, the painkillers for his knee kept numbing the growing darkness too. Never act out of fear and pain, he'd laughed dryly, you'll start to believe all the negative things you tell yourself.

"Hey," he'd said last night, after the phone call. "It's just a check-in, Katie—I'm alright."

I'd nodded, giving him a squeeze. But it was scary, back in April, seeing him grieving, feeling worthless, and seeing him drunk for the first time as he tried to numb dark thoughts. It became a daily thing as he took compassionate leave from his job. He wasn't my Jack—out of it, tired, depressed and irritable. Liam told me his mum's birthday and Christmas might bring up those feelings for him again. I plan to be at his side for all of it, no matter what.

He pauses on the trail to drink water and let me catch up, his T-shirt patchy with sweat. "We're fucking doing it!" He high fives me as I reach him. "You're doing great, Katie, keep hydrated."

He looks so healthy now, his skin fresh and clear, blue eyes bright and lively in the sunlight. I want to comment on it, say how wonderful he looks—my Jack again—but it feels like it might come out loaded if I do.

His phone beeps as we round the next bend, as it has nearly every time we've reached high and open ground—and phone reception—all morning.

I frown. "Who *is* that?"

"Just Adders."

"You've been texting lots. Sure everything's alright?"

"Yeah—he's just catching me up on my god-daughter. He got her in the gym doing dead lifts this morning."

"At eight years old?"

"Just a two-k training bar—she's so proud."

Jack has that smirk on his face, which he tries to conceal by looking ahead, so I don't ask. He's been playful all this trip. It reminds me of when we first met—those days and weekends spent walking in parks and through the countryside, pub lunches, dinners out, on our best behaviour. I remember how we would sit close and keep staring at each other, how his blue eyes had seemed to sparkle.

He's got something of that spark in them now.

We set off again. We're in bear country and I find myself scanning the trees for movement. Jack has the bear spray tucked in his back pocket. All this fortnight I've been determined not to do something stupid and be the ones on the news: "Foolish British couple attacked by bear." And get the priceless bear, whose habitat I've helped plant, shot. The Canadians seem blasé about it, as if only foreigners do daft things.

My knee clicks as the trail descends through a dry rocky gorge, before easing as we wind steeply upwards again into the forest. It's going to hurt on the way back down, I think, just like it has begun to at the end of my long training runs. Yet at the top of the mountainside, the map shows a turquoise glacial lake; I know neither of us will be satisfied until we've reached it.

I'm soon hot and there's just the sound of us breathing hard. I begin to slow, and soon feel Jack's hand at the small of my back, just beneath my daypack, propelling me forwards. Up and round and up, until the trail flattens out again and we get another view across the rich-green forested valley, the muffled white sky from the north meeting the searing blue of the south above us.

"Look!" I pull him to a stop, glad for an excuse to rest.

Weaving through the forested valley below is a torrent of bright turquoise, as cold as water can get without freezing, and full of suspended "rock flour" that the glacier has ground and carried with it over millennia.

There are tracks on the trail ahead, large ones, like elk or moose.

I grin at Jack. "I can't believe the English countryside felt wild when I was a kid."

Jack nods. "I know, right?"

"This is part of the problem, isn't it—so many places being so tamed, farmed, unnatural . . ."

He puts an arm around me. "I can imagine us, Kate, doing this stuff one day as a family."

"Jack—"

"What?"

I laugh. "I don't know—"

"I know, sorry, you're only twenty-two . . ."

I shrug. "I haven't given it much thought yet." I'm not even sure I see myself as a mother. "Can be tricky nowadays." They were discussing the female health crisis in Parliament before we left, including declining male and female fertility too.

He squeezes my shoulders. "Yeah, but that might not be us? I like the idea of teaching them this stuff, showing them how to be kind, having adventures together—"

I laugh. "What's up with you today?"

He shrugs, happy, and I try to imagine what it could be like. Jack with a child-carrier strapped to his front, a little white-blonde-haired child with the same cheeky grin as him inside it.

Jack reaches for my hand, warm fingers interlacing my cold ones.

"Just a second," I say, my heart still pounding from the climb.

"You've done well, all this planting and hiking—all that running has got you fit."

I smile. "I was going to ask—do you think Adders could help me with my half-marathon training? I wondered if some strength work could stop my knee creaking—"

"Yeah!" He's already reaching for his phone. "He does work with some runners too, not just weightlifters and boxers. He'd love to—"

"I want to pay though—he has a business, Jack, I can't get free-bies off him!"

"But he's my bro—"

"Jack," I groan, "to you, yes. Please let me ask, I don't want him to feel awkward."

"Alright." His phone beeps again in his pocket as he sets off ahead of me, still with that sparkle in his eyes. The snowflakes are glancing off my cheeks, the air warm and sweet, as I follow.

12

By late afternoon, a wind has got up, gritty against the windows. Harry and I are standing in the hallway, contemplating our front door, an afternoon behind us of packing what we need and watching the windows. Now there's nothing for it but to go down there to see if I can get the car ready and working.

I turn to the hallway cupboard and open Jack's toolbox tucked just inside on the floor. There, the crowbar. Not used since the first year. I lift it reluctantly, the cold metal reminding me of fighting my way into buildings that weren't mine and jittery rummages through strangers' cupboards, my nose pegged—ineffectively— under my mask. But now the cool metal feels special, like the key, which Harry is clutching reverently like treasure, the spare still tucked in my pocket.

My pack sits ready near the door. Inside it—amongst blankets, spare clothes, toiletries, flask, lighters, a resin candle, lightweight camping kettle and pan, some cutlery, snacks, foraging books and maps—my diary from the year Jack and I first met, that photo of Jack that stood on the dresser stuffed inside it. Things I cannot leave behind.

I'd almost forgotten that my own younger, innocent face smiled out beside Jack in that photo, sun-drenched—the image folded widthways to hide her these last years. I could not keep looking at her, grieving her too. But maybe Harry will want a photo of me one day, and she is the closest thing to that, perhaps.

My waterproof parka and a camping groundsheet are lashed to the outside of the pack. I found the groundsheet in the hallway cupboard—overlooked when I packed the tent for that failed trip in the first year. Harry swishes his fingernails along the shiny water-proofed nylon fabric, making me grimace.

The rest of our stuff—holdalls and sacks full of smoked rabbit jerky, bulrush roots, turnips, onions, apples and more (the musty chestnuts I reluctantly chose to leave behind), and the water-filtering barrel, a few containers of water, sterile cloths, and clothes and bedding—all litters the hallway. All unnervingly ready to re-trieve later, if I can get the car going, or to choose which bags to haul with us if I can't.

Harry stands straighter as I reach for the key in his hand. It feels safer with both in my possession.

"This is the last time I'm going anywhere without you," I say, to him as well as to myself, as I stall. "Stay away from the windows and the front door."

Harry squirms at my low serious tone.

"This is important. Promise?"

He plasters both hands over his heart and nods. "Wholeheart promise," he whispers.

I do it back and reach for the door, the possibility of Jack alive and within reach allowing me to grip the handle with trembling fingers and step out onto the landing, despite Sim and those others being out there somewhere.

Harry, earnest with his promise, is already hurrying down the hallway as I shut the door and pull on my outdoor things.

I stand still a while, listening to the creaks of the roof and the soft clatter of wind against the windows. Vigilant for human sounds.

When I finally step forwards my knees judder, making me hob-ble across the landing to the lift doors. Cool musty air seeps out as I wedge the crowbar in. And with it, that odour of fuel. I lever the doors until there's room for my fingers, and pull, the crack opening up to blackness below. Horror snatches my breath and I stumble backwards. For a second, it's one of Harry's imagined big black holes that might swallow me up, shadows and Balrogs reaching to pull me down and down into nothing.

The lift isn't on this floor. Jack's instructions said he'd stored fuel in the lift, and with the scent of fuel I noticed this morning I thought he might have left it at our level, but of course the electrics would have been out. No knowing where the lift actually is in the shaft . . .

I creep down the stairs, scanning the road out the front every time I pass a window. At the bottom landing, the soft rattle of wind against glass is louder, the front door to the building gaping inwards, forced open, the twine lying slack on the floor. I pull my mask up over my nose and mouth and push the door back inside its frame, rebinding it, but it wobbles alarmingly, like all it would take to get inside again is one hard shove. Opening it yesterday must have exposed the already weakened hinges—iron-red flakes peel off as I watch. Leaves and moths have already blown inside, the breeze whipping up dust particles to swirl upwards in the stairwell. I think of Harry, safe—for now—behind the solid door of our flat, and nearly head back up, abandoning the whole thing.

I force myself around into the dark corner where the ground-level lift entrance is. I feel better here: hidden. But I'm also trapped, should anyone get into the stairwell through that broken front door.

Hurrying, trying not to imagine footsteps or hands grasping at me from behind, I wedge the crowbar into the crack as I did upstairs and eventually the lift doors are groaning open. I shudder as I cram myself through the tight gap—disturbing years-old dust—into the dark, secure, cool spot Jack picked for the fuel, protected from the thick, dangerous air of those first months.

Or so I thought. But the uneven concrete inside is oily and wet underfoot, and it's not pitch-black—chinks of light show above around what must be the bulk of the lift. The fumes are thick and pungent down here, the stale layers of my mask not good enough, no matter how frequently they've been cleaned out. In the gloom, fear prickles, my head quickly woozy. I feel stupid again; Sim might be right: living here with it all this time could have gone very wrong . . .

With gloved fingers I feel around warped and holed plastic containers, the fumes of the leaked fuel stronger as I lean down. There are two containers—metal and in more solid condition—still heavy, fuel sloshing about inside. The lids are tight and intact. I feel a great wave of relief that there is still something here to be found—I blink back tears—this was left by Jack, close at hand and ready for me.

I shake the emotion off, double-checking my mask: the containers are covered with that thick grey coating we cannot take risks with and do not want to disturb.

But I heave both out, dragging them across the ground-floor landing to the door to the communal garage, where I pause to peer through the glass. It's not until I unlock the door and push out into the welcome cooler air that my head clears and the danger of the fumes passes.

I tread through the garage slowly, alert, taking the full weight of the two containers now to stop making so much noise, my arms burning, and I have to keep resting the fuel down. When I reach the corner and Jack's spot, the Cruiser is also coated in grey dust—thickest where the wind and rain don't reach it, along the bumpers and wheel arches. The slightly raised "UN" lettering is still visible across its side, but the car has been sprayed black—rough splodges of it overlap the windows. A white UN car would have drawn too much attention, Jack said.

The driver's door unlocks as if by magic with one of my precious keys, finer dust dislodging from the seal.

The inside smells of worn leather and metal, reminding me of Jack and his old much-repaired Subaru. I remove a glove to reach inside, bare fingers tingling as I brush them across the wheel—Jack's hands have touched this very same wheel. How many times did we sit in that Subaru in Jack's parking spot right here, without thinking of how precious our time was together, without worrying about a workday or a weekend spent apart.

I've barely stood still a minute before the relief and excitement have faded: the time away from Harry in the flat and that broken door downstairs and the possibility of Sim coming back gnawing at me. I try a key in the ignition, just once, out of desperate curiosity, and it fits . . . but of course there's nothing, no hiss or whir, just a painful click. Anything else would have been surprising. Jack's letter makes it clear anyway that even sat for a few months in that awful dust of the first year might have clogged the car, so even if it could start straight away, it wouldn't have gone far without maintenance. Burning now to get back up to Harry, I glance through the letter and start rushing through the tasks.

It takes hours longer than I hoped, the afternoon light fading as I work. I clean out dust and dirt from around the engine and use distilled water to top up the battery, which Jack had actually disconnected and thought safer to leave in the boot, fearful of looters crowbarring the bonnet for it. I spend too long trying to ram that battery—crooked and connectors messy—back into a space it does not want to fit into. I stir additive—left in the boot for me too— into the containers of fuel, hoping it might help the old diesel to burn better and not clog everything. Then I haul each container up and pour it in drips and drabs into the tank—having to rest, sweating, as my arms shudder and burn from the weight. I scrape off old fuel gunked to the pump filter as best I can and tap out the choked engine air intake filter, grimacing away from the thick grey fluff as it floats to the garage floor.

All the time I'm doing this I feel as if I'm underwater, holding my breath until I finish—legging it back upstairs to peer in and check on Harry before hurrying back down—every part of me painfully alert for movement outside of the garage, horrified imaginings of Sim plaguing my mind: of suddenly seeing Harry bundled up over his shoulder outside, face naked to the particled breeze, disappearing across the car park just like I'd seen with my boots and overalls. I keep nearly doing as Harry begs and staying with him, leaving this unfinished.

But we have to see if this works.

Then I'm finally done, apart from the wheels. They too were stashed away by Jack in the back but feel too visible to put on until we're really ready to go. Feeling pleased with myself, I reach in to try a key in the ignition again, hoping—

Footsteps. That horrible regular crunch every fibre of my body was fearful of hearing.

I jump up, easing the driver's side door shut—my crowbar and tools lying on the seat behind the dusty glass. I dash for the stairwell door, realizing too late I've left the Cruiser unlocked. But Sim has spotted me now and I cannot go back: I feel certain I do not want him to know about the Cruiser. I slow to scoop up armfuls of leaves—even as Sim launches into a jog—as if to prove beyond doubt I was never here for any other reason than collecting kindling.

Sim clambers underneath the shutter and gets to the stairwell door first, cutting me off. He has a bulging bag over his shoulder that rattles as he heaves it to the ground—full of paint tins and rollers.

"Not planning on leaving me already, are you?" He smiles at my flushed cheeks and out-of-breath wheezing, like he cracked a joke, and I force myself to stay staring at him, and not look back at the Cruiser, though I'm worrying now whether I've also left tools out on the ground, disturbed too much dust and dirt around the bonnet.

I forgot to bring a weapon! I suddenly feel the absence of even my knife, usually tucked in my back pocket, left on the driver's seat too. I feel smaller, like I'm shrinking where I stand, weak—my breath still catching, my lungs achy and tight from the hard work. My fist curls round the car key, feeling sick to be blocked from the exit and Harry.

"I wasn't taking your stuff, you know, just keeping it safe for you." He rolls his eyes, as if suspecting I was hysterical about it and didn't get that joke either. "You should come up to True Organics with me soon, see how we're fixing it up."

Something noncommittal murmurs in my throat.

And he steps aside, as if to let me go to the door, and I feel freed, trying to cringe past, reaching for it. But his fingers just brush something on my shoulder. Just graze my cheek. And then he presses himself against me, chest to chest, arms wrapping around my back. My whole body stiffens, paralysed, blood booming. The garage around me, Harry, all fading to a blur.

Something moves in his trousers against my leg.

I flinch, clattering backwards against the door, causing a trickle of dust to come down on us. He steps away to avoid it, while I stay rigid, feeling it land in my hair and over my cheeks and nose, my mask hanging from one ear.

The sky is dark grey outside now, the band of intense dirty pink on the horizon disappearing between the buildings opposite.

"Harry's waiting for me." The words wheeze out, thick and nearly incoherent. They seem to do the trick.

"Fair enough. I'll see you tomorrow, yeah?" He seems annoyed but winks, his hand raised in a casual farewell and a blown kiss, as if it's all been romantic. Building to something. And I realize he thinks my words mean "not now."

My lungs burn for air as I unlock the stairwell door, still staring at his now-grinning face. I can't turn my back on him. Not even when I have the door shut between us and the moths are fluttering at my neck.

13

Standing shaking in the stairwell, I desperately wipe dust from my face, berating myself for freezing, for not pushing back, for not doing as that other man said. But it doesn't feel as simple as that.

I stare into the garage through the thin rectangle of glass in the door, fighting against the instinct to run the fuck away. Sim disappears from view, walking towards the unlocked Cruiser.

He's noticed something. He must have. Why else would he be moving towards it, tucked away in the corner? There's nothing else for it now. I press the button on the key fob hard and hold it, praying there's enough battery in it and the Cruiser for this one small thing.

A moment later, there's the loud clunk of the Cruiser doors locking.

And Sim's enraged curse echoing through the garage. He stomps back towards the stairwell door, a pained look in his eyes, arms wide in confusion.

"What the fuck?"

I spring away, heart pounding, hyperaware of that broken front door. I rush past it and up the stairs, that urgency that drove me out of the flat alone to the Cruiser turned into a more familiar terrible urgency to get upstairs and hide, safe. I realize now I never made a conscious decision when I ran back here that first year: days just became weeks, which turned into years.

The garage shutter clangs and clashes below me like it does on stormy days—like a troll in a dungeon—as I sprint the last stretch to our flat. Hurrying to shrug off boots and dusty overalls at the door, I roughly wipe myself clean with the wet cloth I left ready. Harry's pale, wide-eyed face follows me as I dash straight to the bedroom window. I reach through the curtains and blinds to push the dust cover aside and peer out. The dark-grey sky already has a full moon, so low on the horizon that it's an ominous yellow-orange in the haze, like the glow of the sun in the darkest part of a dust storm. There's Sim's silhouette striding away from the garage. He looks back and I jump, the blinds twanging back into place.

That safety I imagined as I raced up the stairs isn't here any-more. Tomorrow is looming and Sim returning in the daylight. I pace by the window in the evening gloom. It's too dark now; I was never going to go in the dark! Yet everything is churning inside me to leave. Now.

Opening the bottom drawer, I slide the engagement ring—the last item I cannot leave behind—onto my finger, where it feels strange yet familiar.

I need light now to finish the prep. Grabbing a green wood stick we use for cooking and a cloth, which I dip in fat, from the kitchen—Harry following—I brandish my unlit torch by our front door, my whole body shaking. Harry bumps against me in the dark, silent and clingy. The Cruiser has to work. I cannot picture us attempting to go anywhere on foot anymore.

But I feel sick. Hot and sweaty one moment, cold and horrified the next.

"Mummy," Harry whines, scared of the dark and my standing here, and wanting the woodstove on—his favourite part of the day.

I have the urge to rush round the flat to touch every familiar thing goodbye, like Harry does before bed, or to find more things to take with us, but that panicky desire to stay put is only going to get worse if I do.

No, we cannot still be here in the morning.

I get the torch lit. The fat-soaked end roars brilliantly to flame, then settles into a flickering orb. Harry chuckles, whooping and excited, mesmerized by this treat. The engagement ring sparkles, bright with facets of colour, my hand trembling. I sit cross-legged in the hallway, Harry in my lap. We wait an hour—re-wrapping and lighting the torch each time it goes out—until I'm sure Sim must be long gone. I stare at Jack's letter, imagining his voice as I rush through the words, needing that sliver of warmth to fill me.

Katie . . .

So, in case you do come back here, I've left all this for you. I know you'll feel safer in that car than on foot. Just keep moving—there will be people on the road, everyone's searching for loved ones and looting. Don't let your driving-jitters get to you—probably no police or military now to stop you anyway!

We've several places to check en route, but I'm heading to Mum's old house soon.

The rest is the instructions for getting the car ready, handwriting sloping and messy, getting increasingly harder to make out by the end.

When I get back down to "Jack," I tighten my grip on the torch. I know that Sim could see its light downstairs, if he is close or chooses to come back tonight. But I cannot reconcile myself to being in the pitch-blackness, nor do I think I'll be able to get Harry to come with me without it. I swing it to and fro, trying not to think about how I froze earlier.

I push Harry's feet into the stiff little Velcro trainers he has never worn.

He grimaces, pulling away. "They hurt me!"

The shoes *are* tight, his toes pushing against the ends. "We have to make do," I remind him. "Socks aren't enough."

"They won't keep bad out?"

"Nope."

We stand at the door. Harry seems to realize we're not having dinner or the woodstove on tonight. But he doesn't yet realize how dark it is out there. The flat is often very dark, even in daytime, once we've shut all the curtains and covers, so it's not always the same outside. The hallway, while shadowy and scary—Harry's eyes darting around at the flickering shadows, transforming our packed belongings into a crowd of restless blobs—is still familiar.

I brace for his reaction, squeezing his hand and waiting until he does it back.

"Remember what we do at night when the rain is really loud? One squeeze is for OK and two is for not-OK and I always know to look after you? This time two means danger or if we spot surprises. Got it?"

"One is OK, two is danger," Harry whispers, squirming on the spot. "And if we're really scared we can run and climb in bed?"

I grimace, guilty. "Remember we have to be brave, together, OK?" I help him with his little pack, which he clutches tight—Luna and his favourite storybooks and pink blanket safe inside—and he nods, a frightened resignation on his face. "Will we see Durby-sher from the window down the stairs?"

"No—"

"Where is it then? In a secret hiding place?" His face is crumpling, his legs sagging. I know if his bottom hits the floor, we're in danger of a tantrum and we'll be stuck longer.

"It's further away, Harry. Like an adventure—"

"Like Simba through the desert and jungle?"

"Exactly. Come on, we'll go one set of stairs at a time, like climbing down a mountain." Blood fizzes through my fingers as I tug Harry's arms into a raincoat of mine far too big for his little body—his pack safe underneath it with him—and his hands into too-big gloves and push his mask, bright blue with starfish-shaped valves, over his face. Crouching, I kiss his cheek. "Will you be brave for Mummy?"

Eyes wide, he stands straighter, trying to be.

Slowly, I open up the front door to the pitch-black landing and stairwell beyond.

"Mummy!" Harry gasps, tugging me backwards, eyes roving around where the torchlight falls on the grubby landing floor and the stairwell through the internal glass opposite—full of shifting greyed railings and walls and deep shadows.

His little chest heaves up and down. "I don't want to!"

"You can have a treat when we get to that door over there—

see?" I point to the stairwell door. "And at every landing. You remember how it looked in daylight, it's still the same." I whisper things we saw: the handrail and steps, the tall glass windows at the half-landings.

"What if there's nasties hiding in the dark!"

"There won't be."

Harry still tries to edge backwards, my arm around his middle the only thing stopping him.

"Nasties don't like fire," I say softly, changing tack. "You always feel safe at the woodstove, don't you? See, that's why."

The two tins of fruit Sim left on the doorstep twinkle in the torchlight.

I pick them up. "These will be the most delicious thing you've *ever* tasted, Harry."

He gasps at this proclamation, despite his fear, and I imagine his joy at that tangy sweetness. Quickly, before he loses his enthusiasm, I wipe the tins as clean as I can with water and cloth. "For you—when you reach the car downstairs, you can eat as much as you want."

I stuff them in my backpack, before getting out a little blue zipped pouch, carefully pulling the rain cover out and over my pack, pulling it tight, worrying how I'm going to adapt my usual habits in order to keep the interior of the car as safe as possible for Harry. And with the rest of my outdoor gear on, I load myself with as many of the bags as I can—realizing I'll have to come back for the last few—and push him slowly out of the door.

Harry moans like a small creature might when being herded somewhere it does not want to go, his legs stiff, each step going no further than I make him. We get to the stairs, his little hands crushing my fingers. And we creep down. Everything is black and faint gleams of silver as I shuffle, overladen, down the stairwell—cold and still, until the orange light of the torch passes and shadows shift and wobble and the air glitters and snaps with the acrid smell of burning plastic dust. Moths flutter round my face, wings singed and smoking as they flit towards the torch.

"Come on," I whisper, as Harry stalls at the next landing, his mask quivering as he chews the hawthorn liquorice and dried apple I promised him.

People don't like the dark either, I tell myself. He won't come back tonight. But even as I think it, I'm searching the darkness for Sim. My eyes keep tricking me, seeing at first human shapes hiding round corners then ink-black tendrils wobbling towards me, the flicker of a black creature disappearing round the wall, the glint of eyes.

Down the next few sets of stairs we go, the metal creaking with our weight, making me shudder and Harry's hands squeeze tighter still.

"I don't want to," Harry whispers as we near the bottom landing.

Hundreds of moths have come inside through the broken door now. Fat finger-like bodies with oily-bronze-coloured wings. Wax moths. *Galleria mellonella.*

Harry yelps, cowering away from the writhing floor—perhaps this is precisely the sort of abstract seething pile of nasties he's always imagined lurking in dark places. Waiting to envelop you and pull you down into darkness, lost.

Wings hiss, smoking next to my face.

"Just little friends, Harry," I say, squeezing his hand once reassuringly, and stepping closer, hating the way they're creeping about the carpet and up the walls. "They're the ones that match the snowberry leaves, look. The only insects I like, remember? The ones that can digest plastic as caterpillars." Reluctant, because I wanted to carry everything directly from the safety of the flat to the safety of the car, as uncontaminated as possible, I put everything but my pack down to pull Harry up into my arms. He clings tight. "What kind of creatures could they make together, like your shield bug?" I whisper.

I step forwards. They melt away from my boots at first, before fluttering back to investigate. In the warm torchlight, they're like a wriggling mass of glittery maggots that squish unpleasantly underfoot as we pass through them, but I describe the golden unicorn foals from Harry's book in his ear, their coats soft and fluttery and nice to touch.

The smell of diesel fumes is strong as we reach the door to the garage—the lift doors close by—and the torch flares with a whoosh, setting off great crackles of igniting dust.

"Mummy!" Harry sobs as I set him down with the torch so I can wince back through the moths for the other bags.

"It's alright," I whisper as I get back to him, Harry twitching and jerking at smoking fluttering wings. I grab the torch and his little shoulder, his raincoat smeared in dust and dirt from the wall behind him.

Shaking too, my skin itching as if I'm crawling with them, I haul us through into the garage, shutting the door on the moths. I squeeze Harry's trembling hand once. "We're OK, see?" I whisper between heavy breaths. "They're gone." I point the torch at the empty dirty ground.

"I don't like surprises," he sobs, hiccuping, balling his dusty fists tight against his masked mouth to keep the noise in. I slip more hawthorn liquorice under his mask, but it falls straight out of his mouth, his appetite gone. "I want to go back."

I feel giddy again, seeing the garage through his eyes. Like a big grey cavern, dripping with dirty dangerous water, and smelling strange, with damp rotten leaves and dust, and glinting bits of glass and metal that could be treasure, a dragon round the corner in the dark ready to guard its domain.

I forge forwards with quiet steps, Harry whimpering, shuffling next to me. My chest is wheezy and gaspy from lugging Harry and all this stuff downstairs, and from being held tight and tense, making my breath too loud in the quiet garage.

But finally, I unlock the Cruiser with a faint click as the key turns and pat down the bags of supplies as best I can before piling them in the already full boot. Opening the driver's door, I hold out the air meter into the interior, eyes darting around us while I wait until it registers green. Then I wipe down every surface with wetted sterile cloths and pull and shake out the foot mats and pat myself down, before peeling off gloves, mask and overalls. I yank the rain cover off my backpack, which turned inside out and with the cord and toggle pulled tight makes a good safe sack for all the outdoor gear.

Only then do I help Harry out of his dusty raincoat, carefully adding it to the inside of my outdoor gear sack, as he stands shuddering, and it's now I realize his trousers are wet at the crotch.

"Oh, Harry . . ." I pull off his wet things too, and help him clamber up into the driver's seat together. Our shoes go inside the sack last of all, which I hang from the excess cord off the back of the driver's seat alongside my pack. Finally, I can tug the door shut, clunking us locked and safe as Harry crumples in my lap.

"We're alright," I whisper, over and over, as I rock him. Slowly his shudders relax into shivers and his cries into sniffs.

I open his mandarins, but he just sits there, hugging the tin.

Yet a weight has lifted off me with Harry safe inside the car. The Cruiser a new safe bubble. The windows are scratched and filthy, with white fractures perhaps from failed attempts to get inside, but they're intact—bulletproof according to Jack's letter. He must be right: every other car in the garage has been smashed into by debris or scavengers.

I abandon the idea of going back upstairs for those last sacks of winter supplies. I can't leave Harry down here and can't face forcing him through the dark again . . . and neither of us will want to come back down if we both go up. And if we sleep in our own bed, what then? Come tomorrow, Sim might make things harder.

The possibility of Jack alive and in Derbyshire swirls inside me. I feel years late, every moment still here painful, wasted. I can't allow Sim to prevent us—anger flashes, making the Fear ebb a bit. Enough that I gently untangle myself from Harry, stowing away his untouched mandarins and settling him in the passenger seat in his dry clothes and just his mask, and make myself climb back out into the garage and into my outdoor things.

"Mummy!" Harry's eyes are wild with the door shut between us, those frown lines that are so like mine creasing his forehead. "The air's funny—I can't breathe!" He sucks at his mask, holding it tight to his face, as if it's a snorkel and the air's been cut off, until I open the door a crack again.

"It's just old in here. Nothing bad can get inside," I say, "just like our flat." I place the air meter on the dash and he peers at it closely.

Slowly he nods, looking around properly, worried eyes returning to mine. "I'm not really Outside here?"

I shake my head. "Just promise not to open anything, might still be dust in hidden places." I leave the door ajar, Harry watching and needing a thumbs-up and my mask lifted for a snatched smile before I step away.

Jack hid the wheels—stacked sideways to preserve the rubber—in the back, inside the hard impenetrable shell of the Cruiser. I cover them with the horrible nylon groundsheet to avoid any flurries of dust contaminating Harry's precious airspace as I roll and heave each one out—thudding awfully to the ground. I strain to listen for any sign someone's heard us as I pull the back seats upright and fretfully wipe at dust in the crevices and grooves of the boot, before throwing the groundsheet down to cover it all, stowing our bags of supplies—secure and stable—on top, and shutting the boot up again. I have a moment of panic, worried for Harry and fighting the urge to rush back upstairs, clean him up properly and seal us inside the flat.

But I focus on the work. The tyres grind unnervingly along the ground in the dark, the torch balanced in one hand. I try to focus on Harry safe inside the secure body of the Cruiser, and Jack's note, and on the training Adders used to make me do in the gym, pushing weighted prowler sleds and lifting kettlebells. And not the darkness. Not something grabbing and pinning me down, not Sim somewhere in Hitchin.

The Cruiser is already jacked high enough to roll the first wheel into position and I fumble for the wheel studs Jack described in his letter.

Moths flutter at my back. I strain, inching the heavy wheel round on the spot until I can feel the studs catching.

I hear Adders's voice in my mind as it clunks solidly into place: *There it is!*

Cheered, I screw on each wheel nut with the wheel wrench until they're tight and the wrench clicks.

As I squat at the back wheel, I notice gouged striations on the fuel cover that weren't there earlier. I reach a hand out to feel the sharp, jagged edges and tug at the cover to reassure myself Sim didn't get inside it yet.

Unnerved, I keep working. And with the last wheel on and the jack stands dismantled, I find a manual foot pump in the boot to top up the air in the soft tyres, despite it not being on Jack's list, and with only a vague idea of how hard to make them. When I'm done, I stay crouched, hands smarting and body aching, breathless again. I realize I am wedged between the side of the Cruiser's dusty bonnet and a caked concrete pillar. The torch throbs. My skin cools quickly, sweaty and itchy under my clothes—only my face burning still and irritated by the dust where it's not covered by my mask and hood. Now that the job's done, fear of the dust and the dark squeeze at me again.

Harry blinks out at me from the driver's window, a little bundled-up grey figure in the pale flickering light.

Guilt wells up. All the times I've returned to the flat to a scared and clingy Harry, and wet floors or nappies when he was smaller. All that I've put him through today . . . and now, trying to wrench him from all he knows.

I grimace suddenly at the sight of a small splintered ribcage amongst the leaves and grit beneath the car, near to the driver's side wheel I've just finished working on. Someone tried to take shelter here. Someone small who was all alone.

Harry's thin little hand on my dusty shoulder makes me jump. He squeezes. Twice.

"Don't touch that!" But I fly to my feet, the torch flaring. "What?" I whisper, straining to hear dreaded footsteps, waving away singed moths and their tiny smoking trails in the air around me.

Harry points. Fingers of dust reach down from the roof towards the heat of the torch, snapping and sparking, making the air thick and acrid. Making me feel ever more conspicuous in this dark corner of the garage. But blinking my stinging eyes, I see what Harry's spotted through the barred windows of the garage. A light. Up high in the far-most block of flats. Moving down a stairwell.

My heart thunders. I force Harry to wipe his hand clean. Then with the torch pulsating and stretching into a thin desperate flame,

I force myself away from him and the Cruiser and towards the shutter at the entrance of the communal garage.

I watch that light moving—second floor. My boots crunch too loud across the ground, my breath hitching the faster I go.

There's no manual crank to wind the shutter up and the reel won't budge when I reach up and try to turn it. I give the shutter a frustrated shove. It rattles, a firm web of thick resisting metal glinting in the torchlight.

The smoky flickering light of my torch picks out long thick nails hammered just under the shutter reel like broken teeth, stopping the shutter from being wound up. Fresh silver scratches mark the red-rusted metal. *Sim!* On tiptoes I tug uselessly at the nearest nail.

I turn, sprinting back towards the Cruiser, the torch guttering out, blackness racing in to smother me.

The bones under the car and the many I know are all around us feel like monsters suddenly waking up in the darkness, joining the chase like that light in the block behind me. I imagine how quickly something undead might pick itself up and close in on me, its bones and rotten flesh somehow stronger than me, smelling of death and musk and man.

I blunder in the dark, choking on panic, reaching out for the Cruiser, until my eyes start readjusting. A flash of Harry's frightened eyes through the windscreen. And instead of black everywhere, I can see greys and edges. A thin spread of moonlight. I find the driver's door and scrape the crisper key of the two into the ignition. Nothing. The Fear throbs. But I force myself to remember Jack left us one last thing to try.

Little fingers cling to my elbow. "Mummy, don't go—"

But I've already pinged the bonnet open with the lever and felt my way to it, locating the battery and straining to get the wires of the jump-starter on correctly in the dark. Right side was red. Red is positive.

I scramble back to the driver's side, feeling for the ignition with the key again, excitement threading its way into the Fear. That light in the distance at ground level now.

But I fumble it, the key slipping loose—a dull flash of silver swimming down into the blackness of the footwell. Frantic, I grope for it, growing hot at the thought of disturbing whatever's accumulated in the crevices and at shedding caked dust from my overalls into Harry's airspace.

It'll start.

Jack's voice is clear and calm in my head. It makes me pause, take a breath.

I rip out of my overalls and gloves in the cold garage, reaching into my trouser pocket for the other key with its worn metal and fat fob, letting my breath out slowly as I feel for the ignition with my finger and plant the key carefully in. As it turns, I brace everything. The engine whirrs twice and then hums into life. We both yelp as it reverberates through us—so much louder than I remember. A gentle glow rises from the dashboard, picking out Harry's face in greenish highlights.

My hands are sticky with sweat as I yank off the jump-starter, shut the bonnet, and bolt back to the driver's door. My outdoor gear—roughly shaken and balled up—is slung inside the sack, a sterile cloth daubed over my hands and face, just my mask kept on.

"OK, here goes," I whisper as I strap us both in.

My feet tremble over the pedals as I try to remind myself how this works: clutch, brakes, accelerator. I switch on the sidelights—though only one works—and not the full headlight beams, as if even now I'm trying to be discreet. The lowest point of the shutter is well below my eyeline.

"Harry"—I stare at it and the too-small gap beneath it—"close your eyes for the first bit, OK?" I want to promise it won't be scary, but I can't. "Remember how we flew across the carpet in the box upstairs?" I reach a hand across to squeeze his, once.

I shove the gearstick into first, then grab the handbrake and push it, juddering, down.

A tentative tap on the accelerator and the engine revs. I hold it, but we don't move—the brake pads must be rusted on after all this time! I press harder—foot to the floor, engine growling, clutch starting to stink of burning rubber—and cheer as the wheels suddenly "pop" and we lurch forwards.

Harry's hands fly to the edges of his seat but he lets out a brief brave—unconvincing and truncated—whoop alongside mine. The wheel joints squeal and the engine pumps loudly as we move through the confines of the garage. We speed up sickeningly, the shutter hurtling towards us.

Then there's an awful squealing of metal as the shutter crumples and we punch through.

14

We're out! I hold my chest, my lungs tight, making my breath shallow and fast. Head fuzzy. Cruiser still rolling forwards.

"Alright, Harry?" I can't move, the seat belt has me pinned to the chair. "Harry?" The dash lights tremble in the dark.

"Mummy!" His little voice is gasping.

I wipe at condensation on the windscreen, but still can't see much through the scratched, dirty glass and with just the one dull and now blinking sidelight on. Except—just there—the shifting and fuzzy glow of a light somewhere ahead. Pressing my foot down again, I weave us forwards, squelching and crunching through bobbing saplings and piles of leaves, branches and roof tiles, guttering and decayed packaging. Harry jerks from his window as we pass night-grey thickets of snowberry bushes. This feels fast, even though the comforting but still trembling dash lights show barely twenty miles per hour. I feel a nervous giggle bubbling inside me. I remember learning to drive and having this same sensation: of going faster than I think I might be able to control.

Harry's cry makes me look up, feeling sick. I flick the headlights on, the dull beam picking out leaves and kicked-up dust in all shades of grey—making me slam my hands across the air vents, but they're all closed already. Through the debris, the yellow-grey light also lands on cars parked either side of us, and four people spilling across the gap ahead, leaving little room for us to get past.

I feel myself lift off the accelerator a touch.

Punch it! Jack's voice shouts. *They're playing chicken with you.*

I think he's right, but I'm not sure I can zoom at people as if prepared to plough them down.

We're metres away now. I'm wound tight in my seat, clasping the steering wheel, the darkness smothering everything but what's straight ahead. Sim is shouting, face scrunched and eyes blazing. And I can't help seeing him as an angry, snarling dog.

There's a split second where I wish I could explain, convince them not to think badly of me. Yet the Fear—overwhelming, blinding—is pounding, my throat and lungs itching. And I pull Jack into my mind, his hand firmly in Harry's. Me and Harry: we have to do this.

And that little warm glow of hope that's been there since I read the letter has me veering right—hard, the wheel stickier and heavier to turn than it should be. The Cruiser bounces over pavement and scrapes along the wall of the next building, the whipping of grass and weeds and mounds of fungi sounding underneath us, leaves and dust whirling. Harry is frozen, silent, face scrunched tight. I yelp, yanking the wheel to avoid a dead tree trunk, plunging us through night-grey vegetation.

Then we're springing back over the kerb into the car park again. Something metallic clangs on the bottom of the car, and clunk, the front end hits a stationary vehicle—our headlights and dash lights wobbling, the other vehicle skidding aside as I accelerate harder.

And we're free, bumping out of the estate and onto Whinbush Road, leaving the shouting behind us. I flick on the indicators by habit, the green glow pulsing erratically: click-click-click.

I snap them off again, wrenching the wheel one way then the next, avoiding bricks and more roof tiles, a shopping trolley, the prostrate shape of something awful. The windscreen wipers are smearing dust and squashed moths across the scratched glass as I wipe desperately at condensation on the inside, heaters not working—finally having to unwind my window to try to stop it fogging up.

Beside me, Harry thrashes to get free of his seat belt, crying.

The streets are dark and grey, empty—but I'm afraid to stop, even for a moment, with the headlights trembling and blinking, giving us only snatches of the view ahead, and making me fear the engine will conk out. So we hurtle through the streets like a dodgem car, derelict parked vehicles along the kerbs feeling—like they did when I was learning to drive—perilously close, and our front wheels clicking and complaining, that metallic clang still sounding from the rear bumper as if part of it is hanging off.

By the time we're heading towards the A1(M) junction, smashing through drifts of fallen leaves and saplings sprouting right from the tarmac, releasing clouds of dust, Harry has wriggled free and is clambering into my lap.

Down the slip road we go, Harry curling into a tight ball, heaving great sobs against my chest.

We swerve past old cars and then speed north on the wrong side, hysterical laughter bubbling up out of me. The accelerator pedal keeps going softer then harder, the dash lights flicking to "electric mode" for a second, only to nearly cause us to stall without any power coming from the electric motor, then back to "fuel engine" with a rev. The sensors seem stuck, showing the battery as nearly fully charged on the dash—perhaps how it was when Jack last had the car running—when I know it must be weak or flat.

"No more bangs!" Harry cries, hands ready at his ears.

"Sorry." I squeeze his arm gently as I search for a way to stop the hybrid system trying to switch to electric. "I promise to tell you if I know a big one's coming, OK? We might have to get used to the little ones though."

"I want to go to bed. Had enough of Outside!"

I leave his words hanging between us, afraid to answer. After a while, my breathing settles and so do Harry's sobs, and I sink lower in my seat, becoming accustomed to his weight sinking into me, and the illuminated yellow-grey patch of road ahead of us. Shrubs, saplings and old cars are black as we zigzag through, a constant scraping and clonking, disturbing puffs of dust and sudden streams of fluttering moths. The night sky is whale blue-grey, flecked with white, just like barnacles on its great back. Shit, I think, I'm tired. And dawn is hours away.

"Are they pushing?" Harry suddenly cranes to look behind us, worried.

It takes me a second to understand he means the men. "No, it's got an engine. It burns—"

"Like the woodstove?"

"Sort of. And that turns the wheels."

"Wow!" Harry reaches to pat the still-white interior metal frame, gently, like he might the gleaming shell of Emer the shield bug.

"There's more trees, Mummy!" He points. "Why are those houses in the dark all short and fat?"

"The buildings near our flat were just tall."

"Which one is ours? Where are the big poplar trees?"

Harry keeps straining to look around at the dark silhouettes, before abruptly hunching over and vomiting into the footwell, his mask flying down with it.

"Does your throat hurt?" I snatch glances down at him, trying to see if it's just vomit or blood too that he is wiping away with his sleeve.

He mumbles a reply.

I panic, mind full and swirling, tears prickling, before I force myself to take a breath.

"Lift your face." I hold his chin up, slowing so I can make quick inspections of his mouth, nose and eyes, the green glow of the dashboard making him look ghoulish and sick. Finding nothing, I help him swivel round on my lap, putting his hands on the steering wheel. "Is it the movement? Sit up properly and look straight ahead, it'll help."

The headlights pick out a mess of leaves and branches, grey in the darkness, sprouting in the road. Squeezing the stubborn wheel firmly, I turn to move round the obstacles, taking one hand off the wheel to wrap my arm around Harry on my lap, but he leans into the movement this time, balancing himself. His little hands reach to grip the wheel too, inching upwards towards mine near the top.

We'll stop soon, in a safe spot. Wait until it's light.

But moving, even the jerky-stiff-rumbling of the Cruiser, feels safer, feels good. Finally moving towards Jack—and I don't want to stop.

"What's inside those cars?" Harry whispers.

"Nothing, don't worry."

"But are they men——?"

"Harry," I snap. Nothing slumped inside the growing lines of cars we pass can be seen clearly or dwelt on as the Cruiser chugs past, not if I don't focus on them.

Pressing the accelerator harder to blur past them faster, I nearly miss the large shapes materializing ahead. I slam the brake pedal, clutching Harry tight. But there's not quite enough time and the car cracks into the concrete just before we manage to stop, and we bounce to a halt, a great curtain of grey specks falling onto the windscreen and bonnet in one go.

Harry screams—a short, sharp one before he swallows it down—turning to bury his face in my chest.

I wrap my arms around him. It takes a few moments for the blocked-up, dry windscreen wipers to unclog enough scratched-up glass to see out again. Moths flutter in the headlights. Tall concrete blocks—black against the dark sky—stand in formation across the road. Reflective fragments of paint glitter: EMERGENCY ROAD-BLOCK: TURN BACK.

My hands are sweaty around the wheel. Sim probably knows all the roadblocks—I didn't even think, it's been so long since I ventured far enough to encounter one. And now his contorted face back in the car park seems more of a knowing laugh.

With a panicky yank of the wheel, I get us off the road, reversing quickly up onto the sloping verge amongst scratching bushes, coming to a stop in the mud, the wheels whirring unhappily, lights blinking, and then the engine finally cutting out. The darkness swallows us up, cold and quiet.

I wind the windows shut and rock Harry in my lap, removing my mask and feeling better once it's over his little face, feeling very aware again of the dust that might still be on me from the garage. He cries silently. Luna is tucked right up under his chin, under his jumper for keeping clean and safe, his wooden hooves digging into my chest. I fish for a make-believe story to stop us from dwelling on the darkness and our own bed, where we should be right now.

"Are there more people Outside?" Harry whispers.

"Maybe."

"How many?"

"I don't know."

He shivers.

"Are they sleeping in the cars?"

I clutch him tighter, trembling, lapsing into silence.

"Will they surprise us in the dark?" Harry whispers urgently, digging tighter into me.

"No," I say firmly. I can feel it again, the weight of all that death, in a way I've been able to forget for years.

I stare out into the dark, half-expecting faces to lurch out of it. Sim won't catch up before it's light, I keep telling myself—he needs it just as much as we do to figure out our next move.

Harry slips, heavy, into sleep on my lap. I listen to the tapping rain and slowly the bushes, cars and pillars begin to look purple-grey rather than black. All glistening with dew and rain. And I can see now that the barricade of pillars stops amongst the lowest bushes of the sloping verge—ahead of us on the steep slope are just the soft purple-grey outlines of bushes and saplings, the ground glimmering with trickling water.

Opening the door a crack, I slip out into my boots and the dawn gloom, getting into my overalls and gear as quick as possible, stuffing the outdoor gear sack back inside without it touching anything outside. Under the now-crumpled bonnet—bull bar bent inwards—the battery is dislodged, the connectors loose. I shove it back into place, tightening the terminals, and attach the jump-starter.

To my relief, the engine roars to life again at the turn of the ignition, the lights no longer flickering, Harry stirring with a jolt and blinking out at me. But once I've put everything away and slid back next to him, ready to go, the Cruiser only pulls, like a dog on a leash, the rear end stuck.

Outside once more in my gear, I feel my way to the rear bumper, the smell of paint confusing until I feel a battered tin half-attached there with bungee cords, all now tangled into metal fencing half buried in the mud and weighted down under the Cruiser's own wheels.

I feel hot and sick again—Sim could be following the trail of paint in the dawn light right this moment, perhaps now speeding up, gleeful at hearing the engine. I yank and pull and untwist, forcing trembling gloved fingers and the crowbar between cord and metal until, sticky with paint and mud, I manage to free the Cruiser. I kick the paint tin clear, harder than I mean to.

Standing shivering in the dark, I strip out of my mucky outdoor things, nails torn and fingers bleeding as I peel off my gloves. I waste a container of water over my hands and face, scrubbing as best I can, frantic to get back in our safe bubble inside, still straining to look for Sim through the trees—splodges of white paint are visible now, down there on the motorway where we hit the barricade.

With my window wound down halfway to keep the condensation from forming too badly, our wheels spin in the mud as we head for the bushes upslope of the last, leaning pillar. I get out twice to rip out foot mats and shove them under the tyres to get grip again in the wet mud. I turn the wheel one way, then the other, mud churning under the Cruiser, as I try to keep a straight line across the slope, giggly reckless energy rising again. We slide past the pillar twisting sideways, driver's side splashing into mud, splattering us through the half-open window.

"Did it get your eyes?" I shout as the rear bumper grazes past the pillar and I lift off the accelerator. "Don't." I hold his wrists as the Cruiser slides backwards down the verge on the other side of the roadblock.

Harry shrieks. Bushes snap as we hit them, the Cruiser wobbling and twisting, threatening to roll.

I grip the wheel one-handed, fighting to keep us straight, before we thump down onto the silty tarmac of the road and our rear end crunches to a stop against a rusting van.

Shaking in my damp joggers and shirt, aware of mud running down my cheek, I wet more sterile cloths and daub them over Harry's face and mine, Harry squirming and hiccuping, half giggling and half sobbing, picking up on my energy. I change our clothes, my blood fizzing from what just happened, and bundle the dirty ones into an emptied holdall so we don't mistake them.

Setting off again, I am lighter and calmer, with Sim behind that firm barrier and Jack feeling a huge step closer. The Cruiser is moving more smoothly too as we weave between rusted cars and bushes in the dawn dark, the steering wheel heavy but not juddering so much, the dash lights and headlights constant and the rear end no longer scraping.

My blinks become long and heavy despite the cold air coming in to clear the windscreen, the sleepless nights and adrenaline finally catching up with me. I keep checking the air meter, the engagement ring then twinkling on my finger and drawing my eye. The bejewelled dress I picked out that matched it rises in my mind, all soft layers of fabric and glittering beads, like any one of the glacial waterfalls we'd seen in Canada.

It begins to feel like this cold dark road is all that exists. I fight against my heavy eyes and the constant subtle tug of the stiff steering wheel to the left, and the pedal as it pushes and sags, making us surge and slow.

I'm straining so hard to see through the dust and scratches and fogging windscreen in the gloom that my head feels like it's splitting down the middle; and the clicking of the wheels, rattling of the car, and scrape and clatter as we pass debris and vegetation make the split fracture round my skull. I press my fingers over my temples—tension tingling under my touch. Jack once told me there are pressure points there, that I should try massaging them instead of going straight for painkillers. He didn't like them in the house.

As we round a bend, I frown ahead at something too bright, like firelight, in the far distance, unable to work it out. Until there's a little more of it and I realize it must finally be the sun.

15

Up yet another slip road, the midday sun in our eyes. Thick, trembling saplings crowd us, their rich red leaves coming loose to spiral down like phoenix feathers, tapping against the windscreen. Harry's hands, itching at his face again, cover his eyes as he shrinks from the windows.

"Harry! Stop touching your face—remember, everything could be dirty now."

He drops his hands. "Why does everything want to get in here, but it didn't in our flat?" He looks out with big worried eyes nearly swamped by my too-big mask round his little face. "Can we stop yet? My tummy hurts."

I pause, the engine idling. Blackened mature stumps peek out amongst the red and golden-orange foliage, like a forest burning. The car still smells faintly of vomit, Harry's wiped-clean mask hanging from the rear-view mirror.

"What do you mean? Do you feel sick again?" I look behind us, but the motorway disappeared as we turned onto the slip road. I wonder how far Sim followed our paint trail. If he's gone back, broken into our flat. I don't know why he would, but I still feel sick at the thought of him touching my things, reading my old journals, or taking Jack's clothes and shoes. I couldn't ever bear to move them from where he left them on his side of the wardrobe, which still smelled like him on opening, even now. I feel heavy again at leaving it all behind.

"I don't like always moving." Harry rubs his head, pulling at the knotted straps of the mask again.

I smile in sympathy, passing him the water flask, and help him lift the mask up for a sip, noticing the red marks the mask has worn over his nose and cheeks. I flick the air meter on, just to check, before reluctantly asking: "Would you stop touching your face if you didn't have that mask on? If you promise to be careful, you can take it off inside the car."

He nods urgently, and I get that treasured little smile as I put the mask in the glovebox.

I don't recognize the layout of the roundabout at the top of the slip road, so we rejoin the motorway. Useless peeling road signs, swamped by vegetation, mark the way. Jack's mum's house was about a two-hour drive, Before. My arms are tired from fighting with the steering wheel as we've driven up and back and retraced roads all morning. I groan and kick the accelerator to push past more fallen leaf litter and branches. Harry yelps.

"Sorry." I rub his knee.

As we plough through the fallen leaves up the next slip road I get a good feeling. It looks familiar—the rise of the road, the angle of the first exit at the roundabout and the long straight road coming off it surrounded by an expanse of dead black trees, young yellow and pink saplings thick around them, that could perhaps be Clumber Park—which Jack and I used to pass as we left the motorway following the signs towards Sheffield, on our way to North Derbyshire and his mum's house in Rothermere.

Once past the forest, I go one way and then another, past a bridge and an old pub, wondering if they look right. We both jump as the Cruiser groans louder, the vibration from the front wheels rumbling through us. Finally, we reach some familiar residential streets full of the dark grey stone of northern villages and I let the Cruiser roll down a hill, clanking and tugging to the left.

"Is the Cruiser grumpy, Mummy?" Harry whispers, clutching his seat. "Nearly time to go to bed now for everyone?"

I smile, scrunching tired eyes into a sore blink, resisting the urge to rub them. "We're nearly there now. We need to keep watch, like you did in the garage for Sim, so we're not surprised."

"Sim the man is here?" He sits up straighter, staring blearily from tree to house to the moving road, flinching every time the wheel on his side groans.

"No, I hope not."

As we rumble back uphill, the streets steepening, I scan rusted damaged road names—where they're not smothered by leaves or dust or algae—for Hilltop Lane, and look for anything familiar. The wheels groan louder, making me pull ever harder to the right to keep us straight.

Harry presses his hands over his face at the spreading hilly views.

I pull them free again.

We push through rust-coloured shrubs into a short, straight cul-de-sac—but this isn't it, the houses don't have steep steps up to the doors. The steering wheel wrenches itself too far left, the accelerator suddenly switching back to fuel-engine mode and revving hard, Harry's side scraping along a garden wall with a metallic screech. I battle to turn us away, but we only scrape closer, the wheels firmly stuck now, nosing us deeper into the overgrown bushes and crumbling wall, until the Cruiser finally stalls.

Still buzzing from the rumble of the engine, the street feels too silent now. I watch for movement along the sprouting cracked tarmac, amongst the rusted skinny hybrids—cables still snaking uselessly under garage doors, and along the rows of houses to either side.

"I guess the last bit's on foot," I whisper. "It's on this hill, I'm sure."

I hesitate, liking the safe bubble of the Cruiser, with its lock mechanisms clicked down.

"I don't like everything still moving when we're not." Harry rubs his eyes.

"It's not really—do you feel sick again?" I yank his hands free from his face.

Eyes wide, he leans away from the bleached-yellow privet pressing against his window, little flying ants pinging erratically against the glass. "Is the blood in my head sloshing about like a flood?"

I frown, beginning to smile. "Where did you get that idea?"

"Is that why flying bugs are so clumsy too?"

I smile at him. "I don't think so. You'll feel normal again very soon anyway."

Taking a breath, I push open my door before the delay becomes paralysing. Mask up over my mouth and nose and shielding my eyes from the fluff in the breeze with my hands, I shut the door on Harry as I hurry my still-muddy boots, overalls and gloves on.

Covering the ground, weeds and winding laces of algae run through every crack in the driveways and tarmac. Greyed particles and dirt cover windows and brickwork like flicked paint, and gappy roof tiling and stubborn bits of guttering sprout with fiery strips of wild flowers. It's eerie the way the ornamental hebes still retain their sculpted globe shapes amongst all this, though they are shabby now, with blonde patches spreading across once deep-green leaves.

Sparrows suddenly chirp sharply from the bushes, making me jump. Then, as I stand still, the throaty peep-peep of a great tit joins in, and the high trill of a wren.

"Why are there so many?" Harry clamps his hands over his ears as I turn back and open the door and help him into his shoes.

"They must have found food and shelter up here." The unexpected birdsong feels delicious and familiar—comforting as I stand here all jittery—though it all sounds hoarser and quieter than Before.

Harry is frozen with his feet on the door-sill.

"It's just little friends, see?" I point to the nearest—a robin, its breast a subdued tatty red. It too is paler and blander now, coat tarnished from exposure and poor diet.

I rummage in my pack for our precious bulrush cakes and crumble a corner onto the ground. Harry finally leans forward to look. The robin hops down, instantly flitting off with a morsel in its beak.

Harry meets my gaze, eyes creasing as if I'm getting a small smile under the mask. He peers down again. "There's so many. What if I squash them?"

Little rivulets of water trickle round my boots, full of tiny beetles and water spiders, with banks of dull mustardy algae writhing with their larvae.

"You won't, come on." I offer him both my hands, resisting telling him to hurry up—he needed a lot of gentle coaxing even when desperate for a toilet stop on the way here.

He carefully steps down and then quickly into his too-big raincoat and gloves I have ready for him, scratching and pulling at his newly dry mask.

"I know yours still smells. Just make do until we get inside, OK?"

I feel light-headed, a little sick, Harry *outside*. But we walk up the hill, going several feet into each cul-de-sac, as I try to morph the speckled and algaed unkempt houses into the ones in my memory. I'm conscious the whole time of leaving the Cruiser further behind, street after street.

Harry stumbles beside me, clinging to my hand, shrinking and swaying with each slight breeze as if it's a dreadful force battering him, and dragging on me as we pass bushes and saplings. He's happiest when we pause to think next to the bare brick of buildings and garden walls.

The next cul-de-sac cuts across a sharper slope, the houses on the right all with steep steps leading up to the front doors.

"This is it!"

I squeeze Harry's hand and walk halfway down, pausing at the bottom of one of those sets of steps—a wind-sanded front door at the top, the corners still that smart burgundy red.

The garage on the right is shut. I have to stop myself from walking towards it. I imagine Jack working on the Subaru in there with his stepdad Ian, both turning to smile at me as I enter, Jack pulling me into a sweaty hug, gleefully explaining all they were doing, always wanting to fix things and create. I wish I'd shown Harry Jack's guitar, let him try it out—something Harry could impress him with now.

"Is Daddy here?" Harry whispers, clinging to my hand, tripping up the steps and wincing at the squish of algae and uneven ground beneath him.

My own legs feel wobbly and weak, head full of what might have happened to Jack and how we missed each other. He will be different, as I am; of course he will be. I feel guilty wishing to find him alone, for him to be mine and Harry's only—at least for however long my chest holds out for . . .

I push on the front door, though the brass bolt is visible in the crevice between door and jamb where everything has warped. I lift my hand, watching the diamond ring trembling with my fingers— wondering now why I felt the need to wear it, as if it's proof of all these promises and dreams from another life.

Softly, I knock. I'm still his Katie. There's still that girl inside me who grinned at him when he pushed that diamond onto my finger, who was by his side on our adventures, feeling free and alive. Who imagined with him all the things we wanted together.

Harry tugs me back from the door. And I suddenly wonder how I'm going to introduce Harry to Jack. How to explain everything— I itch at my ribcage, taking tentative deep breaths. I can imagine Jack's face, oscillating between confusion, elation and grief—when he's already had to grieve for me once before.

"What, Mummy?" Harry whispers, retreating a step down, away from the door as if something nasty might come out.

"I just want Daddy to love you like I do," I whisper, looking up at the dark dusty windows.

"You said he would," Harry says, shrugging, as if it is no big deal.

It is though, I think, now I'm stood here. I'm asking him to take over from me, with a child he's never met.

I glance over my shoulder, feeling exposed here on the front step. The village slopes down the valley to the derelict shops and church and then up the other side. I scan for movement amongst the rooftops and red and yellow foliage, the big dusty presence of the Cruiser reassuring a few streets down.

Yet if Jack's not inside the house, he could be out there somewhere and that glimmer of warmth surges again. Before quickly cooling—in his letter, Jack only said he was heading here soon. Not that he would stay.

We can't just stand here. And we can't wait around the village for long—I can't rest until Harry is with him and safe.

Glancing down, I nudge the rotting doormat with the toe of my boot, rolling it up. Nothing.

"Finders game?" Harry asks, the cracked flowerpot on his step crumbling at his touch with a puff of black specks and dry soil.

"Don't!" I pull his gloved hands back, shaking them out.

"I thought it might be a secret place!" He looks up, eyes watery and worried. "Is it bad dust?"

"Just fungus and algae, I think." There's a lot for them to feed off with all the decaying old leaves and pollution leaching from all the bits of plastic dust. "But the spores—the tiny bits—can get in your airways and be bad just like the bad dust."

"I didn't know there can be so many different dusts Outside too."

I scrape at the bits of pottery and dry soil with the toe of my boot—nothing. Harry is jigging on the spot, shaking out his gloves. I'm relieved he's no longer reaching to touch, but I hate to see him scared, looking down warily at his stiff white trainers, stained and grimy from the little walk.

But I'm already thinking of where else Jack might have thought I'd either hide or look for something. Somewhere only he and I would know.

I walk around the side of the house, Harry's hand tight in mine and little body bumping into my legs. Reaching over the garden gate, I unlatch it from the other side and open it with a hard shove.

Tall purple grasses with feathery seed heads greet us, thick with spiky black-green thistles and brassy daisies bobbing in the breeze, scratching and fluttering. Gone are the neat rose borders and square of bright green lawn.

"Don't go in there!" Harry whispers.

"I think I know where to look—if you come with me, you can do the final guess?"

"The final guess?" He twists on the spot, worried but tempted.

"First clue," I say, pointing at the overgrown steps up into the grass and the rusted fairy figurine paused there in a moment of dance.

Harry creeps towards her.

"Warmer," I say, starting to push into the grass. Harry's grip becomes painful as he stalls at the edge, jerking away from the stiff grass stems and waxy leaves, shutting his eyes against the wafts of hazy pollen.

"Let's pretend it's an obstacle course, just like we play in the flat. Remember how we pretend the chair legs are a thick jungle?"

"This fog is not bad air?"

I shake my head, though I cringe at the thought of dust collected along stems and leaves about to be dislodged as we brush past.

Harry sticks to my side, holding his mask on tight with one hand. The garden is small and we're there, at the back left, in ten steps.

The tree I remember is just a rotten stump now, its cracks and crevices filled with a white fungus that's oozing reddish liquid.

"Very warm," I say to Harry. The grey wooden bird box is still fixed to the trunk, where I put it years Before. The little roof is weathered to fingers.

He nods, face pale, peering at the vines—leaves butter yellow, streaked with pink and purple.

"Is it in the fairy house?" Harry whispers.

"Maybe." I smile and a warm surge of adrenaline makes me grab the delicate roof on its resisting hinges a little too strongly. I think I see something shining inside beneath dry grass and leaves before the whole thing falls apart, scattering in pieces into the grass. I poke around uselessly, Harry whimpering and eyes frightened amongst the tall foliage.

"Perhaps we didn't win this time, Mummy," he whispers.

Disappointed, we push back through the grass to the back door; its thick plastic—rough and blistered from exposure—is as hard, I know, to break open as the solid front door. I size up the kitchen window instead, which is old-fashioned and only single-glazed.

"Stand back." Heaving up the small stone eagle from amongst the menagerie on the overgrown patio, I give the glass a good whack in the nearest bottom corner. Eagle and window shatter. Big jagged pieces of glass and a great cloud of grey sand-like matter come down around me. I scrunch my eyes tight and rush to cover Harry's, shielding him as it settles, and holding my breath even though I've my mask on.

"You're OK." I frantically pat him down, my hands trembling.

"Don't touch anything. Not until we can get you washed properly, promise?"

"I said yes, Mummy," he says, nodding really fast, and cowering from my hands.

I stop. "Sorry."

I help him up over the windowsill, onto the kitchen counter and down onto the floor inside—spongy and wet underfoot and crunchy now with glass. The air meter clicks on in the orange, above ten, the dislodged dust visible in the air, making my blood pound.

"How will you lock it behind us?" Harry trembles next to me, standing stiff, his arms held out from his body. Dust is still stuck to his raincoat, to his hair too. I carefully pick a piece from his eyelashes.

"We can't," I whisper. "Come on, we need to check the house." As soon as we've done that I can clean him properly and make him safe.

Harry is quiet and rigid as we edge away from the dust and the broken window, and towards the hallway.

He whimpers, resisting stepping over the threshold into the hall. "What if someone's here?"

"Jack?" I call out, my voice stiff and odd. "Jack!" Harry and I stand frozen, the house silent around us, smelling cold and damp and uncared for.

Harry's shoulders relax a little. "Maybe no one lives here," he whispers.

I swallow down his words, try not to think. But they come roaring back up into my head, along with all the many cold, quiet, grim homes I've had to go inside. Maybe no one *lives* here. Everything inside me is scrunching up tight, desperate to tear into each room, yet desperate not to. I reach for Harry's hand and squeeze.

16

I turn to Harry, smoothing my voice to calm and slow. "Let's pretend this is the flat."

"I don't want to pretend," Harry mumbles.

I look around the small square kitchen, alert for noises elsewhere in the house, only half-conscious of the opened cupboards with rodent-bitten packets of rice, every grain devoured, shredded paper and card—a stinking mess. Crockery shelves with toppled plates, droppings and spiders. "But, see, on that hook, Harry, we had saucepans like that in the flat, and spoons and forks like in that jar there, and a stove kettle." The skirting beneath the cupboards is bent forwards and I point it out. "See, it even has the same secret places." I try to sound reassuring, but my voice wobbles.

"And the same circle doors." Harry points to the washing machine in the corner.

"Yes." I nod. "Let's come away from this room now," I plead, heading out into the hallway, relieved as Harry allows himself to be pulled along this time, still clutching my hand. Down the dim hallway, we step into the lounge together, and I look first at the spot Jack used to sit in, nearest the window, where he would fall asleep watching rugby with his stepdad on a Saturday afternoon. Disappointment thuds in my chest, as if I'd hoped he'd be sleeping there again now after all.

No note. No sign.

In a daze, I point out the sofas and cabinets to Harry, and he makes me check each corner of the room for any surprises, even though I hurry through it, dragging him to the next room. And the next.

I try not to look at the photographs pinned artistically to fabric pinboards up the stairs, but I can't help it as I pass. Jack as a baby. Jack at ten. Jack at eighteen. His parents. Grandparents. Cousins and people I don't know. All smiling out from glossy rectangles, all ignorant of what's coming. I can't help but touch a photo of Jack as a baby. It comes loose, spinning down to the carpet. His little face stares up at me—white-blonde hair, chubby cheeks and full lips, bright blue eyes.

I can remember Maggie sitting me down in the lounge the first time I visited, the photo albums spread across our laps. She was ill even then—breathing every few breaths from her oxygen concentrator (like so many others) after a nasty flu—and she'd squeezed my hands tightly: "At least he's got his stepdad, if anything happens to me . . ."

We go through the same checks in the first bedroom at the top of the stairs.

Halfway down the landing, the bathroom door is shut, the handle missing. A cold sweat comes over me as I press on the door, my breathing ragged as it won't open.

I kick and shoulder-barge it, the wood frame weak from damp, creaking and splintering until I burst inside.

At first I only see the peach-tiled walls, as if my mind has already refused to look down. Neat and perfectly laid. Jack learned how to do it off the internet, he and his stepdad always willing to have a go at anything.

I see the back of a head of thick desiccated hair, turned grey with dust. A deflated jumper, sunken trousers. Black-soled trainers.

For a second I imagine how he might have knelt over the toilet bowl to vomit or cough up phlegm and blood, all the dust in his lungs doing its damage.

Then Jack's smiling face, alive in all those photos, and my own internal scream are spinning round my head.

I fall backwards from the doorway and pull at the hole left by the door handle to make it disappear. Make it not true. I'm grasping at Harry, trying to make my legs take my weight again so I can get up and get out of here.

At least he's got his stepdad, if anything happens to me... Maggie's rasping voice echoes in my head as I look at Harry, who has no one.

We shouldn't have come. We shouldn't have left.

That balcony railing back in Hitchin and that ground pulsating below flashes in my mind.

"Mummy!" Harry is sobbing, stroking my hair. "What was it? Was it a monster? Mummy!"

I manage to take one breath, then another. I make myself get up. Make myself push the bathroom door open again, keeping Harry back so he can't see. I examine the size and shape of the remains, the type of trousers, the sunken face.

Not Jack!

"Is it a nasty?"

"No, a man."

Ian.

"What's wrong with him?" Harry asks, out on the landing, pulling off his mask and clutching it tightly.

"He's sleeping," I say, trying to sound light. "A deep one, he won't wake up."

I sink out onto the landing floor again, pulling the door shut once more, and crawl away, into the master bedroom, where Ian used to let us sleep when we stayed over, while he took the single in the little box room. Immediately, his face is smiling out at me from the dresser and I turn away from it, my thoughts swirling.

Harry tugs at my shoulder. "Is it lunchtime?" he whispers. "Like in the flat?"

My head spins, bile in my throat. I glance back towards the bathroom.

But it seems the closed door is enough for Harry to forget, for now. He repeats his hope for lunch until I look at him properly, the fog clearing.

Harry is filthy. He has never been filthy. The bathroom still sharp in my head, I strip and wipe him down from head to toe with a clean cloth from the dwindling stash in my pack, wetted from my flask, searching his ears and eyelids and hair for pale grey particles. Then I get the soft brush out to be absolutely sure.

He looks much better in clean clothes and I inspect his nose and throat and eyes for inflammation—making him blink and cringe—fretting if his eyes really are a little bloodshot, or his throat redder than it should be.

He grins when I finally pull out the tin of mandarins from my backpack and let him sit on the floor to eat it. I can't focus on him though, even when he tugs at my elbow with a big grin and eyes half-closed in happiness. I feel numb.

As I clean myself, a small Jack beams out at me from the dresser, a fairy-tale castle cake in the photo with him. Six candles. Pink wafer walls, chocolate finger towers and ramparts, and multicoloured Smarties pressed into smooth glistening icing for the roof.

I've always brought Harry what I can find: leaves and pine cones, cocooned moths to watch emerge, chalks and pencils and paints once too. Things to play or make things with. We read and make up stories. But he's never had a cake or proper toys. I think of Playmobil families and Enid Blyton friendship books—it's all too painful and meaningless. This year I didn't really mark his birthday—only with the first rabbit catch of the year and both of us thin and hungry for the stew. Harry excited and happy with that. And I told myself that without a calendar I'm just guessing the day anyway.

But I should have done it properly. Maggie would have done.

Harry's little voice whispers inside my head: *Do you love me?* He hasn't had enough life yet. Not enough foods or fun or good experiences. Or me.

The bathroom door seems to grow larger out there on the landing. Now what? The words rebound round my head.

No Jack.

Harry's mouth shrinks to a small "O" as he sucks a piece of fibrous mandarin—it must have gone hard and unpleasant. He grins at me as he wipes his nose on his sleeve. The sight of thick sticky snot mixing with the juices round his mouth snaps me from my ruminating. I try to wipe the snot away even as he turns and struggles to keep spooning up the mandarins.

He shouldn't have a stuffy nose.

I stand up, shifting from foot to foot, raking sharp fingers through my hair.

The tin is nearly empty. Now what?

There, on the bed, blending into the greyed sheets. A used brown paper envelope, with HMRC stamped in black in the top left. Harry's eyes are trained on me as I step forwards and frown at the pencil scribble on the front.

Katie

My legs fold beneath me. Harry clatters across the floorboards to fling his arms around me.

In brackets beneath: *Don't go in the bathroom.*

My anguished laugh makes Harry scrape his sticky fingers over my face, mixing with the tears he tries to brush away.

"Don't cry, Mummy. I'll help finders, we can find Daddy. Don't cry."

A creaking and rattling downstairs makes us both freeze, my cry cut off, Harry's sour breath on my face, mandarin flesh stuck between his teeth. I glance down at our things on the floor, clocking my pack, Harry's shoes.

"Did he wake up?" Harry says, trembling.

"Ahoy! Anyone there?" A man's muffled voice. Shouted through the letter box in the front door, I think.

"Hello!" A woman's voice.

Two people.

The sugary acidic smell of mandarins is like vomit at the back of my throat.

I'm moving, the envelope grasped tight, grabbing my pack, dragging a rigid and unhappy Harry, shoving shoes, overalls and masks on, and racing down the stairs.

"I didn't finish the mand-rins . . ." Harry whispers, plastering a hand over his mask, because he knows he should be silent.

He cries out, squirming in my grip, as I pull him out of the kitchen window with me and through the tall scratchy grass of the back garden. I can't stop to see what the matter is until we're safe, so I haul him up and over the garden wall and yank him into a run, tugging him as he stumbles, crying harder, in the too-big raincoat and too-tight shoes, and struggles to keep up.

There's shouting behind us and I surge faster, swinging Harry into my arms and pounding all the harder along the road. Blood. Bright blood is pouring down his face from a cut in his forehead. Its sickening metallic scent right at my nose as my mask bounces loose.

I can't catch my breath, wheezing loudly now, Harry becoming too heavy.

I change direction, careening down the side of a semi-detached house where we're shielded from the road by thick butterfly-bushes, full of yellow papery leaves and soft purple blooms that stink too sweet, and wingless bees that I brush clear as I set Harry down.

The blood is the ruby shade of red that I remember blood *should* be. The bees bumble towards it.

I'm sinking to my knees, lungs whistling—tight and aching, air rushing in and out.

Was it when we scrambled out of the window? When I pulled him down the wall? He's no longer crying, his face is pale, tear-stained, eyes beginning to roll. My hands are sticky and warm as I try to stop the bleeding. But it just flows out between my fingers, seeping into the strap of his mask.

Through the orange willow foliage at the bottom of the garden I can just make out the black dusty roof of the Cruiser. All we need to do is get back to it.

"Hey, we know you're back there." It's the male voice, soft, a forced calmness to it. "We're not going to come in . . . Look, we're sorry, we didn't mean to scare you. It's just, we don't see many people around here. You're one of the few we've seen all year—"

"Yes, people just don't travel about anymore." The woman's voice, less restrained, slightly excited.

It all goes quiet while they wait for me to respond. I try to mop the blood from Harry's face with the bottom of my shirt, but more gushes out. I flick a bee away and waft a hand at the bobbing dust specks in the air. There's so much blood. Why isn't it stopping? My pulse pounds round me, throbbing through my still-wheezing chest. I hold my sleeve over Harry's wound, what else are you supposed to do? I can't remember now. I try to bring Jack's voice to mind again—he's the one trained for this stuff—but it won't come.

17

Four Years and Six Months Ago

"Please don't cry." I'm blubbing, shushing him. "What do you want?" I try feeding him again—my breasts uncomfortable and hard, leaking yellowy milk—but he turns his little face away, his mouth not latching on to anything the way I read it should. I check the towelling nappy. I rock him. "Why are you crying?" And he quietens only to draw enough breath to shriek again, his tiny face and newborn scrunched-up body bright red. And I feel utterly useless. I have one job now, nothing else, just this, and I can't fucking do it!

"Just feed!" I cry. "Or you'll die too! Do you want that?" Sobbing. I wish I could ask Mum what was wrong, why he is so unhappy, what I need to do. I rub my tired eyes, eyelids squeaking.

I hold him tight to my chest, the shrieks at least go right into me then, half smothered by blankets and clothes. Yet it still feels like a siren ringing out into the thick air outside that could draw anyone to us, if there's anyone out there to hear.

I mistime the doorway and smack my shoulder into the frame, peeling skin but not drawing blood. The shock of it drives the heavy feeling harder, and I weave down the hallway, past empty white rectangles where there used to be pictures, my stomach growling, my limbs heavy, and the little boy, eyes wide in shock, drawing breath again.

"I'm sorry," I sob, putting him in the basket I've made into his bed, stuffing the dummy into his mouth and holding it there to try to make it stay, pulling loose the bit of string from the body brush hung by the bath and using that to hold it tight to his face. I watch him suck and fight against it as I step towards the door, feeling pleased with myself for inventing a potential solution. I shut him in the bathroom, duvets and blankets hung off the door and rails inside to try to absorb some of the sound and insulate the small room. I fumble my boots on at the front door, the wailing ringing in my ears.

I shrug on the dust-proof boiler suit that no longer smells of its previous owner—I can't even think his name without a bleak black hole opening up inside me. So I numb the name in my mind, push it down and away, and pick up the mask, gloves and goggles too. Finding myself rushing down the stairs, giddy at the sudden freedom and quiet.

I skid to a halt on the second-to-bottom landing, though, and nearly turn back. His cries are muted now, but I can still hear them as an echo in my head, and my muscles feel tighter and stiffer the further I go, as if I'm pulling against something the more I move away from him.

At the garage shutter, I stop, hood up, and check and recheck all my gear is on and done up, wiping the scratched goggles so I'm not too blinkered. Already the chill foggy air and wide-open space out there is jarring, nipping at me through my layers, buildings towering over me. But I breathe in, reassured that my lungs are clear and no longer tight, and the air not frosty or damp anymore. I have to face all this for that little thing upstairs. I roll my shoulders back. Pull myself straight. I have to go; I've put it off all day. I have no stockpile; I've eaten nothing since yesterday morning.

So I roll under and stagger back up, careful with the delicate areas around my tummy and legs and chest, tuned to scanning windows and the edges of the car park around me. It still doesn't matter how many months have passed: I dread hearing footsteps. Today I crunch through the broken tiles and twigs and trails of dust to cross the street and head towards Hitchin Hill and the estate on the other side. I don't scavenge close to home anymore.

I pause by the wrecked old cottage at the end of Whinbush. The junction ahead is grey and black: the tarmac, bent metal lights, fallen trees and shopfronts, everything splattered and fuzzy, dust like dirty snow in windblown heaps, the sky grey too. All still, all quiet. I cross the pavement and two lanes out in the open, then break into a wincing jog up the alleyway that takes me to the terraces.

Once there, I push on doors—windows are easiest for breaking and entering, but I'm still too sore below to scramble over windowsills. Even walking feels uncomfortable—each stride tugging unpleasantly at unhealed tissue. I wish I could ask someone if it should still hurt like this, if it should still bleed and feel hot. I turn from a locked door, ready to try the next.

And spring back, elbows bashing against the wood.

Someone is staring right at me. Through the grimy window of the once-red now rust-riddled and dust-splattered Honda Civic on the driveway.

My legs shake.

But that person's not moving. There are no eyes in those sockets.

I breathe out slowly, fogging up the bottom of my goggles. They're dead.

My legs are awkward as I force myself to walk past, out of the corner of my eye seeing sunken skin and a full head of dry cropped hair.

"The storm is raging around me," I whisper to myself. "But I am calm." Over and again.

I try a dozen homes before a door opens. I think lots of people fled, sick or scared, without bothering to lock up.

It opens straight onto the lounge. There's a shape on the sofa, hair desiccated but thick and brown still, body covered by a blanket, as if they were vegging out watching TV.

I feel like I can't breathe again—chest tight and breathless like it was up until only a few weeks ago, with winter inflaming my lungs and making them feel worse than they had even in the aftermath of the storm last year. Death. Everywhere around me. I'm trembling, fumbling to shut the door again. Hundreds of flats and houses all around me, hundreds of dead lying on sofas and beds and floors. Some hanging in stairwells. I place a hand on my chest, let the breaths come, feel the free and easy movement of my lungs again—I'm OK.

The street seems to come fully into focus as I walk to the next house. Dead trunks. Grasses and seedlings shooting from the ground like licks of orange-red flame—I scan the brown-grey verges and gardens, like I always do, for something green, for more signs of growth. No sound today. No wind. Just the heavy grey sky and shrouded ends of the street, bigger particles bobbing in the thick air close by. Sun just a hazy glow over the rooftops. No birds. No squirrels. Just me.

The weight of the silence settles in my chest, adrenaline buzzing through me, and I look down the street towards where the alleyway is and home. But I'm already pulling fruitlessly at the next door.

What feels like hours later, but is probably only half an hour, I'm back at the flats, hurrying up the stairs, heart pounding, adrenaline still surging. I can't help it, holding my breath as I struggle out of my outer things and open the door. Then I'm inside our hallway, pushing the door shut, locking it, dead-bolting it, putting the chain across. Pulling on it once. Twice. Three times. Again.

I put the bottle of Worcestershire sauce down, along with the box of panko breadcrumbs and packet of freeze-dried mushrooms. Then I strip in the hallway, washing with the last dregs of soap and the clean water I left in the bowl by the door.

At first I'm relieved to hear the quiet, relieved to feel hidden and safe. But then dread starts pounding. The silence loud and heavy. The thought of death everywhere overwhelming. And I run down the hall, skidding on the hard wooden floor and landing with a thud on my side—the sensitive bits all smarting.

I step into the warm and stuffy bathroom. The little boy is lying too still, too quiet. The dummy has fallen or been tugged out, the string held taut in his miniature fists, bitingly tight around his neck. Shaking, I hold a finger out just over his mouth and wait, feeling the reassuring puffs of air that show he is still alive, and everything inside me relaxes in relief. I throw the stringed dummy to the corner—stupid!—and slap the heel of my hand into my forehead until it stings. Then I stand there shivering, looking at his soft delicate skin—all hot and flushed still, puffy eyes shut tight, short wisps of fine hair on that sweet head.

I pick him up carefully, bringing him gently to the bedroom with me, shutting the door, and with the curtains closed, I climb into my own soft bed, all the muscles in my arms and shoulders loosening and sinking. I rest him on my lap, while I gorge straight from the crinkly packets, shoving food into my mouth, crunching on breadcrumbs and hacking at hard mushrooms, licking at the Worcestershire sauce—tears streaking down my cheeks. Until I see his little mouth making a sucking movement, his head roving as if searching.

And then I get it. I shove the food away, and pull him close, pushing his mouth into position. He does it without waking, sucking and gulping, and I watch mesmerized, focusing on just this, his little features, the way his tiny hands stay fisted and his forehead scrunched as if in deep concentration.

I hope it is a good dream.

18

"We know the little boy is hurt . . ." It's the male voice, raspy and deep. "Let us help you. I'm Andy; this is Sue."

"Hello. Please, dear, we've got first aid things at the house." The woman's voice is smoother, less damaged.

"We can go and get them."

I stare at Harry's pale face, my sticky red fingers over his forehead. "OK," I call, still wheezy from the running.

I hear them walk off. Minutes tick by. I could run for the Cruiser, lock us safely inside, try to drive away, maybe if I pull hard enough the wheels will turn again. But bright blood still weeps out between my fingers and all too soon, Andy and Sue are coming round the corner, he without a mask and she with a camo army-style one. They're both younger than I thought from their voices. Forties maybe. Thin and athletic-looking. His hair is grey and wiry, eyes bloodshot like mine; her face is sadder, eyes lined and drawn. I find myself looking beyond them, as if looking for Jack in their party.

Sue comes straight down to Harry, lowering her mask to reveal a naturally drooping mouth. "Here, help me sit him up. You need the wound above the heart, helps slow the bleeding."

I groan at myself in frustration—of course!—and ease Harry up.

She presses thick white padding over the gash. His eyes are on me and I squeeze his hand, getting one little squeeze back.

"Cuts to the head often look worse than they are," Sue says, as I stare at her weathered fingers gently stroking Harry's dark hair. "It might need help closing up though—I could do it—"

"You don't have to come back to our place," Andy cuts in, standing a few steps away. "But if you wanted to, you can. The boy can rest and get better. We can get us a nice hot meal—bet you both could do with one?"

"Thank you," I find myself saying, if only because Harry's pale face and the blood and a cut out in the exposed air is making me feel sicker and shakier, even if the blood is slowing now.

Andy leans forward, but I get my arms around Harry first and lift him up. His cheek rests against mine, hands digging in to cling tight.

I hesitate, glancing towards the Cruiser, nervous to head away from it. "We're alright." I kiss Harry's cheek. "But remember to squeeze twice if you need to."

The house is at the other end of the village, downhill towards the high street and then up. Harry is heavy and we have to keep stopping so I can rest and readjust, panting, my lungs whistling and tight from the exertion again. But Andy and Sue stay a few steps away at all times, treating me like a spooked horse. I try to muffle my breathing, pressing my mask against Harry's shoulder.

"I'm sorry we scared you at the house," Andy says. "We were just pleased to see someone. There's no one this side of Sheffield."

I nod, disappointment thudding, anxious to read Jack's new letter. My chest is getting sore and achy, my head dizzy, Harry slipping in my arms.

We reach a bungalow—the roof tiles submerged beneath mustard-orange algae and purple thistles—and Andy and Sue lead us up the path to the door.

I pause with Harry to take off our outdoor things, though Andy and Sue only take off boots and masks on the porch.

Down a narrow fresh-white hallway, past a front bedroom with dark wood furniture, then several closed doors, and into the room at the back. Harry's feet now trailing on the floor and my breath rasping, I sink onto the sofa as soon as we reach it. The room has an open fireplace with utensils, gleaming steel pans and drying meats and herbs hanging above it, a sideboard with dishes and bowls and jars, and near the window, a dining table. The walls are a rich warm pink, the wood all sanded pine. It smells of woodsmoke and herbs in here—rosemary and thyme and mint.

"Tea, dear?" Sue asks.

The question makes me tearful again, but I manage a nod.

She smiles, head tilting. "I bet you've not been asked that in a while."

My eyes keep drawing back to Andy. I feel shaky and trapped in the sagging sofa cushions as he steps inside to get the fire going, even though it's the middle of the day, leaning into the open fireplace to arrange logs in a neat criss-cross of increasing size above the kindling. Old ash from the chimney breast catches in his already grizzled hair. Settling back on his knees, he pats down the many pockets of his gilet. I hear a grind of friction, and lean sideways to see sparks effortlessly eating into kindling. I spy the flint and steel, looped together on a blue thread, as he pushes it back in a pocket. How easy that would make things, never having to scour for lighters and matches, eking them out, dreading not being able to find more.

He catches me watching and smiles, but I can't look into his eyes, only down at my feet.

"Don't you worry about inhaling fumes with an open fire like that, or someone seeing your smoke in the daylight?" I don't mean to, but the words burst out of me. Already the room is bitter from the chemical tang of the wood, curls of smoke unwinding in thick white ribbons up towards the chimney. Anxiety makes me tug Harry's mask up, and mine too, glad I kept them on us. Sue opens the back door to let cool air in as the room becomes stuffy, helping the chimney to draw.

"As we said, there's no one this side of the city," Andy says gently, and when he does his voice sounds less hoarse.

I fidget on the sofa, rocking Harry, even though he frowns at the movement.

"Nobody stayed here," Andy continues softly, "and I've seen no one pass through for some time. So, your car was clanking as you drove in. Wheels sticking?"

In my head, I can't help but grasp at other places Jack might have gone—my mum's place in Birmingham after all, or his old army barracks in the north-west? Did he settle in one of them?

"We can take a look at it, maybe it's fixable."

Sue kneels beside us, a wet cloth in her hands.

"Is that clean?" I hug Harry closer.

"Yes, of course—filtered and boiled." She nods at the steel barrel by the fireplace and then shows me a roll of duct tape. "Trust me, it's as good as stitching it. You don't want to leave it like that, love, do you?" I watch her cut a neat rectangle and stick it over the gash. "Does yours need some?" She nods at my hand.

"No, no, it's closed up," I say, though it's not and I don't know why I jerk away from her.

In the next moment, she's placing a warm mug of lavender tea in my hands. Harry fights sleep, head bouncing. The heat seeps into me, and I sink further into the sofa as Harry and I sip it, masks now discarded in my lap, though I have one hand still touching them.

I wake with a jolt to the clink of metal against wood, immediately clocking on to Andy at the dining table, laying out cutlery. I'm curled tight around Harry, T-shirt rucked up, Jack's envelope crumpled in my hands.

"Sorry," Sue whispers. "You look like you've not got much sleep recently. It's nearly done. I've set out a bowl of warm water for you, if you want to clean up."

As I rouse Harry in a blur, I can't help fingering my backpack, the knife on my belt, the Cruiser key in my front right pocket, and sliding the envelope into my left, burning to be read but safe. I touch everything twice over, trying to feel more in control again, despite the swirling dread in my stomach at Harry's pale face, and at being here in this house with strangers, and at the unread letter. Harry winces as I wash his face with jittery hands—the smell of food making me feel weaker again—wiping around the tape and getting at the alarming snotty crust around his nose and sleep in his eyes, my own hands scraped and cut, stinging in the water.

"It's all grown and caught, I hope that's OK?" Sue asks as we sit at the table, relaxing when I nod. "Most people we've met don't trust foraging or hunting, prefer to eat canned food, where they can find it, thinking it's safer. Still used, I think, to packaged labelled food, as if food comes in no other way."

"Scavenging is grim," I say, "and there's not much to find anymore. So I . . . so I found places to forage."

"I don't blame you," Andy says. "You just have to know where to look, know what's worth risking and what's not."

The stew is hot, full of meaty hunks of venison, with beans, tomatoes and wild garlic. It should taste wonderful but nothing registers in my mouth.

Sue offers round bread.

I stare as Harry tears a bit off, dunks it into his stew and nibbles at it. Beautiful, fresh, risen bread. My mouth fills with saliva. It smells comforting and savoury. Wonderful.

"How did you . . .?"

"Wild yeast. I make it with sedge and bulrush flour and water. Did you know if you leave it outside on a calm day covered with a cloth, natural yeasts in the air will get inside the mixture? Eventually you have a live culture to add to dough to make risen bread."

I look at Harry's little face, his too-small frame. "No, I didn't know." Worry gnaws at me though. "In the air?" I can't help inspecting the bread's coarse texture.

"It's nothing like proper bread, of course, but it's something."

Harry grins at Sue, making emotion surge up inside me that I have to blink away.

"The only thing that would top it off," Andy says, "is some nice fresh salted butter. Oh I miss that. On top of toast, melted on potatoes, rich in pastries and biscuits . . ."

"We didn't used to be so lean!" Sue laughs. "But we're managing."

The thought of those foods makes me all the more nauseous. "Are you—did you—did you know each other Before?"

They exchange a glance and I notice Sue fiddling with her sleeves, scars on her wrists just disappearing from view.

"No," Andy says, "we found each other. I saw a light on in a house one night and found Sue."

"We're finding Daddy," Harry blurts, beaming.

My face grows hot, the spoon in my hand slippery. And I realize

Harry's not eating much either, just using his spoon to bail sauce over a dam of meat and vegetables, clear of his sinking bread. He keeps touching his head and the tape.

"Oh?" Sue says, looking to me. "Did you become separated?"

The muscles in my throat stiffen, and I cough instead.

"What does he look like?" Andy asks. "Perhaps we've seen him, if he's passed through. Few have this year."

The silence grows as I don't answer. They *might* have seen him, I realize, five years ago, that first summer After.

Sue grins down at Harry, passing him more bread for his untouched stew. "Hey, I've got something special for you." She disappears into another part of the house and comes back with a small train cradled in her hands, metallic and painted red, the name "Julian" in faded gold along its side. She handles it tenderly as she passes it to Harry.

A strong urge to push it out of their hands rises in me. It's not tatty and worn like Luna the reindeer, but sharp and cold to the touch, I imagine.

"I don't suppose you know what a train is." Sue doesn't look at me to confirm what Harry might know and I shift uneasily in my seat. "They used to run on tracks, carrying people in and out of the cities. You'd sit on there and the countryside would whizz past!"

I wince, the edge of that black hole of grief inside me. Harry doesn't need to know about the past and what happened in it. He gently pushes the train on its wheels, looking up to check Sue's expression. She's teary, but trying to smile—a strange look in her eyes.

We're all quiet for a while, just staring into the crackling fire. Harry slumps against me, getting heavy again, but his eyelids keep fluttering open as if he's determined not to fall asleep.

"It must be hard with a child," Andy says softly.

I swallow. We should leave soon, get back to the Cruiser. I itch for a moment alone to read the letter. It's already getting dark outside—when did that happen?

Andy and Sue are both looking at me.

"I'm trying my best. To make things OK."

"I wonder about my children," Sue says. "About what their

lives would be had they lived. Samuel, my eldest, he was eight. He dreamed about being a footballer and going to parties; I wonder what he would have made of this life. I had three, you know," Sue says to me. "People used to stare! Thrice the joy, but thrice the grief in the end."

My insides twist at her words. It's too dark to head out now.

"He would have adjusted, children do," Andy says. "It's us older folk that cling to life as we would have liked it."

"I suppose," Sue says, her eyes drifting across the room. I follow them, noticing the floral curtains, the large family dining table, and wonder if Sue has clung to her home like I did our flat. Her safe place is within these walls. Even now, I'm fighting between the letter and hurrying to search for Jack, and the urge to run back to Hitchin, lock those doors behind us, and climb into my own bed.

"I wonder how many times we've had the same conversation over the years," Sue says, wincing a little as she smiles at Andy. "The planet was literally telling us, over and again, what we could and could not do, and we didn't listen. How much might they have hated the older generations for destroying the world for them . . ."

Andy reaches over to squeeze her hand. "What does Harry make of it all?"

"He doesn't know—" I stop myself, not sure I want to admit how little of this world Harry really knows. "He knows no different, I guess. He's four."

"And a half!" Harry blurts wearily.

"Really?" Sue says, glancing at me. "He's so small."

I flush.

"Has game dwindled down south?" Andy cuts in, his eyes worried as they look at Sue.

I nod, relieved to talk about something else. "The rabbits have got sicker."

"Andy catches a lot of deer. Great herds of them roam around here, eating everything if you're not careful." Sue glances at the seedlings and pots lining the windowsill.

"The rabbits have plummeted," Andy says, and I get the impression we've hit a topic on which he could talk for some time. "They reached such a number, but their underground burrows must be a magnet for dust and pollution and contaminated floodwater—they looked very sick a few years ago and I gave up hunting them, even before they became so few. The deer seem healthy enough though, despite their gunky eyes and noses. It's a real shame we bred game birds solely for hunting Before—they were stupid and clumsy, used to being fed, lost all of their survival instinct. Not many left at all now, too few to keep the species going at least."

"I never thought much of pheasant anyway, too gamy a taste," Sue cuts in, forcing Andy to finally draw breath.

"She says that," Andy says, smiling at me, "but she still wishes for more variety than venison."

"I don't see why some game birds won't survive," Sue says, "even if a few have lasted this long, they can still breed and produce more."

"Yes, but there reaches a point when the population is too small to last more than a generation or two, not enough genetics. It was the same Before, you know, for pandas and tigers in the wild. Drastic measures were too late, they still dwindled in their special conservation forests. Still disappeared. They reached a point of no return."

"Are *we* too late?" I ask out loud, before I can stop myself, staring at Harry's sleeping face, with those old familiar numb thoughts of not being able to imagine his life ahead. But that awful feeling I had when I saw Ian's body in the bathroom fizzes in my blood too. Could too many years have passed to hope to make things alright for Harry with Jack? It's not like I can call around hospitals, get police to launch a manhunt, canvas doorsteps for sightings . . . if the new letter doesn't lead us to him either. He could be lost still, no matter what, alive or—Ian's decayed body flashing in front of my eyes—dead after all.

I look up to both of them staring at me.

Sue fidgets her hands in her lap and looks away.

Andy looks at me kindly, eyes sliding to Harry. "Perhaps."

Tears sting my eyes.

"You don't know that," Sue says.

"I don't," he admits, worrying his beard.

"You still have a good life though, dear," Sue says urgently, her thin, clammy hands reaching for mine. Her eyes are tearing up. "Every day is hard for me, I can't tell you how hard, but you . . . You've got a good life with your little boy, haven't you?"

She asks with such certainty that I find myself automatically nodding. Yet her tears make mine threaten all the harder, alongside a sliver of anger. She has no idea. My words are wobbly and rising in pitch, bursting out of me. "I've just been trying to keep us breathing and fed and warm, trying not to think, not to feel . . . I want him to survive, for everything not to feel so scary and uncertain and empty for him—I just need to know he'd be alright, if—" The words tumble out, my mouth dry, but I stop myself, suddenly sure I don't want to give Sue any indication that Harry might need anyone other than me. People do strange and awful things in grief—and hers hangs heavy in the room. I press my legs tighter together. I know this.

"You need to know he'll be alright, if this is all there is? I know what you mean," Andy says gently, glancing quickly at Sue, then back at me. "We grew up in a world where we were taught to expect so much more. Settling for simpler things—food, shelter, warmth— well, it's something to get your head around after all we've lost. But we're comfortable here." His smile at Sue lingers long enough to get a tearful half-smile from her.

Except he *doesn't* know what I mean, because I've left too much out. I need someone to give all that to Harry. And to love him like I do. If I can't. All the words and fears that have just batted round my own head all this time are bubbling up inside me.

I glance at Andy, at the strong bulk of his shoulders and arms from what I imagine is hunting those deer and bringing home wood for the fire, the calm look in his eyes.

If Andy were to tell me he was ill, would I focus instead on the grey in his hair, the lines in his face? I don't want them to do the same to me, to focus on my lungs, to imagine me weak. Vulnerable. I don't know either of them at all. Sue is looking down at Harry's beautiful sleeping face, his eyelashes twitching as he dreams.

I lean in to kiss his cheek, obscuring him from her. And trace the outline of Jack's letter in my pocket.

19

Floorboards creak in the next room as Andy and Sue get ready for bed. Andy said they wouldn't come back in here until the morning, looked me in the eye and nodded gently. He only locked the front and back doors at my insistence, though. The keys glint on the coffee table in the gloom.

Katie

I lean towards the venison-grease candle and its wobbling cream-coloured flame, finally picking up the envelope and slipping out the paper folded up inside. Lips raw from biting them. Holding my breath.

I've looked everywhere I could think of for you. Hoping in the end that you did not see the people you loved as I've seen them.
    Maybe everyone's right. Everything I've done has been wishful, desperate thinking. I think this will be the last letter I leave. For my own sanity, it has to be, I think.

I scratch at my scalp and my neck, restless, wondering if Jack left notes in Birmingham—where Mum and Paul lived, or at Uncle Phil's, or at Tristan and Beth's place in Sheffield. I feel sick imagining what he must have seen. No other hope then for Harry and me . . . Even though I knew Mum and Paul must be dead . . . it surprises me how hard Jack's words of them hit.

I'm going north, hoping to settle in Arisaig, near the Old Library and where Mum and I used to camp every summer. A good spot to live out post-civilization! Can't stand to be in the wreck of it.

I don't know if I can live without you, Katie. You were the love of my life. The best thing that ever happened to me. I've regretted leaving since I set foot in London that day and realized the edge of the storm had already arrived and how fucking little we'd actually known about what it was.

We got stuck on the smaller problems, on frowning at annual holidaymakers for taking flights and individuals for not recycling enough. Instead of focusing on big important shifts in how we all lived—wasting resources and polluting, when we didn't need to! I hate how much clearer it all seems—this stuff made you so driven . . . Sometimes the powers that be think panic and truth and change is worse than inaction. Fuck them. Just fucking fuck them.

I smile, blinking wet eyes.

Yet given what I did think I knew, I couldn't not go. I just couldn't, Katie. The kid in for surgery that day that I was so desperate to be there for, he made it. I know it's wrong to think, but Katie, if I could choose again, it would be you. It was always you. Above every human on the planet, I loved you.

The page is smudged and badly scrawled and I turn over, where the writing is straighter and clearer again.

Nobody should face death alone. I should have held you close to the very last. You deserved that. At the very least, you deserved that.

The words are almost illegible again.

You had all my love,
Jack.

I read it over and over until I can only focus on one word. Jack.

Harry murmurs in his sleep, something about dragons trying to wake up sleepy rabbits. "Wake up!" Normally I'd have smiled, his make-believe washing over me, but the Fear is creeping up afresh. I check the letter again, rereading it slowly. I linger over his use of the past tense and the line that reads: *I don't know if I can live without you.* And remember the darkness that settled over him sometimes, his regrets heavy. That kid he couldn't save on that last army tour that left him injured and battling addiction and darkness . . . What if—since he wrote this—I killed him by not being there to be found when he made it back to Hitchin? His guilt and grief too heavy. Or what if pollution or lack of food has got to him? So either way he's dead and we're too late . . .

"Is it from Daddy?" Harry whispers, making me jump. "Sorry."

"It's alright. Yes, it is."

"Did he give a warm clue?"

"Sort of. But it's far away, if I'm thinking of the right place."

"How far?"

With a sinking feeling, I picture it as I last saw it with Jack: the grey low stone building of the inn, its library history remembered in the menus styled to look like book covers. Lists of fancy vegetable dishes, not a single element of the seafood it must have served for generations before. Waves crashing on the beachfront, misted islands in the distance.

My voice cracks at the thought of taking Harry there. "Just about as far as you can imagine." Already I feel sick over taking Harry from the flat, exposing him to the stairwell and the garage in Hitchin, to the risk of breaking down on the road, and all that dust out there! Harry in the open air of Derbyshire, that dusty break-in . . . banging his head . . .

And Jack could be dead anyway.

I remember the warm, hopeful feeling when I opened the letter in Hitchin. Foolish, stupid girl.

"Like as far as the moon? Or as far as the corners of the map, or as high as . . ."

Harry chunters on until his head sags. But he jerks awake so violently he headbutts my jaw.

"It's alright," I whisper, rubbing my numb lip, "go to sleep."

"No!" he says, shrill, as I shush him. "What if I can't wake up?"

"Don't be silly, of course you will." I frown, kissing his head. "Aren't you tired?"

He nods, terror in his little face.

"What if I promise to wake you up in the morning?" With the promise made he finally lets himself sleep again, leaving me thinking and staring at the wick and its hissing thread of white smoke.

In the morning, I hear Sue's voice, whispered and high-pitched—meant for Harry—as Harry tries to shake me awake. For a second I don't want to open my eyes to a new day; I can feel that awful icy heaviness inside reminding me that Jack could be dead after all and the panicky uncertainty of not knowing what I'm going to do now.

"Mummy, wake up!" His voice is so high and scared that I finally do force my eyes open.

For breakfast, we have yesterday's bread toasted with dripping venison kebabs, washed down with bramble-leaf tea—good for runny noses and sore throats, Sue says. Harry, his head still swollen and achy, manages a few bites and sips only. But I make sure he gets down spoonfuls of our charcoal powder and rosehip syrup too.

After that, Andy walks me back across the village and up the hill to where we abandoned the Cruiser. I make Harry come too, though taking him out into the soft hazy morning, with its great clouds of smog visible in the distance, fills me with dread. And despite how pale and tired he looks—and Sue's offers to watch him. The meter showed less than ten, though, and we all have our newly cleaned masks and hoods up, just-in-case.

"Lean into the hill, Harry," I say, fretting about those clouds, and lunging until he copies, still wobbling and hanging on to me, with fearful looks at the steep road falling away behind us.

I'm wheezing so heavily halfway up the hill that I have to stop, hoping Andy thinks I'm only pausing to show Harry the view across the valley and check his mask and raincoat. Even though Harry clings tight and won't look.

"Not used to these down south are yeh?" Andy says.

"Nope," I say as strongly as I can on an out breath. Harry's weight is threatening to topple me over. I crouch to hold him steady. Northern stone villages peek out through the grey smog, along with dead black stumps, yellow and orange-pink young-sters growing around them. Some big trees have survived better, with wind-beaten erratic branches of messy gold and sage-green leaves. But everywhere are the same birches, willows, ash and syca-more. Pioneers, they called them Before, the first species able to colonize.

We all have to be hardy. Survivalists.

"Mummy, what if Sim the man comes to scare us?" Harry whis-pers, wide eyes flicking over rattling windowpanes and swishing branches, settling on Andy.

"He's far away in Hitchin. This is a different place, see? Just like when we read a different book. You wouldn't find Mr. Badger eat-ing Pooh's honey, would you? Or one of the dragons escaping to White Deer Park along with the other animals?"

I get a slow uncertain shake of the head.

"What's the dark green like a big serpent?" he asks, finally frowning out at the valley. Its dark curves seem sinister through the drifting smog, the brightest golds and oranges like a trail of gunpowder sparking around it.

"The River Rother," Andy says. "So, Katie, do you know where you hope to find your man?"

The words are stuck in my throat.

"It's far!" Harry says brightly.

"Is that so? How did you get split up?"

"We . . . missed each other," I say, Andy scrutinizing my face.

"When's the last time you saw him?"

The wind seems to drop, silent, as I conjure up the words. "Five years ago." I start walking again, Harry lunging next to me, the breeze and my sweat and all the doubt of last night and this morning making me feel suddenly cold.

Soon Andy's clomping up the road behind us, and catching up. "You mean Before? Before the storm?" His face is full of confusion, eyes sliding to Harry. "So he's never met—"

"He left me a message. I know it may be too late, I know how stupid it seems—"

"It's not stupid."

"He might not be dead after all . . . I have to try to find him," I say, though my voice wavers, uncertain. I start explaining about the letters and the car, the words tumbling out in a rush, my voice louder and more hysterical than I mean it to be, perhaps because I'm fighting to talk over my wheezing chest.

"I know," Andy soothes. "Not knowing can eat you up."

We reach the Cruiser in silence, our boots slapping over soft algae-covered ground. As soon as I stop, my wheezing becomes a hacking cough.

"It's a very fast, strong car," Harry tells Andy, as they wait for me to recover.

I sip from my flask and try not to let the strain show on my face.

Harry prods one of the big tyres with his shoe.

"Well, let's see if we can't get your chariot fixed for you and your mum."

"I'm not naive," I blurt out when I can speak and my chest feels close to normal again, though there's still that tightness in the cool air. "It's not just wanting to find him, we *need* him—" I spit out. Angry that my chest is failing me and that Jack still feels out of reach, after everything we did to get here. "Sorry."

"Katie, after all we've been through, you're never going to offend me."

"It's Scotland, where I think Jack is. I know trying to go that far north after all this time is . . ." I grope for the right word.

"Reckless?" Andy suggests, a half-grin on his face.

I nod. "Too far"—hundreds of miles—"to risk for a small hope of still finding him there."

Andy goes to squeeze my shoulder, but thinks better of it and clasps his hands together instead. "Loads of people did the same in the first year, searching, constantly walking . . . Facing bad weather—killing weather—smog and rain, blocked roads, always living hand-to-mouth. Katie, just remember—some of them didn't know how to stop. Just make sure you know when to call it quits, you know what I mean?"

I hold his gaze, dust in the air making my eyes watery. He's right—it's foolish. Stupid. And I was stupid to worry yesterday about finding Jack with someone else, having moved on thinking me dead. Him alive after all this time would be . . . everything, miraculous, and enough for Harry. Anything else really doesn't matter.

"Well, you don't have to decide yet, let's have a look at the Cruiser first." Andy hacks away vegetation and jacks the front end up, the wheels coming off with some difficulty. He squints at the axle joints.

"The rubber's split, grease all leaked out—no wonder it's seized up."

"That doesn't sound good."

"Nope, that's why the wheels are too stiff to turn."

"Is it fixable?" That might be it, over, if it's not. I twist the ring on my finger as he lifts the bonnet and tuts over dark muddy engine oil and peers inside at the dash, nodding approvingly but nervously at the three-quarters-full fuel gauge.

He nods. "Yeah, if we can find the grease you need—you want a commercial garage for that though, none round here I'm afraid."

Feeling deflated and fretful, we head back, Harry quickly fading and dragging his feet along the ground, dislodging particles, bugs and spores into the air. Breeze swirls around us, the air meter at the top end of the green level now, and I hurry Harry along.

"If you're serious about fixing the car, we'll need to go into Sheffield—good few warehouses and garages in the retail parks to the north of the city centre. I doubt many people will be after axle grease, but you never know . . ."

Sue is waiting at the window as we finally traipse up the path, and she opens the front door to a basin and cloths set up for us just inside in the hallway.

"We could try getting another car going?" I frown at the electric and hybrid hatchbacks on the nearest driveways, skinny and rusted, bumpers sunk to the ground. Fragile, broken creatures—none of them comparing to our safe, solid Cruiser.

Andy shakes his head. "If I'm honest, Katie, yours is the first working vehicle I've seen since the first year. I tried years ago . . . nothing does well sat gathering dust."

"Especially this dust."

"Aye."

We step inside and I strip Harry and myself of our outdoor gear.

"What if this is as far as you're supposed to go?" Sue says, face full of worry. She has an armful of toys—trucks and dolls and Lego—and Harry twists away from me to look as I try to wash his face.

"Sheffield's not as bad as London, or so I've heard, I promise," Andy says to both me and Sue. "Or I wouldn't suggest looking there." He smiles. "Come on, northerners were always friendlier than you southerners."

We all allow a smile at that, even Harry, who can't understand what we mean.

"How far is it?" I ask.

"About a three-hour hike each way."

"Three? *Are* there people there?"

"There were, years back, when I last went. Many folk who survived headed to the cities."

"Everywhere feels further now," Sue says. "Harry can stay with me, of course, if you want the grease—you wouldn't want him outside all that time, would you?" She smiles at Harry, engrossed in the new toys, looking sickly and tired, and she reaches to stroke his beautiful chestnut hair—my Harry's hair—and Harry looks up sharply.

I shift uneasily, trying to weigh it all up in my mind, fingering the stones along the band of my ring. Maybe finding the grease or not will help me decide if I'm prepared to take Harry north. "We'd be back by tonight?"

Andy nods. "If we leave now."

"It'd be safer for Harry here," I say slowly. As soon as the words are out I feel the gravity of them—eyeing up that pile of toys, Sue's smiling face, Andy's capable figure by the door, the fireplace in the back room, and the racks of meat and herbs and jars of vegetables there, remembering how grim things felt in comparison at the end in Hitchin. I wonder how long until Andy tells Sue where I think Jack is—I doubt she would even consider the risk of going north, the hope of everything I want for Harry with Jack completely fanciful.

"Of course, and better than having to leave him alone," she says, and I wince, guilt flushing through me. Better than the mother I was in Hitchin. Or the one I could be if we go north and find nothing.

Yet I can't help feeling—we've come this far. I have to see if the Cruiser is at least fixable, then I'll decide.

"I'll be back to kiss you goodnight, OK?" I hug Harry. "I love you, wholeheart."

"Right from the middle to the edges?"

I nod. "Especially the soft centre."

He smiles, but it fades quickly. And then Sue is leading him to the back room to lay train track out on the floor. I follow, biting my lip, taking in the open fireplace—unlit for now, knives on the sideboard and pitcher of unfiltered water by the unlocked back door.

"Ready?" Andy calls, hovering near the front door, shoving a mask—navy fabric with two large vents—into his backpack, and slinging a rifle over his shoulder, making my skin prickle.

I glance at Harry, feeling sweaty, head swimming with worry.

"I'll take good care of him." Sue squeezes my hands. The cut across my left palm stings as she does, but I try not to show it. "Just like he was one of mine."

I find myself reminding her that his nose needs blowing while it's still snotty, to make sure that he's careful about washing his hands and touching his face, to keep him inside, to properly prepare water for him . . .

Sue nods, yes, but I say so many things that I can't be sure she'll remember it all. I leave in a blur. Houses and roads float past. I can't help feeling that I shouldn't leave Harry with a stranger. But "stranger" is a funny word now, perhaps, even Sim felt familiar. We've all shared this massive traumatic thing.

We trek across a weedy park, the once-manicured ground boggy and squelching beneath our boots. I vaguely remember the pools and lakes as we pass them, once full of families and children paddling and ducks. Now the water everywhere is puke-green and quiet, the margins grown tall. Bulrush fluff dislodges as we brush past, rising up alongside algae spores and suspicious grey particles everywhere, catching the midday sun. The warm, wet air is thick with it, bitter and unpleasant, making it harder for me to breathe full breaths through the mask—the vents getting clogged. Andy's lead soon widens. I can't concentrate on where we're going, stumbling, pausing to scan the way we've come, not certain at all about how exactly to get back to Harry, not sure I can imagine going north and getting stuck and Harry outside in a place like this. I can't help fretting about what he and Sue are doing. I can't believe I left him.

20

"Come on." Andy waits for me and steers me as I cough—bitter, peaty smoke itching down my throat and into my lungs as I lift my clogged mask. We battle through thick papery-yellow bushes and down to a railway line where the air is thankfully clearer and sweeter.

Andy de-masks there too, and soon I'm gasping in lungfuls, feeling better.

"Fastest route this, takes us straight to the northern business areas," Andy says.

The air is full of wax moths—in daylight and airborne they're better, like tiny delicate grey-white fairies. Caterpillars inch along in the leaf litter, others hang from threads, cocooning. But even after we've walked over the gravel and sleepers for several miles, breathing the heavy sweet scent of the dense butterfly-bushes, I can't help looking back to check for trains. Still that uncomfortable sensation of trespassing, even after all these years.

My steps falter as I check ahead of us. We're approaching the pitch-black opening of a concrete tunnel.

We re-secure our masks, and our boots crunch and splosh as we step inside, red glossy leaves drifting in with us to land in the dark amongst the thick carpet of dust and leaves already there, where the wind can't whip them up again. As my eyes adjust, I see the fuzzy, deeply undulating surfaces of dust-caked walls and ceiling. I draw my elbows in and hunch, afraid of accidentally dislodging any dust. Both of us hold our breath and hurry towards the light at the other end, not slowing until we're ten strides clear.

Tunnels and bridges become more numerous. Some are full of trolleys or bikes or debris that the dust and leaves have accumulated amongst, forcing us to squeeze past, upsetting flurries that stick to our clothes.

"This'll do," Andy says, as we come out of a long narrow one, both of us brushing great gobs of dusty spiderweb off our shoulders.

We scramble up the slope and over barbed wire, and then down through brambles and bushes and trees, over a brick wall, to a road. We head what feels like north and I veer wide past the grey-flecked grim spectre of a church, modern stained-glass windows smashed in. Andy does too, avoiding looking at it, pinching his nose as if it might still smell.

On the next road, grimy terraced houses and fast-food shops leer over us. Bushes have been cut to ground level, perhaps for firewood, and I hesitate.

"Andy, *was* it friendly or was there a reason you didn't join the survivors here?"

He pauses a moment. "It's Sue—she rarely leaves the house—coming to meet you and Harry was an exception. It's not just being outdoors, she'd feel . . ." He scratches his neck, searching for the word.

"Vulnerable?" I say slowly.

He nods. "Outnumbered. She didn't like the thought of it. I did try persuading her once—it can be tough, this isolation, alone with your own thoughts too much, her own grief—it's such a visceral pain, isn't it, losing children . . ."

I murmur an agreement, pulling the hood of my overalls up and tucking my ponytail right in.

"Plus, bartering and sharing the load would have been nice. But I suppose you do get used to your own company, whatever it is. And you can't keep wishing for a version of how things once were. In the end, you have to accept and learn to appreciate what you have—"

"Maybe we should just head back?" I cut in, on edge, and that sickly feeling rising again at Harry being such a long trek behind me, even if Sue is there with him.

"We're alright." Andy squeezes my shoulder. "Let's just stay alert, stay focused."

I stick close to him as we head on, constantly tripping over bulges in the concrete, until the road becomes a dense forest of Japanese knotweed. Violet stems zigzag right out of the grey concrete, their big heart-shaped leaves filling the street with shades of apricot and tangerine. The tight stems and leaves shake as we brush past, displacing dust.

"This wasn't here last time." Andy kicks at the hard ground. "Like triffids bursting from moon rock."

I nod, out of habit cutting stalks as we thread through the least dense patches.

"Edible?" Andy asks.

"Tastes like asparagus when it's cooked."

In the distance, over the sea of knotweed, I can make out corrugated warehouse roofs that must be the retail park Andy mentioned. Low clouds roil beyond them, grey and white, a definite haze growing on the horizon, cool wind flicking spots of rain into our faces, taking all the warmth out of the day. I sniff at the air—just sweet clear rain right now—and pull my mask back up, sliding my waterproof parka over my overalls too, hoping we find the grease quickly and looking forward to getting on the railway line and building up some heat marching back to Harry, though I haven't yet decided what to do even if we do find the grease.

Delicate roe deer are nosing into the knotweed thickets and into alleyways, trying to find cover, increasingly frantic and skittish as spots touch them. The breeze brings their smell—of hay and singed fur.

Two dart right past me, making me flinch, and I step deep into the knotweed with a puff of loose dust. The deer snort, eyes wild, and Andy swipes at their legs with the barrel of his rifle to encourage them away.

"Alright?" He offers me a hand, but I step out of the leaves on my own and shake myself out. "Need to keep your eyes peeled. They're unpredictable these days—like they're in rutting season all year, each generation a little more pent-up than the last. I think the pollution affected their hormones. Makes them reckless."

"I know. And hard to hunt, I imagine, I never tried . . ."

"You can see which might be easier pickings," Andy says, eyes excited and engrossed in the possibility. "Those three rubbing up against the brickwork and nipping each other—they've got caught out in bad smog and rainstorms recently: hides sore, fur falling out, bleeding from their mouths and noses . . ."

He shakes his head. "Just one bad exposure or the long slow creep of frequently breathing it in and getting it on their coats—no doubt it gets to them even when they try to find cover outside—and now they'll just keep getting more ill."

There's a thin one at the back, panting, moving slower than the others. Andy points at it. "That one's lung function is declining, heart's failing, no doubt—"

I look away, my own heart seeming to flutter in response.

Andy continues, oblivious, "—that's what'll make it keel over in the end. Meat's usually still good though—"

Shouts further up the road make me slow, putting a finger up to shush Andy.

"I think we should be open we're here," he whispers, "to at least avoid being mistaken for deer in this thicket? When I came years ago, they were OK with me taking things as long as they knew about it."

I shake my head, sidling deeper into the knotweed and sinking low amongst the zigzag branches, frantically waving for Andy to follow and relieved when he finally does, fronds bouncing to cover us.

The voices become muffled and I wonder if we've been heard. Then the pounding of feet and shouts grow louder again, until I can see bodies moving through the stems, but I also hear the scuffing, heavy breathing and grunts of a fight. They tumble into view on a clear patch of pavement and it's obvious the older guy has something—a silver cylinder—that the younger two say is theirs.

"Give it! Or you'll get a face full of this!" The grey mud in their hands is balled tight, but frothing loose as it dries, drawn out by the growing breeze.

They throw one. It hits the man in the chest, bursting like a snowball. I watch in horror as he tries to turn away from the spray, covering his face with his hands.

"Where's your mask, old man?" And I realize he is the only one without one.

The young guys kick him to the floor and somehow his trousers are ripped off. Adrenaline pumps through me. They do it just to humiliate and incapacitate him I think, and saunter off, with the cylinder swinging in hand, laughing and whooping.

"Didn't think there was much O_2 to be found," Andy whispers. "Maybe they have their own respirators still?"

The old guy stays there, swearing, his hands stuffed over his mouth and nose. The wind aches round the buildings, the telltale rattling of particles sounding against brick and glass. The fisted dustballs are quickly dispersed downwind, like the men are aeromancers letting loose mist. Other people arrive, bundled up in hoods and masks, and more arguing echoes and distorts down the street.

I strain against a cough, my lungs irritated and tight, tugging Andy's coat, signalling behind us. I want to leave. I don't care about the grease. I want to get back to Harry. Now.

Andy presses a finger to his mask, signalling to wait, to be quiet.

But I'm nearly crying, the Fear coming through me in great big waves.

"I'm not going to let anyone hurt you," Andy whispers. "Just wait till they move on."

There's a lot of noise. Every shout and clatter and clonk startles me.

Then the light rain becomes a deluge, making the knotweed dance and twitch. People and deer scatter.

Andy and I rush to the pavement. We push and pull on doors until we find one that opens. A quick check of the downstairs rooms—mouldy wet floors, cracked windows letting in wisps of moist grey, both of us tripping over the sunken form of a previous inhabitant as we step into a lounge. Recoiling, I nearly head back outside but Andy turns and hurries up the stairs.

"Wait!" I hurry after him, dreading what else might be slumped up there, and follow him straight into the back room.

"Whoa whoa, there, who the fuck are you?"

Rain is bouncing on the roof, weighted with dust and so loud we can hardly hear what the man in front of us is trying to tell us, though his gesture is clear. Leave.

The room is bare but for sleeping rolls and a few blankets. A floorboard in the corner has been lifted, revealing the glint of glass bottles in the dim light of their candles. The windows have been permanently boarded up with thick wood, and the door has rubber round it that makes it suck the floor and hard to move on its hinges. This definitely isn't a home; it's a bolthole.

"Can't we wait out this storm with you?" Andy is saying, as I try to stay in the shadows behind him. And the others are shaking their heads.

"Not enough room. And we don't trust outsiders: *fuck off.*"

"We have to wait out the rain."

And I can smell it, coming up from the cracked windows downstairs and with us on our damp outer layers—a bitter chemical scent.

I start to shiver.

"Fine, whatever, but not in here."

We are ushered out of the room, and the door slams.

Andy goes straight to the front box room. The window is a tiny dormer and still intact. The heavy rain has created a semi-twilight outside, milky-grey raindrops streaking down.

I imagine how many steps it is from here to Harry.

"We should get back," I say, looking out at the rain and the thick grey-white air drifting along the street, buildings now getting lost as if in a mountain whiteout. I wonder if we have time to reach another building or hurry to the end of the rainstorm, even though I know it will penetrate my outer layers—and, crucially, my mask—if I'm out there too long, and that that smell is bad. And I don't have my cap and nearly useless, scratched goggles, which I wear in winter to protect my eyes when I have no choice but to go out in thick bad air. But not in rain like this, I'd never risk this.

Little grey eddies make it through invisible cracks in the window frame. The more I stare out, the more I can imagine wind wraiths and ghosts drifting out there, ready to suffocate poor victims and snatch your soul away. Nasties, though I really don't think Harry's imagination has specific names and images like mine does. I shrink back from the window.

"This looks set in!" Andy shouts over the rain rattling against the glass, leaning towards me. "It might rain for hours. We have to stay put."

A horrible anger runs up my spine, alongside this irrational feeling that Andy is trying to keep me from Harry, or has brought me to this house on purpose. But there's fear in his eyes too and I swallow the thoughts down. I know he's right.

He searches the wardrobe, divvying out baby-blue and white knitted blankets. Two rodent-nibbled teddy bears tumble out from amongst them, only one eye between them. And we each set about wadding up the edges of the window and around the door.

I grimace, imagining if I had brought Harry with us today. Or if we do head north soon. At the flat, I would never, ever have risked Harry even close to a window when it's like this outside. Let alone consider travelling hundreds of fucking miles to Scotland out in it! I'm trembling in the gloom as I reach for the side of the little child-sized bed and sit in the corner. Cursing myself for leaving Harry. After everything I promised!

"They'll leave us be, with any luck," Andy says, as I try to read his lips—his voice lost in the drumming rain.

Slowly I nod, as Andy pulls his hood up and a blanket around him and gets comfortable in the opposite corner on the floor.

It's a long dark afternoon and night. The men in their sealed room get louder and drunk enough that I can hear them over the rain, and I can smell food cooking, my own stomach growling and contorting. Their laughter and voices slowly become strangely comforting—human against my imagination of outside and that prostrate shape we tripped over downstairs.

I keep trying to weigh up the sickening gamble of going north.

At some point I doze off, and dream of Jack up in Scotland, his body hanging, swinging as I open a door, and later, of him alive and angry, shoving Harry away from us, out into the dangerous smog.

I wake—desperately trying to shake off that new horrifying nightmare as the rejection stings me, the unsmiling expression on dream-Jack's face alien and awful. Jack would never . . . never . . .

Yet all the ways Harry doesn't look like Jack suddenly thud, heavy, in my chest. Jack's mum's photos clear in my head. He's not like Maggie's fair-haired little boy pinned on those boards in her stairwell. Or the grown-up Jack I'm carrying inside that diary in my pack. I feel guilty wishing—even for a moment—that he was, as if he's not enough or wrong as he is and it would make things easier, simpler. The love I crave for him more certain.

I blink, becoming blearily aware of my surroundings, realizing it is the low throbbing glow of a gas flame in the pitch-black room that woke me. I begin to open my mouth to ask Andy what he's doing. But the eyes glinting at me are not his, nor are the sharp contours of the forehead, cheekbones and square fabric mask. The rain has slowed to quieter tapping. So much so that I can hear the wet regular slapping inside the room.

I feel frozen again, small and powerless. Trapped in the corner of this little bed. The knife I slowly pull from my trousers seems feeble—short and slender. I can feel the wall behind me, nowhere to escape to. As I shift he takes a step closer, the pounding getting faster. So I stay still and don't look away, not wanting to make things worse. In case this is all he wants. *Just let me have this.* The words there in my head already. I just have to sit here and take this. Like I am nothing again.

The hiss and smell of burning plastic fills the room, the gas lamp's flame jumping and bulging inside its glass orb like a little trapped fire demon. Trails of dust from round the wadded dormer window reach towards the heat like ghostly fingers, fizzing and burning in the air as they near the lamp, and orange glowing embers begin to dot my mattress. I yelp, hot stings biting through my clothes, and I slap the blanket across the mattress, putting out the sparks.

When I look up again he is gone. I think about getting up to wake Andy, who I hope is still on the other side of the room. But with the rain still tapping and the bedroom door left open, I feel numb and afraid to move. And as the minutes roll by, those fresh worries of my nightmare keep returning to keep me company. I pull my stinking, still-smoking blanket tighter around me, knowing I'm not going to get any more sleep.

21

Five Years and Four Months Ago

I heel the last tent peg into the ground, swaying—the tight prickling sandpaper feeling of my lungs inhaling and exhaling making me feel sick and weary. I feel watchful, in case it gets worse, like it was in the first few months, when I dreaded each cough—terrified of one day seeing blood on my hands—lungs hot, tight and splinteringly painful.

It's dark now, but I can feel the dry crisp grass beneath my boots. Hitchin is a few weeks' slow, breathless trudge behind me. I'm tired of dead brown grass and leafless dying trees, everything withering and winking out, brown and black, the sky an unsettling thick grey haze that blocks the sun. And still that dry, unpleasant chemical taste to the air. I feel about ready to choke on the death everywhere.

I can hear the group that I passed lower down the hill—only male voices seem to carry to where I'm standing. I wonder if some are friends that survived together. That hope burns inside me, of what I'll find when I get to Mum's house in Birmingham. Please. Let her be alive.

It feels safe to be within calling distance of those voices, like we have some unspoken agreement that proximity is comforting. I have this urge to go down to them and tell someone about Jack. More than anything I want my mum to put her arms around me.

But even a stranger's acknowledgement of it would mean something. To have some sympathy and understanding for the awfulness. There's been no one to share my pain with, no one to say things out loud with, and now I fully understand why they call it bottling up your feelings. I feel ready to burst. But I don't know how to begin. So I climb inside the tent, finally pulling free of my mask, the heavy exhaustion in every limb from the day's breathless walking like a thick smothering blanket over the grief.

The swift grind of the zip, from bottom to top, wakes me, but I feel so groggy that I don't even open my eyes.

I do to the crinkle of the groundsheet as my sleeping bag is yanked out, my legs tangled up inside.

"What the fuck are you—" I find my croaky voice only to be smacked across the jaw. My face throbs. Numb pain grows in my gums, something warm running from my nose. His face is a blurred shape in the dim twilight. He's shouting, but I can't focus on the words. His skin is rough and greasy as I struggle, like that of a teenager, but his voice is deeper and hoarser—damaged. He's tearing, pummelling, but it dawns on me that he doesn't know what he wants.

His boot slams into my stomach, crumpling me.

"Stop!" I'm wheezing, trying to suck air in, then coughing and gasping, my lungs becoming hot again like they were months ago. I try to protect my chest. His hands are in my hair, yanking my head back onto the hard earth. I feel myself waver between here and unconsciousness and I fight it. Feel my hair tear at the roots.

He figures it out. There's a hand on my crotch. My whole body responds to the unwanted touch, vomit churning at the back of my throat, my fists flailing. He tugs at my trousers. Tears at the buttons. I feel cold air on my pelvis.

"Stop it!" My scream is ragged and inhuman, reducing me to something less: an animal. I don't care. I'm kicking, punching.

But he's heavier than me, stronger.

"Please. Just let me have it, I just need—" His voice is muffled as we struggle. His weight keeps me pinned down, the pressure on my tender lungs making me feel like things are beginning to spin.

Panic thickens. I feel him shove his way between my legs. Heat flushes through me.

I try to twist and kick, remembering suddenly that I need to use my knees and elbows if being overpowered. I try, twisting and heaving, but I can't get free enough to jab in.

The sharp sting of teeth cut into my bare shoulder, like we *are* animals, like I just need to be subdued.

"Why aren't you her? It's not fair!" Elbow or head, don't know which, comes at my face. "You're nothing compared to her. Nothing. Stupid useless bitch." I don't feel it, not really. Just numbness. And warmth trickling from my nose, from my mouth, dribbling down my chin.

And he carries on. Desperate now, his breathing deep and fast.

And I begin to drift away. Something inside me has shrunk and tried to hide, even though there's nowhere to hide. I'm not moving anymore. Can't feel anything. Even all the grief has numbed down and I find I don't want not to feel it—that pain is Jack and I want Jack.

I scream at myself to fight harder. But there's nothing left.

So maybe I am a useless bitch.

Nothing.

After all, I'm nothing to anyone anymore, am I?

22

In the dawn darkness, I keep looking back the way we've come, convinced there's movement amongst the shadowy mass of zigzagged fronds—but the pale yellow glow on the horizon is barely enough to see by, my eyes still adjusting from the bright torchlight we used to navigate the warehouses.

The night Harry was born swims in my head, that second spring After. My mind travels backwards from there, through nine months of scavenging in Hitchin and bodies and the Fear and a growing bump, to that awful day in May or June of the first year, making me happy to hurry after Andy's quick footsteps in the dark.

And that crack inside me opens up as I force myself another four hungry harrowing months back to Jack and January and the storm.

I keep blinking it all away, focusing on treading softly and making it back to the railway line, where the wet crunch of gravel and squelch of leaves and mud greets us underfoot. Neither Andy nor I have bothered with masks—the air is deliciously clear and fresh, the rain having damped down the dust.

It's jarringly still on the tracks this morning, no breeze, and the ground littered with sodden dead moths and their plastic-munching "waxworm" caterpillars.

Andy catches my eye, flashing a small smile in sympathy. "They wreak havoc on the remaining bees, though, don't they? Eating beeswax too. One problem just triggering another and another . . . the world unbalanced and swinging like a broken chandelier."

In the dark silence between our crunching boots, my lungs wheeze and gasp, catching at each end of my breath. They're not just itchy now, but prickling as if lined with sandpaper—aching open and wincing as they deflate. The inflammation is worse after last night and I can't dislodge Andy's observations of the suffering deer from my head.

Andy looks back the way we've come, and even in the gloom I can see his smile falling away.

"What is it?" I stare at the long grey silent track. Around us, the thick embankments are full of deep shadow, and dripping gently from last night's rain. But I cling to the thought that we'd hear the rustle and snap of vegetation if someone was there.

"Nothing." He forces a smile that makes me hot and alert—and I wonder if this is how I make Harry feel when I pass things off as nothing. I stick close as we keep a brisk pace. "Don't break into a run, Katie," he says at one point, "we're not scared."

But I'm getting breathless, grimacing, and I have to slow, hunching over to gasp and cough.

Andy absently pops blackberries—straight off the bush—into his mouth as he waits, eyes darting behind us. My own stomach rumbles, but I'm surprised he would risk that coating of fresh milky residue—all the details of the vegetation becoming more visible in the dappled but growing light.

"Let's keep moving," he says.

I look over my shoulder. "What is it you've seen?"

He shakes his head. "If we stay calm, I think we'll be alright." He swallows another berry, smiling, and I feel myself grow irritable.

"You shouldn't eat that," I say as I get going again.

"A few probably won't hurt, just this once. The chemicals leaching from plastic dust reach everything we eat through the soil anyway, don't they, and dust is in the air everywhere, so even if we pick from sheltered spots and wash things and are careful with masks and gear—it's all gradations of contamination, right? But we're still surviving, aren't we? So is the world"—he gestures around at the lush cherry-red and golden dripping leaves, fresh shoots springing up after the rains—"everything's fighting to survive."

"Nothing's thriving, though," I say, that wave of irritation stronger at whatever it is he's not telling me. Does he think I'll panic? I want to scream that *I* was right not to want to be near those survivors last night—but I don't want to draw attention, if he doesn't know what happened. I fear it being brushed off, or resulting in questions, or worse, bringing up all the other nightmares of last night.

"Most things don't grow over head height," I say, "constantly dropping leaves, that colour—anthocyanins and carotenes, reds and yellows—the trees put that out in autumn Before, so they could gasp last breaths before winter. Or give young fragile shoots in spring a fighting chance. And everything is sweeter but less nutritious—" I wheeze, face scrunching at that prickling in my chest. "And the skin of that blackberry *is* probably worse than what's inside—it's just rained grey."

"You're right, it's a gamble I don't usually take," he says softly, reaching a calloused hand to squeeze my shoulder—a warm, solid, good hand, like Jack's, which makes me crave to feel it—but I cringe away.

We continue on quietly for some time, until we reach the stretch of butterfly-bushes, the sweetness damped down by last night's rain too. I flinch as Andy suddenly tears off his jumper. Ripping shreds from it and wrapping them round the end of a thick stick, he then trails this through the moist dust accumulated along the tracks—layer after layer—finally lighting it. It sparks into a foul-smelling flame, the thick white smoke following us as we move.

There's rustling in the bushes.

Andy lights a second torch and hands it over, raising his hand. Stop.

I freeze. I see nothing at first but the narrow railway line, shadow-grey and yellow-ochre leaves fluttering thickly either side, and the tremble of a few stray moth wings emerging into the pale dappled light.

Shit.

I clamp a hand over my mouth to smother the gaspy note of fear, keeping it there even though my hands are unwashed and dirty.

Long legs and heavy feet creep out through the flutter of wings and shadow. A ruffed neck that makes its face look broad. A grizzled grey coat. And two eyes shining greenish orange, pinning us to the spot.

I grip my torch tighter, wishing I had hold of Andy's rifle, which he is slowly manoeuvring off his shoulder one-handed while swishing his torch to and fro.

The first animal is pure wolf—I'm sure of it. The others emerging around us look mixed-breed, smaller and paler, but all with the same wolfish shape and face—pointed ears, serious eyes and long nose.

"Looking for victims of last night's rain. Easy meal. I guess they think we might be it," Andy whispers, as we both back up. He motions for quiet.

Hot with panic, I try to muffle my wheezing chest, all those gleaming eyes making me feel like I did last night: small and stuck and easy prey.

"I'd hoped we might've come across something by now."

As the wolf darts towards us, Andy leaps forward to swipe his torch across its path, raining down sparks and foul smoke, the wolf-dogs whimpering. The wolf keeps coming, looking for a way under our defences.

Jaws snap at my leg, snagging my trousers and teeth just scraping my skin—making me slip to one knee. I thrust my torch towards the snout, a whine marking the retreat of those teeth, though the pack surges towards me. Andy is there, waving his torch in a circle around us and hauling me up with one strong tug.

They lunge at us as we swipe and whack with our smoking torches, the flames dwindling. We edge down the railway line, metre by metre.

"Aha! Knew there'd be something, torrential as it was last night—keep coming, Katie, if we can get past this . . ."

Both of us stumble backwards—hanging on to each other to stay upright—through the weeping torsos and stiff legs of a dozen deer, which likely tried to shelter amongst the bushes. Bloody foam trails from their mouths and noses, the air flitting with flies. Crows pick at the bodies, making shrill calls as we approach.

Yet I'm focused on the pack, whose eyes are still fixed on Andy and me. Andy draws his knife and slashes and pierces hides as he passes—the rotting stink he releases making me gag and feel faint, the smell tied to that first awful year.

Crow wings flap past me. I yank my own knife free and copy Andy. The wolf bares its teeth, the wolfdogs dashing forward to sniff and bite the deer, whining. Then the wolf issues a low warning, and all the dogs back up, heads low and whimpering.

And we keep moving off too—the wolf chewing and tearing at deer hide, eyes on us as if making sure rivals now are leaving—until we have shrugged backwards through an underpass and jogged the next few hundred metres of track, adrenaline making me move despite my queasy stomach and wheezing lungs.

We come to an abrupt stop as we emerge out of the bushes into the northern end of Andy and Sue's village. I blink into an intense bleeding orange-pink horizon, the wonderful warmth soaking into my cold face. The whining of the pack is distant now, *both* of us gasping as we catch our breaths. Our eyes connect, and smiling, relieved, neither of us can help starting to chuckle.

"You knew that was out there?"

"Sorry"—Andy grins—"I didn't want to scare you. Some folks must have freed one years ago; I've seen 'em before. If you start behaving like you're scared, with something with so much wild blood in it, you might be interpreted as prey. Never been so relieved to be tripping over dead bodies!"

I laugh, harder than is warranted—Andy too. Until I'm bent double, coughing and dizzy.

"Katie, are your lungs bad?" Andy asks. "They heard and stalked *you*, I think . . ."

I grimace, gasping and forcing my breathing steady again, to its prickling inhale and wincing exhale. I start down the street.

"Is that why you're hunting for Jack?" Andy says, following. "After all this time? I know it must be hard, as a parent, you worry about what happens to them . . ." He trails off, voice cautious, as we fall into step again. "Just make sure you're not grasping at straws," he says softly. "Sue would be glad to help you."

I nod. Harry would be fed and warm at the bungalow, perhaps. I try to feel glad that he isn't alone right now, and grateful that there is someone to keep him safe and care for him. But all these blanks keep coming to me—all the unknowns about Sue and Andy and all the big and little things you don't know about people you've just met or the place they live . . . and these survivors in the city . . .

"But I don't doubt there's no substitute for the people we loved and imagined we'd share our lives with."

I realize he's right. And that tub of axle grease bouncing in my backpack—though heavy over the morning's trek—now feels a comforting weight. I'm glad Andy convinced me we might as well look, though I'd wanted to forget it when I'd finally nudged him awake in the silent dark of that grim bedroom, relieved to still find him there in his corner.

We didn't find any more fuel yet, but with the grease, the sunlight on my face, the dangers behind us, Harry close again, and an easy downhill stretch easing up that unpleasant prickling of my chest, somehow the Fear and doubt of last night and the last days has faded to the back of my mind. Replaced by that little bead of warmth that's inside me again. Everything feels possible and clearer again: I imagine the Cruiser moving once more, and Jack's arms around Harry.

"Listen," Andy says softly, smiling as we reach the centre of the village and veer up towards where his and Sue's road is, "don't tell Sue about all the excitement last night and this morning, or she'll be even less easy to convince on leaving the house and garden."

I wince a smile, nodding, but I can feel the stinging in my calf now, my trouser leg draughty, and I'm picturing that wolf circling the bungalow with Harry in it, a persistent fairy-tale nasty.

Anxiety surging, the distance left to reach him squeezes at my chest. I try to pick out the bungalow among the rooftops as I speed along the squelching streets, Andy keeping pace with *me* this time.

"Hey, should we take something back?" Andy slows, grinning, and I follow his gaze to a lone stag, sprawled, dead, a little way up the next side street—unusually sturdy and beautifully branched antlers drawing my eye. Andy rushes to inspect the carcass. "It's not spoiled—still warm. Something for dinner!"

I nod, reluctant to stop—but we can't not take advantage of it.

And Harry and I *have* been eating Andy and Sue's stores.

Bringing home good calories does normally make me feel better for leaving Harry behind too . . .

The nostrils and mouth have bloody foam around them like the earlier deer, the jaw opened wide in a last rictus gasp. I twist the ring on my finger, shifting from foot to foot.

It didn't occur to me that the rains might have spread so far. I worry if Sue kept Harry indoors and safe. If she helped him feel less afraid of the shadows, and knew to list everything in the room still there, even in the dark. Or to imagine our own bed in the flat. If she knew what to say so he didn't worry I'd disappeared into a black hole. Did he sleep alone on the sofa, or . . . ? I feel a growing bitterness: it should be me there to do that, always. Jack rises up again: I know what his love felt like. If not me, I want that for Harry. Only that.

Once Andy and I are pulling the stiff body behind us on a piece of tarp, I keep moving, even as my prickling, heaving lungs beg to drop the weight of meat and the heavy backpack, feeling with each step the loosening of that thread between my chest and Harry's.

There's no face at the window when we get there, and I push past Andy, shrugging off overalls, boots and backpack to get inside, hurrying down the empty hall to the back room. Empty sofa, bare rug floor, cold fireplace. The Fear reignites, pumping through me, and just as I'm about ready to scream, I hear their voices in the garden and crash through the back door to see Harry sat at Sue's side as they weed her potato patch. Harry is chuckling—it's soft and over so quick and I savour the sound, wondering what she did to make it happen. He has a shy smile on his face, his hand rising for a high five. Heat surges inside me as I rush towards them. Neither have their masks on.

"Harry!"

Sue stands up, smiling at us, leaving Harry hanging, that shy smile fading, lost.

I take in the turned-over soil, and despite the plastic polytunnel, imagine Harry disturbing grey sand-like particles that then drift up towards his exposed face. "He's safer inside," I say, a hard edge to my voice.

"I was careful to watch him," Sue says kindly. "You wouldn't have wanted me to leave him alone indoors, would you?"

"Mummy?" He pounds across the covered veg patch towards me, sobbing—his eyes puffy and face pale like he hasn't slept. "Why didn't you come? Where were you?" He stops a good six feet short, glancing—worried—back towards Sue.

"I'm sorry, we got stuck because of the rain—"

"You should have tried harder," he sobs, like he thought he'd never see me again. And I stop myself from sweeping him up—even without my overalls on—thinking of all the rain and dust I've been exposed to. He flinches as Andy steps out behind me.

"Is it Sim the man?" Harry whispers, glancing between us all, confused and scared.

"No, it's Andy, of course," Sue says softly. "Harry's not great with faces, kept mistaking me for you . . ."

"*I'm* your mummy, Harry." I kneel, tugging at his arched little shoulders. "I'm going to be your mummy, always," I say, tears pricking. "Always, always . . ."

No longer able to resist, I draw him into a tight hug—Harry hot and stiff but slowly softening, sobbing into my chest. "Why didn't you sleep with me?" He clutches his little head, shuddering. "What if I couldn't wake up and I needed you?"

"I know, I'm sorry, I'm here now," I say, repeating it as I carry him indoors to the washbasin in the hallway, Sue and Andy following.

Sue makes a show of being overjoyed by the venison. "We usually cook up something to eat straight away, hang some, and smoke some," she says, smiling at Harry and me.

Andy butchers the stag on the driveway. The air is clear and sheltered by the house, but I still grimace at the raw flesh so close to dust and algae and invertebrates on the ground. He wraps different cuts and the lacy fat from around the entrails inside oiled cloths, calling in to me to show me how to collect the thicker fat—hard and waxy—from around the kidneys and inner cavity, which Sue uses for soap and candles.

Harry is tired and grumpy and getting harder to persuade to stand still while I wipe his face.

So I don't notice Andy walking up to the house until he is at the door holding up the impressive branched antlers, which he has sawn free to keep. He's beaming. "Look at this, Harry!"

Harry's face flushes red, his eyes big, staring at those dripping antlers.

"You hurt him!"

"He's dead," Andy says gently, "nothing can hurt him now."

"It's just meat," I say, trying to turn Harry's face away from it and back to mine, "we eat it at home—not deer, but rabbit, fox, a dog once too!"

"I didn't know you had to make him dead, Mummy!" He's crying hard now, shoulders shuddering, face scrunched up, gulping out his words. "That's mean! What if he wakes up without his head!"

"You don't know what dead means. I'm sorry, Harry—"

Sue kneels, reaching for him while he pulls away from me. But I know there's no consoling him now and she doesn't notice his stiffening arms and he flails, arms windmilling into her face. I pull him away from her. But there's a sharp sting—teeth in my bare shoulder—and he runs off down the hallway to the back room.

A hot sick feeling goes through me. "You don't bite, it's bad to bite . . ." Even when he was very little I never let him.

A red mark rises on Sue's cheek. But there's a small oval of red lines and arches on my arm making me feel dizzier and dizzier, because just a few inches higher are a larger oval of older scars that feel like they're stinging too. Throbbing. Bleeding as they did when fresh.

Harry's loud sniffling from the back room tugs me to the present. Andy and Sue are silent, watching me. "I never explained. About death . . ."

"Can't blame his fuss," Andy says with a small smile. "We didn't eat meat Before, did you?"

181

I shake my head, speaking in a daze. "We gave it up—waste of resources, mass production causing all that pollution, deforesta-tion . . ."

"And bad for health."

"We thought it seemed cruel—all that death," Sue says.

I nod. The word feels big and ominous again, hearing "dead" come out of Harry's innocent little mouth, as if it conjures the overwhelmingly awful days of the storm.

"Now it's a necessity," Andy says firmly. "Easy calories."

Sue nods fiercely. "Needs as much as you can give him."

"You should clean that straight away," Andy says gently, sur-reptitiously looking down at the tear in my trousers and the graze on my leg underneath, before nodding at my shoulder. "Bites, even from people, can get badly infected."

"I know." I'm shaking as I reach for the washbasin once more, glancing down the hall at Harry. He's sat on the hearthrug now, tear-stained and sulking, stomping Luna the reindeer around Julian the train's track. His soft chestnut hair half obscures his face, but I can still see his dark lashes, the shape of his rounded little face, the small delicate mouth. His eyes flick up once to meet mine—those beautiful melting amber-brown eyes pink-edged and wet.

The basin wobbles, water and soap slopping over the floor, and I slip down to hands and knees to soak it up in rags and towels before it runs in all directions across the hardwood of the hallway, taking any dust and spores from outside with it.

Those worries dream-Jack's rejection of Harry sparked last night come back fully formed now. And I cringe, imagining an adult face with Harry's amber-brown eyes and chestnut hair. As if Harry's biting is a glimpse of some dark trait . . . and all of it a reminder of something awful that has *nothing* to do with him.

My own bleary image looks up at me from the slick floorboards—grim-faced, narrow, with its small mouth and full sad lips, messy mouse-blonde hair, and almond-shaped eyes, always the stormy sea-grey to Jack's Mediterranean blue, framed by his blonde mop.

And I remember Jack, cross and eyes blazing just like in that nightmare, as he squared up to some woman who'd sideswiped my car but thankfully only left me whiplashed. How *Linda* became a curse word for Yaris drivers after that—good or bad—simply reminding Jack of that unrepentant woman who had hurt me and could have killed me.

The pounding rises into my head, worrying who Jack will see if and when he looks at Harry's little face. What he'll think. Would he be able to *just* see this precious person I know? But all this stuff—

"It doesn't matter," Sue says, taking the rags from me and mopping up the floor herself, smiling gently.

I jolt at her words; I've pretended for so long and things have felt so desperate that I haven't really thought if it does. All my hopes feel like they're spinning in my head again. My voice is low and flat. "He'd take care of him for me, wouldn't he? Love him? No matter what?"

Sue is staring, mouth opening again, anxiety drawing the outside creases of her eyes down and sad—when all I want is for someone to agree. "What do you mean?" Her hand reaches for mine.

"Don't touch me." I can't bear it—I shrink away from her, breathing gaspy breaths, the wheezy notes loud in the hushed hallway. Itching at those scars, at that fresh bite.

"Oh, honey," Sue is saying in a quiet voice.

Andy catches my eyes and I can see everything I've said about Jack unravelling in his.

"Was it someone else?" Sue whispers. "Is your Jack not Harry's—"

"Sue, if Katie doesn't want to talk about it . . ." Andy cuts her off, his eyes too understanding, but I've already rushed out of the front door to avoid the question that might come after the one she's started—tell me you weren't . . . ?—scratching at that shoulder like it's burning, like I can get *him* off me, and gulping in clear cool air.

23

As I step back inside, Andy and Sue fall silent at the other end of the hall.

"Who wouldn't care for that darling boy?" Sue whispers when I approach, her hands reaching to close around mine.

I look at Harry's little face—tired and puffy from tears—blinking up at me from amongst the toys on the hearthrug in the back room. I can't help thinking Sue must be right. And his eyes are almond-shaped like mine, he has my frown, my smile—usually shy, closed lipped, our cheeks dimpling—something of me too. And if it were the other way around, I'd grow to love any child Jack loved, wouldn't I? *Wouldn't I?*

"If I were you, though, I might let it go. You can't think a journey like that would be safe for Harry, you can't. I've had to live with so many would'ves and could'ves for my boys—but you have him, a healthy beautiful boy, and you have to keep him safe—"

"That's what I'm trying to do!" Tears spill down my face.

"Sue," Andy cuts in, a warning note in his voice.

I step past them to join Harry on the rug, where he shimmies closer, still trembling and upset, but allowing me to put my arm around him. He eventually lets me finish stripping and washing him, but he's quiet and rigid, won't put his favourite red trousers on afterwards.

"How can I make it better?" I whisper as he sits on the sofa in the stuffy back room in just T-shirt and pants. I glance warily at Sue's pile of sentimental toys. "What about a game, any one you like?"

"How about a storybook?" Sue says, getting up from the fire she's building to make a late breakfast for Andy and me, and a second one for her and Harry. "I'm sure we'll have one that you won't have read. I kept everything . . . couldn't bear to get rid of any."

My smile is frozen. "It's alright, we have our own—"

She scurries off, coming back with an armful.

"I want a new book!" Harry hurries to look, picking one with an old man and his dog in front of a lighthouse on the cover.

"Shall I read it for you?" Sue pats the rug beside her.

Harry rubs tired eyes and rushes back to me. "I want this one."

I hesitate. But I sense I have just seconds before Sue makes another offer.

"OK." My fingers tremble over the cover. But even the first sentence leads Harry to ask what lighthouses and sailors are, who it means by "family," why the sea is so blue, the sky too, and then what all those buildings and little figures are on the seafront sketch on the first page. It feels so complicated and painful to explain. My eyes fill with tears, but Harry stubbornly waits for me to continue. " 'There's going to be a storm, Dogger, and a fierce one at that!' said Bill." And then I'm sobbing.

"How about I tell a different story," Andy cuts in softly.

Harry reaches up and wipes my tears. "Sorry, Mummy, maybe I don't like this story with people either."

"What stories do you like best, Harry?" Andy asks.

"Dragons and animals and make-believe."

"OK . . . well, the only one about a dragon I know is the one about a greedy dragon and a dwarf king and a hobbit." He winks at me as he launches into it. He ends with the dwarves finally getting their mountain home back from the dragon and how happy they are. In his version, no one dies.

"Home makes me think of the flat," Harry whispers sadly.

"Me too," I say, twisting the ring on my finger, but it's Jack's arms around me after a long day at work that I think of. Maybe he and Harry would build a home of their own one day.

185

Brunch is a feast: thick meaty venison steaks, roasted burdock roots, mashed sedge seeds, and greens—knotweed, plantains and nettles. We sit at the table like we're here for a dinner party, a smoky foul-smelling candle at the centre. The food eases the hunger that's been building since yesterday and lifts my mood. The burdock roots are crusty, with fluffy hot centres that taste wonderfully like something between a parsnip and a potato.

Harry tucks in, though he still chews the meat suspiciously.

Hungry, I shovel down the food, though I glance guiltily at the half-full jars and patchy drying racks in Andy and Sue's back room that four mouths have been depleting faster than two would have. I shift in my seat as soon as my plate is clean, restless.

Andy watches me, a bit of sadness in his eyes. "So, you've decided? You could wait, you know? Spring would be better for going north. Clearer air, less chance of flooding . . ."

"If you found out that someone you thought was dead might actually be alive, could you wait?" This prickly discomfort and tightness in my chest is bothering me even sat at rest now, the sandpaper linings itching open and closed. Suddenly the time here feels a hindrance, full of scares—a fraction of how it felt leaving Hitchin, urgent to make a dent in the journey towards Jack. A nasty thought pushes its way into my head too: what if I weren't well enough to go when spring came around? What if this is it, now? For me. For Harry to have Jack. While the mild weather lasts.

Andy nods grimly at my words. "Just don't take risks with your health, OK? Stay warm, stay dry, or what good are you to Harry?" He flashes Sue a warning and I see her swallow down whatever else she was going to say.

We get the Cruiser's split rubber axle boots glued together, and the joints greased and turning, drain and refill the engine oil with the bottle Andy lugged back from the city, and I correct the tyre pressure under Andy's guidance—which should also help keep the pressure on the repaired wheel axles more even too. Sue packs extra supplies in our boot, and replenishes our water barrel. And when Andy and I have spent an hour trawling the streets unsuccessfully searching fuel tanks and garages for more diesel (or any fuel at all), Andy imparting advice on routes and roads, it's finally time to say goodbye.

"How did any diesel cars even still exist?" Andy sighs in the hallway.

I shrug. "Perhaps because it's a government—UN—vehicle?"

"Wonder if they and big business were still using jet fuel too. One rule for them . . . You *will* need more, I reckon."

"The electric motor was still trying to kick in on the way here," I say hopefully, but he's right. Jack said diesel fuel keeps for longer than petrol—though much longer has passed than the "up to a year perfectly well" he suggested. And I know a hybrid could have gone up to Scotland and back on one tank Before, but I can't trust my three-quarter-filled tank of old fuel or the electric mode now.

"Aye, that technology might stretch it, if it can build more charge as you go," Andy says. "Use what diesel you have and then gamble with whatever you can find. Sometimes engines will run awhile on the wrong fuel—just make sure it's not stuff that's gone too gummy with age or the engine will clog sooner rather than later."

I nod, picking up my backpack, ready to go. I find myself touching the walls of the hallway goodbye as I peer into the front bedroom, and pressing my fingers against the now-familiar sofa and dining table in the back room as I look behind and under them for Harry. But Harry is suddenly nowhere to be found.

"He's not here," I say breathlessly, beginning to panic about all the time Sue has had alone with him. And that mountain of enticing, heartbreaking toys.

"He won't have gone far," Sue says, calmly. She and Andy head out the back and front to look. I follow Sue, dread rising in me.

I finally spot him at the bottom of the garden under the polytunnel, amongst purple, bruise-coloured runner beans. Stood with Luna and Julian in each hand. He has on his too-big outdoor raincoat, trainers and the red trousers, the cuffs neatly turned up— I realize Sue must have done it.

She is there before me.

"I don't want to go, Mummy!" Harry says to her, frowning at her features.

"I know, I like it here too," I say, striding up close so he realizes it's me.

"Then why do we have to go? Sue is my friend. She has good games."

"Harry could stay here, you know, while you go look for your Jack? And if you find him or not, you can come back. It's much more sensible—for the same reason you didn't take him to Sheffield?"

"Andy thinks he's dead anyway, I heard him and Sue," Harry says.

I bite my bottom lip, my whole body shivering.

Sue's cheeks are flushing, eyes avoiding mine, but her hands are reaching for Harry's shoulders, like mine have so many times, just trying to touch, as if that will keep him safe.

"They don't know that," I say, forcing my voice level, and tugging Harry away. "If we go now, you'll be able to see the views in the hills—you like high-up places like the flat, don't you?"

At the Cruiser, we do another round of hugs, though I keep my hand in Harry's the whole time.

Sue whispers to him, as if forcing herself to, "You . . . you might see the train tracks up there, you might even see a real train."

Harry beams and I help him up into his seat, stowing away his outdoor gear.

"If . . . You keep that precious boy safe," Sue says to me, eyes red-rimmed, pressing a child's blue snowsuit into my hands— only thinly lined with fleece but protective—which Harry grabs and hugs to himself. "I'll think of him when I bake my bread, that happy little smile, and when I'm in the garden."

Andy steps in front of her to show me a rifle and box of bullets. "A spare I had." He packs them in the boot for me.

"Thanks."

He nods, handing over the maps we looked through together earlier as he walks me to the driver's door, the Scotland OS maps tatty ones he retrieved from his old house just for me. Arisaig on the west coast of Scotland is just a far speck—the four hundred miles to go make me feel sick and reckless. I try to keep my face turned from Sue's, in case she sees.

"You might catch yourselves some deer up there," Andy says.

"And if you need to, protect yourself with it, Katie, OK?" He shifts on his feet then, and I grow hot and sweaty. "You'll always be welcome." He squeezes something small and metallic into my hands.

I find I can't speak, but I nod.

When I turn round, stow my outdoor gear and get in the Cruiser I don't look back, even when I look down and see the flint and steel in my lap, even when Harry twists in his seat to wave goodbye as the car rolls down the driveway. Even when I hear Sue's awful sobbing wail, so like Mum's at Dad's funeral, when we had to hold her up on her feet and I realized how deep inside you grief goes. I indicate to turn left—that habit again—and the houses blur past as we weave slowly enough through the broken roads for the "electric mode" light to keep blinking on, white lime-tree pollen smearing down the windscreen getting stuck in the scratches and pockmarks, and sodden leaf litter squelching beneath the tyres.

"We could have st—"

"No," I cut in. "Andy and Sue are strangers." Though they could have been more than that, I know, if we tried. And now I look in the rear-view mirror, trying to pick out their bungalow amongst the roofs and autumnal foliage.

Yet, I feel my heart tugging towards Jack in the same way it tugs towards Harry when we're apart. Andy was right. No one else is enough.

Please. Please let him live.

24

Five Months Before the Storm

Jack brings the breakfast tray over to the bed, the wooden floors squeaking. He does a silly jig as if he's walking the plank and about to overbalance into the sea.

Rolling my eyes but breaking into a smile, I sit up, pulling on the fluffy white robe against the chill of the air-conditioning unit.

Yet there's a lump in my throat as I sip the black coffee.

"It's all going round your head again, isn't it?" he says gently, reading the look on my face.

I nod. The infection Dad got, and the way he then chose to die.

"The infection was bad luck. And it was more complicated than just that—you couldn't have foreseen—"

"I know . . . but I wanted . . . we could have had more time. If I'd just—"

"So many family members at the hospital feel that sense of guilt, no matter how someone dies. It's not your fault, Katie. Likewise, if anything happened to me." He gently nudges my face up to meet his, his eyebrows raised. "Right?"

"Right," I croak.

"Hey, come on, look where we are." He pulls the curtains back to bright sunlight and tugs open the sliding glass door. A shock of blistering air laced with salt and sun blasts into the chilled room—Sardinia is under an extreme heat warning. I get up from the bed, following Jack out onto the balcony, the heat hitting our bare skin.

It's mesmerizing, the sea sighing as it draws back and rumbling as it rushes up the beach again. I try to stare, make it feel real, make it feel as beautiful as Jack sees it, his face all lit up at the sight of it. The sky is clear and infinitely blue. But I feel numb.

"Let it all go, for a bit," Jack says. "Be present. This beautiful place will make the day worth seeing through, won't it?"

I nod. I so want to appreciate this—as if I have to live for Dad too now, to make extra sure I don't take any moment, any joy, any beauty, for granted.

Jack kisses my head.

I sink into him, trying to focus on those crashing waves. But it's only been three weeks . . . "Is it OK that we're on holiday right now?"

He shrugs, beginning to smile. "Perhaps it's when we need an adventure the most?"

I can't quite smile back. This trip was already booked and paid for—another plan we made to make up for not going on the year out—so we just found ourselves getting on with it. That almost-carefree trip to Canada earlier in the summer when I was only worried about Dad seems a very long time ago now.

"But this year's been a shitfest, hasn't it? My mum and your dad should have coordinated not to die in the same year, the buggers!" He squeezes me tighter. "Next year will be better."

I nod. "We'll *make* it better."

"It *is* OK to feel how you feel, though, you know? Don't be rushed." He kisses me again. "But you're right—losing Mum hasn't got any easier, the grief doesn't shrink . . . you have to grow stronger instead, grow around it, *make* things alright again."

"Like with addiction?" I whisper.

He hesitates a moment. "Yes, a bit like that."

Later, in bikini and shorts, as I walk with Jack down the beach, feet sinking into soft white sand, I feel glad, for the first time, for the distraction of this trip. A welcome sea breeze touches my hot skin. The trees lining the beach are green still and lush, but back up the lane we've just walked down, they are skeletal and bare, the scorching heat and hard thunderstorms making the baked leaves fall and disintegrate off the trees. It looks eerily as if the town has

191

fallen to winter while the beach still enjoys summer, but every-where is oppressively hot. We squeeze past sticky bikinied tourists with ice creams and street sellers offering sun hats and seaweed water bubbles. Jack and I smile sympathetically at each other; this is not our typical getaway location, but the hotel's a good base for the sea caves and also hikes into the rugged interior.

I can't help sighing at the plastic wrappers and washed-up bits of fishing net. I feel more worried and irritated by it all since Dad's death, like everything inside me is worn thin and I'm more deter-mined to get everyone to do better with their lives because Dad doesn't get to be here to live his. I've been more vocal in meet-ings at work, arguing with developers and landowners, even started looking up activist groups I could join. We treat the world like we can just throw it away.

Jack curses at the rubbish under his feet, making heads turn, as he blinks and rubs away the stinging mix of sunscreen and sweat from his eyes. But I'm thinking about how we too could do better. This trip, however green the plane, feels unnecessary.

"Sorry," Jack says, forcing his voice lower. "I'm too damn hot!"

Jack's stories from his time in the army have begun to haunt me—the people having to leave places that weren't liveable any-more: the victims of climate injustice. And the scale of further looming conflict, displacement, hunger, illness . . . I feel weary: the problems so big and progress so slow.

"Let's get a tandem," I say, to think of something more uplift-ing, and I point at the boat-hire sheds we're aiming for through the sticky bodies and sun lotion, perfume and sweat.

"And I'll paddle us home if your arms go to jelly." When he smiles, that bright easy grin is back.

"Sounds good." The mass of open water—all those waves rip-pling in the sunshine—does look inviting, if daunting. I inhale a big lungful of warm, salty air. "Should we take face masks?" I look at the sign on the side of the nearest shed. A handful of people on the beach are wearing them. "The Med Whirlpool, they're calling it here, blowing smog around the coast."

Jack shrugs. "If the pollution was bad here, you'd at least see a haze." He points to the clear blue horizon. "And these civilian tourist masks are cheap trash, useless—"

"So . . . don't waste our money?" I say, smiling, before Jack gets irritable again. I examine the pretty patterns on the thin cotton masks, remembering reading somewhere that inhalable dust is seven times smaller than the width of a human hair anyway.

Jack lowers his voice. "Better to donate proper ones where people actually need them."

Waves bounce the kayak as we set off. Once we get a few hundred metres from shore, heading towards the cliffs round the coast, I imagine the water a hundred metres deep, or more. I shiver despite the hot sun—the breeze out on the water a relief from its heat. Jack chants a rhythm behind me, and I slice the water with my paddle to match him.

We near the first of the cliffs riddled with caves, water sloshing and tinkling inside. We glide into clear glittering water, salt spray splattering my hot face. The sun is like a big white heat lamp on the back of my head as I pull my cap off and rake my fingers through my hair. The sandy bottom is visible under the surface now, undulating and untouched, the reefs like abandoned cities of white crystal, beautiful, though at the back of my mind I know it should be alive with colour and fish. There's a fluttering in my stomach, a delicious feeling bubbling to the surface which hasn't been there for the last awful weeks. It makes me smile.

"We're doing it!" Jack whispers. And I just know without looking that behind me Jack is grinning, and that he knows there's a smile on my face too. And maybe, just maybe, this, us, together, will be enough to get us through all that's to come.

When we get back to the hotel and I look out again, I have this horrible fretful worry. All that deep water. My mum needs me more now. I have a feeling of responsibility, that I must remain safe and well for her.

"Could she come and stay with us, if it would help her a bit?" I say.

"Who? Your mum? Yeah, of course."

"You wouldn't mind your mother-in-law moving in?" I smirk.

"Family is family, and I like your mum. I'd love anyone you loved—within reason!" He laughs.

I remember how he has hugged her, so effortlessly, just like he would his own mum.

"Thank you—Paul's not moving out any time soon, so she's not on her own, but it might be good for her to get away from that house and its memories." I tug Jack's hand out from his pocket so I can hold it. I take a deep breath. "Also, when we get back I'd like to do some wedding planning together."

"You sure?"

"Yes—maybe it'll help to plan something good. I don't want to postpone it. And it's not long to go now, less than nine months."

"OK."

I think about all the excitement and planning that stalled because of Dad. The "Save the Date" cards still need posting, and there's the cake, the flower supplier, the bridesmaids' dresses and actual invitations, and all the other tiny insignificant decisions to be made that somehow now feel piled together in one big mountain of decisions, suddenly making me feel a bit sick. I try instead to think of how it will feel in that sparkling dress—wispy and dripping in beads like a waterfall—and seeing Jack's teary-eyed face as he sees me in it for the first time. And I'll walk towards him, eyes locked, all of the details blurring behind that wonderful face.

Then we have the whole of our lives to learn how to be happy again.

25

I'm driving in a daze, scuffing decayed tree trunks and fresh saplings, snaking between rusting cars, wheels wobbling over kerbs, bricks, toppled power lines and vegetation. I keep the speed as even as possible, lifting the accelerator when the hills do the work for us and avoiding the brakes to save fuel. We check the map at each junction, choosing the most likely routes north, trying to aim between Leeds and Manchester, but without road signs the steep northern roads feel like a maze.

We start meeting fallen trees, and then roadblocks, which I hope mark the outer limits of the cities, and zigzag north, past a lone surviving sign for Rochdale and Burnley, and through village after village. I'm holding my breath and not slowing until the houses fall away, and the roads become narrower and drystone-walled, and the Yorkshire Dales spread out ahead, straw-yellow hills eerie with a sunlit haze drifting through them. The reek of peat smoke and burning plastic manages to penetrate the Cruiser.

Harry cringes, hands up at his face again.

I yank my water flask out and wipe his face with a wetted corner of cloth. "Remember, your hands aren't clean unless you've just washed them. Don't touch your face."

"Everything is always bad outside the flat?" he asks, gripping his seat tight, those two frown lines that are mine fixed between his brows.

I bite my lip, wanting to say yes to make sure he's careful, but hating the sight of his fear, as if that proves Sue right and we should never have left. "I never said *everything*. It's just really important not to get dust in your mouth and breathe it down into your lungs."

We emerge from the smoke to a hilltop, a river below bending through the hills into the distance—the River Eden, I check, glancing quickly at the long meandering blue thread along the bottom of the brown-shaded dales on the map.

A soft drizzle blurs the windscreen as I drive downhill, drenched moths crowding the sills and vents, looking for cover.

"Mummy, don't leave the walls." Harry shrinks down in his seat.

Up ahead the drystone walls are in ruins, rock strewn everywhere. The wind buffets us as I come off what's left of the tarmac to drive round the debris.

"It's OK. This was probably flooding"—yet I imagine ferocious wind full of grey, funnelling down the valley—"or a bad storm."

"Is that why you didn't like Sue's storybook? Did a big storm disappear people from the houses? Sue said—"

"Harry!" I say it sharply and his mouth snaps shut. I feel instantly guilty, but my hands are shaking on the wheel, trying to concentrate over the rough ground, and I can't bear to talk about this. I wish I'd never left him alone with Sue. "We don't need to talk about Before." But I have to add something, to try to placate him. "These walls might have been pushed over by the big storm, yes."

"So stronger things are left?"

"Sometimes it's strength, sometimes it's luck."

We drive back within the comforting lines of the drystone walls on the other side of the collapsed section. We scrape past the first few fallen big oaks, the road thick now with caramel-brown saplings, while beyond the walls either side of us, the fields have become full of yellow and gold willows, the floodplain of the Eden wet around them. Then we come to a halt, a thick trunk wedged across our path.

Rain thrums harder on the roof, those saplings swaying and fluttering around us like seaweed in a current as I reverse to one side of the road to turn around, my feet tired and aching against the pedals. I can't help glancing at the map laid out on the dash. Fretting over whether we can get through the dales to the M6—if we do, perhaps the way north might get easier.

We lurch backwards, the wheels whirring in mud.

"Mummy!"

I prod the accelerator with a numb foot, the car suddenly switching itself to fuel engine again—the abrupt increase in power shooting us forwards across the road, slapping through caramel-brown leaves.

Before a line of brighter blood-red saplings tremble a warning, my foot still finding the brakes, and we dive down with a thud into the ditch at the base of the drystone wall the other side of the road. The steering wheel jabs my lungs before the seat belt can catch me. Harry screams. Pain roars through my chest. Stone and mud crash and splatter down onto the windscreen.

Buried in semi-darkness, the engine is still humming, and slowly everything comes back into focus. Harry is crouched in the dark depths of the footwell, clutching his head. More debris taps and splats and cracks onto the roof. Water is breaking through the damaged wall, gushing around the sides of the Cruiser.

I breathe slowly. The ache is hot and tight in my already sore lungs.

"Does it hurt?" I gasp, hauling Harry up, the effort making me dizzy. The tilt of the car makes him slip instantly forwards as I clip the seat belt in and let him go. There's a lump on his forehead that we both feel with our fingers. "You're OK." I kiss his wet cheeks. The engine's hum deepens, becoming muffled.

Sue's wail at the house blares in my head. *You could have killed him!*

The front wheels spin beneath us as I try to reverse, the Cruiser shifting wildly from side to side in the wet.

I cling to the steering wheel, foot pressed on the accelerator, yet we only shift around more violently, Harry crying and shrieking.

The car's capable of four-wheel drive, Katie. Jack's voice in my head. *And only the front wheels are working. Think.*

Squinting at the dash, my seat belt cutting into my sore chest, I can barely think past my pulse throbbing through me, the sound of rain and debris, and the growling engine. I can make out buttons I haven't looked at before. There. One shows four wheels, front ones wonky, a cross between front and back axles.

I hit it and tap the accelerator. The back of the Cruiser pulls instantly. I push my foot down harder and the Cruiser jumps backwards up the edge of the tarmac and bounces to a stop on the road, water continuing to slosh around us. I adjust my grip on the wheel, take a breath.

"That was scary," Harry proclaims, bottom lip wobbling. "How did you know?" His eyes are bright as he examines the buttons and dials on the dash.

"Daddy told me." I smile, twisting the ring on my finger so that the stone is front and centre again.

Harry narrows his eyes. "How?"

"I heard his voice." It felt so real—that familiar warm tone and Yorkshire twang. "Let's leave that button on!" I feel giddy, as if hearing his voice is a sign that trying to find him was the right call. It feels good to push the doubt aside again, even for a moment. "You alright?" I kiss Harry's bump softly and he nods, still looking thoughtful.

"Not dizzy? Or sick?"

He thinks a second, then shakes his head.

The windscreen is fractured now, the crevices filled with mud. I sit hunched forward, squinting through the clearer bit in the bottom corner.

Through the broken wall and across the muddy part-submerged field of yellow-gold saplings, I can see powerboats bobbing nose-up, and the posts of a submerged quay, water slapping against the rusty corrugated metal warehouse of a marina. A muddy village is beyond it, bright with ephemeral feathery pink and red aquatic grasses and willowherbs.

The twitch of the fuel gauge needle draws my eye. The water around us is settling below the wheel arches, the wind carrying the rain cloud south.

Fewer people may have looked for diesel here.

I wish Andy were here to go with me. From where we're sat, the marina warehouse looks like a rusted island, a dark damp cave-like opening at its centre.

You need diesel.

I twist my fingers in my lap.

"Stay here," I say, as I wind the window down and sit on the ledge to put my legs through my overalls, and my boots on, tying them extra tight. "No matter what, you don't get out of the Cruiser, OK?"

He nods.

The water is brown and rippling, suspended grey specks catching the light.

"Can you be lookout for a bit?"

He looks up properly. "Do we have binoculars?"

"No, sorry. Harry, if you see anyone—you probably won't—but if you do, you sit tight and hide behind the seats, OK? And if they come towards the Cruiser, you come to the front and press this here—that will make a big hooting noise. Do you understand?" I say it over again.

Harry nods. "Stay here. Hide if there's people. Press hoot if they come."

"I promise I won't be long."

He whimpers as I lower myself down into cold and mud, which quickly soaks through the thin but usually water-resistant overalls, and I'm drenched up to my knees. I hesitate, looking at the half-submerged warehouse doorway. But it's done now; I'm in contaminated water. I pull on the top half of my overalls, zipping and buttoning them up, and don my mask and gloves.

"No one can get inside, the Cruiser will be locked, safe." Andy's rifle crosses my mind, but it's bulky, heavy to carry, and I haven't even worked out how to load or use it yet—I'm not going far and it feels derelict and wild here. If Harry hooted, I could be back faster without it.

"I don't want you to go," Harry whispers, staring at my disappeared legs.

"Think how far we've come since we left the flat. You even slept in a strange house and not our own bed. You can be brave again while I go and look for diesel—for food for the Cruiser—can't you?" I pat the window arch.

Harry sucks his bottom lip and slowly nods, stroking the dash, and for a moment it does feel like the Cruiser is a large black-scaled loyal creature.

I wait as he winds the window back up and I click the Cruiser locked.

The water sploshes, my boots sinking in mud, as I wade deeper through the quiet willows. Soft fingers of algae clutch at my legs, and I turn, breathless and horrified—relieved when I see Harry's face at the passenger-side window. But the tight feeling doesn't go. Even when he flashes me his hands and backs up from the window to show he's not touching. There's only the Cruiser's old rubber seals between him and that water, and that elastic between us is stretching tight leaving him there.

The water is at my waist as I reach the warehouse and push through dangling brown algae at the opening and into shadows inside, forcing my eyes wide open so they adjust quickly. The windows are smothered, the air thick, a dank whiff coming off the surface scum of dead black algae and leaves.

There's a flash of movement above—pointed wings and a long tatty tail with odd tufts of pink feathers—heading towards a crack of daylight. A kestrel! The first I've seen, since. I stare as she disappears, wishing Harry could have seen her, but it might have only frightened him, and I shiver in the dank darkness, the excitement fading fast.

Black ripples spread outwards as I wade carefully towards the shelves at the back, making the shadows shiver, my legs bumping against slimy solid shapes under the surface, and I keep yelping, imagining a whole host of dead floating here. I glance behind me, as if they might rise up and cut me off from Harry.

I poke through the shelves. Nothing useful for us—outboard motors, power connectors, rotten ropes, buoys, paints . . .

But my heart leaps at the metallic clunk of my boot against a metal drum. The "diesel" embossed lettering is still visible on the rusted top—jackpot!

It takes some bashing and tugging before I manage to unscrew the bung and peer in. There's a film on the surface—thick, sticky grey. I squint about me in the heavy gloom and fetch a long thin rod with a fluorescent flag on the end. The diesel feels thick and viscous as I push the rod down into it. It hits something harder, before bursting through and pinging on the bottom. When I pull it out there's a thick black sludge covering the bottom few inches. That doesn't look good. Would boat diesel work in a car anyway? I put the rod down on the nearest shelf and scrape the flint and steel over it—the fuel does not light. I sag, disappointed.

But then black smoke thickens along the length of the rod, soon rising from the dark waters around me too. I back up towards the exit, afraid in case the fuel is better than it looked as dust in the water burns, fizzing across the surface and around the outside of the opened drum, the smoky fumes able to get past my mask and making me feel faint and start to cough.

Gulping outside, I remember what Andy said. I can't turn that fuel down, no matter the state of it—and at least the nosedive into the ditch that led us to this spot and the getting soaked will have been worth something. So I wade back to the Cruiser for the fuel containers that Jack left me, the fizzing and snapping dying away behind me. I'll take as much as I can store and hope we find something better and we can dump it.

Harry is nowhere to be seen as I approach. I scan the soggy yellow hills and water around us, the cool air nipping right through my wet contaminated clothes. I thought he understood he had to be lookout!

I peer inside to see Harry scrunched in the footwell with all his things, head down, hugging Luna and Julian to his chest, rocking gently as if to soothe himself.

The elastic twangs: I don't want to leave him like this to go back inside there for dodgy fuel that might be useless anyway.

You need it.

To get Harry to Jack. Or even back to Sue if we run into too much trouble. The gauge is down to one half. Still three hundred miles to go . . .

I call out encouragement to him as I grab the fuel containers from the boot, wading back to the warehouse faster now, improvising a siphon to collect from the middle of the drum when I get there—the best I can do. And with the containers full and heavy and unwieldy, makeshift siphon pocketed for future use, I rush to get out of the dark warehouse, my head stuffy and pounding from the fumes.

Before I know it, I'm skidding backwards, head slapping through the surface scum, and I thrash, underwater. For a second I'm disoriented, unsure which way is up. Then the one heavy container I'm still clinging to hits the bottom and I push against it, breaking the surface.

I stand up, frozen in shock, dripping with foul water, one hand still pinching my nose and my mouth scrunched tight. I abandon the other container, somewhere under the surface. I'm fleeing across the flooded, muddy ground outside, gasping in air, arms burning with the weight of the container I still have. Finally I'm yanking open the back of the Cruiser, where I swill and spit clean water, shakily scrub my face, wash out my eyes and ears, douse my hair and strip out of my sodden clothes, letting them disappear in the turbid water.

Finally, as clean and dry as I can get myself, I sit in the boot, bare skin goosebumped and rubbed raw, the Cruiser clicked locked, and the container of fuel strapped in beside me. I'm trembling, still scouring my face with the last clean cloth we have. Harry is kneeling on the back seats, watching, his little hand squeezing through the headrests, hoping for my hand.

26

At last, we're making headway on the cracked sprouting tarmac of the M6, "electric mode" blinking on successfully for a weak trundle a few miles at a time now. The pink hazy glow of the setting sun meets the distant dark blue hills of the Lake District on our left, the cracks and scratches on the windscreen dazzling and hurting my eyes.

The Cruiser is tugging left again, the steering wheel heavy; even the working sidelight has drooped, as if our loyal car is weary and ready to pull over too.

Thick leaf litter crinkles under us as we weave through dull mustard-yellow birch saplings to the highest point of what might once have been a motorway services car park. Silence as I turn off the ignition. I stretch my arms up to the roof, my stiff muscles aching into it, and Harry copies, bouncing on his seat in order to hit the roof. We both yawn.

"Are we going in there?" Harry peers out towards the service station.

I shake my head, the shock of the boat warehouse still buzzing through me.

"Did Daddy tell you not to?"

Frowning, I snort out a laugh. "No, Harry." But then I consider how Jack might do this, and I re-park us—the engine still warm and roaring back to life straight away. I feel better once we're pointing down the slope towards the exit. Ready to go. I wipe us down again, obsessively checking my bloodshot and stinging eyes. My hands shake. I'm still horrified at how easily I could have swallowed or inhaled that untreated, dust-filled floodwater. I wipe the seats and dash, windowsills and handles too—the dread not easing the more I do it.

We nibble on Sue's bread, the bumpy road having shrunk our appetites, our stomachs still swirling, and sluggishly brush our teeth. Harry resists getting ready for sleeping but eventually allows me to help him into his pyjamas, before I make a bed of blankets across the back seats and tuck him in, a feather-stuffed pillow of Sue's propping up his head.

"That bump's gone down already," I whisper, soothingly, because he's pressed against me and quiet.

His fingers find the square of Sue's duct tape instead—covering the cut on his forehead—and pick at the edges.

"Will Daddy speak in my head too?" he says in a small voice. "Is that what happens when you disappear, like a magic?"

I swallow, realizing he misunderstands what I meant. "No, it's only because I remember his voice, and what he might have said."

"Will he look like in the picture?"

"Maybe a little different, but not much."

"Maybe the shadows will be stuck to him, like how you look in the dark, all faded and grey?"

"Harry, he didn't fall into a shadow, that's not what happened."

"Where did he go then? And the children from Before? Sue said—"

I take a sharp breath in. "Harry—" The dread floods back.

"You never tell those stories," he whines. "Are daddies bad?" he whispers, eyes glinting in the growing gloom.

"No, they're not bad."

I try not to show it on my face, the little jolt I feel at Harry having picked up on the idea of his father being "bad." I shake my head. When all I want for him is the bright warmth of Jack. "Before . . . before the big storm, children lived with mummies *and* daddies, or just mummies, a bit like us, or just daddies, or with lots of other sorts of grown-ups."

"Why don't Andy and Sue . . ." He stumbles over what words come next.

"They're too old now. But Sue had some children Before."

He frowns. "She said they went to sleep forever in the garden. But I didn't see them—did they get disappeared?"

I squirm, not wanting to answer. "No, they were there, Harry, don't worry about it." I press a kiss into his shoulder to hide my grimace.

Harry is silent, fighting against sleep, like he doesn't believe me. "What is it?"

"Nasties can't get inside to disappear *me* while I'm sleeping, can they?" he whispers. "Can't we shut out the dark Outside, like we do at home, just-in-case?"

"No, there's no such thing as 'nasties.' And I'm sorry, we don't have curtains here," I whisper, but instead, like I wished I could have last night, I make-believe our own bed, our own duvet and our own familiar room, our fingers touching every familiar thing.

"And Daddy's magic buttons that save us from falling down."

"Yep."

We keep going, adding bits of the Cruiser into our safe bedroom, until Harry sinks heavier against me.

"Is the glass strong, Mummy?" he whispers, jerking himself awake again.

"Yep, we're locked in and safe." And yet I press my fingers against the glass. It shifts on its base and I think of all the slumped shapes in cars and in this very car, I realize—it was this car I spotted in front of the supermarket, through the binoculars, that day I first saw someone again, months after the storm. "Put your mask on and pull the blanket up, Harry, over your head—that'll . . . help keep nasties out—like our big fluffy duvet over us at the flat."

With that, Harry sinks down, calmer. "And you'll make sure I wake up?"

"Of course I will."

"What about all the other children, Mummy?" he whispers. "Can we go and get them? Just-in-case bad daddies get them or there's no one to make sure they wake up? We could take them to Andy and Sue to be safe?"

My throat tightens. "Sorry, we can't go looking for them."

"You're going looking for a daddy." His stubborn exhale under the blanket has a slight whistling to it.

"That's different."

"Why?"

"Because Jack's already mine." I freeze as if I've given the awful truth away. "Ours, I mean."

The heavy weight of darkness keeps drawing me out of sleep, making me feel like I'm suffocating under the weight of dust-filled water again. I stare out of the window until I can spot the soft glow of one of the brighter stars, which are still visible on clearer nights.

I shrink tighter around Harry's warmth. All night there are scrapes along the ground, rustlings, and, near dawn, the soft pitter-patter of rain unburdened by dust. I keep checking the doors. I keep dreaming awful familiar dreams. Jack dead amongst debris at his London clinic, or one of the long-dead with his hair dried and skin desiccated, slumped in a rusting car. But those dreams keep warping to a Scottish cottage, Jack hanging in a rustic doorway, or slumped in his shattered Subaru in the Highland air. Harry starved in my arms. Crows picking at our decaying flesh. I keep waking myself up, horrified, the Fear flooding and choking me at the thought of having killed them both by virtue of not being there to be found five years ago and by gambling for *everything* now.

I keep trying to shake off the images, try to refind that warmth of hope inside me.

Until Harry is tugging me awake.

I'm alert in an instant, eyes gritty and uncomfortable. The tight prickling of my lungs and aching everywhere my new normal as I haul myself up. Blinking against the dazzling red of the sunrise, I stare into the dark otherwise all around us. I've woken in a nightmare caught between my own fears and Harry's.

Outside, ten metres away, the grim fuzzy outline of a tall shadowy creature bounces with rain in the darkness. Long hair drips out the bottom of a hood. I imagine the spots where its eyes should be staring right at me through the glass, its hungry evil thoughts in my head, ready to grasp and touch and tear and hurt.

"A nasty!" Harry moans.

"Just a person," I croak firmly. "Stay still." I scramble forwards into the driver's seat.

The windows are so wet and scratched it's hard to make my eyes strain through them. The figure takes a step towards the car, leaning as if trying to see inside. In my right hand I finger the key and plant it in the ignition. The engine clicks, but doesn't roar to life.

Please. I try the key again, and again, until there's not even a click anymore, conscious of the figure staggering closer, face pressing against the window—grey skin and black shadows for eyes and mouth.

Dread churns my empty stomach. The figure shudders with a wet rattling cough, pulling at each of our door handles.

In the rear-view, I see Harry slip down in his blankets, holding them up over his face.

It seems like we sit there a long time in the drizzling rain and early morning gloom, the sun slowly rising, that wet faceless figure watching us. I keep searching the darkness for others.

I finally shuffle to the passenger seat and into my mask. I can't just sit here anymore. With that face still staring in through the driver's side window, I quickly squeeze out into the cold wet air, just into my unlaced boots, my knife held tight in one hand, the jump-starter in the other, locking the Cruiser after me. The wet figure surges round the car towards me, coughing in fits and starts that sounds almost like speech. I keep moving round the Cruiser to avoid them and eventually they seem to get the message and pause a few feet away, wobbling, waiting.

I keep my eyes on them as I get the bonnet open and jump-starter fitted, losing sight as I step round to the driver's side and try the ignition. But there's no wonderful hum of the engine starting— and I recall Jack's instructions: the emergency jump-starter will only work once or twice, then it's flat.

Fingers grasp at me and I yelp, jerking my sleeve free of the weak bony grip.

"What do you want?" I shout.

They stagger back, hitting the ground, hunched over, croaking and coughing, like an animal fighting against drowning.

I slam the bonnet shut and jump back inside, ramming boots back in their place.

Pulling up the handbrake, we roll slowly down the slope, ignition on and Cruiser in gear, just like Jack instructed for a bump-start. We pick up speed halfway down, engine silent and saplings snapping under us, and I gently let the clutch out and press the accelerator down, holding my breath as we plummet towards the end of the slope. Suddenly, both pedals seem to catch and the engine lurches back to life.

I glance at the wet figure shuddering to their feet in the rearview mirror. But in the next instant, they're lost in the gloom and rain as I snatch my foot from the clutch, thundering us along the slip road to the M6 again, afraid to let off the accelerator.

I replay the incident in my head, wondering now what they were doing outside in the rain like that. Would Andy and Sue have taken them in, offered help? Now that I'm safe inside the moving car, with the engine rumbling comfortingly, the Fear has ebbed and I feel guilty. Ruthless in a way I felt during the storm, eking out my food and never answering the knocks or screams.

What if I'm wrong to ask so much more of Jack? The question rings accusingly in my head as I glance at Harry, and swallow, my own throat and lungs so tight and itchy. Even if Jack is alive and smiles at Harry like I imagine him smiling at me, it's hard to find enough food, to stay safe . . . he will just be trying to survive himself, might have others to care for already . . .

When I cough, the sound is so like the wet figure that Harry jumps, startled, a look of horror on his little face.

27

Bright gold leaves slap the windows.

"Mummy!" Harry yells.

I'm still so jumpy, even after miles and hours weaving along the M6, that I swerve. The front wheels jostle sideways into a deep crack, just as the Cruiser switches to electric mode, the accelerator sagging alarmingly this time and the engine nearly stalling, before I manage to right us, squinting hard through the fuzzy glass.

"There's no way to avoid them," I tell Harry, trying my best to navigate the thickets of saplings growing up out of the broken tarmac. "We have to be careful, no more shouting, OK? We can't afford for the engine to cut out!"

He nods, tearful, Luna tucked under his chin, but cringes as another sapling bobs past his window, its giant creamy-yellow leaves of a size and shape that are almost face-like. And suddenly I too can see the sea of grey faces veering towards us.

"Touch the window on the next one—just this once. See? Even if it slaps the glass, it's not coming inside."

Gradually the trembling gold saplings thin out and I can see broken offshore wind turbines on our left—and then the estuary of the Eden! We must be past Carlisle—nearly in Scotland! Yet when I look ahead again, something shimmers across the road in the hazy afternoon light and my heart sinks.

A thick mesh fence.

"What is it?" Harry asks.

As more of it comes into view—flowing over the blue-grey grassy hills to east and west—I realize: "The Scottish border, I forgot about the fence . . . I haven't seen it before, only on the news."

"On the *news*?"

"A place people used to tell each other stories, mostly scary ones."

"Like where the deer are for hurting?" He sniffs.

"No," I say, only half listening as I let the Cruiser slow. I lean forward to examine the passport office and two watchtowers.

"Do you see anyone?" I whisper.

Harry's arms are folded stiffly, but he squints out. "No," he whispers back.

"OK then." I dare not turn the engine off as I step out into boots and towards the gate, looking from watchtower to watchtower. The gate is seven feet of vertical, solid metal bars. Dark grey like steel at first, but up close clearly bloody with rust. The faded imprint of a sticker still declares "This is Scotland!" with "SNP" and a silhouetted Scotsman planting the Scottish flag. I push on the gates, wincing at the clang, but they're bolted shut.

Turning back to the humming Cruiser, I feel uneasy, the watchtowers casting their shadow over me. I'm trying to remember how many gates there might be and figure out what the chances of them all being locked shut are.

Back ensconced inside with the engine ticking over, I look east at the steel mesh fence dipping and swelling across the hilly ground. Fluffy seed heads catch the light as they bob over the grey-blue grass—more grey fairies.

The car's made for it, Katie.

If Jack's past this border . . . we have to try.

Taking a shaky breath, I lurch us off the crumbling moss-soft edge of the concrete forecourt, and we dip down alarmingly into sodden ground, the grasses revealing their bright yellow bases. I slam the brakes, blood pounding in my feet. The weight of the Cruiser shifts towards me, Harry's side rising, air beneath the wheels. Lifting off the brakes instead, I groan in relief as the wheels bounce back down and we level off.

"I don't like it!" Harry says, scrunching his eyes shut.

"It won't roll," I say, squeezing his knee. I remember images of four-by-fours thundering up rocky slopes, wobbling at all angles, but staying upright. Only, I know I don't know what I'm doing, and the ground ahead is full of milky pools and fiery-yellow grass stems—this low boggy ground a conveyor of groundwater and dust.

I stick closer to the fence line, where the ground is flatter and drier. Our tyres find old tracks—deeply rutted and grown over.

When we stop for a break, Harry climbs in the back to refill our flask and select a jar of sharp sweet hawberries. He gulps water down, while I take a few careful sips—mindful we won't be stopping to collect rainwater to filter and boil, not until we reach our destination.

Hours are lost trundling along this fence, the sun gone nearly three-quarters of its arc now. Harry looks woeful and tired, clutching his seat. There must be another gate on the A68, the other side of what used to be Kielder Forest Park, but we're wasting fuel going so far out of our way. Down to a quarter of a tank now and still over two hundred miles to Arisaig. Only one container of dodgy backup.

I bring us to a halt. Easily missed if I weren't staring desperately at the fence—a vertical gash in the mesh.

The air is still and clear when I step into my cold boots and get out—the sky only grey and hazy in the distance. From my sack of outdoor things, I pull out my waterproof parka, since I chucked the saturated overalls back at the Eden. The engine idles with a thrum, drinking fuel, but I find my shoulders relaxing, a relief to leave the noisy lurching cabin, claustrophobic with the two of us all day. It's like being on a big open plain here too, no buildings or trees crowding me. Like prey able to get a good view all around, just-in-case.

"I don't like it!" Harry calls through the glass. His eyes grow bigger as they rove round the big open space, blinking at the expanse of grey sky. He is pale and small, swamped by the navy-blue hoodie of mine that he's wearing, flinching at flies and mozzies buzzing near the windows.

I step towards the fence, a bitter chemical odour rising as I squelch.

"Don't leave me alone, Mummy!" His cry yanks on that elastic between us, makes me stop and turn. His eyes are full of tears.

"Just keep watching me. I'm not disappearing anywhere," I call, wincing at my poor choice of words.

The wire is thick and heavy, fighting to spring back as I pull it. I think a second, then undo my boots and use the laces to tie it back as far as I can haul it. The gap between the steel posts still might not be enough.

Harry throws his arms around me—jostling my tight irritated chest—as I sit back in the driver's seat. He's all clammy and warm, his heart racing, like I've been gone longer than a minute.

Winding down my window, I pull in the mirror. Then lean to do the same on Harry's side. "It's OK." I show him the air meter. "It's good, clear air."

"I want to!" he says, excited to press the button to make the glass move. But he yelps as cold bog-dank air rushes inside, and sinks from the hoverflies and a beetle it brings with it.

"I thought they were your friends?" I waft them away from his face.

"There's too many and too fast Outside."

Once I've pulled Harry's mirror in and wound the windows up, I contemplate the gap again. There's no guarantee the A68 gate will be open.

"Harry, remember when we left the garage at the flat—"

"No!" He thrashes, unclipping his seat belt, swiping at my reaching hand, catching the not-healed cut so it throbs. "You said not again!" He glances at the back seats, the only place he can stomp off to.

"I said I'd try." I shake out my stinging hand.

Harry bounces on his seat, purposefully banging his head back, his cheeks getting redder.

"We don't hurt people, Harry."

"Why not?" He folds his arms.

"You know why, it's mean." I feel myself trembling. Harry's amber-brown eyes are angry and hurt, glaring at me. I imagine

Jack staring into them too, that anxiety that came to me at Andy and Sue's flaring, before I blink the feeling away.

And tears are pricking Harry's eyes too, his bottom lip wobbling.

"It might be a bit scary, but we have to try, don't we? We can't keep wasting fuel and time. Or we'll never reach Daddy."

He considers this. "The Cruiser might get too tired?"

I nod. "If we make it keep going in case of a better gap . . . Can you be brave? You could wrap a blanket round your face, might make any noises hurt your ears a bit less?"

He looks so tired, sat staring at the fence ahead, slumped low in his seat, eyes puffy.

"It'll be over quick, I promise, straight through, and then you can have a treat from the boot?"

He shakes his head.

"You like berries—" I twist, ready to scramble back for them.

"No, I want a game. A new one." The flush in his cheeks has spread to his neck. A beetle taps against the glass and he cringes away from it.

"Alright, whatever you'd like, we'll do it. You've been such a brave boy."

There's a small smile at this.

I bite my lip as I reverse a few feet. It's going to be very tight. The Cruiser leaps forward as I slam the accelerator. There's an awful scraping and squealing. We slow, the wheels whirring in mud, and I'm holding my breath. Then suddenly we burst out and up.

I let the Cruiser roll to a stop.

"We're through!" I grin, giddy, the squealing still in my head.

Harry is silent a second, as if he might cry, then lifts his hand, ready to high five.

Grinning, I don't leave him hanging this time.

"Let's not do it again," Harry says, rubbing his ears, and eyes blinking. "What's the new game?"

"How about I spy? We played it in the car when I was little." I explain the rules and follow Harry's gaze to the billowing rolls of purple and grey rushes and the mass of wine-red woods in the hilly distance. The sky yawns across us, grey with cloud except for a dirty orange-grey horizon.

He looks back down at Luna. "Everything's too big."

"It's . . . it's just the same as Sue's garden, just leaves and soil and sky. You liked it out there in the end, didn't you? Couldn't keep you in!" I tickle his side, relieved when he squirms and breaks into a smile.

"Can it be a make-believe game?" He sits up, wiping his nose on his sleeve and glancing outside in small quick looks. "You have to guess what I'm imagining."

"But it could be anything . . ."

A cheeky grin lights his face.

"OK, go on then."

He looks outside, eyes flickering over the rushes and pearly white water in the pools and dips between them.

"Is it an animal?"

He nods.

"A beetle?"

"No! That's not a make-believe!"

I try a few others, watching his face as I guess wrong, growing anxious to move—we're still wasting time. He's clutching his Alistair the dinosaur T-shirt through the deep V of the hoodie, the faded red scales all higgledy-piggledy in the folds.

"A dinosaur?"

He blushes; I'm close.

I sigh. "A dragon?"

"Yep! It's daddy dragon Smug—"

"Smaug? Like Andy told us?"

"He's curled up in the bottom of a white pool, just his nose and the tip of his tail showing—black shiny scales like a black beetle. And he's got lots of food in the bottom in the mud, and there's tiny children all hungry trying to reach it, but they can't, because the daddy dragon has big mean eyes."

I press my lips together. "What if it was a friendly green mountain dragon, from the north? And he's a bit lost like the children, and if they ask him nicely, he might pass them up some of the food?"

"Yeah and maybe he can breathe his fire a bit to dry out the food and burn away the bad."

"Alright." I smile, getting out to retrieve my laces, the fence swinging back as I do. Turning back to the Cruiser, I notice how scratched the paintwork is—and that there are deep scores along the tyres! One's hissing . . .

Panicked, I rake around the slightly damp boot desperately—Harry must have spilled some of the flask water when he filled it—but I already know it—there's no spare wheel.

"What's wrong?" Harry's little voice calls. And I rush to the glovebox. Pulling out—from under the foldable warning triangle—an emergency puncture foam kit.

"But this won't fix the wheel. It's for holes, not rips."

He shrugs. "We have to make do with what we can find."

That makes me smile. "Yes, we do." I kiss his cheek. "Maybe it'll get us as far as we need to go." I fit the canister to the wheel valve and the wheel fills with foam and air, a bright line of white bubbling out through the very fine but inches-long rip. It starts hardening instantly.

And we get moving. I can feel that foam spinning in the wheel, spreading, and that side of the car feels loose and bouncy.

"Harry, you know what Andy told me? He said things don't have to be scary just because they're different. I think maybe he's right, maybe we can both be brave and—"

"No! Don't squash the green dragon!"

"Oh, Harry . . ." But I go around the pool in front of us anyway, the tyres churning through the wet ground, making us bob from side to side in our seats.

Eventually, Harry asks: "Was it lots different Before?"

I think carefully before finding a safe answer. "Yes. Greener."

"Wasn't it boring, *everything* green?"

"Well, there were lots of different greens."

We play a game, naming all the types we know, and ten miles into Scotland at last, heading west to refind the motorway, I start to relax as we finally put a bit of distance behind us today. The game moves across the rainbow, keeping us going until we reach the relative comfort of motorway tarmac, firm beneath the layers of silt and leaves, and now I feel how unruly the Cruiser is. The front wheels are sticking and tugging left, back right wheel soggy and pulling right, accelerator pedal sinking with weak power each time the electric mode kicks in before surging again with the diesel after a few miles.

Up ahead the M74 is lined with trees, and we both gape at pine boughs—rich deep green—peeping out amongst the coppery beeches. There's the sound of water flowing somewhere to the right, getting louder as we drive. I go slowly and carefully as we start weaving between lower-reaching branches and crunching over rotted trunks again, my eyes on the wing mirrors and our tyres.

I keep stopping to consult the map, Harry keeping the first of the Scottish OS ones spread out on the dash for me so I can trace my finger northwards. The ground has levelled again—we're in the Central Lowlands of Scotland now, approaching Glasgow.

"Does the orange mean more slippy bog plants?" he asks, working his fingernails under the duct tape on his head.

I pull his hand away. "No, on this map it shows a city." I touch the outermost fringes of it. It extends further than I thought. If we want to avoid it all, we'll have to go east, past Carluke, and then up, following minor roads in a big loop around Glasgow, ending up on the A82 up the west bank of Loch Lomond from where we can head north-west into the Highlands and towards Arisaig.

"Is the flat there?"

I shake my head.

"Will we never be there again? What if the Cruiser gets too tired and we haven't found Daddy yet?"

"It won't, we'll be OK," I say, but only Andy and Sue know where we're going and they can hardly launch a rescue if we run into trouble.

We need to cross the River Clyde at some point to avoid the city, so I take the next turn-off, scraping the Cruiser through beautiful green pine branches, needles clattering against the windows, the sound so like windblown toxic particles that we both grimace.

"It's fine," I say, watching carefully for big branches that might punch through the already fractured glass.

"Why are you staring so hard, then?" Harry leans away, his yawn interrupted by another clank.

We come down a steep bend, emerging from the trees to a little arched stone bridge. Beneath it, what must be the River Clyde in spate.

The brown water is high, dragging bankside trees into the swells. It slaps the underside of the cracked bridge with a rumble.

"It looks wonky and broken, Mummy."

We both sit high in our seats to peer down. "I don't know, might have been that way a long time—stone is strong." Better than something more modern of wood, concrete or steel, which would have needed us to maintain it.

I look again at the map. We might be where I think we are. The curve of the road we took down here looks right on paper, we could have missed these other marked adjoining roads amongst the spreading pines and beeches, and the "historic bridge" symbol is there. There are a dozen river crossings close to the motorway though, and no road sign to confirm this is the way to Carluke.

I sigh, frustrated. The long hazy descent into evening is already here. We've lost so much time today. I peer at the dash; the fuel gauge has dropped again—around a hundred and seventy miles still to go. I think of all the crevices and trunks the already bad wheels have gone over; we can't afford to check out all the crossings and make sure.

"Are we going that way?" Harry whispers, eyes wide at the rushing water.

"Yep," I say, more decisively than I feel.

28

Rolling the Cruiser towards the middle, the gushing water under the bridge reverberating through the car, I force the wheels as straight as possible. Both of us smile as we reach the orange-pink alders on the other side.

The trees continue into the soft yellows and warm caramels of an ash-oak woodland that leans across the road on our left. Loose leaves swing and twirl across our path, making Harry frown and cringe again.

A small garage marks the start of a village on our right. And beyond that, a field of straw-coloured grass, peppered with purplish weeds, a row of houses at its furthermost edge.

"Am I coming this time?" Harry asks, as I scramble over the seats to the boot—my turn to fetch some food to keep us going—before I head outside. Everything's really wet now back here, turnips and bulrush roots sitting in puddles. Clothes damp. I glance at the dripping tap of the water barrel.

"Oh, Harry," I mutter, closing my eyes a moment, before clicking the tap fully off. The inch left inside slaps gently against the sides.

"What?"

A sweat comes over me as I climb back and hand him the bulrush cakes and apples. But Harry didn't mean to. "Nothing, it's alright."

I gobble a few mouthfuls before getting outside and into my gear. The air meter throbs on and off—long enough to see it's safe.

Harry clambers carefully after me.

"I'm just going to that service station there. You see those pillars holding up the roof?"

He blinks up at the sky.

I let out a slow breath. I don't want to discourage him from being brave. "It will be ten steps at most, to the nearest one."

"OK."

He recoils at the thick rustling leaves as his shoes touch the ground and squirms in the puffy all-in-one snowsuit. He insists on taking his pack, unzipping it on the floor first to check all his things are there. Luna topples over on the uneven leaf-strewn ground.

"Never put stuff on the floor!" I yank his pack up, patting the material down while he checks his blanket and toothbrush are secure and safe inside.

I lock the Cruiser and we take two steps before Harry stops, fretting with the straps of his backpack.

I continue on past the charging ports towards the pumps, letting the gap between us widen. Until I hear him gasp and hurry to catch up, bumping against my legs, the backpack snugly on his back.

Feeling guilty, I work through the emergency hand pumps in quick succession. They all whine: dry.

The orange glow of the dipping sun makes me squint and Harry lean as if to bury his face in my parka despite my constant warnings about face and hands. It's too quiet here, the air still now. Harry frowns at the row of houses across the straw-yellow grass. I follow his gaze. And as I blink, I too notice the shape hanging from the roof, second house to the left.

The wince shudders right through my sore chest as I pull short. I tug Harry back towards the Cruiser, breaking into a sprint, cursing—I should have noticed that!

"Is it a man?" Harry gasps, trying to keep up.

"Yes."

"Why does he look so—"

"Fire might have got to him," I say, my boots sploshing through the muddy colonies of moss on the tarmac.

"Why is he up there?"

I force the ugly word sprayed below his swinging body out of my mind.

As soon as we're both in the Cruiser, I push down the door locks, the sack of outdoor things bulging again on the back of my seat, and wipe our hands and faces with a nearly dry though no longer clean or sterile cloth. I long for the flat. Dust of some sort floats inside the cabin. The meter still hasn't charged back up. I tap my fist against my forehead in frustration, closing my tired eyes.

"Mummy!" Harry pulls at my arms.

I snap my eyes open and drop my hand. We can't rest yet, not here anyway. We head on, the sunset lighting up all the cracks and scratches in the windscreen again, forcing me to peer and squint harder. Through the next village, which I hope is Carluke, though its rows of houses seem over too quick. I try to look at the lichen- and rust-crusted vehicles, wondering if vans might be more likely to have diesel, but now I'm seeing that swinging body over every door. And Harry keeps hanging on to my elbow, head leaning on my shoulder—hot and clammy. My chest is tighter, breaths shallower.

I stop abruptly and scramble out, shutting Harry in behind me, and walk towards a small British Wind Power van. Harry's amber-brown eyes burn in my back as I go. Yet I can't turn around, gulping in cold air without my mask.

And I wonder if I left him so often in Hitchin not just to keep him safe—I needed a moment to myself, to breathe.

I'm sure Sue wouldn't. Maggie wouldn't.

Bitch. Guilt churns the sickening Fear round in my stomach.

At the van, there's a strong whiff of fuel. Electricity companies needed engineers to travel for miles and for that you often still needed fuel, even them. But nothing wets my Eden marina siphon as I push it down into the tank. I'm gasping in breaths now. The street is full of shadows, the orange sky silhouetting black roofs and bushes. Harry's face is bleary behind the glass, and now, like hundreds of times before, I feel that tug between us, that thread, and I run back.

"We're wasting diesel looking," I gasp, after shrugging back out of my parka and boots. I squeeze Harry tight even though it hurts my sore chest and he wriggles to free himself. "We've got *something*, anyway." I feel Jack's judgement in my head, but I shrug it off.

It's a relief to move forwards, winding through the shadowy streets. Though I'm not sure we are where I thought; there should have been one main road to follow, but instead I'm jumping from one narrow lane to another, old roadside tree trunks like dark monoliths against the darkening grey-orange sky.

"Mummy! I can't find Luna." Harry's face is suddenly caught in agony. "He's gone!"

"Have you checked your pack?"

"Yes!" His terrified wail resembles the one I'd hear as I raced up the stairs when he was a toddler, knowing he'd woken before I'd got home from foraging.

My foot feels heavy on the accelerator now, but wobbly, Harry's cries right inside my chest. I remember Harry putting his pack down on the ground. I blink slowly. And Luna too. Fuck fuck fuck!

I let my foot ease up, and we drift to a stop. Harry's whole body trembles as I hug him close, lungs expanding in lurches. Hot tears wet my T-shirt.

There is no way we can waste more diesel and the last of the daylight to go back. No way.

Yet I turn us around and speed back the precious miles we've come, Harry still in my lap, blubbering. My hands throb around the steering wheel, eyes avoiding that fuel gauge.

We keep going the wrong way, houses and roads looking unfamiliar, though the silhouetted saplings and bushes all look the same.

It's quite dark by the time I find Luna in amongst the buttery-yellow leaves, but the tension in my shoulders loosens at Harry's relieved tear-streaked face—even if that word, letters in dribbled red paint, lodges back in my head. RAPIST.

Harry curls up in the passenger seat, exhausted, staring tearfully at Luna, who I won't let him touch yet and have wedged instead in the cupholder. I keep the lights low as the evening draws in, driving slowly down the darkening streets, moths and particles dancing together around the working sidelight. I feel an urgency to keep moving, to make up for the wasted time. The sky isn't black tonight, instead it's dark blue, full of stars. And in the distance, lights flicker. A handful have the muted but constant glow of something with power. It's about the direction of where Glasgow should be—though they seem much smaller and further away than they should. The fuel gauge, close to the last few bars, glares at me from the dash.

"Is it dinner time?"

Harry's voice snaps my attention back to the road ahead, just as something moves in the darkness—low to the ground—twilight catching reflective eyes and a long snout. I slam the brakes, dozens of eyes blinking behind the first.

When I realize what I've done, I fumble to check the locks. In my tired mind, I'm still morphing them into silhouetted and unnerving human shapes.

Harry strains towards me against his seat belt, hands over his eyes.

"Harry." I pull his hands from his face. "It's just badgers, I think. Mr. Badger."

"Not nasties?" He refuses to look anyway.

The eyes disappear and I don't wait, foot hitting the accelerator. Squinting into the dark, the shapes of old cars, bushes and trees, a coat caught on a fence, keep wobbling into monstrous things Harry might imagine—swallowing shadows and nasties hiding in dark places, and those I fear—man-sized figures, dead bodies, tree trunks blocking our path, or clouds of smothering dust. My foot keeps shoving the pedal harder.

Drizzle smears the fractured windscreen, but I put off wasting fuel to power the wipers. I should stop, though. Park somewhere that feels secluded. But the road and houses around me are grey and black shapes in the dark, that handful of Glasgow lights closer now and unnerving. And I don't want to stop here.

"Hungry," Harry says, kicking the dash.

"Climb in the back and find something if you want, we can't stop."

I feel robotic. Staring into the dark, turning the Cruiser this way and that. Trying to stay on this main road, and keep those lights still in the distance and at nine o'clock.

Harry rummages in the boot, skidding about as I turn, though I'm only going slowly.

"Hurry up," I call. I don't want him to hit his head again. "Make sure you don't touch everything, Harry, just what you need to!"

"I need you to open it."

There's the swish and scuff of him clambering back, noises that bring back that vomity shock I felt in that village earlier, and pull me towards unwanted memory. A flash of lying on the ground in darkness. The hiss of the tent being unzipped. Hands grasping for me.

Something is glinting in front of the car and I frown at it, Harry's monsters and my own all jumbled up in my head. But there's sloshing, a silky surface rippling as we move, pinpricks glittering in it. My chest tightens—we're surrounded by water! I can't tell if we're still on a road. The tyres still have traction, so maybe we are. But now it's so black outside—I can hardly see anything, not even those distant lights! This was stupid.

Harry pushes against my shoulder and the gearstick as he climbs back to the passenger seat.

"Can you open it?"

"Not yet, Harry."

He plops a large jar on my lap anyway, the cold glass pressing against my legs.

We should have waited out the night, continued on in the early hours when I can actually see. But I'm afraid to stop now—what if we got stuck here? I can imagine it thick with particles, miles of it.

"It's too dark," Harry says, his voice small.

"Well, you were brave to go and fetch the jar. What are you doing? Sit down please."

A fence post looms out of the dark, like a thin skeletal figure, and I jerk us away from it. Harry topples sideways into the passenger window; the jar in my lap bounces up and wedges between my seat and the gearstick.

"Harry, sit down, seat belt on."

"I want the light! It's too dark, I don't like it."

I shove the jar back to my lap and finally flick the headlights on to better light our way. And stupidly, in my tiredness, I switch the radio on too, to distract us like my mum might have done with us when we were small on long journeys.

The blast of white noise makes us both cry out, and I turn it off again.

Should I try to back up the way we came, out of the water? It doesn't seem to be ending. I don't know, though, how long we've been chugging along through it.

No, keep moving.

"I'm hungry."

Keeping an even pace in the dark, watching the black skin of water rippling ahead of us, I balance the wheel with my knee, try to open the jar. It's on tight. The water outside gets higher, inching up the side of the Cruiser to just below the windows.

The jar lid is too wide, keeps slipping from my fingers. I wipe my hands on my trouser legs, try again, and feel the thread start to shift.

The bumper crunches into something, nudging me. I grasp the steering wheel, swerving us away from it. Wet seeps across my trousers and drips into the seat, the smell of onions becoming pungent.

When I focus I can see the remains of a drystone wall breaking the surface of the black floodwater, like a snaking grey spine in the dark, particles in the air picked out by the headlights like crackling specks on old film. I stay close to the spine, follow it as it weaves ahead.

"Can I have one?"

"I need to concentrate, Harry." But I pat my lap, wet round lumps rolling away from my fingers and onto the floor. I grasp the jar instead and lift it across to him. "Wipe your hands clean first."

"Is there any water to drink?"

"Later, Harry."

I jerk the Cruiser away from a tree, but the wheels are tugging left and right, and we skid. I try not to panic, try to focus on the direction in the dark we were heading in, keep my foot evenly on the accelerator.

"Mummy!"

We grind along the tree, before the wheels find traction again and we keep moving forwards, slipping and sliding, the Cruiser lurching up and bumping down. I'm cold now, wet trousers clinging to my skin. My eyes are heavy.

The water is thinning though, a heavy sloshing at the wheel arches, rather than halfway up the door. I keep going. Harry crunches and slurps beside me.

The back of the seat presses against me, the ground jostling us upwards, and there's a scratching outside like we're driving through a giant hairbrush. The sloshing has gone, until we dip abruptly with a splash at the front bumper.

"OK, we'll stop here." I reverse a few feet, till we're clear. The handbrake judders up, and, after a nervous pause, I turn the engine off, taking with it the comforting dash lights. Silence and darkness engulf us.

My hands buzz, my whole body trembling. All we can see outside now is a patch of dark grey night sky up ahead, and the topmost spikes and bristles of vegetation around us, silvery and wet.

"How do we know it's safe? We should keep driving, Mummy."

I shake my head. "We need to stop. We're out of that water at least."

"What if there's scary faces out there in the night?"

"Nothing can get inside the Cruiser, inside the glass, remember? I promise."

I set up Harry's blankets on the back seats and drag myself over the armrest to lie with him. For the first time, I feel too exhausted to wipe us down and clean. I wonder if it makes much difference right now, without even spit available to me to dampen a cloth it's either on our skin or just going to be dislodged to add to what's in the confined airspace surrounding us. Instead I just pull Harry's mask up, happy when he shrinks under the blanket. Curled up tight against me, I feel each of his flinches as waves of rain hit the roof—if not dust-laden, then propelled by strong gusts, and at the scratching and swishing so like fingers trying to get in.

I whisper in his ear, imagining the soft comfortable mattress at the flat, the big rectangle of the wooden bedframe.

"Why didn't Daddy come find us at the flat? Why do we have to go so far?"

My stomach squeezes tight. "He tried," I whisper. "But he didn't find us."

"He wouldn't be good at finders, would he?"

"He might have thought I was . . ." I grope for a word other than dead—"lost."

"In the shadows Outside!" Harry says, his voice full of understanding and awe. "He might be scared, looking Outside."

"He might have given up."

I tug at my bottom lip, worrying it until it cracks. *I can't live without you.* Yes, you can, you must have. Please.

I wake with the now-familiar aching in my cold chest, prickling as I take a first breath, my whole body stiff, my trousers still wet.

The first glow of dawn glitters across the fogged back window. Everything else still grey and black. With a jolt I realize I'm alone, and sit up, cracking my neck.

"Look." Harry's up front, smearing condensation off the windscreen.

I frown through the be-dewed thorns and leaves caught silver in the twilight, out at a vast flat skin of grey loch the Cruiser is half-nosed into that I was not expecting to see, distant mountains on the far side a muted grey-blue.

"Shit." I wince, grabbing the map from the floor.

29

Stinking oniony liquid weeps down the dash as I peel open the sodden map. I trace my finger where we might have come, past the east of Glasgow and up—wasting fuel going the wrong side of Loch Lomond, heading north-east, and not to the west coast.

Well at least you stopped when you did, no harm done.

"Shit," Harry says.

"Don't say that word."

"You did."

"That must be Loch Lomond," I tell him, my throat dry, nodding outside and pointing on the map.

"What does it mean? What does shit mean?"

I open my mouth and hesitate, instead pulling off my wet trousers and rummaging in the boot for something else. My hair falls loose out of its ponytail, greasy and stiff around my face.

"It means I need to do better."

As I shuffle out of the Cruiser into wonderfully cool fresh dawn air—sharp inside my prickling lungs—the air meter flashes on for long enough to show it's safe. I take a shaky breath, wedging a door open so fresh air circulates inside the stuffy cabin.

"I want water," Harry says, hurrying on his outdoor gear and following.

"In a minute. We'll have to find some."

Gorse thorns snag my legs as I fret about water and fuel. Yet the sight of familiar low bushes cheers me—perhaps we'll find some fruiting in the upland heaths soon and Harry will get to try blueberries too.

I spin on the spot—Harry's not by my side. Braver than I'd like now, he's further down the slope, crouching at the edge of the murky brown floodwater we came through last night—it stretches out beyond him, bushes and trunks and debris breaking up the still surface.

"Harry!"

His head snaps round and he shoots to his feet as I race down to him.

A few seconds later I'm swiping his dripping upturned mug from his hands.

He fidgets with the cuffs of his too-long sleeves as I pull his mask back up. "My mouth was dry."

"Please say you didn't drink it?"

"There was like a rainbow and Sue said her children went up the rainbow bridge and wave at her sometimes if she spots one, so I thought . . ."

Oily drops swirl on the surface in the pale dawn light.

"Water isn't safe unless I tell you it is! You know that—" I stop, Harry trembling.

He stays close as we walk back to the car. I steady him as he trips, clumsy amongst the rushes in his too-tight shoes. Why couldn't I have kept the angry tone from my voice?

He touches his gurgling stomach, making a face.

"How—how much did you drink?" I say as softly as I can.

He fiddles with his cuffs.

"A whole mugful?"

He shrugs.

"Two? Three?"

He doesn't answer.

I stop. "You have to try to be sick, get the bad water out."

Harry shakes his head, backing up. "I'm sorry, Mummy."

"I'll help you." I clean my hands as best I can. He's still shaking his head as I press my fingers into his mouth. He squirms as they hit the back of his throat, but I have my other arm wrapped around him, pinning him to me. A dribble of vomit splutters up. "Is that all?"

He shrinks away, coughing and heaving.

"I'm sorry, Harry. Bad dust and tiny bacteria can be in the water outside. You know this. And it gets collected and grows in floodwater and rivers and ponds," I try to explain in a softer voice. "Water is like a big train picking up dust as it moves, and the bigger it is, the more passengers it collects. You understand?"

I pick up Luna from his cupholder prison and brush every crevice and curve out. He's accepted with a very quiet "thank you" when I finally hand him over.

Yet Harry still avoids my eye, grimacing as he swallows as we sit in the front seats spooning up cold preserved runner beans. We drink the foul-tasting gloopy water they're sat in too and Harry has a spoon of moistened charcoal powder. I wish we could have woken earlier and got a fire going to heat up the beans and filter and boil-clean some water for drinking—it would have avoided all of this. But it's getting light now, rays like warm honey punching through clear patches in the rear windscreen. And I think of how it was in Sheffield, and how close Glasgow is.

We have enough dried meat and preserved fruits and veggies to last about five weeks. More than enough to get up to Arisaig. A hundred and thirty-odd miles to go. But even if the roads are good and the engine hangs on, the last bar of the tank isn't going to stretch much further—electric mode working or not. I fret about that container of old gummy fuel.

Harry looks flushed already, though that could be from the forced vomiting. What we have could get us part of the way back to Derbyshire. Sue might know what else to do for him. I flick through my foraging book, for herbs that might make you empty your stomach, all the time feeling hot and worried that maybe she was right: I shouldn't have brought him here.

I check the map and the route south to Balloch and—just the other side of the village—the start of the road that heads north on the west side of the loch. I make a decision. The engine stumbles into life on the second try and I let out my held breath. Turning us around, I let gravity help us drift downhill. The wheels slow as they hit water and I press the accelerator gently until the water ripples softly either side of us. The tyres pull left and right again, threatening us off the edge of the submerged road, and I grip the wheel hard.

"Why are we doing a zigzag?" Harry says.

There's a whine in his voice that makes me choose a careful, light tone. "It's the wheels, and I'm also trying to stay on the road—we're less likely to get lost again if I do. Or sink."

He clutches his stomach. "I don't like it."

"Sorry." I squeeze his knee, looking ahead towards the cluster of houses at the southern tip of the loch.

I find myself watching Harry in my peripheral vision. My foot taps the brakes as I see Luna going up towards his mouth.

"What are you doing!" My blood fizzes, but I try to quickly soften my voice, especially as Luna is as brushed clean as I can make him. "Not in your mouth, remember, it's a bad habit in case things are dirty."

His face crumples, hugging Luna and his knees to his chest instead.

By the time we get to Balloch, the road is still several feet underwater and both of us are still fractious, my mouth dry and my head aching. Wrecked houses loom out of the water, seaweed-brown with mottled grey growths like huge riverbank toads.

Where the Lomond Bridge should be there's nothing but warty brown pillars amongst the churning dark water of the river mouth, resembling river demons poised to strike.

We take the flooded side streets slowly, the strange, deserted, sunken village putting me on edge, both of us falling silent. The next few crossings are missing too, and we soon head out into puddled heathland, the river on our right.

The fuel gauge has hit red and the engine is gasping.

Fuck. I keep checking the map, and Harry's flushed face. Glasgow growing bigger again in the windscreen. Everything inside me squeezes tight in panic.

Focus, Katie.

Time to gamble on the crap boat stuff.

I keep the engine running as I pour it in, drops of viscous fuel spitting out at me.

The Cruiser feels worryingly different immediately. The engine groans and hisses against the oncoming wind and the right pedal feels less responsive, the ball of my foot aching as I press ever harder as we wobble towards an old flat stone bridge at last, rusted iron railings on either side.

A tangle of tree trunks and branches and rusted cars bar the way across, the railings torn open in several places.

"Keep watch," I whisper.

Squelching through silty puddles, I pull bigger branches clear, eyeing up a route weaving between the three larger trunks. The rusted car in the middle needs to turn out of our way. A decayed shape is slumped across the back seats, smothered by algae and weeds, tatters of cloth showing through. The front driver's side window is wound down, not cracked or shattered, and for a split second I feel sick. The railings are full of padlocks—some in the shape of love hearts. I can picture it: the driver choosing this special spot to die and lie forever alongside someone they loved already dead in the back.

But there's no body up front as I reach my hand in to yank up the handbrake and force the steering wheel round. And when I straighten up again, I look at Glasgow in the distance and I wonder if the driver saw that too and saw hope, chose to live instead, and bundled up against the storm, fought their way there.

The car rolls after a good push and tips off the edge—I watch it, wondering if I'm right—that beloved person going with it to sink into the muddy water below. I regret not burying them properly.

And in a daze, I don't notice the sour smell of vomit straight away as I get back in our Cruiser. I swivel round—a brief guilty sort of relief that maybe he's now fully expelled what he drank. But he's curled up on *our* back seats, looking sweaty and pale, holding his stomach.

"Harry, you OK?"

He shakes his head. "Feel cold and bad."

"You'll be OK," I say breathlessly. Repeating it. "Good you've been properly sick. You'll feel better soon." I try to smile, reassure him.

Yet I poke about in the vomit in the footwell, unable to not search for specks, as if I need to confirm my fear. I know they might be too small to see, but I look anyway. They might have lodged themselves inside Harry's stomach, might right now be grinding against the walls of his intestines, finding their way into his bloodstream, getting gushed along through arteries and veins. Orbiting his heart, his brain.

I scoop the vomit up with the onion jar lid, flinging it out the window, and pull the blankets over Harry though he soon complains he's too hot.

We're closer to Arisaig and Jack than Derbyshire now. I tell myself it makes sense to keep going.

"It's OK," I repeat. "We'll get you somewhere warm soon, get you clean water and a hot dinner. You'll feel better then." I try to convince myself that drinking particles isn't as bad as breathing it in. Worse odds then. If it's swallowed at least there's still a chance it could pass right through you and out the other end. Not get lodged in the labyrinth of his lungs. Cause inflammation, scarring that'd make his lungs harden, taking his breath away . . . nor get pumped straight from his lungs to his heart . . . narrowing and stiffening it, making it race . . .

I watch Harry's pale shivery face in the rear-view as we wind through and rumble over the bridge and onto the road west. Finally, we turn north, and mountains lie ahead. A glimmer of hope and excitement warms inside me, a fraction of what I might have felt when Jack and I came on our adventure to Scotland. I wonder if Jack remembered that feeling. If he came this way.

The old road is layered in leaves and silty puddles. Old ash and pine from the banks of Loch Lomond are bedraggled and spreadeagled across the right side of the road, dull yellow and brown, and squelching as we pass.

An old layby is almost hidden amongst the trees on the left. Harry peers blearily out at the crisp white trunks and bright pure yellow leaves as I pull into it, deep orange bracken carpeting the ground.

I hesitate with the engine running, more nervous than ever to turn it off with Harry ill. Yet the instant calming silence when I do soothes my terrible dehydration headache, and I scramble over to check on Harry. His skin is clammy and hot, though he shivers in his blanket.

I get him to sip the last dregs of liquid from the runner bean jar, which dribbles out the corner of his mouth. And I try offering him peas and fruits. He tries a few bites, grimacing as he swallows.

The lingering damp aroma of vomit doesn't make me feel hungry either.

I search for something else that might tempt him. My mother always made me toast and chicken soup. Brought me digestive biscuits and hot lemon tea. Jack and I swallowed activated charcoal and antibacterial supplements. I finger the jar of ordinary charcoal dust and pick up a spoon again.

There's a soft splashing in the distance, coming from the south.

I freeze where I am, crouched in the boot.

The noise gradually gets louder.

A band of fear tightens my lungs, making it hard to gasp in a breath.

I scrabble to the driver's seat. Shove the key into the ignition, but I don't turn it. Don't make a sound. The layby should curve to rejoin the road ahead, but I haven't checked to make sure I had another exit. And now the yellow and white birches feel too close and choking, even as they feel safe and sheltering at the same time.

The gentle whir of what must be an electric car, its tyres spinning on the ground, passes by and gradually disappears up the road, heading north, with a silky splashing sound as the wheels pass through the shallow floodwater.

30

Seven Months Before the Storm

"Don't cower," Adders shouts over the din of London outside: trams, hooting cabs, sirens and a drone whizzing overhead. The air drifting in through the open sash windows brings a thick waft of exhaust fumes, lime blossom, and chip-shop grease.

He bounces on the spot, tall and broad-shouldered, grinning as our eyes meet. I feel suddenly how much I want him to like me. Jack's best friend—*best man*—like a brother, Jack always says. They're the same age, though Adders looks slightly older; I think it's the brown hair peppered with grey and his deep smile creases. He reads a lot too, always has interesting perspectives on things and that same stoic calmness as Jack.

"That's it, straighten up: if you feel weak, the brain will follow suit." He chuckles at whatever look Jack behind me has just given him.

I didn't know Jack was coming today—I feel even more awkward with him watching too. Though it was nice to arrive together, with Adders excited to see us and gush over the ring, which my finger feels odd without, having taken it off for the first time since Jack gave it to me two weeks ago.

I stay on my toes and try to copy Adders. He said we'd do prowler sled pushes and lunges—functional strength training for my running—but wanted to box to warm up and build confidence. I need more of that. I feel a little like I do in my meetings for work.

With Adders and Jack toned and muscled, just baggy shorts on—*confident* and sure of themselves. And me: skinny and stiff, awkward, like a *girl* with silly tree-hugging ideas in rooms full of mostly men.

"Your mind's elsewhere," Adders says suddenly, stopping. "You OK?"

"Yep." I wipe my sweaty forehead on my sleeve. Now that I'm here, I'm not sure I'm prepared to swing punches at Adders, even with gloves and pads on. "I'm just . . ."

"Preoccupied. She's two weeks into the dream job," Jack says.

"Yeah, I guess. I want to make it work, I'm just not great under pressure."

"Well," Adders says, "you got through the interviews and landed the gig, didn't you?"

I nod, wondering if Jack's mentioned to him all the many embarrassing and unsuccessful interviews before that . . .

Which is why I signed up for this event. "I used to love running, and I thought this half-marathon would be a good achievement for me—"

Adders nods. "So that confidence spreads into other areas of your life."

"Yeah." I smile, relieved to be understood. "I don't want to blow this chance with this job—I need to sound knowledgeable, convince landowners. I've worked so hard, all these boring retail jobs, the volunteering and internships since graduating. If I can make some of these rewilding projects get off the ground, I stand a better chance of being signed on for more time after my four-month contract is up." I finish with a small grin, embarrassed at having rambled on like this in front of Adders.

"I get it," he says, nodding. "Come on then, let's build you that backbone."

"Feeling like you could do someone damage might give you that, I reckon!" Jack chuckles behind me.

"That's what the army gave us, Kate," Jack adds as we spar again, making Adders and me shoot each other quizzical looks and laugh. "Backbone!" Jack laughs too. "Not easy fists!"

And I feel myself relaxing a bit, moving less awkwardly, my muscles warmed up, less self-conscious now as I hit the pads.

"*I mean*—bar the events of the final tour"—Jack continues— "doing hard things out on tour, whether physically or otherwise out of my comfort zone, made me feel capable the next time, helped me go on and do other hard things."

"I did take up motivational speaking!" Adders nods between punches, laughing again. "And Jack must've told you how much that makes me sweat. God, I feel sick each time. The trick is knowing you can walk through that fire your anxiety tells you is there."

"It's all just energy, isn't it?" I say, hitting the pads, one two, one two. "Nerves? If I can just channel it."

"Absolutely, use it, flip it round," Adders says. "If the thing's worth doing, it feels amazing afterwards."

One, one, two.

"So, *if* you had to fight"—Adders continues, correcting one of my uppercuts—"chances are they'd be bigger and heavier than you. If you don't know how to get around that, they'd always win by that advantage alone."

"I guess I would just aim for the throat or between the legs?" I get a good strong jab in, making a satisfying smack on Adders's left pad, and I feel like I'm starting to enjoy myself.

"That's wishful thinking," Jack says. "Chances are they're not going to be standing still, an easy target."

"Get your chin down, fists up," Adders calls. "That's it. Now rain knees and elbows at them—they're your best weapons if they're outpunching you or have you trapped and there's no room to swing a punch. Aim for the jaw, lower ribcage—ought to hurt!— solar plexus to knock the wind out of them, neck and groin—soft tissue!—and yeah, balls too."

I practise the movements. Jabs with the elbows. Thrusts with the knees.

"Feel free to bite too," Jack adds.

I laugh. "Do you think I'll need this at my landowner meeting tomorrow?"

"If not, maybe at the half-marathon!" Jack laughs, mimicking the start line with his elbows out.

"No, seriously"—Adders laughs—"it can be a scrum at the start, don't let them push you over."

Jack jumps up and suddenly his arm is tight around my neck. "You need to believe you're capable of doing it. Now, come on, you amazing woman, how do you get out of this?"

I'm giggling, it feels almost too playful and intimate in front of Adders, Jack's breath on my neck, his mouth right there, his other arm around my middle. "Jack—"

Adders is laughing. "Sort it out, lovebirds!"

"Get out of it," Jack insists. One of his legs hooks around mine, threatening to tip me.

I struggle against him, grasping the arm around my neck, trying to prise him off.

"No," Adders says, "it's no good trying to use your strength against his. Wriggle and struggle until you can get an elbow in."

I do, twisting and sweating against Jack.

"Nearly."

We tussle a bit more, getting hotter and more claustrophobic, and I twist harder. A gap opens up. I snap back my elbow and hit something firm.

"There it is!" Adders says—as Jack grunts—full of warmth, the words ringing in my mind.

Jack lets me go, gripping his side, and they're both grinning at me.

There's no way I'm ever going to need to elbow someone in the ribs for real, but I feel better for it, laughing and grinning too.

31

The night is black outside. Leaves rustle all around us. I can't sleep. Don't want to. I'm listening for the car. I am almost certain it hasn't come back south, that I haven't drifted off and missed it. The longer the night goes on, though, the more I doubt myself.

Harry has finally fallen asleep in the back, bundled up in all our blankets and coats.

We push on to reach Jack, or we turn back.

Not that Jack, Andy or Sue could help if plastic microparticles are careering around Harry's bloodstream.

I try not to think of the flat, of the careful ways I filtered water and boarded up the windows on breezy days. All my efforts to forage enough good food and build winter stockpiles. How I managed to keep him fed and hydrated every day. And safe.

Jack. Turn back. Either way, I need sleep so I have enough energy to face whatever needs facing tomorrow. For Harry.

I sink down across the front seats, the gearstick digging into my stomach. It's miserably cold, making my chest ache as it settles inside me. The faint smell of vomit and onions still lingers. I should curl up with Harry, but the only way I'm going to sleep is if I'm within touching distance of the ignition.

When I wake, my eyes snap open to yellowed daylight.

Harry is coughing on the back seats.

I scramble over to him—wincing at my prickling lungs—and

lift him to sitting, bringing the preserved jar of peas to his lips so he can sip the disgusting liquid. It dribbles down his chin in globs. His head sags against me, skin sallow in the light filtering through the leaves.

"I'm hungry, Mummy."

I pass him the hard bulrush cakes and Sue's smoked venison jerky.

He sniffs at the food. "Was there more mandarins?"

I glance in the back. "Tell you what, if you eat this good protein and carbs to stay strong and you're careful in the car today, tonight you can have the whole tin of mandarins."

His face lights up. "If I follow the rules?"

I nod—showing him that second tin of fruit crammed in my pack to prove it—and smile as he works his jaws on the jerky.

It's possible I missed the car going back south since I fell asleep. Yet I'm sure I would have woken to the tyres cutting through the floodwater.

"Your face is scaredy again." Harry grimaces as he swallows the tough meat. "Are you sure Daddy's not going to be angry like Sim the man?" He rubs at his throat.

"No, of course he isn't . . . And you know I wasn't really *angry* yesterday? Just worried." I put my arms around him. "You know how good our hugs are?"

Harry nods.

"That's how good hugs with Daddy felt—all warm like this, his chest moving up and down as he breathed, just like yours is now."

"I can hug you, Mummy," Harry whispers. "Wholeheart."

"I know, my sweet boy." I kiss his head. "But I'd like you to have Daddy's ones too. It's other people I'm scared of, not him. I'll tell you a secret," I whisper too, making him lean closer. "Daddy made Luna. He carved him out of wood with a knife."

"Really?" Harry sniffs, lifting Luna from his lap to examine.

I touch the wood, seeing Jack's roughed-up hands working at it with a penknife, his mouth blowing away shavings as long thin limbs, a rounded torso and sloped neck emerged, then the rough suggestion of snout, ears and antlers.

"Come on," I say, "let's get moving."

The engine is coaxed into life with three tries and a heavy foot on the accelerator.

Steering through the trees, we slowly pull out onto the road, into an unusually clear, pale-blue day, my spirits rising. Yet as we drive up the A82, I crane forward anxiously at the winding road ahead through the cracked and scratched windscreen.

Harry slumps under his blankets in the passenger seat, frowning, fingers tight around Luna.

We finally reach the end of Loch Lomond. I slow to ford a tributary.

"Mummy! Strong things!"

I jump. On slightly higher ground, there's a huge house, its whitewashed stone gleaming. The windows show heavy repairs, the sturdy shutters pushed open. I spot bookshelves and chandeliers.

As we draw level, I see two children through the trees. Oblivious to us, they jump across a painted hopscotch. I can hear them laughing and the high notes of a piano tinkling indoors. Beyond the children, a huge steamed-up greenhouse has dark green leafy shapes pressing against the windows from inside.

I keep going, gently accelerating away—the electric motor quiet but our unruly wheels clicking and rumbling.

Harry twists to stare back.

My eyes are half-glued to the rear-view mirror too as the miles tick by. Once the diesel engine switches back on, I'm going faster than ever before, faster than the hissing engine wants to. Harry gasps as we bounce over crevices and skid round bends.

"Mummy—" His little face is pale and sweaty.

"They were being looked after there—"

"But children! I wanted to meet them!"

But I think of the rifle lying in the boot. Andy's words as we parted.

My foot gets heavier on the accelerator.

"I don't like it so fast," Harry says, clutching his seat. "Why is the ground so big? Is it going to fall on us?"

I glance at the colossal mountains rising up all around us, making me feel giddy, beautiful god rays breaking around the peaks.

"Your face is scaredy again. You have to tell me!"

I snatch a glance at his little face—serious and studying me.

"Of course not—"

My foot stamps the brakes, everything shunting forwards with a thud, including us. The smell of burning rubber fills the car. Boulders and the rubble of a previous landslide swamp the road.

"I don't like it!" Harry glares at me, though he manages to keep his fists scrunched tight in his lap instead of covering his eyes.

"That doesn't happen often . . . and no harm done," I say, repeating Jack's words aloud.

Making sure we're still both strapped in, I set off across the glistening yellow-orange expanse of Rannoch Moor, up unevenly over rushes and bog myrtle, and tilting down into sponges of golden peat moss.

When the grey granite terraces of Fort William come into view, it's a relief. We drift down the high street, shopfronts peeling and cracked, mustard and brown algae along the pavements and streaking up the encrusted glass and stone in uneven waves from frequent flooding. No abandoned cars. Fort William was a tourist town Before—a hub for outdoor sports—perhaps empty anyway off-season in mid-January. Green algae spores bob towards us from the top end of the street with the breeze, making it feel like we're underwater, watching diatoms and phytoplankton float by on the current. White mushrooms grow in the gaps between cobbles too, like current-smoothed pebbles.

There's a pharmacy halfway down, a big sweep of dried seaweed covering the bottom half of the window. I glance at Harry, now slumped low in his seat, eyes closed, mouth hanging open.

The engine conks out as I slow, dithering. So I stop and decide I might as well go and look. I lock the doors and linger, watching Harry's pasty drawn face, sliding the key into my trouser pocket.

I pull myself away, check my mask is tight and tug the hood of my parka up. The shop door is locked. That reckless feeling that's become familiar since we left Hitchin surges as I wiggle loose a cobble from amongst the algae and mushrooms. The glass cracks as the cobble bounces off it, but it doesn't shatter. I glance at the Cruiser and hurl it harder, then hammer with a larger brick, until the glass turns brittle and white, and I can kick through it.

Inside, strings of dark algae creep around tipped-over shelving, bottles and packets scattered, as if the place has been underwater a lot and everything dislodged. I pick through the disintegrating boxes in a rush, peering at unreadable bottle labels. Harry needs better, *activated* charcoal, and antibacterial metals tablets to fight off the other crap he swallowed in that water, the stuff they touted as alternatives to the almost-magical antibiotics that I remember still working when I was little. What else? Paracetamol? I finger an empty silvery cardboard sleeve amongst piles of "female immunity boosters" melted into the carpet.

My fingers tap a jar that could be multivitamins. Don't know if they'll be any good after all this time, but I stuff a few jars into my pocket.

I find the shelf for activated charcoal—two small jars of black powder sit right at the back, wedged where the shelving above has collapsed. I grab them, my hands buzzing, a smile tugging up the corners of my mouth, imagining all the microparticles Harry may have swallowed getting soaked up and carried safely out of his body.

I spring out of the shop window and across the cobbles to the Cruiser. Harry is still bundled up in the front passenger seat—he seems peaceful now, the sleep healing instead of worrying. I pat my pockets gently, the jars clanking reassuringly. Fort William is still silent. I consider the outdoor clothing shop next door.

Harry does need proper boots up here, to go with Sue's all-in-one. A few minutes more won't matter. I grin to myself. *I* can get him good ones.

I scan the overturned racks and wander into the back room, imagining Harry's face when I give him the boots. In the chaos of misshapen and crumbling cardboard boxes, my heart leaps at the sight of a child's pair of walking boots. Rifling through, I find a few sizes—grey with bright rainbow laces—and stuff them, along with the pills, into a cloth bag. As an afterthought, I take a pair of size six Berghaus for me too—brand-new, brown vegan leather, suede ankle collar. My current pair are still wet and dank.

It suddenly feels like I've been gone a while. I hurry outside— I should just wake Harry up and feed him the activated charcoal now.

I go five strides towards the Cruiser before there's a tingle down my neck. I hear the slap of boots across the slimy cobbles behind me.

Two men march in my direction from a clean, if beaten-up, Volkswagen—gleaming solar panels attached to the roof bars, a cable snaking inside through a window. They close the twenty metres past cafes and shopfronts before I can shake the shock out of my legs.

"Hey! Why didn't you stop way back on the road?"

The hope in his voice makes me pause, as if maybe we know each other and I failed to realize. The man who's shouting is athletic, strong-shouldered, and with a wide, weathered face. Both of them have rounder, healthier faces than us, or Sim, or Andy and Sue, or anyone else I've come across.

"You driving about in *that*—you must have supplies: fuel, grease, power?"

He's only a few steps away and now I can see his eyes are blood-shot, irises dull and cloudy. His hand searches the air to his side as if expecting to find something there.

"I'm here, Bill." The other guy runs to catch up.

"I can still see you," Bill snaps. He turns those eyes back on me. "I need supplies to fix up some of our turbines, keep our glasshouses running—get more of it operational. I have a kid, and a growing little community, we're trying to ensure they have a future they can survive in." I can almost imagine it—all the books, music, company that Sim spoke about, and crops grown systematically in well-lit, irrigated and temperature-controlled, safe soil. And those children, playing with Harry. And yet I'm inching towards the Cruiser. Jack could be so close.

"I don't know if I can help you, I—"

"Of course, a fucking *English* girl." He rolls his eyes, chuckling.

"Easy, Bill," the other guy says, "she seems spooked, probably one of the hiders." He smiles at me without blinking, sharp blue eyes with heavy lids and grey messy brows.

"Come on, girl," Bill says again. "You know, if we make it right for them, it won't have been an end, not really, and we won't have to worry about dying ourselves—nothing's so bleak if we know things continue? That we haven't been wiped off the face of the Earth and obliterated?"

"Always trying to outrun death." The other guy smiles, like he's well used to Bill's philosophies. "Bill here was always colour-blind too, poor cunt can't see yellow or red—world's all grey to him now!"

"At least it allows me to see how shit it is!" Bill grunts. "Simplified, even the leaves look the same shapes to me, same fucking species—I turned up to the protests Before, I know diversity was what made so much life possible. Now we've got to save it from the brink. It's going to take a long time for the world to recover, so we have to work hard to grasp a life for our children, our community, for the future." He wheezes, trying to catch his breath. "And they can thrive, you need more than food and water and solid innovation to really survive, people need community and culture too—"

"Sorry, I can't help," I say more firmly, glancing sideways at the Cruiser, trying to catch sight of Harry.

"We *should* be helping each other, not keeping things for ourselves—what good is that? The kids are the future! We fucked it up for them already, but we have to leave them *something*." His misty eyes narrow as they scan my face, drifting down the rest of my body. "*You* especially should be nurturing this future community."

My boots crunch on a loose cobble—the top of Harry's head is visible in the passenger seat. Bill grabs hold of my arms from behind, fingers digging into me.

"Please, don't just run." His hot sour breath is on my neck, his warm solid chest pressing into my back. "My wife didn't make it, but she helped the first month—she would have dug in still if her lungs hadn't been so burned and she got to live. What's your name?"

As I hesitate, he thrusts his arms around me instead—one around my stomach, the other around my neck. Tight. He's heavier than me. Stronger.

"I'm not going to apologize for not being her!" I find myself shouting, a sudden rush of hot anger making the words spill out. The other guy is peering in the back of the Cruiser. Harry's little head is moving between the front seats. "I didn't get to decide who lived!"

Bill's body stiffens and the other guy's head whips back to me.

"You can now!" Bill says. "Is your life worth more than my kid's future? Thomas, that's his name. And there's more, there's a group of twenty of us now, five children. *So far.* Don't you see? It's not really the plastic we have to worry about—we have to live with it, maybe one day more and more of it will be buried, only dangerous if it's disturbed—the climate crisis was always the bigger bugger and it's still coming, we have to at least make sure they can survive!"

I don't answer.

"Let's just see what you've got, what supplies. You hiders are selfish little snowflakes, as if some horror has been landed on you and only you. Wake up, bitch."

Bill's arms still pin me to him as the other guy feels down the outside of my pocket. He finds the key, starts inserting his fingers to retrieve it. Grinning at me. "Why are women always so hysterical?"

The pressure of his warm hand against my thigh sends another hot wave through me. My T-shirt has come untucked, my stomach exposed to the cool air and Bill's hairy forearm. I can feel his fingers on my bare hip. I can smell his sweat and the scent of woodsmoke and something metallic on his clothes. The Fear pumps up through me—thick and paralysing. I'm holding my breath. I can't see Harry anymore.

The other guy grins, unlocking the boot, pulling out our things: boxes of roots and jars. Andy's rifle.

"You've been able to forage," Bill grunts.

"There's still food out there," I find myself saying, trying to sound calmer, more placating, "you just need to know how to forage, where to look, how to grow things . . ."

"Nothing looks like it does in the books. We're just relying on propagating veggies, keeping a few animals. *You* could help us." His deep voice is right at my ear.

I open my mouth, but the words get stuck in my throat. His rounded gut moves against my back as he breathes, his heat and sweat all around me, my leg still tingling from the unpleasant retrieval of the key. Muscles all squeezing tight.

Everything feels bleary. I'm shrinking into make-believe. I'm

245

not here. Sinking into a dark hole, away from fingers and pressure and sweat.

The hooter blares from inside the Cruiser, ripping me back to the cobbled street, eyes clear. Bill flinches, his grip slackening. The other man is making for the driver's door, Harry's desperate little fingers trying to push down the lock.

I throw myself into a twist, my forehead catching Bill's chin. Yanking myself back the opposite way, I find enough movement to jab my elbow into his ribs. He grunts.

There it is! Adders cheers in my head.

Once more and Bill is wheezing. The arm around my middle disappears, my face squashed against his shoulder with the arm he still has around my neck. Harry is being yanked out into the street like a ragdoll—both men cheering as if he is a trophy to bring home.

"One more for our future!"

I'm not conscious of reaching for Dad's knife from my belt but suddenly the cool blade is in my hand, and my arm jerks almost of its own accord. Hard. Pain shoots up my wrist as the blade connects with flesh and scrapes into bone. Bill howls, folding forwards. And I run. Towards the driver's door. Towards Harry.

32

The other man turns and pulls away just as I slash upwards, so the knife bites across his shoulder instead of the hand that grips Harry. But it's enough for him to let go, to stagger back a few steps. I bundle Harry up into the Cruiser and throw myself in on top of him, slamming the door against the hands still trying to stop us leaving. I don't care that they crunch; I slam until the door shuts and I can force the lock down.

"The other key!" I croak, groping with my free hand for the one I lost in Hitchin.

"Mummy!" Harry cries, pulling something shiny from between my seat and the gearstick.

I grab the silver key, plant it into the ignition. I hear more of our stuff being dragged out behind us as I try the key once, twice, jars smashing, the water-filtering barrel bouncing on the cobbles. Third time lucky.

"Bitch!"

Punch it.

The Cruiser screeches forwards, the boot door bouncing up and down behind us. The cloth bag is still tangled round my shoulder, wedging me forwards in the seat.

Harry is crying, gasping.

My right arm is covered in sticky too-dark red, the bloody knife in my footwell.

Disappearing in the rear-view mirror, Bill is on his back, the other guy stumbling on the cobbles, loading the rifle. Bitch. The word cements in my head with the crack of the rifle firing. The bullet slams into a back passenger window as we lurch round benches and lamp posts on the pedestrianized street. Snatching a glance in the side mirror, I see the glass whiten and splinter—resisting and catching it.

He bends to reload. I watch to see if Bill gets up.

I am a bitch. Another crack. Another punch to the back of the Cruiser, making me more grateful than ever for Jack's protective choice of car.

Harry squirms out from beside me and scrambles over the gearstick to the passenger seat. The Cruiser is wild, tugging against me, the ripped tyre finally blown out and flapping and slapping as it spins. We swerve, crunching along walls, the wheel rim rumbling. Another crack and the exhaust bangs, red sparks in the rear-view. Harry's terrified face catches my eye.

Energy bubbles up through me, making me suddenly laugh, even though the horror of my knife slicing into another person's chest is replaying in my head.

Concentrate, Katie.

"You did great," I say to Harry, squeezing the dimpled leather of the steering wheel, trying to force it straight.

"Did they bite you?" Harry whispers, clinging to his seat. "They were bad men."

I want to agree with him as I glance in the rear-view at our empty boot. As we career through the streets, banging and rattling. As I feel the unpleasant fizz still in my skin from hands and arms and gut pressed against my body.

Yet it's not my blood. And I felt Bill's determination; he had his own hope to make things right.

It takes a few turns after leaving the high street, as I ease off the speed and untangle myself from the cloth bag, for me to understand: Bill won't be getting back up. The bubbling-giggling feeling goes cold.

I can't help wondering about Bill's glasshouse community as Harry examines his new boots, lovingly stroking the bright laces.

And about how skinny and small Harry is compared to those children playing hopscotch, how he could have been one of them.

I shake my head. It doesn't matter. Too late now. And everything but Jack is low-hanging, but less sweet, fruit.

My hands are clenched around the steering wheel.

We need to get out of here. Make it to the dense, dizzyingly bright yellow trees at the edge of the loch. There's probably enough food in my pack for today. We might make it to Arisaig on the fuel we have, if the engine holds out—it's still grumbling, shooting bad fuel straight down the exhaust to pop and bang. All we have to do is reach Jack.

Bitch. My thoughts feel jumbled, but I know it used to matter to me, Before. Fixing the world, leaving it better, being helpful.

Squinting through the shattered windscreen, the blood drying and itchy up my trembling arm, I smudge away tears. I wonder if one of the children playing was Bill's Thomas.

"What is it?" Harry turns, frowning out through the bouncing boot door.

"It's only . . . thirty-five miles west . . ." I gasp out the words with each breath, guilty for feeling like getting to Jack will make it all feel less wrong. ". . . to Arisaig . . . to where . . . Daddy . . . said he'd be."

"Is that far?"

Breathe. Push the word out: "No." And yet the past five years all pile up in my head, heavy: yes. And I'm suddenly sinking, exhausted. Everything I might say crowds my mind, and what Jack might think, if and when he looks at Harry.

Blackness edges my vision. I try to suck in the fresh salty air whirling in from the back of the car.

We reach the trees and the lochside road and I press my foot down harder again, as if my speed right now—as if every moment—after all this time, matters.

Loch, trees and rocky heathland rocket past in a blur of black and yellow, the Cruiser bouncing and pulling in all directions, wheels clicking, groaning and slapping, the road disappearing beneath loch water.

As we near the end of the black water of the second loch, the

Cruiser judders through the floodwater. Spray hits the windows. Harry flinches.

The diesel engine sputters, making me press ever harder on the accelerator. Yet we keep slowing down.

The hum of the engine suddenly cuts out and the drag of the water pulls us short, leaving us in silence.

I sit tight, still gripping the wheel. Just waterlogged trees and loch on one side, sheer cliff on the other.

Harry is holding his breath. "Mummy?"

Water ripples just below the windows. I try the ignition, over and over. Nothing.

Harry leans away from his window, scrunching his eyes shut, and even to me the ripples could be something looming towards us under the dark surface.

The Cruiser soon feels cold and I find myself smoothing the steering wheel, tapping the gearstick, breathing in the scent of the old seats.

Harry watches, his expression sad. "Is it too tired?" he whispers in the silence, running a finger over the four-wheel-drive button.

I nod, cleaning the dried blood off myself, and reaching for my backpack hung on the back of my seat. Everything's gone from the boot—food, water, clothes—except the groundsheet, laden with glass shards, and I lash that back to the outside of my pack.

"Put them on." I nod at the new boots that look closest to his size and hand him the all-in-one from the outdoor gear sack, as I lace up my own new boots, their gleaming waterproofing and Gore-Tex label reassuring with all that water outside.

"They're too hard! And I told you this is too swishy, I don't like it." Harry still has a wild look in his eyes, glancing at the still-bloody knife in my footwell.

"You'll get used to them." I wipe the blade and put it away on my belt, before pulling his legs and arms into the suit, lacing the boots and pressing the toes. "Plenty of room." I thread his pack onto his back.

He sits motionless as I wind my window down. The air meter shows green, though it's breezy, and I glimpse overcast sky above the trees and rock.

"I know you still feel sick, and what happened back there was . . . scary. But the Cruiser's stuck; we have to go this last bit on foot." I study the Scottish OS spread out still on the dash. The dark green line of the Fort William to Arisaig road is only the length of my hand; we must have already travelled a good portion of it. We've gambled this far; if we can just make it to Jack . . .

"We might be there in a few hours." I feel a surge of that energy that keeps eclipsing the horror behind us.

"Will Daddy have a warm fire like we did in the flat? Like Andy and Sue?"

"Yes, probably."

Harry sighs heavily, frowning at me and up at the steep rock, squinting. "What if the mountain falls on me?"

"You'll be fine . . . and don't forget the mandarins I promised."

He sits a little straighter. "But isn't it bad water?"

"I'll carry you through the worst bit."

Unhappy in his gear, he is stiff and unhelpful as I struggle to pull the mittens attached to his sleeves over his hands "for not-touching." Eventually I agree he can hold his mask for now, but only until I say he must put it on.

He's still craning to scrutinize the rock as I get out first, getting instantly drenched up to my knees. With my backpack on my front, I help him out onto my back, his little feet hitching to avoid the water. Staggering forwards, the ever-present prickling ache in my chest is soon a sore breathlessness. My new boots pinch and rub, cold seeping in at the ankles.

The inundated road bends round the cliff, and as soon as there's a bit of exposed yellowed grassy slope, I head up as far as I can to get away from the water, before having to set Harry and the bag down. The hillside spreads out around us to the west, low mountains to the east, that breeze picking up.

"It's wet!" Harry stands with his feet close together, teeth chattering, looking very pale.

I nod. I can't speak yet, still gasping and wheezing.

Grey droplets land on my coat sleeves.

"Where's your mask?" I cry.

Harry flinches, hands at his ears as if feeling for it, and I rifle through his pack and mine. Looking back at the glimpse of the Cruiser between cliff and trees, I see the loch water has risen fast with the tide, now splashing in through the opened window.

"You had it in your hands!" I scan the water, as if I might be able to spot and retrieve it, but I know it's gone.

Dread clogs my throat. The sky is thick with grey, the haze blurring the furthest slopes.

Yet in the distance, down towards the faint blur of the sea and across the folds of rich orange-brown hillside to the west, there's a promising cluster of white specks. Arisaig is the only village in this direction—those may be the outermost cottages.

I don't wait for my breathing to calm. I tie my adult-sized mask tight around Harry's little face and strip out of my T-shirt to fold and wind the thin woven fabric around my face in as many layers as possible. We start scrambling upslope over the tufts and spongy mounds.

The rain plinks down on our hoods and shoulders in sharp heavy droplets. I keep plunging knee-deep into blood-hued cushions of wet moss and peat, and just catching Harry before he stumbles.

We have to rest further up when I can't gasp another wheezy breath in, pins and needles starting to numb my hands and feet. Harry slumps to his knees in the damp grass, retching as I croak in breaths. Breeze spirals round us, ruffling our hair as I pull his hood up again and lash it tight, grey rain dripping from our coats.

"Is the wind angry, Mummy?" Harry's mask-muffled voice is snatched away.

I twist the ring on my finger in frantic circles, slack dead bodies whirring in my head.

We just have to reach one of those cottages. Jack is not far now.

More clouds roll in, turning the grass and moss grey and billowing, and the afternoon dim and shadowy. The air is cold and damp, sharp and stinging inside my chest as we move again. The small cubes of those cottages in the distance fade into the grey downfall, but I try to stare exactly at the spot, so I won't lose it.

33

I'm trudging through the gloom, sploshing across rushes and peat-bog, knees juddering, threatening to give way. My pack is heavier than ever. And I'm dragging Harry, holding a blanket over us to keep the rain from his face.

I stumble and land on my hands and knees in something wet and cold. I've lost my gloves. Rain pummels me—cold hard loaded rain. My lungs are hot, the irritation that has felt like sandpaper scraping open and shut since that night in Sheffield now feels like a ball of thorny bramble sat inside my chest, growing bigger and sharper as I inhale. I shouldn't get cold and wet. Or what good am I to Harry?

Harry! There, a foot. Then the soaked heavy weave of the blanket and the slick snowsuit. He's limp and exhausted. I haul him up.

And I freeze: pain flares. A hot angry squeezing pain as my heart beats. Like it never has before. Not even last winter when it first gave that wince of pain that so terrified me.

Lightning flashes—once, twice, then all around—the storm heading towards the sea, which is suddenly visible again over the next rise. That row of cottages is close. I fold an arm over my chest, pulling Harry across the wet boggy grass. He yelps as his boots splosh through puddles, the grey matter on the surface swirling artistically like a watercolour.

The pain is making me dizzy, like walking with an arrow through my chest. Making me remember those dead deer, stiff on the tracks, putrid flesh.

We reach the remains of crumbling tarmac as the rain eases on our hillside, the grey storm still all around us, and I imagine Jack and his mother—and later in Jack's teenage years, his stepfather too—trundling up this last stretch with their caravan. Arisaig just beyond these first cottages—they would have seen rows of white-washed houses and steep winding streets, deep-green gorse thickets with lemon-yellow flowers on the windy cliffs, views down to pale sandy beaches and blue waters. That harbour and the Old Library Lodge.

Jack knows this area well, perhaps that's why he picked it. Less chance of other people too. Perhaps he took to hunting like Andy; I can imagine him with a rifle and stores of meat. I squeeze Harry's hand.

"I don't like it too big," Harry whispers. We can smell it now, the salt on the stiff sea breeze.

I remember that jealous feeling that came over me at the house in Derbyshire, quickly replaced by the dread of finding a body. I wouldn't have really wished Jack alone and lonely, not really. Finding him alive is everything, no matter what.

No matter if Harry has a new mummy in the future; he'd have Jack! I'd have one last hug.

My head spins. "Maybe it's best if I go alone, first. Make sure it's safe. Explain. Y-you stay here?" I help Harry onto the brick wall next to the road, out of the wet. His new shoes are covered in mud, dulling the bright rainbow laces.

"Don't go where I can't see you." He shivers, those amber-brown eyes bloodshot and weary—worrying me—as he looks out at the sea and grey around us. He shimmies further under the branches of an elder bush.

"I won't."

Alone, I slog on along the last bit of road, until I reach the row of cottages overlooking the sea. At first I don't know what I'm look-ing at—a blood-red fringe to the coast, not visible back where I left Harry . . . algae, thick and clotted. The road forks, right and upslope to the cottages, and straight ahead to the harbour road, which then bends right and down, straight down to a drop into nothing, just choppy seawater below.

Trees and bushes with slimy black leaves bob in the red water amongst green-black kelp and rubble. The red meets the deep blue of the sea a few hundred metres out, finger-like tendrils bleeding out.

My stomach lurches. The steep hairpin road should zigzag down through rows of homes to the seafront where the Old Library was. Jack and I parked the Subaru right next to the harbour, the yak of gulls all around us.

I stumble along the row of wrecked cottages, forcing my way into each. Only the furthest one, on higher ground, hasn't been completely flooded in the past and caved in. All stink of damp and decay. All are empty.

I lean against the doorway of the last cottage, trying to swallow, but the sea air is blowing right through my T-shirt mask, leaving salt on my lips, and itching down the back of my dry throat, pulling those thorns tighter in my chest.

There's still one stubborn "Talk to us" Samaritans plaque screwed into the brick wall near that hairpin to nowhere. I imagine it mocking Jack too, if he stood here, perhaps as he waited for me to come—his last just-in-case hope. Heavy with guilt and loss. I wonder if that road was quite so eroded away—if he saw that drop to a bloody shore?

I hope not.

A sound rings in my head, like when I hit my head at the flat. I stare at the red water, my legs and arms starting to shake. Crawling up from the pit of my stomach, the Fear pulls at my ribcage and the hot pain of my heart. I look again at the wall. At this row of cottages. This can't be all that's left of Arisaig. It can't be gone. There can't be nothing here.

An awful inhuman wail bursts out of me, quickly becoming a spluttering cough.

The wind buffets me as if in response and I rock on my feet, shivering. I should have known. I should have realized that it was Jack who left the Cruiser in the garage downstairs, should have found the key, should have found him sooner . . .

I almost had hold of him!

The cold sea air is burning my lungs, that squeezing pain of my heart hunching me over. I cough up more yuck, coating the inside of my makeshift mask.

There's nothing to do but turn back for Harry. So I turn on the spot. Put one foot forward, then the other.

Harry is still there where I left him, under the brown-splotched gold of the elder shrub, feet dangling from the wall. So small. Sometimes in the flat I forgot how small he was. He seemed to fill the rooms, always be at my side, tripping me up, his hands touching whatever I was touching. But now . . . the low mountains spread out behind him, the massive ash-grey sky pressing in on us above and all around us, and the great mass of black loch and dark sea . . . it all swamps him. That sky rumbles again, threatening more rain, startling him. He's so fragile and small in the midst of it all.

How could I have brought him here?

"Was Daddy there?" Harry asks brightly as I get closer, swinging his legs from his perch. How could I have ever doubted that Jack would have helped him? This precious little person. No matter what.

"No, the sea swallowed everything up." My voice is cracking, flat, and Harry stills his legs and stares fearfully out at it as I pull him down from the wall as best I can, grimacing, and cast around me desperately for what to do next.

34

When I wake up, it's because my chest is burning—lungs like torn bellows rattling open and shut, my heart beating too fast, and flaring with that sharp wincing spark every other beat. My eyes won't open. My mouth is claggy with dry phlegm and the taste of blood.

"Hungry." Harry's voice is muffled under blankets, but he repeats himself as I rub at my crusted swollen eyes until I can creak them open to slits. I half expect not to be able to see. But the room is brighter today as I squint around at it, enough to see clearly the black smattering of mould up every wall in the once-cosy sitting room. Cold leaches out from those damp walls. The fire I lit last night is out and I crawl to it to get it going again. We're soon coughing from the smoke, flames licking through scavenged wood—floorboards from upstairs that I yanked and hacked up yesterday, my fingers still stinging from my clumsy use of the blunt tools I found in the shed outside, a splinter in my thumb throbbing.

The days feel long since that first awful night here, drying out by a fire made from the OS maps for England as kindling and dismantled bits of wood furniture that could be wedged into the fireplace. Sitting close enough that I could feel dust specks sizzle on my itchy red skin as I tried to clean us up. Smashing open the corroded jars of vitamins and charcoal tablets to pick out the least mouldy ones to swallow. Harry, forehead and eyes blotchy and pink, feasting on that last tin of mandarins—happy—and the little food in my pack, not yet knowing all I'd found in the cottage was a decade-old empty bottle of tomato ketchup.

The cottage is oddly quiet today. I go to the window and pull back the curtains and blankets we used to cover the seaward view and stop little eddies of grey damp air from seeping inside. The sky is a brighter hazy grey. After days of pounding rain, it has stopped, though the bucket in the corner still plinks.

"Hungry," Harry repeats, pinching my arm hard, leaving a red mark on my wrist.

"Hey!" I groan, flinching away, the movement burning across those sore bellows of my lungs. Those amber-brown eyes of his are tired and desperate, and I hate how hungry and tired I am—that it seems to make bitterness rise in me, making me have to blink away that faceless man in the dark with Harry's hair and eyes.

Yet it's my fault Harry's suffering. My fault we're here.

I crumple on the floor, striking my forehead with my knuckles, the dull thump bringing a sort of relief. You useless shit, Katie.

But beside me, Harry copies—delicate knuckles hard across his own head—before his face creases and he hugs his empty tummy.

"No, not you, never you. I'm sorry . . ." I rub his head better and kiss his cheeks, guilt rippling through me. He copies *me* after all. No one else.

He looks very thin. His skin grey and tight to his cheekbones. His fingers, clutched round Luna, like spindly birch twigs. I've not looked at him properly for days. Not enough light in the barricaded room to have noticed his eyes sunken and bloodshot, trails of red still weeping from the inside corners. Even his hair is dull and lank. And the cut on his forehead that Sue duct-taped is now exposed, a jagged angry line.

I pull him closer to examine his little nose and mouth—relieved not to see redness and inflammation there too, though his nose is snotty and his lips cracked.

"There's nothing to eat," I croak, my mouth dry too. We've not drunk anything for days either.

I haul myself up and across the sitting room, and out into the hallway to the front door of the cottage. Everything hurts. Even the cut on my hand has opened up again, red and raw, though not bleeding. I imagine it's the same inside my chest—everything red, raw and swollen, stiff and scraping and blistering each time my lungs inflate and deflate. Yet while it's dry, I have to go out; find water, if nothing else. I take a saucepan from the kitchen to collect "dirty" water in and pull on my damp smoky parka. And there, underneath where I'd hung it and my boots, I spot a tin.

"What's the shiny?" Harry asks as I tug out the crinkly plastic-wrapped contents.

I smile grimly. "Plastic."

Harry freezes, peering down at it.

"It's OK, it's not bad like this—quite useful and precious actually. Keeps what's inside preserved and dry."

"We needed that for the stinky chestnuts." Harry sniffs the tin. "Is it food?"

"It's for animals," I say, reading the label. "Winter bird energy balls."

It says clearly *Not for human consumption*, but I scan the ingredients: cut wheat, wheat flour, beef suet, cut maize and black sunflowers.

I shrug. "I guess."

We share a ball. It's greasy and sticky—hard to swallow.

"Is Daddy dead?"

My stomach roils. I can't answer.

"Are *we* going to die?"

I cough on the last bit of fat stuck in my throat.

"Is winter come now and we can't go out?"

"Not yet," I mumble as I shoo him back from the door. I tighten my belt a notch, zip up my coat and open the door before there are any more questions.

It seems so bright and cold as I step out, compared to the dark smoky warmth inside. I close my eyes until I can bear it. Icy air scratches inside my lungs. I shut the door and sit on the step to take shallow careful breaths, heart racing and squeezing with its hot pain.

The track along the front of the cottages has disappeared under a run of brown and grey floodwater and undulating mud—almost indistinguishable from the choppy seascape below. At my feet, the mounds of saturated moss—gold and glistening in the sunlight with ribbons of water oozing through them—make it feel like I'm sat at the very edge of the endless dark sea itself and if I took a step forward into that mud I'd actually plunge straight into its depths.

But I get up. There's nowhere to go but up the slope behind our cottage. So I set off. My boots sink into the grey-red mud, the ground seeming to bleed and rust-coloured specks and midges floating up into the air around me. I pull my mask over my nose and mouth.

When the pain makes me feel faint, I stop, gasping in breaths. Behind and below me now, there's the roof of our cottage and, visible from here, the point where brown floodwater along the coast mixes into the dark blue of the sea, globs of broken-up red algae afloat through it. And ahead of me, I take in the hillside to north, east and south—all wet mustard grasses and purple-black rushes with occasional lumps of granite, fading into the brown of flooded lochs. Water. All around us.

Feeling sick, I hug my chest and start scrambling across the hillside, slipping and sliding, legs soon slick with mud, my sleeves and hands too.

Up and down, inspecting pools and runs looking for clearer water, and leaves for edible plants. I zigzag one way and then another, over unpromising grassy mounds and dips. The stunted pines have stiff thick needles—all vivid red and orange, curling in tufts like old Christmas tinsel that's been dipped in wax. I stuff my pockets full. Hopefully still rich in vitamin C, despite the colour and texture.

But I stagger to a halt, stomach growling. We need more than pine-needle tea!

Harry's probably sat by the fire, his pale skinny face and hungry bloodshot eyes watching the door, waiting for me.

Pressure tingles around my eyes, my face crumpling, tears stinging as they break through blood-crusted ducts.

I look back towards the cottage, head in my hands, taking slow careful breaths, but the pain is dizzying. Tears flow freely down my face, my nose getting snottier and my chest throbbing hotter. I feel myself sway.

There's nothing I can do now, is there? The word rings round my head: NOTHING. Stupid useless bitch. But I don't clunk my idiot head with the heel of my hand like I want to, thinking of Harry's little forehead.

You have no idea what to do now? You do, you always have! Jack is loud in my head, like wearing headphones with the volume too high. It makes me flinch, makes my whole body buzz. *You're going to keep living until you're dead. You're going to keep fighting for yourself. And for Harry. You're not going to watch him die like I did Gale. You're not! You're his mum. Fighting is what you do. You know this.*

But there was food in Hitchin. There were people to help in Derbyshire. God, even Bill might have been useful ... I blink, eyes skimming across the landscape.

Andy and Sue were right: I didn't know when to stop.

I wanted Jack to hold *me*, to love *me*—as well as love Harry—because *I* was scared of dying, wasn't I? I couldn't bear not knowing what had happened to him. I couldn't bear not trying to find him. And now Harry's going to die and it's my fault because I couldn't let go.

That man in the dark was right.

Stupid useless bitch.

Every choice was the right one—your best effort. Just because HE said those things doesn't make it true. YOU know how strong you've been to make it through that, to make it through this. To hell if nobody else knows it! You know it. I would know it, the second I laid eyes on you.

He was wrong. You're not useless, you're not nothing.

I can feel all the dark places I've been—all the grief, fear, hunger and pain—piling on top of the hopelessness now, weighing me down heavier, sinking me into this mud. And I can understand why Jack turned to pills to numb all his darkness, his depression, after that awful last tour, to make it feel possible to cope with. I can feel now how hard it must have felt to get out of that mess, to keep fighting back to health.

To survive, quitting on you and Harry has to be taken off the table. Because then it's simple, there's only one choice, you have to dig in no matter what. Get through today.

I stand up. "I am not useless, not nothing." It becomes a mantra, a rhythm to keep me walking. And I feel a sort of stubbornness right at the rock bottom of my guts giving me strength. "Not useless, not nothing, not fucking dead yet . . ." I even find myself breathing into the hot pain in my chest without fear. Let it come. I'm going to live till I'm dead. I'm going to walk until I have food for Harry. "Not useless, not nothing, not fucking dead yet."

35

I'm sleeping too much. It's morning again, the days slipping by, and I feel groggy and weak, my tummy bloated with pine-needle tea and pushing on my diaphragm, heart pain soaring and ebbing as I breathe. The warmth makes it a little less sharp. The embers hot still in the fireplace.

I scramble up and squat outside in the chill air. Harry has kept pinching himself and me awake, still scared to sleep. He's yawning and blinking out at me from beside the fire, a pile of scavenged books and magazines next to him. He's tearing the pages out, crumpling them, adding them to the basket next to the fireplace, for kindling. Every so often he stops and looks at the page.

I go back inside just as a coughing fit gets going—dialling up the pulsing pain until I'm doubled over in the hallway, struggling with my boots and coat. I force myself up, gasping, to filter flood-water through the old gauze and crumbling carbon block of the tap-attachment in the kitchen—which is better than nothing—before hanging the kettle in position in the fireplace. I try to distract myself by layering small bits of wood on top of the embers, followed by a few choice still-damp branches.

"Mummy, what happened to all the people?"

My arms shake as I lean to blow on the embers.

"In these books the pictures show lots. If they didn't get disappeared, where did they go?" He holds out some glossy advert for housing.

I bat the page away, trying not to look. "They died. They all died." I regret saying it instantly—the sheer weight of death: parents, siblings, friends, co-workers, neighbours, strangers you'd see hurrying to work or serving your coffee or reading the news on TV. Everyone.

Harry twists his mouth to one side, considering this—or does he? He can't understand the vastness of all that death. It's like us looking at the ruins of Pompeii or something; we couldn't have ever understood it.

"Oh," he says, eyes wide, scratching his scabby forehead in confusion. "They went to sleep? In all the houses, like that man?"

I nod. "It means they're not ever going to wake up again."

He slowly nods, his eyes growing larger. "Are we going to die too?"

I push the pages from his lap, and nudge his little face up to meet mine. "No, not yet. I won't let you."

He picks at the scab on his forehead, rocking on his heels. "But . . . will it hurt?"

I wonder—sick—if he glimpsed Ian's gasping face in the bathroom in Derbyshire . . . or if only I saw enough of his face and its decay and dust to imagine that. I moisten my lips, the saltiness on the cracked skin making me feel sicker. I can't help it; I can almost smell the stench of all that death, the reek of decaying flesh lingering in stairwells and houses, the metallic odour of blood. The horrifying flurries of greenbottle. How, in the first months, I used to lie awake at night unable to stop thinking about Jack, wondering if he was alive or dead, about how fast or slowly or painfully he might have died or even if he was dying right at that very moment. I imagined him staring at his phone—as I had mine—unable to connect to me. The pain of wishing for that one last chance to say I love you.

It's better to say goodbye than not, isn't it? More bearable. I let myself hope too much. That after all, there might be a chance for that.

"I'm four and more than a half and I've been lots of brave since we left the flat. You have to tell me." Harry folds his arms. "Then it won't surprise me."

"I don't know," I say. "Sometimes, I think—" I look at Harry, his insistent, grown-up little face. I don't want him to know how painful it could be. How I heard people gasping last breaths, hacking up their lungs, screaming, falling from windows. In that first year, all those awful remains on sofas and in bedrooms, or in the street, where they must have just dropped.

Or the recent crunch of metal into ribs.

I imagine all the awful ways we could die here—starved if the floods stay up, poisoned by the water or the food, or suffocated by the fumes of the fire or fresh contaminated rain blowing in. "But sometimes life is painful too, isn't it? Like when you scrape your knee or when you hit your head or when you feel really sad."

"I guess."

My stomach gurgles. Harry's pops as if in reply.

I glance outside.

"It's OK, Mummy, I can keep the fire warm. I did it yesterday," he says proudly.

I feel the sharp pricks and painful pulse of my chest squeezing tight; I didn't even notice. But I smile at his piles of kindling and semi-damp wood sorted into sizes. I fidget, wanting even now to leave him cold until I get back, to be safe. "OK, be careful?"

He nods, pulling his own make-do mask up—the smoke often curls into the room, thick and bitter.

"There's no more drinking water until I get back. Don't touch the kettle—it'll be a while until the fire is hot enough to heat it anyway. You promise to not go outside?"

He nods, a flicker of fear in his eyes. "Wholeheart promise."

He comes in for a gentle hug, knowing by now he has to be careful with me.

"I love you," I say, determined now to say it every time. "Wholeheart, Harry."

Once outside, I slog north, past the ruin of Arisaig and then along the water's edge on the grassy dunes, too sore for the muddy slopes of the hillside today. I feel buoyed at first because the water has actually gone down by a few metres—piles of dead grass and leaves and decayed birds along the trash line. Maybe we might be able to make it back to Fort William soon.

But I can't imagine the water not still being high there, so low-lying at the meeting of loch and river. And even if it weren't flooded, what then? Holiday homes make for poor scavenging.

No way we could turn to Bill's community now in any case.

At a copse of still-standing ash and birch, I stare at the thick, spongy leaves, bright acid yellow with threads of red veins.

Yet maybe Andy's right, and everything just grows differently now and this lurid yellow is just as alive as the green once was, even just here, where these trees seem to be fighting hard against the dust and toxins to breathe. Perhaps it's still worth risking some-times. I pull my mask clear to spit-clean the grey film off a leaf. It's bitter and tough in my mouth. Yet we *have* eaten them before, when desperate.

I get dizzy as I pick handfuls, and I feel myself sway, pain pulsing stronger.

I concentrate on three careful breaths before I continue moving down the shore. Foods I haven't thought of in years keep popping into my head: chocolate fingers, Victoria sponge with sharp rasp-berry jam and smooth cream, chips with tomato ketchup, salted caramel ice cream . . . Harry would love it all; I imagine him stuff-ing it in his mouth. Giggling. Full of energy and sugar.

I rub my stomach, trying to soothe the aching.

And keep going, up and down the rises and dips of the dunes and fields, following the shoreline, until I can't see the cottage anymore. The sun inches up overhead. Hauling myself up onto a boulder to rest, I scour the landscape. No cottages on the slopes or other copses to search, just low muddy orange grass and bracken, grassy dunes and rocks.

Yet in the distance, way north of where Arisaig should have been, there's something. I frown, trying to work out what it is. A brown rectangular shape, half in the shallows, half resting on the rocks.

I chew on another leaf, cringing at its bitterness, but it keeps me from feeling so dizzy and gives my mind something to focus on other than pain. I have to rest four more times before I reach it. Halfway there I understand what it is—a shipping container.

I keep moving, enjoying the leaves itching at those infuriating points down the back of my throat as I swallow. This is the west coast, anything brought in from the sea has to come from the Atlantic Ocean. I start imagining American candy bars, wrapped safe forever in cellophane and sealed plastic boxes, preferably from a time Before when America refused to ban such plastics. Or preserved fruits from Brazil stored in syrup and cans—pineapple, peaches, mango . . . smoked South American jerky, intensely salty. Californian dates, gooey like toffee.

As I near it, a strong salty-metallic tang that even my blocked nose can smell comes off the container. Completely rusted with brown-red flakes, the container glistens where the tide has splashed it, translucent crabs scuttling inside rust holes as I give the door a useless tug. Then hit it with my fist as hard as I can bear to. The rusty bolt rattles but doesn't come loose.

My hand throbs in time with my heart as I look around. Just rock and mud, and a few miniature orange-red pines and yellow-brown birches.

Trudging all the way back to the cottage, I haul the heavy blunted axe I found in the shed to the container, stopping less frequently than I did before, despite my whole body burning with the weight.

It takes a few swings before I get enough height and momentum to bring the axe down hard enough on the bolt. The jolt runs right up my arms and down into the centre of my chest.

"Fuck." I drop the axe, buckling to hands and knees, sucking in air, red-brown flakes showering me.

I shake myself out. Think of Harry. I swing again—boom—and again—boom. The bolt swivels, flecks of rust flying off. I try to tug and wiggle it open. I keep swinging until part of the bolt sheers off and clatters on the rocks. I have to kneel on the ground clutching my chest, grimacing as my heart throbs.

Yet the doors remain stubbornly closed. I pull and pull, wedging the axe in the small gap I make and trying to lever it open.

Sweating, there's enough room now to glimpse inside: a mess of boxes and crates and shiny plastic in the gloom. Hope soars. I yank the door again, enough to squeeze my head and shoulders through.

Ziplock plastic bags, vacuum-packed. I tear the nearest one open and a woollen, exotic smell bursts out. It reminds me of holidays, staying in bed-and-breakfasts with someone else's laundered sheets. I pull out the coloured fabrics. Staring. Not able to comprehend what I'm looking at.

The material is thick, heavy and otherworldly with bright pigments. Neon pink and electric blue, shot with bright apple green, all in geometric repeated patterns.

I shove myself further in, my hips stuck at the opening.

I tug open a box and the smell of plastics is overpowering. Flip-flops. All varieties. Violet, covered in flowers. Gold with rhinestones. Green with tropical fruits. I stare. Opening box after box. Flip-flops. Full of fucking flip-flops!

Tears run hot down my cold cheeks. Two pocketfuls of leaves isn't enough. Nowhere near.

I'm sobbing before I realize it. Hard sobs like a child—my whole body heaving and clenching. Coughing and spluttering. Tugging my mask clear of my face again. Clutching my burning heart as I slump to the ground, still half inside the container. Piles of plastic flip-flops half burying me. When I start laughing I find I can't stop. Laughing and groaning, bloody phlegm hacking up on my sleeves, a ghostly metallic echo inside the container.

Something outside on the rocks nudges my boots. I rein in my coughing and tears with a gasp, and try to sit up. A shape moves along the shoreline, tugging at seaweed. A red deer by size, her coat greyed and ghostly, limbs long and delicate. Ethereal.

She's rooting amongst the seaweed with her snout for tiny, dead washed-up fish and limpets. Maybe the grasses taste too bitter and contaminated and she's drawn to scavenge instead, like the roe deer down south. The fish seem to disintegrate to grey mush as she bites them—would a few fish be so bad for Harry and me? Better or worse than starving? Seafood was banned years before the storm hit. Microparticles and toxins literally gobbled up the food chain. And the seas too damaged by overfishing.

I don't move, wishing I still had that rifle. One shot right now and I could have fed Harry a feast, venison broth and steaks, heart and liver pancakes.

And yet . . . she looks ghostly, like a forest spirit who's lost her woods. Her belly is rounded, too rounded for her not to be pregnant, unless it's just from eating so much crap. I could have done it, though. I look at the blunt axe on the rocks by my feet. I did it to Bill, didn't I? Hurt another parent. Another sick, desperate parent. I could do it to her, for Harry.

She flinches as if she senses my thoughts, those eyes turning to stare at mine. Pale and cloudy like Bill's, lined with flies and caked with dust so that she blinks furiously. They widen, as if she'd thought me nothing but inedible clothy flotsam a moment earlier.

She seems lit up by the soft yellow light, the rising and resettling insects all around her like a halo. I notice her soft pointed ears and the curve of her back, the relative delicateness of her thin but powerful legs as she paws through the wet sand and mud back towards me. Fully sunk to her knees, foreshortening those legs, and her head carried low as she strains in the mud, she looks so like what Jack captured in Luna the reindeer, with his stumpier legs and lower, heavily antlered head. I remember Jack smiling up at me, in the midst of carving.

I love these creatures; they're like really useful, friendly pals, aren't they? Can survive anything.

The red deer mouths at my legs, teeth scraping along my shins. I kick, my shouts echoing round the container. She balks, ears pricking and eyes losing their confidence, becoming wider again in fright.

I stare as she bounds up the slopes away from the sea, my thoughts racing.

I know where the reindeer are in Scotland.

Fucksake, Jack.

36

One Year and Eight Months Before the Storm

"They're semi-tame," the volunteer says, "but they can be a bit oblivious, so just be aware of the antlers." We're stood outside the Reindeer Centre at the guide kiosk.

"Are they actually Scottish?" Jack says, leaning against the counter.

I bite my lip to hide my smile. It's early—dew burning off the pine canopies in the morning light—both of us still sleepy from the huge Scottish cooked breakfast we got in our guest house back in Aviemore, just a mile or two away through the dense Cairngorms Forest.

"Well, no, reindeer went extinct here about eight hundred years ago. These were reintroduced from Sweden to help save the Scottish heathlands—grazing the rank grasses, bracken and shrubs helps keep the heath itself rich."

"Increases resilience," I add.

"Climate change?" Jack asks and I nod. "So, you want to feed these *Swedes*?" he says, as if this was a swizz to have got up early for.

I roll my eyes, smiling. "Yeah, of course." I playfully punch his shoulder. "The Highland Zoo is different! Reindeer *were* native to Scotland once."

"They roam free too." The volunteer grins at Jack. He's gangly, with dark dishevelled hair, a slightly pink wind-scorched face, and thin fingers that he taps on the price card. "Two pounds for a bag of feed." He looks up at Jack like I've seen many people do—enjoying his easy chatter. Jack's tall, his blonde hair pulled back in a topknot, eyes bright—always appearing confident and sure of himself.

I hand over the money and Jack smiles at me as we head off. It's a few miles through forest and over a bridge, before our boots clomp across a boardwalk, lush green heath on the mountainside around us.

"You love this stuff, don't you?"

I nod. "I like seeing how the Earth can clean itself up if we just find a way to let it." This trip has been good—both of us loving exploring wild places. I know we talked about it and planned and dreamed, but I'm glad we've been excited by similar things out here on our first proper trip together: the hikes, the forests, that feeling of being on an adventure in the wilds. Having the time to sit and have deep conversations about life.

The ground is hard and dry beneath the boardwalk, the summer sun warm on my face, even if the mountain breeze feels cool. Jack slips his hand into mine—our fingers interlacing tight—as we follow the other visitors and guide ahead. I feel good in my faux-fur-trimmed jacket and tight black jeans, make-up done with cute winged eyeliner. I definitely overpacked, wanting to look nice every day. Jack smiles at me, head leaning to one side, his eyes bright in a way that makes me feel it was worth it.

Our first few months in the flat together have sped by. I start my Wildlife Trust internship when we get back and a new part-time job at the garden centre. Not quite landed where I want to be yet, but it's been a novelty these past ten months since graduating to have some money for once in my life. I feel like I'm a bit more grown up, an equal in Jack's world, not just the younger, broke, long-distance student girlfriend anymore . . . and I like that feeling.

As we go uphill, the reindeer join us, slotting in amongst the convoy of people. There's one right behind us. Her antlers brush the nylon of my backpack as she bends her head to follow the path. The velveteen covering is coming off now at the end of the season, leaving bloody stains on the antler bone.

"What is that?" Jack says.

"That clicking?"

"Yeah." He makes a face. "Sounds like time ticking away too fast or bones cracking . . ."

"He just said, Jack, it's their ankles. It's how they stay in contact if they wander into snow or fog."

"Kind of sweet, I guess," he says, with a grimacing smile, and it makes me laugh.

"They eat vegetation and mosses in summer, and lichen and fungi in winter," the guide is saying, signalling that we can offer them our pellet feed now. "They can survive thick snowstorms and fluctuating temperatures: their hairy noses warm and filter the air they breathe in, and their thick oily fur repels snow and rain . . ."

I don't hear the rest. The compressed pellets of animal feed are barely in my hands a few seconds before she hoovers them up, warm breath and warm tongue on my cold fingers.

Jack takes endless photos, framing me between heath and mountains and a clear blue sky.

The reindeer mill about amongst the visitors, nosing in the heather for fallen pellets. Someone gets close enough to touch a reindeer flank, unable to contain a squeal at the soft fur. I edge forwards, wondering if we're allowed.

"I could live here," Jack says, breathing in the view. "Peaceful. Majestic. Makes you feel so fucking free!"

And it does. I feel as if my soul has been recharged up here with Jack. I feel alive in a way that only endorphins and fresh air seem to make you.

"Could we handle the isolation, though?" I say, chuckling. "I'd miss our little flat and town and life down south."

He rolls his eyes. "Katie—"

"You know I'm right." I laugh, leaning into his warm chest.

He presses a kiss onto my forehead. "Well, if we ever wanted to start over, leave it all behind."

It's a moment before I realize we're alone. Everyone else has drifted off back down the slopes, out of sight.

"Maybe one day we'll do a year out of travelling instead?" Jack whispers. "Get away? Two weeks is over so fast. And I don't want to wait until we're retired to have bigger adventures, what if we're dead before then?" He laughs. "Somewhere like Scandinavia maybe—like Scotland on steroids!"

"Maybe." I smile. "But I've got so much I want to do first." The breeze ruffles my T-shirt, bringing with it the rich scent of pine from down the valley. I think about the rugged Norwegian mountains and fjords, Jack's Subaru, perfect freedom, and all that time together. "One day, though. I think I'm catching the travelling bug."

And just then it starts to rain—thick, heavy, warm summer droplets—like it hasn't in months. We both lift our faces and arms into it, laughing, getting soaked. I can taste it on my tongue—soft and fresh, reminding me of sudden summer showers and garden parties where everyone makes a dash, laughing, indoors—and down the slope I can hear the squeals of delight from the rest of our group just out of sight. The warm heath seems to steam with rising moisture, even as it rains. We catch each other's eye and everything seems to pause and I know I'm going to remember this moment, this feeling, always.

37

"Outside? All the time?" Harry stands in the hallway, munching a last piece of baked seaweed, as I help his bony little limbs into his outdoor gear. Our stomachs whine, bloated and uncomfortable but filled with a dinner and breakfast of seaweed, leaves and tiny rush and grass taproots. He wants to wear his newly treasured South American poncho too—I took one for each of us from the shipping container, just for something to bring back. I let him, even though it's heavy and stinks of woodsmoke and plastic fumes from our fire now—it was the price of getting him to stand here and allow me to put his boots and snowsuit on, and my too-big mask as tight as I can around his little face.

I nod, feeling sick. Though we were up before it was light, it has taken us hours this morning to get organized and to the door. "But you understand we can't stay here? Winter will come, we'll probably get stranded again, it'll get colder and damper. We'll both get sicker . . ." For all his questions about death, I can't bring myself to actually say things so starkly.

I put my own gear on, the warmth from our fire already leaving me, making the pain in my chest rise sharper again. I shift on my feet. We could stay, sleep and starve until we slip away. For a second that feels tempting; an easier way to go.

It's a long trek east across the Highlands to Aviemore in the Cairngorms and the reindeer herd. We marked it on the Scottish

OS maps. About a hundred miles. It's just as far to Bill's community though, and four times that to Derbyshire.

"We should give Daddy one more chance," I whisper. "Then we stop. One last finding game for Daddy, OK?" I open the door before he answers, pulling up my own makeshift mask and donning our pack—Harry's pack left behind and his few precious things consolidated into mine.

Harry blinks at the onslaught of cool salt air.

"How about a story as we go up this first slope? A new one that might help."

He looks up at me. "A good one?"

I nod. "Before, there used to be these special big fish living out at sea. Every year they'd come to shore to—"

But Harry is motionless in the hallway, flicking at his tassels, eyes heavy and dark-circled—glancing back inside.

"Wait, let's pretend they were sea serpents! Big long snake-like creatures—covered in shiny scales—some of them blue, some green, some red. With mouths full of teeth, horns on their heads, and spines all along their backs, right down to the tips of their arrowhead tails."

Harry looks up and I turn, stepping away from the cottage.

"I read a good story that went like this once. They lived at sea, eating fish and eels, and one day, in the autumn when green leaves used to go yellow and brown and fall off, they all swam to the coast and up a particular special river. The water was flowing to the sea, the opposite way, so they had to thrash their tails hard to move against it. They came to big rocks and fallen trees and had to squeeze through or leap over them. Sometimes they even swam up waterfalls . . . When they reached a special sandy beach up in the mountains, they cocooned themselves with mud and pebbles and they slept. In the springtime, the cocoons were hard and, like all the moths, they wriggled and pushed their way out—beautiful, colourful, winged dragons."

"Wow!" Harry is following my slow shuffling steps.

I imagine more and more. But by late afternoon, I'm so tired and chest-sore that all I can do is focus on the next step forwards.

I have to move my tongue around my dry mouth before calling: "Come on, Harry, well done!"

I wait as he catches up, traipsing through hummocks of purple bedraggled rushes. His boots and the snowsuit are damp and flecked with mud. His poncho drags over the vegetation. He tugs on a snag, staggering as he pulls it free, still walking in exaggerated strides like he expects his feet to be heavier than they are. I reach out, just in time, to steer him clear of a jutting rock that he hasn't noticed.

"Mask back on," I say, tapping the air meter, which shows we're borderline here.

He frowns. "You're not wearing yours." He sits and pulls off his boots, and his socks too, revealing little blisters. I can feel the same on my feet.

"Ouch. Yes, sorry, I'll try it again now." The thick triangle of blanket must do a better job than the thin T-shirt I used before—though nothing like the military-grade layers of mesh and charcoal Harry has got. But it makes the effort of walking—of sucking in enough air—unbearably hard, my heart racing and squeezing in pain, as if I'm about to suffocate.

I join him on the rock to re-secure our masks, my warmed-up breath briefly soothing the sharp prickling of my tight lungs. I blow a kiss to Harry's foot, tearing a piece off my already ragged shirt to wind round his sore big toe, the heel already having had the same treatment a while ago, and help him put his boots back on.

Looking back west, the coast and its red bloom have long disappeared. Yet specks of red drift in the air with the wind.

"Warm enough? Want your hat?"

"I'm hot."

"Well, don't get too hot, you'll sweat and then you'll get cold." I reach for his poncho.

"No!" He flaps it out to one side to avoid my hand, like stretching out a wing.

We each take an unpleasant sip from our flask—no amount of filtering and boiling floodwater has destroyed that taste of mud and algae. A third of it's gone already; we've stopped to rest almost every time we've come to a rise on the undulating heath. I feel dizzy, as if no matter how much I try to catch my breath, my lungs just can't do their job.

The sun is dipping as we reach the mountainside bothy, marked on the map, that I'd hoped would still be here—just a tiny stone hovel with a camp bed, bench and fireplace—and we set up inside, the damp grey walls and smoky meagre fire feeling similar to the cottage at first as we eat our rations of last night's baked seaweed. But the fire never warms us, quickly going out. All I have are the covers and sections of the maps we don't need as kindling and a few handfuls of twigs. Harry's so tired he does eventually sleep, cocooned with me in our groundsheet on the rusty camp bed someone long ago must have left here. He clings tight for ages though, afraid to shut his eyes and let himself go. I barely sleep—cold and anxious about dust I can't see, of drifting off and bad rain or wind starting up and coming in, and about making some ground on this journey while we still can.

The next morning, so tired, stiff and chest-sore, I almost can't bear to get back up. Yet I remember Jack's warm hug. And how, once, on a sunrise hike, he'd surprised me with rich, sugary hot chocolate from a flask in his pack.

Harry and I manage to get up and out. The next stretch east for several miles is a long downward slope. But the heavy rain has caused a landslide, it's mud-slicked and slippy. Tears prick as I contemplate how long this will take us, how much effort, to pick our way slowly and carefully.

I stare for a while before sliding the crude wooden bench out of the bothy, and upturning it. Harry's face is frightened and pale as we sit and cling on and I shunt us forwards, remembering how many times we have imagined a sledge ride or a flying rocket as I've pushed Harry along the hallway in the flat. We start to slide downhill.

It jars my chest, my feet sticking out to control our descent, and each jostle, adjustment in course and abrupt stop to prevent us careering into rocks. Harry squeals, both frightened and thrilled, but it feels worth it and makes me feel lighter to quickly cover ground that would have taken us hours on foot. We abandon our sledge at the bottom of that mountainside—Harry touching it solemnly and whispering goodbye—and we scramble on.

We hunker down amongst slabs of rock and grass in the dark on that second night, which I hope isn't the remains of a barrow, but I'm so relieved to find some cover—*anything*—that I also don't care if it is. The stone keeps off the wind but there's nothing to get a fire going. Wrapped in our groundsheet again, anxious, hungry and restless, I whisper to Harry about an imagined castle instead as he shivers, cold, and scared as the wind hisses freely around the tops of the stone.

Then it is the third day out—and we are still going—the slopes not so steep and the day's walking not so bad, if we'd not been so tired. All too soon the sun is sinking at our back again as we reach a scattering of birch trees—not thick enough cover for tonight. Beyond the slender white trunks, I see leaf litter on cracked grey asphalt and after that, a wide expanse of running water. I consult the map, thick golden triangles splatting on the paper as we stand still. It might be a B-road and the River Lochy running down to Fort William—we're now level with the town!—a few miles south of us.

"We've done really well to come this far," I tell Harry, squeezing his shoulder. Nearly thirty miles in three long days, winding through low mountain slopes and round flooded ground, though I feel sick it has taken us so long. It has taken all my willpower—knowing there is no alternative—to keep us moving. We've barely eaten. Are nearly out of water.

I pinch off fresh shoots as we head through the trees—bright like creamy honeycomb—and spit-clean them for something to chew.

The light is changing, the air getting colder—and there's the dreaded scent of coming rainfall on the breeze. I finger my knife, growing heavy on my belt; I don't like to be near this road and the way south. Just-in-case.

In the distance, an open-sided metal shed peeps out amongst bushes at the edge of the bloated—brown and silty—river. Fungi and dust-laden winds have taken bites out of it, and the roof is half-sunk into the slapping current.

We reach it just as the first drops of *clear* rain hit my face. Empty storage racks for canoes and kayaks jut out from the central pillars. One canoe remains, its plastic hull half-submerged in the mud that's washed inside. The wind shakes the roof, showering dust specks down on us.

I pull Harry's hood up just in time. It's too exposed here and too close to the rising water. Dark ominous clouds are rolling in from the north—my eyes slide off them and to the opposite river bank. A wave of giddiness washes through me, blowing off a little of the tired, hungry fogginess.

"Mummy?" Harry pulls at my sleeve, staring too.

Across all that roiling water and up a muddy slope . . . a beautiful, dark green mass of pines! Reaching twenty metres into the sky, and spreading across the hillside to north and south. The largest, richest bank of green I have seen in years. Unable to stop staring, I start tugging at the abandoned canoe, trying not to focus on the worry seeping from the back of my mind of why it is the only one here.

"We should keep moving—we might search a long time for another way across the river." All the lochs have burst their banks with the heavy rain—I can't imagine it will be any different up- or downstream of here. "We can have a good fire and make a nice cosy camp—it'll be safe in the green pinewood." Even as I say it, I don't know why I feel so strongly about it—that the green marks a safe place. A primal sort of desperation makes me want to get there.

Harry frowns at the water. "It's too big."

I run a dry tongue across my teeth, my mouth sour. It's maybe sixty metres across, and suddenly I feel Harry's panic. It looks impossibly far and the water too fast, full of eddies and ripples and bubbling upwellings, and boat-toppling branches being carried downstream, the water coursing with plastic dust.

And to the north, those dark clouds have burst, a great sheet of grey blurring the hills and sky. The river will only get worse.

It could rain hard again for days or weeks. My eyes flick to that tall wall of green. And then drift inward to Jack, who could be somewhere beyond it.

I dig at the pale-blue canoe with the heel of my boot—to keep from raking my bare hands through the likely contaminated mud.

It's mucky, battered, and crawling with ants, but looks solid enough. I start dragging it towards the water.

"I don't want to go there!" Harry's voice is hoarse and shouted, and he stomps back up to the road, his little body hunched and weary.

I wheeze after him, spots of rain landing on our shoulders.

He kicks at fungi on the crumbled tarmac, black ooze and orange spores sticking to the toes of his boots. He slumps to his knees.

"Harry, come on, get up off the ground." I tug on his poncho.

"No." He twists away. "There'll be nasties in the water, Mummy." His cheeks flush, face scrunching up, his gasping wail muffled as he stuffs his masked face into his fetid poncho.

"Harry," I say quietly, my voice low and worried. He stiffens, lifting his face. "We're both so tired and hungry, we can't argue. We can't stay this side of the water, with the rain and nightfall coming and so close to the road south. We could be brave and paddle across in the boat—Daddy is that way." I point east across the water, still staring at that bank of dark green, trying to believe it's real. I break off into a horrible rattling wet cough.

Harry gets the flask from my pack and presses it into my hands, opening the top for me. I sip the brown unpleasant water and keep coughing. I cough until my chest feels like it might tear apart or my heart burst, and I have to crumple to hands and knees.

I take more sips, the flask emptying. Keep trying to stop.

Finally, exhausted, I lie on my side—even though I shouldn't lie directly on the ground—breathing ragged breaths, my chest shuddering.

"OK, Mummy, I'll try." Harry is crouched next to me, watching.

I reach up to rub his shoulder and he launches his arms around me, jostling my fragile chest. I squeeze a hand over my heart, pressing my lips together against the groan, and rock him, hugging him tight.

The wind is whipping round the boathouse as we get back down there—the dark clouds closer. Harry lets me pack his precious but permeable poncho away and put his raincoat over his snowsuit against the wind and rain, Harry shivering now we're stationary. We drag the canoe to the river's edge. It rocks in the water, clanking against the fallen roof. My initial estimation of sixty metres is wrong; it's at least a hundred metres to the other side. I pick a V-shaped branch from the bank, cutting a strip of groundsheet and wrapping it to and fro until I have a crude paddle.

"What if the water swallows us up like you thought happened to Daddy at the sea?"

"We'll be OK as long as we get across before those storm clouds hit."

"What if the boat falls over?"

"I won't let it."

"But what if it does?"

Weary, my legs shaking, I step into the canoe, one foot still balanced on the muddy bank. "Then we'll get wet," I say, smiling grimly.

Harry's eyes are big. "Will we die?"

Ribbons of grey swirl in the swift brown current, glittering specks, clods of dark algae gunked at the shallows. A flourish of still-clear rain dapples the surface.

I close my eyes. No way would I be doing this if we'd just left Hitchin.

Yet I take a breath and draw him gently closer. "I'll look after you," I say firmly. "I won't let anything happen to you."

Finally, Harry nods, face creased in worry, and I help him clamber in and under the groundsheet to protect him, guilt and warmth flooding me at how easily he follows.

The canoe rocks with both of us in it, trying to turn into the wind, and Harry making it worse by clutching the side nearest land.

"Harry, let go, sit in the middle . . . there, see, it helps balance it if you sit there."

The wind is an insistent push southwards at my shoulder as I push off with the paddle. Sat balanced on the one cracked, sagging seat, I keep both legs out straight, my boots hooked around a stiffly huddled Harry so that he doesn't slide about.

As I paddle across the current, the turbid water sloshing with slimy black leaves, my arms tremble, muscles soon tiring. My chest begins to burn from bracing and rowing, my pulse getting frantic again. Rain taps on the plastic hull and the groundsheet. My ring glitters on my left hand, slipping down my cold finger. I wish I had my gloves still. I wish we had life vests. I wish we had full-face diving masks just-in-case we do fall in! I glance at those dark clouds, the surging river all around us, and at the shoreline drifting away, and just too tired for this and my heart bursting a beat with white-hot pain, I feel a stab of panic and dread that makes me freeze. But we're in the middle now, it's just as much effort to turn back as it is to go on.

"We're doing it!" I whisper to Harry, like Jack used to say when we'd planned an adventure and were finally out on the trail in the mountains.

"Mummy! A sea serpent!" Harry leans, making us wobble, as he peers out from under his groundsheet. I spot the weave of a long slick brown body swimming upstream.

I open my mouth to say don't worry it *is* actually only a grass snake, but I shut it again. Harry's sitting upright, not frightened, but looking at the moving water excitedly now. If make-believe makes him brave, I'm not going to take it away.

Buoyed, I push into the next stroke. But there's a sudden jolt: the nose of the canoe crunching into something beneath the water. The canoe swings violently, Harry and I crying out. The huge trunk of an old oak bobs up through the murky water.

The river ripples either side of us as we lurch, sparkling particles in the upwellings boiling to the surface. My arms are so heavy, my fingers barely gripping the wet sides as the wind and rain suddenly lash harder.

"Maybe it's a dragon cocoon that got washed downstream," I say breathlessly, wincing, and I see Harry's shoulders relax a little as he considers the log.

"We should push it free, Mummy."

With a small smile I push as hard as I can bear to with my paddle. We leave the log to bob south while we continue on towards the east bank. My muscles are soon burning again, my left hand with the unhealed cut stiff and nearly useless, and I'm wheezing and wincing with each stroke I try to lean into, barely getting any power into it at all now, and the wood of my makeshift paddle flaking off and the groundsheet blade getting loose and flabby. I'm sweating in my warm clothes, my heart a hot lump pulsing in my chest.

The shore is several metres away still. Just a few more strokes.

"Mummy!" A long hairline crack at the nose of the canoe is seeping, Harry shuffling back from it.

I cut the paddle into the water, pushing and pulling, my body screaming to stop.

The seep becomes half an inch of murky water, then an inch, reaching my boots, Harry crouched and swaying.

As soon as I can, I grab hold of a silvery bankside willow and hang on with numb fingers, heaving us closer to the bank with every spent burning muscle. The canoe swings away from me as I step out onto the mud, the nose beginning to sink under the surface.

"Mummy!" Harry slips in the canoe, scrambling on hands and knees away from the water.

My heart is squeezing white-hot constantly now, the pain making me feel faint. But I hang on to the plastic hull with one hand, grabbing Harry's little hand with the other. "I got you!" The mud glitters around me, pocked with grey deposits.

I'm slipping and sinking deeper in the mud, sweating and gasping at breaths, blackness edging my vision.

"It's getting me!"

I let the canoe go and swing Harry up with a grunt, falling backwards with him into the wet earth as I try to hold him clear. But my left foot stays stuck in the mud at the edge of the bank, my ankle popping, a horrible dizzying numbness instantly throbbing through it.

"Mummy?" Harry is screaming as I open my eyes again, the fuzziness still slipping from my head.

"I got you," I groan, forcing deeper breaths, "the mud's bad."

Harry stares down at it and back at my foot, bottom lip trembling. "Did it swallow you?" He cringes his own boots clear, his knees digging into my thighs with all his weight, as if there might be fangs under that undulating surface of muck too.

Hissing between my teeth, I sit up, try to pull my boot out of the sucking mud. I cannot sprain my ankle.

"It's OK," I say, in my best everything's-alright voice. "It's just really deep and my foot got stuck."

Eventually I get up, holding on to Harry so his boots don't sink too much, and try placing my boot on the next bit of more solid-looking mud. I can't. The ankle is too numb. A hot, sweaty light-headedness is coming over me in waves. I focus on holding Harry upright—though he is beginning to get heavy.

"It might not be so deep up ahead. If you fall, don't touch the mud with your mittens, alright? And especially keep your face clear. Promise?"

He nods solemnly, checking his mask. Yet even as I say it, the wind is pummelling us with still-clear rain, those dark clouds overhead.

He sinks to his waist on his first step, shrieking, and I hurry to yank him up, his hands and face held as high as he can away from the mud.

We go with small hop-steps, so my bad ankle doesn't take my weight for long. I keep wobbling, yelping every time I have to reach a hand down into the glossy mud to steady myself. Harry tries to follow where I place my feet on the more solid bits, slipping to his knees every other step and awaiting my help to haul him back up.

"You're doing great," I tell him, panting.

"I know," he says, his tired little legs trembling. "I can do it."

When finally we make it up across the mud, the ground slowly becoming firmer and then drier and sandier, we pause before we enter the darkness of the pinewood. The trees tower high into the sky. Rich beautiful green—the needles glossy with their protective waxy coating, just a peppering of orange and yellow tips amongst the outermost needles. There are windblown dead trunks at our feet. They look orange-brown and bent—the soldiers taking the brunt along the woodland boundary. But the trees still standing look thicker and healthier the further inside the wood I look, trunks wide like great barrels, crowded in rows and lines, tall and straight, shading out the light, like they've been able to thrive together in the post-storm world.

"This looks an old wood," Harry whispers, his face worried, eyes flicking at every creak and rustle.

And I know he's thinking of the Wild Wood, that finally, this is it. To me, even though it's old timber plantation and not wild pinewood, it still looks prehistoric, like we've looped back in time to when everything was gigantic and lush and green. This is the very sort of place I'd expect one of Harry's dragons to come out of the shadows for real.

"Big woods can protect themselves," I whisper back. It's why lonely city trees and tiny copses died during heatwaves or pollution events, Before, and there was a desperate rush to rewild and replant lost woods. Bigger became better. Dips in oxygen levels at higher altitudes overseas fed that rush too—after new waves of climate refugees arrived.

Limping awkwardly over the thick exposed roots and old needle litter and into the pinewood, I worry, even in these foothills, that *we're* higher than we've ever been. The rushing river and growing wind are muffled inside the trees, the air still and heavy, and it takes a good few minutes before I can catch my gasping breath and my heart is bearable again, and I can reassure myself the air is still breathable. I don't blink, waiting for my eyes to adjust. Harry stands close, mask hanging down from his neck already.

My ankle throbs against my boot and I'm suddenly anxious enough to forget about the air and stinking mud on my clothes, and to ease myself down to the ground. My ankle tingles with numb pain as I pull on the heel of my boot, and it is all I can bear to just loosen the laces instead. The flesh is puffy and swollen, the skin itchy and tight.

"How can we make it better?" Harry says quietly, leaning over like he wants to kiss my ankle like I would with a scuffed knee or splintered finger of his, back at the flat, but he stands with arms and legs held awkwardly, eyes big.

"I don't know," I say, my voice wavering as I try not to cry. "Other than rest it." I remember Jack fractured an ankle once, had lots of exercises to build strength back into the ligaments, but I can't picture any of them now—not that those would help me walk tomorrow.

"It's OK, Mummy." Harry pats my shoulder.

38

With my ankle resting on my backpack, it's Harry who collects the pine branches from the gold and green moss and needle floor and drags them to our camp, carefully brushing down his mittens each time. It's Harry who finds softer fir branches to make a mattress with. I let him rummage in my pocket and pull out Andy's flint and steel.

"Do you know how to do it?" I rasp.

He shows me, scraping the steel along the flint.

"Harder and faster," I whisper.

He tries again, his fingers trembling but face determined, and after a couple of goes, gets a spark and looks at me triumphantly. He lights the dry needle kindling all by himself and sets it under the branches, blowing until flames lick up through them.

The warmth takes the edge off the pain in my chest and the throbbing in my ankle.

I fall asleep without meaning to.

I wake to the welcome sound of the kettle whistling. It smells of pine-needle tea. The filtering tap-attachment I took from the cottage kitchen lies next to the fire.

Sitting up, dried mud crumbles from my clothes. I peer around me. "Harry?" The pinewood trills and chirrups with tiny birds, flitting between the old creaking trees. "Harry!"

"Coming!" I hear his voice and relax back against a tree trunk.

Harry comes back to the camp, and I have to laugh. Pale-faced and tripping on his clothes, yet he's hauling the "dirty" saucepan, which is filled to the brim with pine cones, mushrooms and long fleshy green leaves.

He grins as he sets it in front of me. "I've been finding dinner."

I smile. "I can see that."

I tap the air meter until it flashes a reading—it's OK just here, and Harry's face bears red marks from his too-big mask, so I don't tell him to put it back on. I should have taken him foraging when we were in Hitchin, shouldn't have kept him cooped up.

"The water, where did you get it?"

He points. "Over there, it was trickling up through the rocks and grass."

"A spring?" I think of going to investigate, to make sure, but my ankle throbs a warning.

He shrugs. "It wasn't muddy or dirty. And I put it in the saucepan for dirty things first and poured it through the tap into the kettle, for filtering." He fidgets, looking worried as I brush myself down as best I can.

I pour a mugful. The water comes out clear, a hint of green from the pine needles. All groundwater must be contaminated. But there's no unpleasant smell. So I smile and take a wonderful warm mouthful.

As we clutch our tea, I wash our faces and hands with warm water and brush down our clothes, the ritual making me feel a little better. It's the best I can do right now. My hands and legs are itchy and red where they've touched the mud; thankfully Harry is OK.

I pick through Harry's findings. The cones have to be bashed open with a rock. Inside, the pine nuts are encased in their own hard shells, and so tiny, my heart sinks.

"The shells will still make good kindling for the next fire," I tell Harry, who's looking mournful. I stuff handfuls into an outside pocket of my pack.

I pick through the mushrooms, but I've never trusted my ability to identify them—too many with awful reputations. I look at Harry, the shadows making his little face bony, lacking any of the lovely roundness his cheeks once had. Maybe we're that desperate.

The bracket mushrooms and the brown and red umbrellas look too difficult to identify. But the third is more unique; the size of my fist, and shaped like an egg, if softly dimpled. Feather-light but solid, and a startling clean white—in the gloom of the forest, it almost seems to glow.

"So magic egg ones might be food?" Harry whispers in awe, squatting at my side.

I smile. "No, it's the colour and shape, see . . ." I point to the image in *Wild Foraging*, scanning the text. Even edible mushrooms can be very bad, if they're decaying, or contaminated—which I always felt ruled everything out.

I'm already imagining this roasted, covered in the crushed wild garlic leaves Harry found—a brilliant green the colour grass used to be. Though now I sniff them, I can't smell anything at all . . . perhaps it's something dangerously similar.

My brain's too fuzzy to think.

Harry examines the little umbrella mushrooms. His fingers come away covered in black soot-like dust.

He freezes. "Mummy?"

"Wipe it off. Mushroom spores could be poisonous."

He kneels, his hand sweeping a frantic arc across his just-cleaned snowsuit, until I have to tell him to stop.

We drink more tea. At least we have plenty of pine needles—plenty of vitamin C. I flick to the pages on Scots pine. Just-in-case. I grin at Harry, who's watching the fire dejectedly, sipping at his tea. "It's called 'famine food'! We can eat the inner bark of the pine trunk, a carbohydrate!"

"What's a carbohydrate?"

"It means energy food!" I grab my knife and hobble to the nearest pine tree. The outer bark takes a bit of scraping off, blunting my blade, but underneath I can see the white film of the inner bark. It peels away from the wood in rough strips.

"Has it got poisonous dust inside too?" Harry asks. Grey-black granules of oil pepper the white film. The book doesn't mention them, so I assume it's new, since the toxic storm. I scrape the granules off as best I can and wash the strips with tea water from the kettle.

We both munch a piece. It tastes sweet. I make my way through the nearest few trees, until I'm hacking with the knife completely blunt and I'm barely able to grip the hilt anymore. All the trees have the granules.

Pleased with the haul, we eat strips raw while I experiment with roasting some over the fire and sharpen my blunted knife on the most suitable rock I can find.

"Tastes better cooked," Harry says, smiling.

"Everything usually does."

"I think I feel the energy!"

Darkness has crept in as we've been eating—the thin strips of food barely touching that gnawing hunger. When I look up I can't see anything but black surrounding us.

Harry scoots closer still, practically sitting in my lap. He fights to stay awake, but I soon feel him getting heavier and hear his breathing slowing and I slip his mask over his face for the night, leaving me with just the fire and the darkness.

The silence and the crackling fire are good. Restful after all those days of storm and crashing tides and wind. And the heat seems to make breathing easier, soothes my chest. And if I don't move, my ankle doesn't feel too bad. This reminds me of so many nights spent staring at the woodstove with Harry, feeling finally safe and relaxed for the first time that day as we watched the flames, even if we are outside now. Reminds me of mountain camping with Jack too—cosy and happy and looking forward to sunrise views.

I am exhausted, but again I barely sleep. Pain keeps pulling me out of it. Rain drips straight off the pine needles onto us, filling the air with a sweet damp smell. I hold the groundsheet over us, leaning forward towards the fire, which is fuelled well enough that the drips have yet to put it out. Despite the warmth of the fire, there's too much cold and damp, and soon there's no position I can fidget to that helps. Worry nips at my earlier relief and peace. We're not eating enough food to sustain us, my ankle might not take my weight in the morning, and how long can I keep going with my chest? What if this rain's not clear but milky and full of pollutants that I can't see in the dark? All night my mind turns over the problems.

I try to imagine Jack in the Cairngorms, not moved on or dead, but just standing at a rustic front door, waiting for us. Me and Harry walking towards him.

We have to make it.

And that makes me relax again despite everything. There's nothing to decide.

Something wakes me later. I ache with cold. Harry's sleepy form is snugged next to me. The fire is a low pile of embers, still smoking, and the rain has stopped, though it drips still from the needles.

The trees creak around us.

I lean forward and stoke the embers, adding more semi-damp branches. The fire grows again, sparks in the air fizzing and smoking.

There's a deep, short "hoo-hoo" and a scratching in the pine-wood somewhere.

I shiver, still wary. The thick cushions of moss near the fire have dried soft and fluffy. I feel for Harry next to me, his skin cold, and carefully start piling the dried moss around him like a duvet, just as I feel hot moist air on my cheek. Teeth yank at my hood, tearing at my hair.

My scream is garbled. I grab a smoking branch and thrust it wildly into the darkness, jumping to my feet, all pain forgotten for a moment, expecting to see lupine eyes. A sparking grey circle of frantic branches imprints in my eyes instead. I can't see anything else.

After I've settled a bleary but frightened Harry again, I bank the fire up and sit alert all night, staring blindly out at the darkness, wondering if my blocked nose really can smell musk and hay.

It's not until dawn light filters through the thick pine branches that I look around and spot the prints in the mud. The owner walked in a half-circle around our camp before continuing.

Harry gets up and peers over my shoulder. "Don't worry, Mummy," he whispers. "Some dragons are friendly."

The prints have blurred in the mud. Elongated and distorted, and as sleep-deprived as I feel, they could look reptilian.

But I think I can see two toes, like a deer, not three or more. Or I convince myself that I do. My head is too foggy to not take Harry's thoughts seriously.

"Whatever it was," I say, "it was bold, came right up to our fire." I shake out my blanket-mask, perturbed by the dust wafting into the air.

I keep Harry close all morning as we hobble through the quiet pines, looking over my shoulder at every rustle and squeak. Vigilant, like I was in bear country in Canada with Jack, knowing something bigger and stronger might be watching or following. I keep startling at antlers that turn out to be just pine branches. My ankle feels sickeningly loose, like my foot is hanging to my shin by a thread. I managed to get the heavy walking boot off this morning and have it tied to the outside of my pack—my left foot cold but not throbbing so much in just a sock. Harry finds me a good—if spiky—stick to lean on.

We're slow, though, and we pause at the top of an incline, where the pinewood turns orange-red and abruptly ends in saplings and fallen trunks. Wind gusts in our faces. There's a flooded town below us, water gushing through it. Golden gleaming tree trunks with deep red canopies on the banks, dripping bloody palms into the water. We slump down in the shelter of a fallen pine and consult the map. The road that should run through the town and north-east parallel to the River Spean is also flooded, criss-crossed with streams and tributaries into the distance—the tops of its nearly submerged snow-time marker-posts winding north-east. That road would, in sixty-five miles, have taken us straight to Aviemore in the Cairngorms.

Instead, I trace an alternative route across the squares of the map.

"What's all the brown?" Harry asks, leaning in.

Dark to indicate height.

I swallow, sinking, the jagged bark digging into my back. "Mountains."

39

As we near a ridge, days later, a hoarse bellow carries through the damp silence of the Highlands. I drag Harry down on his front into the rushes—my ankle sparking as my foot hits the ground. My mind leaps from lions and bears to wolves and lynx. Instead, as I peer over the rocks, two stags face off, with what must be the peaks of Creag Meagaidh above them. They stamp the ground, sending a tremble up the slope. They are silvery instead of red, like the hind at Arisaig, limbs long and delicate, antlers branched but crooked and broken off in places. Tufts of fur float from their backs as they move—maybe they shed more often than Before, like the trees.

Another roar, louder this time. It rumbles right through my inflamed chest, drawing out the point of pain where my heart is.

Harry shivers, whispering through his mask, "Do they eat people?"

"No," I whisper back, wrapping my arms around my chest, but remembering that hot breath and those teeth.

"What are they doing?"

"Fighting over the females, I guess. See, over there." I nod at the hinds on the opposite ridge. Silvery-grey, their coats shimmer in the breeze, their eyes glinting in the daylight. They're all small and slender. Malnourished and young, as if their life cycle is faster than it was Before. Several stamp their feet or paw at the ground, like they want to join in with the stags.

"Why?"

"What? Oh, to prove who is stronger and who should have the . . . be the leader of the females." I jump as one of the calves suddenly launches down the slope in a furious stampede, right into the path of the heavy thudding antlers of one of the stags.

Harry yelps.

Eyes and ears twitch to look right at us. The stags shake their heads, hooves stamping.

I pull Harry away.

"But why does he want to—"

"To make baby deer with them."

"How?"

My cheeks flush and I stumble over my words before rushing to get it out. "They'll rub against each other, and . . . and he'll put something-inside-her-that-helps-grow-a-baby." We shuffle down the way we came. The sound of hooves over the ridge makes me sweat and rush, ignoring the sharp pain in my ankle and horrible ache in my pulsing chest.

Harry nods. He has that wide-eyed look of make-believe on his face as I tug him along towards a sharp dip in the mountainside where a boulder must have dislodged and thundered downhill. Harry might well have believed flying storks or spontaneous whole-animal-mitosis—I needn't have said what I did.

Down in the hollow, the wind whips round the sandy basin left by the boulder. Below us in the mottled yellow and purple valley there are now unnerving smears of mist or cloud or smog, it's hard to tell which. The flooded A86 we're trying to follow is still visible down there by the glint of the reflective snow-time marker-posts amongst the broader expanse of the Loch Laggan waters now. Having crossed the Spean at a high footbridge in its lower, steeply valleyed reach, the days have blurred together again, as we traipse painfully up-slope and down, always trying to refind and keep sight of those road markers as they weave through the Spey Valley. When we come across streams, we wander until we can find passable stepping stones. We sleep in hollows or thickets under the groundsheet, hungry, tired, cold, and eyes irritated and bloodshot, though thankfully my mask is keeping Harry's lungs safe. Aviemore is still forty miles or so up the Spey Valley.

I peep over the rim. The stags have locked antlers. A few hinds still look in our direction. The calf hasn't got back up.

"Was my daddy the strongest?" Harry asks, his voice almost lost in the wind and the clashing of antlers.

That old sickly feeling squeezes inside my stomach.

"He was strong . . ." I remember the muscled shoulders my hands would always cling to when Jack and I had those proper warm bear hugs. But also the way he cried when he broke down, the struggle to not resort to pills anymore, but to get better and forge his career and thrive. "Yes, he was strong." And then I think of the weight of that man I didn't know, pinning me down, the way I couldn't make him stop.

"Am I as strong?" Harry stands straight.

The sickly feeling swirls. But in the end I smile. "It doesn't matter about him, you're your own sort of strong."

He grins, but it fades quickly. Mist is drifting in around us.

"Come on." We cut south to loop around the deer and weave through the mountainscape, sticking to the clear parts, but we're soon surrounded by mist.

Harry whimpers, eyes wide, next to me.

The air meter won't turn on.

"What does it smell of?" My own nose is too blocked and sore.

I help Harry lift his mask, just a little. "I don't know," he frets. "Just Outside."

"Not bitter and bad?"

He shrugs. "I don't think so."

We scramble up and down peatbogs and heath, the haze-muted orange and honey-yellow of miniature bushes and grasses and bare black mud at our feet the only things we can see. I try to keep an eye on the pale glow of the sun too, but soon I lose sight of it, all white everywhere. The cold wet air stains the map and soaks my blanket-mask, my hot pulsing lungs gasping for air. I find it's better to keep going slowly than stopping and starting, more bearable. So we inch our way up and down, trying to find a way out of the whiteout; it no longer matters if it's the right direction; I've no idea which that is anymore. Just get out.

We splosh through an icy stream and follow it downhill. Exhausted and with the afternoon drawing in, we finally emerge out of the hazy dreamlike night world of the whiteout and back into the clear waking world. Harry flops to the ground instantly. A flatter heathland spreads out ahead, a strip of green in the distance under a grey sky: the deep greens of tall healthy pines, with a scattering of glossy bright-yellow young birch.

"One more bit," I wheeze, biting my lip as I help him back up.

"You said that already," he says, but he stumbles to his feet and follows my slow limping pace across the wet, rocky heath until we reach the trees and pause at the first cluster of old dead trunks.

Burrow holes emerge around their bases. Muddy trails exiting them peter out into the mountainside around us. Harry cranes his neck to look up. Scuffed paths run up the wet and sloping blackened trunks to widened cracks and holes higher up, where small tunnels must be dug right into the rotting wood. I gape at a rabbit sat high up like a sentinel, his nose twitching. He soon dives down a knothole and disappears.

I snort. "I never looked up! I always thought the rabbits in Nathan's Coppice, in the winter, either dug in somewhere else drier if they could find it . . ." Or drowned. "What if they learned to do the same?"

"Didn't they always go up Before? Looks safe. I like high up."

"No, people controlled the rivers and sea then—or tried to—so it didn't flood as much. Big walls and hard channels and gates and things. Floods used to be a surprise. And the floodwater now is probably full of bad dust."

Harry frowns. "That's silly, isn't it too big for trapping? I bet that made it sad or angry. That's why it swallows things."

"Wild places aren't sad or angry, Harry. They don't feel."

"They do!" He whines, nodding his head, as he slips a hand free of its mitten to rub his tired eyes. "The wind and rain *are* sometimes angry. Like you when you sometimes slam and bang . . . things . . ."

Harry kicks his heel into the ground.

I watch, my thoughts already returning to rabbits. "A pitfall trap! It might work if we check it regularly. Otherwise, they'd soon dig themselves out."

Harry sighs, sinking to his knees. "Why are we making a trap?"

I swallow, avoiding answering, and instead stab the ground on one of the rabbit trails with a stick, scraping away soil, careful to sit upwind as the grey layer beneath the rich topsoil gets carried off by the breeze. I dig until my arms have nothing left. Harry helps me find twigs and leaves to cover the pit, before we brush each other down as best we can.

"Bait would help," I tell Harry.

"What's bait?"

"Like food—something the rabbits would like."

We explore the green and yellow copse, me hobbling in Harry's wake.

Deeper amongst the trees, my ankle throbbing with each snag and every part of my body begging to rest, I spot hazelnut shells amongst the thick layer of fallen leaves. And soon, the double-toothed papery leaves—yellow with red-black smudges—of a hazel tree. I show Harry the unripe, pale green nuts in their crinkly coverings. Anything ripe must be taken straight away by squirrels. So we pick the unripe ones until our pockets are full.

With the trap baited with hazelnuts, we set up our camp at the other end of the copse with a view east of endless rolling mountains, which scares me as I frown at the blurred sodden map, not sure at all which mountains are which now. No snow-time marker-posts or roads visible either.

Huddled under our ponchos and the groundsheet, the fire taking, we listen to the hard pummelling rain coming down, and cram hazelnuts in our mouths. Most are too hard, like crunching into dried peas, but soaked a bit in hot water, they're edible enough and have a sweet vegetable taste.

We doze, exhausted, the nuts only making me more aware of the terrible emptiness in my stomach. I wake to the fire snapping as Harry adds another branch to it, face bare and intent on the task. The rain has slowed and the light is fading, the distant black ridges backlit with lurid pink and orange.

The pain has crept back up, the adrenaline of the whiteout long gone, but we need to check that trap. I grimace as I force myself to sit up. Heart squeezing in sharp searing pulses. Lungs feeling raw and papery thin as I gasp in breaths—the ball of bramble I imagined in my chest in Arisaig, expanding and shrinking, now gorse instead, with its long stabbing thorns for leaves. I try to contain the wet coughing, bloody phlegm splattering the dirty cloth I use as a handkerchief. This feels unbearable. Tears prick my eyes.

Harry is weary, hypnotized by the hungry flames, and snuggled into his poncho and blanket. The firelight exaggerates the hollows in his cheeks, his sunken eye sockets.

Maybe if this is as far as we manage to get, it was my best. Maybe I've fought as far as I can fight. The pain fills my whole chest, and I rock, exhausted and holding myself together with my arms folded.

But as I watch Harry, eyes dancing with orange flames, something screams inside me. Can't give up yet. Not dead yet. I focus my hope on the pitfall trap—not counting those first few days of rationed seaweed, or our taste of inner pine bark, and leaves and tiny lingering and sour haw and buckthorn berries picked as we've trekked, this is the closest we've come to finding a proper meal that filled our bellies in nearly a week. And that last hot meal with Andy and Sue feels an age ago. I try schooling my voice to a calm, hopefully playful, tone. "Can we play a finding game? One more before dinner?"

"Too tired," Harry says, his eyes flicking up at the word "dinner."

"Please, Harry. A brand-new different game, I promise."

Finally he wobbles to his feet like a sleepwalker, shoulders hunched and yawning as he nods.

"Good boy. Can you find me as many different plants as you can? One of them is magic—see if you can find it."

We call out to each other as Harry scrambles through the undergrowth. He totters back frequently, looking brighter now he's up—though I know his energy will sap quickly—asking if the wilting yellow in his fist is different. A nettle and a willowherb, a horsetail and a dead stem of something indeterminate. I check everything off as he brings it to me, still clutching my chest, just trying to focus on each gasp in as it comes, each rattling breath out, each painful pulse.

"Wow, that's fifteen now, Harry!" Sensing him tiring, I risk a hand up from my chest to high five. "Getting warmer!" The pain spasms as he slaps my hand and goes off for more.

Please let there be something.

40

A lemon-yellow flower. Harry presents it in a straggly bouquet, before slumping down by the fire. I know I've seen it before.

I flick through the book. There. Common evening primrose. Flowers open only in the evening in summer and autumn. Four bright petals.

Pain-relieving properties.

"This is it," I tell Harry and he squats to examine it. "Can you find more?"

"Too tired." He slips lower under his poncho.

"Harry, please?" I croak, fear creeping into my voice. "It's got magic that might make me hurt less."

He wobbles to his feet and eventually I have several handfuls. Double-checking my identification in *The Wild Flower Key*, I test some in my mouth, nibbling it. No swelling or immediate reaction.

I oversteep some in an inch of hot water and sip the bitter tea.

My heart still squeezes painfully, but slowly, my lungs do seem to ease. Enough that I can sit up properly and feel less dizzy. I don't care if it's a placebo; I try not to think too much.

The light is fading now. I meant for us to check the trap hours ago; it could be too late. I limp slowly round the copse to the warren, pausing every time my chest spasms. When we get there, we find the trap fallen in on itself, the leaves gone. A rabbit darts out of a freshly dug hole not far from it, dashing up one of the warren trees. But a second rabbit is huddled in the leaf litter inside the pit-fall trap, munching on exposed roots. Its ears flatten. I squeeze my hand twice and Harry freezes.

The newly dug escape tunnel is just to the rabbit's left. This animal is almost white and has extra-long guard hairs, making it fluffy. It could have passed as a pet, Before.

This is going to hurt.

I glance at Harry's windswept shabby little figure.

I dive. Eyes focused on those hind legs. The rabbit launches up the escape tunnel, but I get one hand around a kicking foot as I slam into the cold, hard earth. Claws gouge through my sleeves. Pain explodes across my chest. The rabbit pulls and thrashes, digging claws into the damp tunnel soil; I groan and gasp, stubbornly holding on. But my fingers are weak, slipping.

Black spots blur my vision; I feel sickeningly dizzy and faint. I force a desperate grip with my stiff left hand, and suddenly I have two hands now around the back legs. I drag him back into the trap pit, inch by inch, against his panicked thrashing. Get my left hand around his neck.

One sharp yank and there's a pop.

The rabbit sags in my hands and I crumple. Even to myself I sound like a wounded animal—gulping at breaths and moaning. Harry tugs desperately at my legs spread on the grass above, but I can't speak yet, my face smashed into the soothing damp cold of the soil, soft warm fur pressed into my neck. White noise swirls round the fringes of my head and I feel on the edge of falling into it.

Harry is a shadow crouching over the hole. "Is it sleeping?" His voice is small and unsure.

"No, it's dead," I whisper on an outbreath when I finally can. Harry's face is drawn together in horror and confusion, his eyes teary. I take a careful breath in, and whisper. "Important to do it cleanly. Don't want the rabbit to feel pain and be terrified."

I haul myself up bit by bit, until I'm kneeling on the ground, the precious limp rabbit held tight in my lap. "We're so hungry, Harry, I had to." I stop to catch my breath again, wait out the pain. "You understand?" I gasp. "We kill only so we can eat." Another breath. "You feel bad for the rabbit, don't you?"

Harry nods, bloodshot eyes full of tears.

"That's good," I mumble. "We *should* feel bad . . . shows we have proper respect for it."

I try my best to clean myself up, wiping my face and hands with a spit-wetted corner of my T-shirt, but I don't feel clean.

Harry winces as I show him how to skin the rabbit—"It's dead, Harry, it can't feel it anymore"—and to cut and whittle hazel stools to make skewers to cook the meat over the fire. Harry has to help—I keep having to rest, crumpled forwards, biting my lips, and my knife keeps slipping, my left hand not gripping. Harry picks up the whittling quickly, chewing on the first cut skewer as he concentrates. Jack would love teaching him to carve and create things.

Soon, my mouth is watering at the smell of roasting food. Even Harry is grinning now.

This is how hungry we are: we eat every scrap of meat, until we are so full, neither of us can move. Maybe you're supposed to build up to such a big meal after so long. And what if we don't find anything more in the days to come?

I don't care. It felt right.

"I love you, Mummy," Harry says, his little hands resting on his tummy.

I smile, feeling better too. "Wholeheart," I whisper. "Sorry I didn't let you . . . help more before, Harry . . . I wasn't alone, was I . . . Always had you as my little partner, didn't I?"

Harry nods vigorously.

I smile more. We settle into our blankets, watching the fire. I sip more oversteeped evening-primrose tea, conserving a mouthful of water for the morning, as I shift, trying to get comfortable. The rain is delicate, swirling in the breeze and getting us beneath the groundsheet anyway. But it looks clear for now. Harry helps me find more wood before everything gets too wet and then we get the fire going really well again by disturbing the glowing embers.

Harry points. "Look!"

Above the fire, yellow-white sparks snap like a fairy fireworks display.

"This is a good place," he sighs.

I finally find a position that's bearable, the warm mug pressed against my chest and soothing, my stiff left hand and sore ankle held towards the wonderful warmth of the fire. Harry is sat cross-legged, all bundled up in his steaming poncho, his face full of joy as he watches the sparks. I don't remember the last time I felt this content, like I do just now—I don't think I've been able to imagine that feeling being possible in the world After, not really. Everything's still painful and scary; death hanging over us. But that makes the good feeling of being warm, fed and finally resting under cover together all the more intense. I feel hopeful that tomorrow might bring another meal and a fire, and we'll get to rest and be warm together again. I feel almost drunk.

And *alive*—in a way I only ever felt Before with Jack on our adventures, when things felt brilliant and intense and eye-opening. That's why those moments are what I remember most when I think of him. I don't mean to, but I can feel a tear sting its way out from a blocked duct and roll slowly down my cheek. This is the feeling that makes the rest of it all worth living, all the stuff that we've been through and all that may happen next. I wish I could have had more of it with Harry.

I blink, aware again of the crackling snaps of light, and, frowning, tug my mask up, the air meter still unresponsive, and signal Harry to do the same. Yet I miss his smile and feel sad for losing sight of it, though I can tell it's still there by the glint in his eyes. And why shouldn't he enjoy this? He is of this new world just like the strange deer and the fiery trees. I'm the only one stuck in the past, thinking of the way the world once was, looking at it all as if it were alien and bad. Why shouldn't he enjoy its strangeness? Why shouldn't his favourite colour be yellow? We watch the sparks until the breeze changes direction, the orange flames shooting up higher.

"When we're asleep are we dead for a bit?" Harry asks suddenly, as if it's something he has been thinking about a lot. "Like the man in the house by Andy and Sue, and the people in the books at the cottage?" His face is serious and scared as he looks out at the dark around us, as if imagining all the dead people sleepwalking about in the pitch blackness.

Or rather, I realize, as he worries over Sue's "disappeared" children, the "sleeping" deceased Ian and the butchered deer . . . imagining falling asleep here and having one of those nightmares you really want to wake yourself up from but can't, whilst in real life monsters drag your defenceless body down into unfathomable terrifying darkness—lost forever—or people carve your flesh up to eat. And you'll never wake to see the daylight and trees and mountains again.

"Oh, Harry," I say, feeling horrified. "Is that why you've not-wanted to sleep? I thought you were just afraid outside, away from the flat." That guilty lump clogs my throat. "No," I say firmly.

"But how do you *know*?"

I rub his shoulder. "That man we saw wasn't sleeping, I shouldn't have said that. Dead isn't like sleeping at all. It means the body has stopped working, like the rabbit when I broke its neck. Sleep is just resting because we're tired."

"He was broken like the rabbit?" He glances sideways at the "clean" cooking saucepan, the lid clipped down against the elements, the rabbit bones safe inside it for a breakfast broth tomorrow morning.

I nod. "And Andy's deer," I say gently. "All things die eventually, even if someone or something doesn't stop them from working on purpose."

He stares into the fire, thinking hard. "And when you're dead you never wake up again?"

I shake my head.

"Then we're dead forever and ever like all the people in the books and all the people in all the houses?" He sniffs, the weight of that horrible understanding on his little shoulders.

I remember sitting in the flat alone before Harry arrived, a not dissimilar numb weight of understanding hitting me. Surrounded by all that death, the *one* life I got to live ruined beyond repair by that storm. It made me feel like all I had left was waiting to face the void alone, one way or another.

And yet I kept trying. Each day. Surviving. For now. For myself.

And then I had to survive for Harry too.

I clutch my chest, trying to think of something good to say for Harry, so he's less afraid. The fire pops and sizzles, and I think about our day today, and how there were really hard bits and then this little perfect good bit. Same as life overall.

"No," I say, "that's not right. You get to live every day, you only die once."

Harry nods, but he's too little still to really understand. And yet perhaps I have to try. He filled in the blanks of what I was not telling him—my fear obvious—with something scarier than the truth. I imagine him growing up, not understanding things at all, filling in the blanks with stupid or dangerous ideas because he knows no better, because I didn't teach him. I should have told him about Before, how people lived together, how they got along and how they didn't, how diverse human beings are, all the stuff they knew to keep us healthy, how we can get ill, how the weather works, how the Earth moves, their predictions about climate change because of how we lived, all of it. Even if I get him to Jack, I might not have done enough.

What if, one day, he thought bad rain or storms or heatwaves came down as punishment or that things with "magic" rainbows and sparkle—clear rain or glossy mushrooms or glittering water—were good and safe. Like some supernatural nod of approval.

I was right to try to explain how babies are made. One day, if we make it, he'll be a grown-up human, not a little child. I should have been raising a future adult all this time, not fearfully keeping my little boy safe.

"Harry . . ." I look into the fire, wondering where to start and, still, if I can bear to. "Those sparks are bits of plastic dust catching fire really easily—the people that are gone made plastic and it all got ground down into small pieces and spread about in the air, and everywhere. That's what bad air is. It's different to natural 'dust' like mushroom or algae spores, or the bits of skin and clothes at our flat. Do you understand?"

Harry makes an "oh" sound, as if this seems all the *more* magical. "Why did they make it? How big is everywhere?"

"Remember when you got sick from drinking that bad water? Or when I get sick and can't breathe? Well, the people Before made the world a bit sick . . ." I start to tell him about how we lived, Jack and

I. Where food came from, how we had power to turn on lights and cookers, how planes—like cars in the sky—flew to very far places, just how many people there were, how plastic was made and what we used it for but how we didn't treasure it . . . How scared everyone was when they realized the rivers and seas were getting sick, how it got warmer in some places and more prone to droughts or wildfires, or more stormy in others. How it used to be so green . . .

How they started to find plastic dust in rivers, soils and even the air—and also in the vast oceans, millions of pieces per square metre, washed there like it was a great big watery garbage dump. All containing their own chemicals (poisons) to make each piece a particular colour or texture. How other poisons we threw away got stuck inside the tiny bits of plastic too, and all of it leaked out again at will. Because we really were pigs, weren't we? How hurricanes— big massive storms—got bigger and bigger, until several huge ones all at once carried so much dust out of the ocean they covered a continent in it, then blew the toxic dust around the globe. And it will always be here—it doesn't break down, can't disappear. It will be in all water, all soil, all air, affecting all life. And that's how all the people Before died—they breathed it in during the big storm . . .

Once I start, everything begins to run off my tongue. I'm not sure how much Harry will understand, but he's listening like he does to a new story, and I figure it will all go in and the questions will come. And I resolve, this time, to answer them.

41

We stumble on, long wet days heading what I hope is north-east by walking slightly north of where the sun rose. We keep the bigger peaks on our left, hoping we'll find the Spey Valley again soon—Aviemore somewhere along it—over the next rise or ridge. Days run into each other, the taste of cooked rabbit a dream we talk about every night as we chew tiny heathland herbs and grass seeds—most of our handfuls going in Harry's belly, at least one of us slightly less empty. We stop now at every boulder; I focus on them as we slip-slide across scree and bog. Just get to the next boulder. And the next. We frown at the map every other one, desperately trying to match up peaks and streams, but nothing quite fits. I'm breathless now even when we stop, heart still winking its squeezing pain, making me feel faint and sick. My cough is no longer wet and bloody like it has been since Arisaig, but dry and tight and raw. We stop to sleep when it gets dark and force ourselves up when it gets light.

Over a ridge we hit the welcoming muffled quiet of a green pinewood—not old dark plantation with needle and moss floor this time, but naturally regenerated forest, with beautiful spreading wonky-branched pines of all sizes, letting in more light, and the ground lush with hummocks of bilberry and heather. We lose ourselves in the deep depths of it, free from our masks. Eating inner bark and drinking pine-needle tea. When we reach a clear spot, the trees go on to left and right, but fade out to shrubby old farmland below us, a clear arc of yellow further down in the valley that might once have been a railway line. And beyond it, a vast plateau thick with mostly green forest, surrounded by domed mountains—the Cairngorms! We consult the map, chilled fingers hovering over marked forest and railways, and I blink, giddy warmth rushing through me. I know exactly where we are! For the first time in days—since we got lost in the mist.

Harry smiles. "Did you find us?"

I grin, splitting my bottom lip again. "Yes! Overshot Aviemore . . ." I can see glimpses of the town to the south. "But . . . can follow that train line I think." I sob, still grinning, sagging against the nearest tree, Harry patting my back as I focus on breathing.

The warm spark of hope and relief—we could have wandered and never found this—fuels the slippery trudge downhill. By midday, we're down on the old tracks, kicking through pale gold Himalayan balsam. Seed pods explode at the slightest movement, the pink flowers bobbing. We eat the immature flowers and seeds, peeling back their unripe cases and eating scraped-out slivers of soft mush or nuttiness inside.

"Mummy!" Harry cries, pointing, and I grimace to straighten myself up. A blue carriage, its big dark windows marred with dust and algae, is nestled in the balsam, a blanket of vomity grass on the roof.

"Don't look inside," I whisper. Telltale awful shapes are slumped on the seats; I see snatches of desiccated hair and creamy-yellow bone before I manage to look away.

"Why?"

I spit out the trickle of blood sitting in my mouth, and heave a dry cough as I try to speak.

"Nasties?" he says quietly.

I'm tired but I try to pick the right words. "People from Before—"

"Disappeared dead ones?"

He stares up at the nearest window and then immediately drops his head and shuffles close, determinedly looking at the ground as we pass the length of the carriage.

"What if they wake up?"

"They won't, remember?" And I feel myself needing to say more. We stop and I struggle down to his level. "The rabbit wasn't a nasty, was it?" My voice is scratchy. "Nothing dead can hurt you. The people inside the broken bodies are gone."

"Where?"

"Nowhere. Just gone." I lift his mask to kiss his cheek, his face still confused by where they might go.

The afternoon is almost over by the time we emerge next to a pretty wood-clad Victorian train station and I feel a surge of excitement and relief. Just like I did with Jack after we'd arrived on the overnight up to Edinburgh, and then the local up to Aviemore for a holiday, mixed up now with a burning longing and familiar dread.

He has to be here. All or nothing.

Our best is a constant shuffle now. Everything hurts; each step of the many scrambling miles behind us feels like a triumph.

I know if I stop, it's hard to start up again, so I focus on each step closer, feeling that magnetic pull of Jack somewhere not far away now, putting as little weight on the smarting bad ankle as possible, balancing on the large stick Harry found me. My lungs are so wheezy and painful and breathless that I concentrate on that too; breathing feels like trying to suck air in through a straw, my mask long since discarded. Going this slow, and the pain ever-present, I'm sweating and cold.

"Mm." I have to stop once more, a thundering pain in my heart.

"Come on, Mummy," Harry says, tugging me on again.

The houses along the sleepy high street are grey and pale pink stone and slightly battered, with pines growing up rich and green around them. I don't know where Jack and I stayed, but it was a bed-and-breakfast that looked like these houses.

Yet I remember more forest. And this converted-bothy pub at the end of the high street! The air suddenly seems to smell of roasting vegetables and rich gravy. To ring with Jack's voice and the bustle of a busy pub. I stop to rest again, and when I shake my head, the imagined scent and sound is gone.

We turn south round the corner of the pub, heading deeper into the Cairngorms Forest, which spreads out in a glorious carpet of rich green and mottled yellows and oranges. We pass a primary school with faint hopscotch squares—purple, pink and blue—still just visible beneath the leaf litter in the playground. Maybe tomorrow, we could come and play there. Past that, the pines have grown so tall and spreading that we are constantly in solid shadow.

"Big trunks, Mummy—lots of famine food, see, don't worry," Harry says, spreading his arms wide across a lichen-hairy trunk.

The air is thick with the scent of pine, and clear and still under the trees on what's left of the road—maybe the cleanest air we've breathed. Even so, I hop slowly, sucking breaths in.

"We're doing it!" Harry says, smiling as he zigzags next to me, touching the glossy green pine needles tipped with fiery orange and examining the yellow-streaked bracken. A pair of ravens keep cawing and following, landing in the road and then flying ahead, watching me, it feels.

A few miles down the road, we stop. A jolt of warmth and desperate hope spreads through me. The Mountain View Inn—its sign, repainted recently, visible above the door—sits amongst the Scots pines. Pale grey and pink stone, steeply gabled roof, tall gothic windows.

"Is this the house?" Harry whispers, tugging my hand after a while and it's almost as if he's woken me up. I don't know how long we've stared.

"It looks familiar." My voice is raspy and thin; it hurts to push the words out. I remember laughing on this very spot—it echoes inside my skull. Tears streaking down our faces. Jack weaving up the path ahead of me. We'd fished out the keys and were still trying to control ourselves as we stepped inside. I don't remember now what made us laugh so much.

The pain in my chest only pulses hotter as I limp the last stretch to the solid pine door—there's a carved wreath of leaves and fruits in the wood. I reach out to touch it, the pain and exhaustion-fuelled fog clearing from my mind, every part of me sharp for sound or movement, for Jack. A rusted tripwire and bell lies in a pile beside the step and the door smoothly swings open as I push on it. Tiny pieces of glass inlaid, or blown, into the wood sparkle as it moves, like dew.

We creep into a hallway, letting the door close quietly behind us,

Harry pulling free of his mask. We can still hear the creaking and soft rustling of the pines and the cawing of the birds outside, but it's muffled. The hallway is dark, all the doors shut, perhaps to keep in the warmth.

Harry sticks to me as I move forwards. A skylight casts a grey glow over the banister rail. At first I think the pale wood has rotted, but as we step closer, I can't help reaching out to touch it. A twisting river is carved along the first span of horizontal rail—the golden grain flowing and rippling, and around it, beautifully detailed roses, trees, mountains, two figures holding hands, the sun setting over a sea. I can almost smell the delicate sweetness of roses. There are turrets and castles—their names inscribed finely beneath each. The tartan-carpeted stairs are soft underfoot. I stop every few to clutch my ribcage and catch my breath. To press my fingers along the tiny shape of a canoe in the river carrying two figures. Harry is scratching at the collected dust in the lines of a carved bear, rearing up between trees.

I shake my head and he snaps his hand back to my waist.

Upstairs, the doors are shut too, and dread hardens my stomach. It seems airless up here; I'm gasping, body tingling from lack of air, lungs desperate.

"Is it OK, Mummy?" Harry tugs at my hand, making me wince. "Sorry."

I nod and hobble down the hallway. At the end, there's a room marked "Norefjell" with tiny carvings around it: of mountain peaks, a sprig of heather, a dipper perched on a river pebble, a beautiful fish. My stomach gives another lurch. Tears threaten to blur my vision and I blink them away as I reach for the handle, fingers trembling over the tarnished metal.

"Shouldn't we call out?" Harry whispers. "So we won't be a surprise?"

I nod, but my throat won't work.

The door moves smoothly on its hinges and we step inside. The room is gloomy, heavy purple curtains shut, the air dry and smelling of wood. I stare, refusing to blink, willing my eyes to adjust. Harry is at my hip, clinging to my belt. The four-poster is there. Dark, carved wood, drapes missing. The headboard is upholstered in Scottish thistle fabric. The bed is unmade, greyed sheets runkled and tangled. There are shoes at the foot of the bed, a pair of fur boots, one tipped on its side. I bend to touch them—supple leather on the inside, soft thick fur on the outside, seams hand-stitched with thick waxed thread. Some clothes are strewn in the corner of the room: jeans, a few T-shirts, pants. Blinking, tears sting out from my crusty eyelids.

I hurry as best I can round the corner. The bathroom too is empty. Towels are draped over the sides of a cast-iron bathtub as if to dry off. Harry leans away, pointing at the big brass paws of its feet, as I try the dripping tap, surprised when clear water flows out, groaning in the pipes in another room.

"I don't like it in here," Harry whispers, pulling at my sleeve.

I turn back towards the bedroom.

There's fear nipping at me now. It might not be Jack at all, and what will happen when not-Jack comes home, which could be any minute?

And what if Jack *was* here. What if this is years old, and I'll find him in a downstairs room hanging from—

Stop it.

I try to breathe, suck the air in and push it out. My heart pumps with its squeezing hot pain.

I brush my fingers over the table and the posts of the bed—they come away caked in dust. I shake my fingers free of it and pull us both back. The sheets are greyed. The boots are dusty. The spread of the dust in the room is light and regular though, not eddied around the window frame.

We stand there uncertain in the doorway. The house creaks around us.

"OK," I croak, "we'll just explore a bit."

I open each room with a wave of fear and hope, holding Harry back, just-in-case. Downstairs in a sitting room that's dark and snug, the walls are covered in thick tapestries in regal blues and reds too fancy for a house like this. The floorboards, too, are covered in thick rugs, with big soft Chesterfield sofas angled round a fire-place. There's a wooden train set in the corner—brightly painted— the little train trucks linking together with tiny brass hooks. There are little sprigs of pine cuttings, stiff yet still green in a pile next to them, like tiny fallen trees. I shiver at the sight, feeling guilty and greedy yet hopeful. Turning to see a half-finished wooden cradle in the corner.

Harry is soon absorbed in making Julian and these trains skip across the rugs on their miniature squeaking wheels. My thoughts are beginning to race; Harry's face, dead on this floor, flashing in my head. But I tell him about the great train with sleeping cabins we could have ridden to get up to Scotland, about the narrow corridors you have to walk down—I tell him this, all without that wincing feeling talking about Before used to give me. I tell him about the chug-chug-chug sound of the train, the screech of the wheels, the toot-toot of the whistle, the gentle buffeting movement. All the places and scenes that move past you out the window. All the sorts of people you might see.

"I think I would like it on the train," Harry says, his little face smiling, making me jump, my mind still stuck on that image of him dead.

"Yes, I think you would have." I feel I'm either going to cry or use what's left of my voice to scream, but I hold it in, I want him to see my smile, to feel safe, to be able to just play, at least a while longer. In my mind I'm counting down the rooms left to look in— the kitchen, perhaps, next door, a pantry next to it maybe, and the front room. Three rooms in a silent house.

My hands shake, everything jittery.

We find a rolled-up carpet in the corner with a scene printed on it of countryside and villages and a train track in a circle all the way around it. I try to focus on Harry as he empties a box of little wooden bridges and larger metal army figurines that are not part of the same set, but which Harry lines up across the fields, like old tree trunks, or a growing looming invasion. But those three rooms press in on me.

When we hear footsteps outside, a soft crunch made by metal mud grips, we both freeze and look at each other, my heart—hot and painful—speeding up.

"Stay here," I say hoarsely to Harry.

"Me too." He stands up.

"No, stay here, play with the trains." He looks forlorn, but I kiss him on the cheek and leave. As I turn to close the door, he's watching me, Julian gripped tight in his hands. I hold back more tears until I'm out of the room. And then they're streaming down my face again, tears just overflowing from my eyes. I know that walk. The weight and pace of those steps. Or, I think I do.

The evening breeze is sharp down my throat, whipping all the soreness back up afresh, and throwing loose strands of hair into my eyes. But every cell in my body is tugging me towards the road. The light is fading, the houses opposite getting sucked into the shadows of the pines.

I can see the outline of a man.

When he crosses from shadow into the fading light, I think he looks tanned, and taller and broader than I remember, and he must have grown a beard.

I know that face.

But it's not Jack's.

42

I stand there blinking, air hissing between my teeth as I put weight on my bad ankle without meaning to.

"Katie?"

The shock of hearing my own name makes me stare harder.

I suck in air, exhaustion and pain fogging up my mind.

"Adders?" I connect the pieces in my head. I can't help smiling, lips re-splitting and stinging, and I stagger towards him, suddenly lighter. There are shadows under his eyes, the twilight exaggerating them, morphing his face from the one I remember. His hair is almost fully grey but still thick, messy and flattened at the top from the woolly hat that's in his hands.

"Is Jack—?" I whisper. "Is he . . ."

His face is crumpling, his mouth turning downwards, his eyes remaining wide. That small shake of the head that makes my head spin.

It's hard to get any air in, my legs wobbly beneath me. The street, the houses and trees, it all blurs, everything smearing as if viewed through a dirty wet windowpane. The sounds are muffled, my ears thick—just the rapid pumping of blood through my eardrums. All I can see is Adders's anguished shocked face.

His fingers drag through the grey-brown wiry hair across his jaw, and I can't help wishing he had Jack's blonde-brown beard and blue eyes. That Jack was here smiling at me. I'm shaking my head, not wanting to believe that Adders is here and Jack is not. How can that be? Adders is crying. I've never seen him cry.

Before I know it, the space between us has disappeared and he's standing right in front of me, enveloping me in his arms, my face pressed against his chest. I can smell the smoky-earthiness of his army jacket.

"Katie, how . . ." His voice trails off. His arms squeeze tighter and I can't feel the ground anymore, can't feel anything, can't think, except the thought that Jack isn't here.

Too tight. Pain and no air. I feel myself sinking.

"Are you alright? Can you stand?" His voice sounds far away. He's holding me up.

"Yes." I nod, but swaying, sucking in air.

"You're really hurt, Katie—" When he speaks again his voice is high and anguished.

But then his eyes slide right and I look back up towards the house. Harry has followed me and is a little trembling figure in the doorway, peeping out, eyes wide and glinting in the gloom, the last of the day's light falling on his face. The sight of him sobers me up a bit. I realize how tall and large Adders is beside me, a foot taller, and much bigger, his shoulders bulking out the jacket. And his arms are around me still. I force myself to stand up straighter and smooth some of the pain from my face, to smile.

"It's alright," I rasp to Harry, beckoning him over. But he knows by my voice and my face that it's not, and he stares at Adders.

"Is it Daddy?" he cries out. He takes a step forward, shifting into grey, then hesitates.

Adders is looking at me and then at Harry, scrutinizing his features in the gloom. I can feel Adders tapping fingers one by one against his jacket, as if counting up the years. His posture suddenly stiffens, his chest moving faster.

"Is he Jack's?" Adders whispers in confusion.

I shake my head, barely. Words won't come out, not enough air. And I realize I've not said the truth, ever, not out loud. It's been a make-believe. But I never intended on pretending to Jack, I guess I was always going to say it. Say it all. When we reached him. After a moment, I can muster a hoarse crackly whisper, the words running out in a rush, thick with that grief that's roaring up to the surface inside me: "I wanted him to be."

Adders's eyes don't leave mine. I see a wave of understanding dawning in his face—sadness and pain and guilt—muscles taut as he still holds himself tight.

I'm struggling to get more words out.

"Oh, Katie," he whispers finally, hugging me tighter, still waiting, but my throat is making a choking noise. "Someone forced themself on you?"

The word squeezes itself out: "Yes."

My heart and his heart seem to pound against each other as we stand there—mine fast and fluttery, his strong and booming. All that I've carried, all the pain and tension inside me, sinks into him as I let go.

"I'm so sorry." Slowly, he releases me from the hug, his hands still squeezing mine—calloused and warm, in case I'm not steady after all. And there's a glimmer of pride and awe forming as he looks at me—eyes boring into mine. "I can feel how strong, how brave you've had to be . . ." His eyes flick beyond me to the house. "What's his name?" he says under his breath.

"Harry," I whisper hoarsely.

Adders kneels down on the ground, and when he does, he doesn't seem nearly so formidable. His hand finds the small of my back as I start to tilt again.

"Hi, Harry," Adders calls out softly, as if he's known Harry's name all along, and Harry lights up like I did when I heard my name. "I'm a friend of your daddy's. And of your mum's. It's so wonderful to meet you."

I see the fear drop out of Harry's shoulders and he takes another step out of the doorway.

I can taste my own tears as they run into my mouth.

And I know: this is what Jack might have done to put him at ease too.

No matter what.

43

The fire is crackling, gorging itself on the pile of logs in the hearth. The room smells richly of smoke and pinewood. I'm so tired, yet so awake. It's as if I've been walking around in a dark muffled hole for the last five years, and in the last weeks I've suddenly been beautifully and painfully awake again. The stuffy heat of the room is thick and comforting, the bitter tea Adders brings me soothing. Soft golden light pours across the room from the wobbly glass windows, warming the rich wood-panelled walls and red-orange arabesque rugs covering the floorboards. We're curled up beneath heavy wool blankets, Harry and I, Harry blinking at the flames and around at the room, finally awake too. My lungs lurch sharply with each gasped breath.

"Morning," Adders says softly, relieved, as if afraid he might not have got the chance to say it to me. He replaces the fireguard and settles once more in the armchair. I can't help but stare at him.

"You want another hot bath, and the solution to wash your eyes?" he asks.

I smile. "Later."

"Then, Katie, I think I should—"

"I'll," I say, my voice husky, "go first." I can't bear yet to know what happened to Jack. So I fill him in on my last five years, my voice raspy and thin, the effort of talking almost too much for my lungs to take. I skip the parts about Harry that aren't for Harry's ears—not yet—though Adders catches my eye and nods as if he's picked up on what I'm not saying anyway.

He's a good listener, watching me intently, nodding along, occasionally agreeing or asking questions. Then we lapse into silence.

Adders clears his throat. "He got ill in the first week, badly . . ." His eyes flick over me and away; I didn't talk much about my own health, not with Harry listening. "Wrecked his lungs—we both eventually made it down to the Circle line, found each other there. London Underground became a refuge for many initial survivors, I think. He was a tough bugger though; he slowly seemed to gain strength. And we set off, a bunch of us. Spent three months searching out loved ones, moving."

"Until you ended up here?"

"Katie . . . he told me he knew you were dead, that we'd looked every place you might have fled to. He never forgave himself for leaving you that day."

"What happened to him?" Every muscle is tensing inside me, making my chest all the more uncomfortable, heart burning hotter. I just need to take this bullet and then maybe it will ease a little again.

"He loved it up here, but . . . his lungs got worse that first winter, and his heart . . . with the cold and the pollution pushed lower— and just as spring was showing—when there were finally signs of life again, orange-red shoots and fresh leaves . . . He was glad to see that, it felt hopeful, didn't it?"

I nod.

"Then he went."

I wince, curling over my knees. "He went, and Harry came." The coincidence is both painful and comforting. And that memory of imagining Jack's hands in mine at the very moment when Harry was arriving, eerie.

I sob, triggering more coughing and an awful rattling in my chest and throat as I try to breathe. Harry, overtired, cries too and we stuff our faces into each other's shoulders: snot and tears and blood and wool.

"Katie." Adders's hand touches my shoulder, as he breathes with me until I revive a little.

"It had been four months . . . so I thought . . . But we could have—" My voice breaks, the coughing fit making me heave. Jack and I could have been together all that time, we could have survived or died, together.

Adders hands me a mug of water and after a few sips and lots more coughing, it finally eases, and I rest back on the sofa, my lungs feeling splintered, focusing on sucking the air in.

"I'm guessing you wouldn't have had this handsome little man," Adders says, "if things had worked out differently. Sometimes things happen for a reason."

I cringe at those last words, as if everything we've done was controlled by fate and meant to be. All of us just passive lumps of flesh and everything bad really something good in disguise. I don't believe that.

"Or at least," Adders says, correcting himself, shifting uneasily in his seat, "you don't take one door, but another one opens up, perhaps not the one you wanted, but it led to something good too— eventually. Katie, he too reached a point where he knew he had to stop looking for you."

"What was . . . car then?"

Adders smiles knowingly. "He left the car in Hitchin as a foolish hope, that's how he saw it. Just-in-case."

"A just-in-case? We do those too," Harry says. "To make sure."

Adders grins at him. "Katie . . ." His smile fades as his eyes return to me. "I'm so sorry. If he could see us sat here now, he would want me to—"

"It's OK." He wants to apologize, on Jack's behalf, for leaving that day, and I know Jack would have said it too.

Adders runs a hand through his hair, yanking at a knot. I can't bear to hear it, can't bear to go over any more what-ifs and maybes and painful should've, would've, could'ves.

"Nothing to forgive . . . We missed each other . . . that's all . . ." Yet I can't help picking at one more scab. "Ever since I realized . . . he hadn't died . . . I've worried he might have suff-suffered. That he might have spiralled down . . . until he couldn't . . . see a way to live? And if he'd have died like that . . . when I was really still out there . . . when I would have done anything to be there for him, to show I loved him . . . that's just too . . . so cruel." Breathless, I push the last words out, head spinning.

Adders nods. "I worried for him too—he had that empty look in his eyes that we probably all did in the first shock of it all, only I'd seen that bleakness on *his* face before, in normal life, and it scared me. I couldn't bear to lose him, not after losing everyone else . . ." Adders sobs and reaches over to wrap his hands around mine. "To make it through that alone, you're braver than I would have been, I think . . ." He shakes his head.

I feel an urgency to say things, all the things that really matter, before it's too late. "Thank you—for teaching me to fight."

Adders smiles through his tears. "No, I gave you a few tips, looks like you taught yourself. As it should be!"

"I'm sorry too," I croak. "Evie and Rachel?"

He nods, wetting his lips as if searching for a change of subject. "He did drink, Katie . . ." Adders says softly. "But he kept pulling himself out of it—memory of you helped, and me at his side, I hope."

"I saw him do that . . . after his mum died."

"I think his struggles Before made him tougher than the rest of us, he'd already found the ways to cope when life feels bleak and impossible. The rest of us had to learn. He was a pillar of support to me that first year, an absolute rock. He didn't lose hope."

"Hope?"

"That things would feel better, that the grief wouldn't swallow him and each of us up quite so often. As I said, the car was a foolish hope, but I did used to catch him talking to himself as if you were here, just telling you something he'd done that day.

"He carried you with him. Thinking of people we lost was painful in the early days—we needed distraction and purpose to find any peace, but I think it gave him comfort in the end.

"He was the bravest guy I ever knew, until you two turned up." He winks at Harry.

"I hope I can always make you happy, Mummy," Harry says. "I still don't like the dark but I can be brave."

Adders and I both chuckle at that.

"Katie . . . what can I do?" Adders says, sobered again. "What do you need most from me? Name it."

Harry does a belated forced little laugh to match ours.

"Love him," I whisper, so quietly Adders leans in, ear right to my mouth.

"Of course I will." He clutches my hands, eyes wet. "You have been so loved too, Katie, hold on to that. You were like family to me too, you know, not just Jack."

The sky is bright out the window—no clouds yet moved in. From here I can't see the houses the other side of the road, just the rosemary and fiery orange of the pinewood beyond them, dew evaporating in a rising mist, and birds flitting, and over the tree-tops, rich rosemary-green hills and peaks.

There's something about today that feels a bit like Christmas, in the later years, Before. Cold outside, warm inside. A bittersweet, sad-happiness, because there were always people missing then too.

Adders guides me through the house, propping me up as he shows me things he and Jack started to put together in that first year and that he finished off. The woodshed by the back door, and the shelves in the kitchen now lined with jars of preserved vegetables and dried herbs, sealed jugs of rosehip syrup and rosemary oil, and smoked meats. I love the excitement in Harry's face and the warmth in Adders's, Harry stuffing reindeer jerky and shovelling dried blueberries into his mouth.

We don't go back upstairs to the room that was Jack's, and I'm glad, for now. Adders and I pause in the hallway, watching Harry return to the hearthrug to bask in the heat, Luna beside him.

And yet there is one more place I need to see.

Adders catches my eye and nods once, as if he knows.

Outside, the air is so cold it stings our skin, all three of us blinking watery eyes. I breathe tight, painful breaths under a thick fleece scarf, the shock of cold doubling me over again and again, fighting for breath, chest rattling, heart sparking.

Adders supports me, his arm locked under mine, as I shuffle down the middle of the road, Harry sticking close. We pass a whisky shop, three wooden crosses in the grass beside it.

"Not everyone managed to recover and keep going," Adders whispers.

They make me shiver but my eyes soon drift to a row of houses that are clearly lived in. The driveways are pruned and neat, the roses and apple trees all cut back, and I picture Harry getting to smell and eat them next summer. The windows are clean and inside the first house I can see a stock of wood next to the fire and washing airing.

"They've all gone to the loch to hunt," Adders says.

"They?" My voice is paper thin.

"It's OK, don't look so worried. They've been—they are—like family to me. To Jack too. A couple of them live in our house—with their little 'un."

Like family. Harry's never known *family*. Not like this.

"Hey, Katie, this isn't working . . ." Adders pulls me to a stop. But even stationary, leaning against him for support, my short shallow wheezy breaths and the grimace on my face make him frown. Our eyes connect, the wind dying down just enough that it sounds even worse.

Just as I think he's going to suggest it'd be better if we go back to the house, Adders says, "Wait here."

"Where are you going?" I whisper, embarrassed how clingy I sound.

"To fetch help."

My face must pale because he stops moving off and comes back to me.

"No, you can meet them later, if you want. I meant—just a reindeer. Gerry, one of the old guys, he worked on the hill with the herd Before, and was really keen to keep it going—for meat, fur, company—Jack spent a lot of time with Gerry and the reindeer. We've kept a few down here in town, for pack animals. You can ride it."

"Ride it?"

Adders nods. "Some are feisty, but if you give them shelter and clean food, they're more good-natured, trainable."

"Alright."

Harry and I move to the side of the road, where he helps me sink down to the kerb to wait.

"Mummy, look." Harry points a short while later.

A reindeer pads across the road behind Adders.

Harry gasps, inching behind me, as I too feel myself cringing back.

"Are you sure?" I whisper.

"Of course," Adders says carefully, pausing a few feet away, the reindeer rubbing her head against him. "I promise." He turns to Harry. "This is Louise. Have you ever met a reindeer before?"

Harry nods slowly, lifting Luna up to show him.

"Louise?" I ask. "There was glacial . . . lake called Louise . . . in Canada."

Adders smiles. "I know."

Adders pulls out a handful of grey sponge-like lichen and Louise starts munching on it. I get up—Harry trying to steady me—and reach out to touch her flank, my fingers sinking into deep thick fur.

Louise is easy to ride, once I'm up. Harry bravely insists on sitting on my lap rather than walking next to Adders, though he scrunches his eyes tight as Adders hauls him up and we both sit there tense and wary.

"Ah!" Harry grips my legs as Louise starts her lolloping walk. "What's it doing?"

"It's OK."

"It smells funny."

"Yes," Adders says, leaning forward to whisper to Louise, winking at Harry. "But don't worry, Louise, the other reindeer won't mind."

Harry almost smiles, but looks away instead.

The road is long and dappled amongst the pines, and after some time it curves round a loch and we enter an old car park. Adders's shoes and Louise's hooves squelch across the moist cushions of moss and algae. Past what must have been a visitor centre. It all looks vaguely familiar.

We head up a steep incline, crossing a fast mountain river by a rickety wood bridge, and follow the trail through the heath on the opposite slope. Louise slows over the lumpy ground, the coarse grass and bell heather brushing against my boots—most of it's orange, but here and there, there are pure green tufts with lingering dainty, bell-shaped purple flowers. There's just the sound of birds warbling, the wind through the trees, and trickling water.

"This is where the wild reindeer are?" I point to a print in the mud.

"Yeah," Adders says. "Semi-wild. They've been here since the fifties I think. We feed them every month, most of them still come back for it. They're quite a large group, over two hundred at the last count."

"Feed them what?" Harry asks.

"Lichen. We collect it in the woods. Clean it too."

We reach the top of the hill and Adders sets me down so I can take it in: beautiful green—lush emerald green—forest, only peppered with orange, and a surprisingly clear loch in the valley below, rolling mountains all around and fading out as far as I can see. Only a few midges buzz in the air around us. The sky is heavy white, though, and in a moment, the air thickens with white flakes.

I pull Harry towards me, pulling his mask tight. Adders stares at the sky, eyes wide, freezing to the spot.

"It's alright," he says at last, "it's only snow."

And I realize he's right. I loosen my grip on Harry and when he looks up at me I grin back. "Real snow this time."

Harry stands stock still, though, shaking, until Adders suddenly laughs, turning on the spot. I find myself doing a spluttering chuckle too, and soon Harry's little giggle joins in, and he copies Adders, trying to catch the flakes in his mittens.

"Magical isn't it?" Adders says. "Bet it's been too mild down south for it."

"I know all about magic!" Harry tells him. "Though make-believe is not-real and bad, I think." He stops dancing.

I kneel, whispering. "Don't stop imagining, Harry . . . it's good to dream and hope and think differently . . . but learn as many real stories as you can too." And I picture Harry with questions about all sorts of things and imagine Adders there to help answer them.

Harry nods and spins in a wild pirouette, giggling.

I'm smiling, another little chuckle, because the snow must mean that winter is actually here—coming earlier, up in the mountains—and that dread in my gut that winter usually brings just isn't there.

Adders leads us over the boardwalk, and I recognize this. This is where Jack and I walked, with the reindeer up here. We leave the boardwalk, Adders gently carrying me across the rough ground, traipsing further downhill through the hummocks of purple-green heather and dark rushes, to where the wind is less fierce. Harry squats to examine the snowflakes settling on the delicate white rush-flowers.

"This is it," Adders says softly, setting me down. He squeezes my shoulder gently. "I'll just carry on a little way."

There's nothing to distinguish the patch of mottled orange-green grasses and black rushes in front of me, but amongst it is a large irregular rock, the size of one of those big Pilates balls. It's smoothed almost to a polish, mottled pink and dark grey granite, like the ones in the river we crossed to get here. I imagine Adders lugging it up here, for Jack. His name is chiselled crudely near the top.

Jack Henry Conners.

I read his name over and over, a chant in my mind. I stare at it for a long time. It feels strange to see it written there, sort of confusing, like I'm Harry's age again and don't really understand what death is or that I won't actually be seeing Jack again after all. I understand why that woman in the red coat in the flat opposite had cried "Ryan" like that, over and over. Something in the mind can't accept it; I can feel the conflicting thoughts in my head: understanding and disbelief. I had hoped, against the odds, against reason, that I might see that beautiful face again.

There's a glut, just to one side, of tiny purple flowers amongst the dark green hummocks of heather. Harry has knelt to look at them and at an electric-blue dragonfly perched there. Others buzz around him—the noise like packs of cards being shuffled—but he doesn't flinch.

I kneel in front of the rock and trace my fingers over Jack's name. Tiny flakes of snow catch in my hair and on my eyelashes. And

I remember standing here with Jack after the other visitors had left and the herd of reindeer gone on their way, and it was just us and that view of mountains, forest and loch. And I'd thought at any second, at any moment, he might get down on one knee. He'd locked eyes with me, and in that second I knew that he wouldn't, that he hadn't got a ring with him, hidden in an inner pocket, and that he wished that he had. Instead, he'd saved up after that, to buy the ring he dreamed of getting me—expensive diamond, reflecting light at all angles—and he'd knelt next to that glacial lake in the Canadian Rockies. But this spot, here, is special anyway because of that look, which said you are it; you are my favourite human being.

Happy warmth and sad hot tears at the same time. I press my hands against the cold stone where his name is.

"I love you too," I whisper.

Adders has come back and helps me to my feet.

"Alright, Katie?"

"I wish . . ."

"Yeah, I know." He stands closer and tentatively puts an arm around my shoulders. The cold is growing in my chest, forming an icy lump, burning, making my lungs shudder and I'm so tired, Adders has to brace me, holding me up. "I like to come up here sometimes," Adders says, "feels good to visit, comforting, to know he's here. And to think of him gone to be part of the mountainside now—in the earth and bushes and grass blades, the birds and dragonflies just here."

Adders stays by my side, glancing at me every now and then, like looking for the right moment to say, *Come on, let's step away now.*

"I think, when I . . . I'd like to lie next to—"

His hand gently squeezes my arm. "I know, I know . . . you got it. Katie, I think you need to tell Harry."

"He doesn't need to know yet."

"I think you know he does," Adders says softly. "He needs to understand what's going to happen. It will help him, now, and—"

"After?" I rasp. "When I'm gone."

"Yes," he whispers, gently dabbing my nose and mouth for me as Harry runs over to us—dark blood staining the grey cloth. And

325

to my surprise, it's Adders who lifts him up from the ground—just like I've seen him swing little Evie up so effortlessly so many years ago—so that Harry can wrap his arms around my neck.

"Look, Mummy." Harry holds a sprig of green too close to my face. His cheeks are flushed, his eyes bright.

"Ah, you've got bell heather there, Harry," Adders says, "smells nice, doesn't it?"

Harry immediately slides his mask up and sniffs long and hard at the earthy herb-like scent. "Like dragons' feet!" He chuckles.

"Is *that* what it smells like?" Adders smiles, glancing around to show he's looking for other signs.

"Of course! See, Mummy?"

I smile; I can almost feel it. That flutter of magic in the world that Harry sees.

I pull my ring from my finger and place it amongst the rushes by Jack's stone before we turn back. The inscription on the inside of the band glints, black on silver: *Wholeheart.*

"Come on, Mummy!" Harry tugs my hand.

And I think, I think he might be alright here.

EPILOGUE

Dear Harry,

When you read this, I wonder if you'll still love stories about dragons as much as you do right now. Did you know that people used to believe that when dragons left the world, so too did magic? So maybe it all once was real. Or maybe they are just the best of stories that can teach us something we need to know.

I want you to remember something, when you feel sad or alone or lost, or if and when someone or something makes you feel small or worthless. Or when you struggle with finding meaning or with the idea of dying one day. I hope you never feel those things, never struggle, but I'm not so foolish to think that sometimes life won't be hard for you. This is true for all people, in whatever time they are lucky or unlucky enough to live. So, remember this: dragons have fire in their bellies—pure energy and heat. So do you. Remember it when you wake up in the morning and remind yourself how magical it is to be alive at all, to see out the day ahead.

Live, Harry. You will always be my Harry, who I loved every second with my Wholeheart.

Your Mummy XX

Note for the Reader

When life is difficult, support and resources for mental health in the U.S. can be found with the National Suicide Prevention Lifeline and many other helpful organisations. Resources can be found on 988life line.org and you can call or text 988 for free, 24/7.

Support and resources for mental health in the UK can be found with Mind.org.uk and Samaritans.org. You can call the Samaritans 24/7 for free on 116 123 or email them at jo@samaritans.org. Resources world-wide can be found on Befrienders.org.

Acknowledgements

Firstly, thank you, dear reader, for picking up this book and reading it. I hope our souls have met somewhere between the pages. May you find resilience, hope and love in your life.

Writing and being published have been my big dream. This story was inspired by adventure, our planet, love and the depths of grief. The dark, light and wild. And the finishing of it is emotional. Thank you to all who helped along the way. I wanted to say special thanks—

To the wonderful Harry for choosing *Not Alone* and being an ace agent—editing and working with you has been a brilliant experience. Thank you for making it happen and for all you do. Thank you too to Helen and everyone at DHH.

To Carolyn and Gill, for your overwhelming encouragement and joy in *Not Alone*, and all the work you have put in. I feel grateful to have had the benefit of two brilliant editors at once, in such a nourishing editing process. Thank you for understanding and celebrating the soul of *Not Alone* and helping me lift it to the surface. Thank you too to everyone at Doubleday and Picador (and wider Penguin Random House and Pan Macmillan) for their much-appreciated work and support. It is a joy to see behind the process of a book being published.

To Anna Davis and Curtis Brown Creative for your support and encouragement, and the brilliant Charlotte Mendelson for your wisdom and warmth. Also thanks to Sara Starbuck and others who have inspired and helped along the way.

To my husband, Rich. For our adventures and love, which very much made it into this book. And for supporting my artistic aspirations, being gracious in gifting me space and time to work on this, and for listening to deliberations on plot and character and meaning. For being my consultant car-nerd and co-explorer on locations. For sitting outside literary workshops and events, waiting for me. For the jump-up-and-down celebrating when there was good news. And so much more. I'd go the length of the country to find you too. Always.

To my brothers, Matthew and Duncan. Duncan, for sharing the love of those special books and films that made me want to write and create—the brilliant Ian Irvine, Garth Nix, Philip Pullman, Studio Ghibli and the cinematic pull to the east we felt. You were the only one I shared my first attempts at novels with. You are the big hole in my heart that will never fully mend—I sat at my computer and bled. And Matthew, for being the comforting big brotherly presence that has held me up in darkness and made me proud on bright days, and for all our word games. I always aspire to be as articulate and intelligent as you.

To Mum, for all your love, care and energy given, for memories and experiences, for a house full of books and trips to the library. For all our travels and adventures. You inspired Katie's deep fierce love and determination for her child—I am grateful to have such a wonderful mother. I have no doubt of the lengths you would go for us.

To Dad, who sadly isn't here to see the book published either. Your childhood nickname, "Harry," captured the most fun side of you. Thank you for sketching with me in the Pitt Rivers, letting me watch you sculpt, for the magic of Manorbier Castle, knights and stories, Portland Bill read with all the voices, and reading perhaps my first—Bambi-inspired—story, aged eight. I'll always wish for more, but all of it mattered.

To my friends who in their own ways helped me and this book come to life. With special thanks to my writing friends for reading early drafts. And to Katie and Charlotte—the first to read the very first rough draft of chapter one—for encouraging me on my way and being there on amazing and tough days. And finally, to Joe, for your friendship, for reading early chapters and listening to deliberations, for helping me find strength, bravery and myself again after loss, and for all those chats about life and books.

Thank you, from the centre of my heart.

The following two poems are included to honour Duncan and Dad. They mean a huge amount to me and my family, and feel powerful, beautiful works on themes of deforestation and nature as a battle-ground, which seemed poignant and relevant to this book and to the times we live in. Duncan's was written whilst on a conservation research trip to Madagascar, aged eighteen, and Dad's is one of many musings looking out at his back garden.

The Forest by Duncan Hodgetts (2008)

A tree so white it seems to glow,
So vast, so picturesque,
It sits upon a bed of leaves,
That sway around its chest.

So beautiful the forest.

True love lies in a lullaby,
That scents the air with tone,
A flap of wings she flutters hither,
A bird in here this woodland grown.

So beautiful the forest.

A harsher note has pierced the air,
A thud, a bang, a clash!
Man has come with fire and axe,
Upon the ground a white heart smashed.

So fragile the forest.

Without a heart a forest dies,
A slow and lingering death,
The bed of leaves becomes a tomb,
As beasts and angels draw last breaths.

And as the forest fell, I wept.

Snowflakes Landing by Tony Hodgetts (2021)

Fearful curtains slid aside,
on capitulating hooks.
The bunker bedroom blazed,
scimitar hit by silent flares,
from war-heavy parachutes,
assassins en-masse miming daybreak,
dark crack troops in aim and guile.

Greens and browns succumbed,
to bridgehead evil fluttering,
battalions everywhere at once.
No wind assisted axis here,
only remorseless gravity,
kept helpless gardens flattened,
suppressed indigenous colour.

Accoutred with falling spikes,
frozen pikes and spears linked,
invasion iced a victory cake,
including field, roof and shed,
obliterated hope of cease-fire spring.
The tops of pots and regular posts,
bristling hexagon gunneries.

Acknowledgements

White spite ruled, naturally,
dangerous and pristine,
hard blanketed, universal
encroachment, domination.
Would blade or sod be seen again,
path told from peace time lawn,
all underneath lie dead?

But out of the strong came forth weakness,
the first drip on flag resistance,
watery runs down wood,
piled up look-outs lowered,
dendrite bonds broken.
Barometers rose up and
the corps d'élite surrendered.

A NOTE ABOUT THE AUTHOR

Sarah K. Jackson is an ecologist specialising in botany, and has a keen interest in human–wildlife coexistence, conservation, climate change and microplastics pollution. Her job has taken her all around the UK, scrambling through woodland, paddling up rivers, squelching through mountain bogs, and also sometimes overseas. She studied psychology and criminology at Cardiff University, before doing a master's in conservation ecology at Oxford Brookes University. *Not Alone* is her first novel.

A NOTE ON THE TYPE

The text of this book was set in a typeface called Aldus, designed
by the celebrated typographer Hermann Zapf in 1952–53. Based
on the classical proportion of the popular Palatino type family, Aldus was originally adapted for Linotype composition as a
slightly lighter version that would read better in smaller sizes.

Born in Nuremberg, Germany, in 1918 Zapf also created the
typefaces Comenius, Hunt Roman, Marconi, Melior, Michelan-
gelo, Optima, Saphir, Sistina, Zapf Book and Zapf Chancery.

Composed by North Market Street Graphics
Lancaster, Pennsylvania

Printed and bound by Friesens
Altona, Manitoba

Designed by Anna B. Knighton